The
Memory
Man

Acclaim for Lisa Appignanesi:

'Her novels are high-profile psychological thrillers ... gripping reads, but also deeply reflective'
– *Independent*

'It is the process of investigation and of excavating the past that appeals to her sensibility ... those pockets of time in which the boundary between sanity and insanity is broken down'
– *Guardian*

Losing the Dead
'A compassionate and intelligent memoir ... This dramatic story, written with a generosity of spirit and gorgeous flashes of wit, is a voyage of discovery both for the restless dead and Appignanesi's own brave spirit'
– *The Times*

'Distinguished ... Appignanesi has a sharp eye for the details of everyday life in the Warsaw ghetto. Read *Losing the Dead* and you begin to appreciate what life must have been like during the long nightmare of the Third Reich'
– Robert McCrum, *Observer*

'Remarkable ... beautifully told and permeated with the wisdom of those who survive against all odds'
– *Financial Times*

The Dead of Winter
'Appignanesi paces the mounting emotional atmosphere beautifully ... *The Dead of Winter* becomes, gradually and grippingly, not just the tale of a search for a woman's killer, but an exploration of obsession and guilt that leads to a shocking conclusion'
– *The Times*

'Rivetting, thrilling, sexy, intelligent'
– *Evening Standard*

'Appignanesi skilfully manipulates the reader through a maze of suspicion and fear to a tense denouement ... she writes so well that she sweeps you along'
– *Sunday Telegraph*

Memory and Desire
'A monumental novel, intelligent and well-written. Appignanesi's tight plotting and confident style make this a superior version of the blockbuster'
– *Sunday Times*

'A superbly plotted saga of passion and heartbreak. Appignanesi will keep you guessing until the last full stop'
– *Cosmopolitan*

Lisa Appignanesi

The
Memory
Man

A

ARCADIA BOOKS
LONDON

Arcadia Books Ltd
15–16 Nassau Street
London W1W 7AB
www.arcadiabooks.co.uk

First published in the United Kingdom 2004

A catalogue record for this book is available from the British Library.

ISBN 1–900850–89–3

Typeset in Stempel Garamond by Northern Phototypesetting Co. Ltd, Bolton
Printed in the United Kingdom by J W Arrowsmith Ltd, Bristol

Arcadia Books distributors are as follows:

in the UK and elsewhere in Europe:
Turnaround Publishers Services
814 N. Franklin Street
Chicago, IL 60610

in the USA and Canada:
Independent Publishers Group
1045 Westgate Drive
St Paul, MN 55114-1065

in Australia:
Tower Books
PO Box 213
Brookvale, NSW 2100

in New Zealand:
Addenda
Box 78224
Grey Lynn
Auckland

in South Africa:
Quartet Sales and Marketing
PO Box 1218
Northcliffe
Johannesburg 2115

About the Author:

Lisa Appignanesi was born in Poland, grew up in Paris and Montreal before moving to Britain. A university lecturer, she was a founder member of the Writers and Readers Publishing Cooperative and then, deputy director of London's Institute of Contemporary Arts. She is the bestselling author or eight novels and a number of works of non-fiction, including the family memoir, *Losing the Dead*, *Freud's Women* (with John Forrester), and *Cabaret*. She is also a noted broadcaster, critic and cultural commentator. Lisa Appignanesi lives in London and has two children.

'I realized then, he said, how little practice I had in using my memory, and conversely how hard I must always have tried to recollect as little as possible, avoiding everything which related in any way to my unknown past ... I had constantly been pre-occupied by that accumulation of knowledge which I had pursued for decades, and which served as a substitute or compensatory memory.'

W. G. Sebald, *Austerlitz*

'Days in the past cover up little by little those that preceded them and are themselves buried beneath those that follow them ... Our self is composed of the superimposition of our successive states. But this superimposition is not unalterable like the stratification of a mountain. Incessant upheavals raise to the surface ancient deposits.'

Marcel Proust, *In Search of Lost Time*

Present Tense

1

Had Bruno Lind known what awaited him when he returned to the city of his birth, he might not have made the journey. As it was, he wasn't quite sure what had brought him to visit a Vienna he hadn't set foot in since childhood. He put it down in the first instance to an old man's vanity. The city that had once chased him away was now wooing him back. He relished the whiff of perversity in the city fathers having remembered him because they were holding a conference on memory.

He was a scientist of considerable reputation and more years, not that he suffered from them unduly. He prided himself on the fact that his limbs still carried him unaided, that the pull of gravity wasn't yet excessive, and that he didn't normally experience a blind panic when trying to retrieve a name or a bit of knowledge from the recesses of his mind. The deposits the years had left on his brain still seemed to allow some current through, and thoughts were produced. The only difficulty was that he had the sense time was running and running out at an ever-quickening pace. And the past had begun to haunt him, sometimes plague him with its unfinished business.

At the Vienna-Schwechat airport, a man with a bristling moustache came to meet him. He carried an identifying sign that bore the word 'Memory' in curling Gothic print in three languages above Bruno's name. He didn't laugh when Bruno said he was happy he had remembered to collect him. In fact, he gave the distinct impression that none of the three languages on the sign were his own. Driving, not conversation, nor jokes, was his business, and he drove the large limousine with sedate pomp.

Bruno was left to his own devices. He leaned back in his seat and, with a hint of reluctance, looked out the window. The city rose into view through some internal mist then quivered into dim familiarity. Bruno stared at old narrow streets, at buildings of pale stone, at arched sculpture-strewn doorways, at voluptuous goddesses and expansive gods, at graceful domes and vaulting spires. He began to feel they were hieroglyphs in a lost language poised to reveal a long-hidden secret he hadn't known they contained.

The animated hotel roused him. The lobby was a confusion of voices and tongues, muted only by the chocolate-box padding of walls and curtains and chairs. Luggage trolleys purred across thick carpets. Youths in dove-grey uniforms signalled to straying guests. Beside Bruno, a woman with an operatic bosom insisted on tickets for that evening's performance of *Parsifal*.

The pert, curly-haired attendant behind the registration desk welcomed Bruno with respectful enthusiasm, adding the 'Herr Dr Professor' to his own unadorned 'Lind' and smiling as if she had been waiting for no one else all morning. She explained that his hosts had graced him with their best suite. That if everything was not to his satisfaction, he should ring immediately. Bruno returned her smile with a cordiality he was, in fact, beginning to feel under the shower of her attention.

It was in the midst of all this, while she was handing him his key and a brochure, that he heard the name. Heard it from behind, so that it insinuated itself into his mind and clutched at him like some tentacle born from the reverie the streets had induced and now given a vivid, unnatural, daytime life.

'Aleksander Tarski?'

The syllables coiled round him and forced him to turn. Somewhere in him, it seemed, the fear was still alive, despite the passage of years. He stumbled, had to lean against the counter to catch breath and composure like the old man he stubbornly refused to be.

What was that name doing here rolling off a woman's lips and abutting in a question? What was it doing here ahead of him?

He saw now that the syllables had been tentatively aimed at a man who had just risen from one of the silk-cushioned armchairs.

He was tall, really far too lank-haired and bedraggled to be standing in this hotel with its veneered pretensions to good taste and better discretion. The woman was more in tune with her surroundings. A slim, rather angular creature with a haughty expression and a long flower-like neck, she was carefully suited and coiffed – yet nervous, judging by the hesitation in her voice.

The tall man acknowledged that the name had found a home. Bruno relaxed a little. He was curious now and followed the couple with his eyes. This particular 'Tarski' had a soft, slightly distracted air, despite the large features and cavernous jaw. His hair was of an indefinite colour. His shoulders in the worn tweed jacket sloped slightly, as he allowed the woman to lead him away. He was both too old and too young, Bruno judged, though judging people was no longer what he did best.

He took the mirrored lift up to the fourth floor. In his room, he pushed the thick brocade curtains aside and opened the window. The excited noise of the narrow pedestrian street rose towards him. He watched the scurry of passers-by for a moment then stretched out on the bed and closed his eyes. A brief rest would restore him.

But there was no rest. Images from the dream that had plagued him this last while leaped before him with the grainy effect of a battered old film on a loop. Figures kept falling: one after another, larger and smaller. Their faces were turned away from him. They refused recognition. The ground opened beneath them making a short fall into a terrifying drop. Deeper and deeper they fell, against razor-sharp granite walls, so that he had to open his eyes to stop the plunge and the barrage of German voices that accompanied it, like the deafening incomprehensible rumble of gunfire.

Bruno rose to look out the window once more. The name of the street came back to him. *Graben*. Trench, that's what it meant. In the plague years, it had served as a grave. Someone had told him that. Only the Viennese could turn a communal trench into one of their principal pedestrian arteries. A pleasure haunt for consumers positioned on top of a mass grave.

'Tarski.' That name overheard in the lobby had come back from the grave too. He, himself, was a dusty ancient dig now.

Contained generations of graves, some shallow, some vertiginously deep. Had he been right to come here? After so many years pretending the place had nothing to do with him. Not only the place. The whole region. Central Europe. A cemetery. For years he had been a Canadian, a Californian, a Bostonian, a New Yorker, latterly even a Londoner, which might be a little closer. Anything but a Viennese. And, above all, he had been a scientist, which made him part of a country without borders or geography.

Bruno glanced at the conference brochure the hotel clerk had handed him. His own face stared out at him in full colour. Blue eyes glinted. The shock of white hair rose from a face where the lines were deeply etched, a road map of the character he had become. Uncanny how it was, yet didn't feel like his own image. Like some self-deluding woman, he never altogether recognized himself anymore. He skimmed the details of his long scientific career and the précis he had submitted of the keynote speech he would deliver this evening. He had a need to familiarize himself with a life that here, now, no longer quite felt like his own. They would have robbed him of it. But they, he reminded himself, were no longer here.

The organizers had deftly noted his Viennese birth, alongside the list of honours and titles he had become. Of course. He had entertained no illusions when he accepted the invitation that this was a meeting with a difference. A conference with only a slightly hidden political intent. He would allude to that in his asides. Keeper of the new analogue neurosteroids that promised so much for the ageing individual's cognitive powers, he had been brought here to prod Austria's sluggish, often faulty, collective memory into action. Or at least to make it appear to the rest of Europe that Austria wanted to prod at it a little itself, so as to become an acceptable member of the wider community.

He leafed through the pages of the brochure. There were open sessions aimed at a general public and closed presentations geared specifically at the scientists. Some of the usual suspects were here with papers on semantic dementia and cognitive amnesia, the different processes involved in knowing and remembering. There were others on aspects of synaptic plasticity, the cellular correlate for learning and memory, on APP-related peptides, on intra-cellular calcium and caspase cascades, on Alzheimer's plaques and tangles and APOE, that molecular chaperone that many thought escorted the evil beta-amyloid through the brain. The field had so burgeoned in this last decade that even its supposed members sometimes had difficulty understanding each other.

It was a far cry from the naïve and all-too general question that had seemed so urgent all those years back and which had propelled him into memory work. Why was it that, although our brain cells are always changing, we remember even when we want to forget?

But the world had been transformed since then. Wanting to forget had been replaced by wanting to remember. Maybe there were too many products on the market, products that didn't count as pharmaceuticals, to induce oblivion – even if not always reli-ably. Alcohol, cannabis, Ecstasy, a welter of harder drugs, plunged you into the welcome waters of Lethe more or less at will. As for enhancing the mnesic function when it had grown recalcitrant, there was nothing yet to deal with that. Except perhaps his lab's synthetic neurosteroids, which had done well so far on the rats. 'Viagra for the brain' one of the competing labs had dubbed the compound, though he himself was far more cautious. Slightly worried too about the hype that had infiltrated even his world.

Bruno searched down the participants' list until he found the name that had sent him reeling in the hotel lobby. A pharmacolo-gist. From the Academy of Sciences in Krakow. He was leading one of the parallel sessions on Alzheimer's. Professor Aleksander Tarski. The name hadn't been on the original participants' list. Or had he somehow missed it? Or, far more troubling, subliminally seen it and still come here?

Nothing important, he thought, just an image that fell on his retina, an association: some signals carried by neurons, that's all. No reason to be agitated. He could almost feel the signals running, leaping from axon to axon across those synapses, after all, he'd examined all this so often, he could almost trace the pathways in his brain... Though this had to do with sound too. 'Tarski' 'TARSKI': that was what did it, the name... He'd have to check the pathways of words as opposed to images, especially names.

Were they supposed to stimulate the same amount of hormonal outflow, or only in certain cases, certain kinds of cases? And what kind of case was he dealing with here? Did it make a difference that it was himself?

But no one really yet knew exactly how perceptual filtering took place. No one. No matter what they said or pretended.

Before he realized he had quite made up his mind to it, Bruno Lind was out in the streets and hurrying along with no particular destination. He needed a walk. He needed it more than he needed to return the two voicemail messages that had been waiting for him. Stillness wasn't his natural mode, though too often of late he found himself in it. Probably because his future was now all in the past.

The Vienna air was close with the closeness of land-locked climates. Slightly foetid with its very distance from sea. The sky above was too bright. He let the jostle of the quick-paced crowd propel him and found himself in front of Demel's. The café window brimmed with an astonishing assortment of moulded pastries and rich cream cakes. In a moment, like some child who had been given permission, he found himself greedily inside amidst the imperial grandeur of chandeliers and highly polished wood and a pervasive smell of chocolate. He wondered at the eerie sense of familiarity the place induced in him, despite the dizzying passage of years. The menu still wore the imperial design of the dual monarchy the café had served. 'K&K. Kakania. Imperial and Royal', his father had explained so very long ago and simultaneously made it a word to giggle over in modern Republican times.

Bruno ordered Sacher Torte and a mélange, half-thinking that the first might serve as Proust's madeleine for him, though would probably only give him indigestion, and not because he had secretly to confess that he had never read the greatest of the literary memory men. The scales didn't fall from his eyes with the first bite and invest his past with new meaning. Even though it was a scientific truth, now wrested from nature, that taste and smell did indeed lay down some of the earliest synaptic connections. Maybe recollection was the last thing he needed to focus on in his time off. Far better to glory in the sheer sumptuousness of chocolate: so often self-denied. Rich, fragrant chocolate mingled with the tart sweetness of apricot jam.

Bruno picked a newspaper off a corner rack and read and ate. He was surprised to find that he had selected a local paper, not the *Herald Tribune* displayed with equal prominence. He learned that the right-wing Austrian Freedom Party, which so blithely married alpenstocks to laptops, nationalism to grasping professionalism, had embarked on a new patriotic strategy. In their leader, Jorg Haider's, stronghold of Carinthia, the road signs would announce only destinations outside the country – presumably so that any of those South Slav foreigners could find their way quickly home or at least to Italy without any prolonged stay in the pure local villages.

The paper made him aware of the people around him. Apart from the evident tourists, they were mostly old, like him, even older. Thin-lipped but jowly, with small suspicious eyes, their clothes far too warm for the season. A voice screamed inside him: Did you? Did you eat cream cakes while others were torn from their families, shot? Did you hold the gun?

He dropped some money on the table and raced out. On the street, a young woman caught his gaze. A young woman with red-gold hair and a spattering of freckles. It came to him that she was addressing the same question to him as he had to the Demel's clientele. He was the right generation after all, old enough to be her grandfather.

Bruno laughed out loud. Curious looks came his way. He wondered if he passed as a native? Could one say of a country abandoned at the age of ten that it was one's native land? Others seemed to think so. But so many places liked to claim him when they chose, when his particular assets suited. Canada, the US, now Britain. They could just as easily not choose, of course, could choose instead to close ranks and call him foreigner. Like these men on a bench here. Raggedy, smoking, too dark for native taste, cast out. Outcasts.

That name, encountered with no forewarning, had thrust him into a strange state. He even felt, now that he emerged from

enclosed streets into the vast neoclassical grandeur of the Helden-
platz, that he had grown smaller and needed an adult hand to cling
onto. He felt insubstantial, powerless. He had to force himself to
look up at the curving façade of the newest imperial palace, finished too late for the Hapsburgs, but in time for that malevolent
usurper of power to stand on its columned terrace and declare the
unification of Austria and Germany. *Anschluss*. He may not have
witnessed Hitler's rallying cry to the Austrians then, but somehow
it had etched itself with pictorial realism on his mind, so that he
could see the huge massed crowds, the arms lifted in salutes, hear
the raucous, hate-filled voice, the stomp of boots beating out a
unified rhythm. Like New Yorkers, who vividly remembered the
destruction of the Twin Towers as a real event, whereas in fact they
had only witnessed it virtually. Did the brain distinguish between
registering real death from real-time death, as death on television
was oddly called? The answer probably lay in the level of fear –
recurring fear.

It was soon after the *Anschluss* that his father had disappeared.
He had never returned. Bruno was no longer sure he had missed
him at the time. Not right away in any case. There were his mother
and his sister to tend to. With his father gone, he was the man of
the house, self-important despite his short trousers. He revelled in
the new responsibility. But later, much later, when he was already
in his forties, older than his father had been at the time of his disappearance, an acute sadness had taken him over. It was when the
San Diego lab had won that huge investment and he had all at once
recalled – for the first time – that it was his father who had first
shown him a drawing of a nerve cell, so intricately branched that
it trapped the eye like a lure.

Early spring, it had been. They had all spent the day in the country. A family picnic. At one point he and his father had lain under
a tree together and looked up, marvelling at the intricate fretwork
of boughs and branches, not yet in leaf, through which the sky
glowed a deep clear blue. When they got home that evening, his
father had pulled a thick book from his library shelves and shown
him a delicate drawing that repeated the spread of branches and
boughs. This, his father had told him, is a neuron, a cell in your

brain. Bruno had gazed at the spun-sugar delicacy of the drawing: a mysterious tracery that his father told him mirrored the complexity of human thought.

Yes, it was his father who had infected him with the excitement of science, had even way back then talked of sending him to the technically progressive *Realschul* instead of the more classical Gymnasium. Perhaps it was he who had spoken of science as a search for principles of law and order in the universe. Perhaps not. Bruno no longer knew.

He wasn't looking at the palace any more. He was walking, walking quickly, his summer jacket ruched, his hands balled into fists. Walking with his head down, like an angry lad or an absentminded don. He walked past chestnut-lined gardens and statuary, bronze horsemen and flower beds, past regal arches and towering spires, past a roll-call of names: Bankgasse, Lowellstrasse, Schottengasse, Warhingerstrasse... How he arrived at the particular street with its uniform stone buildings, he didn't know. His body had taken him, and it was the sudden slope that alerted him. Memory triggered by his legs along ancient pathways to the cerebellum. He was staring up, up past decorated stonework, at a second-floor window which was home. The curtain fluttered. A woman appeared. Her soft, gold-brown hair curled slightly at the shoulders. Her summer dress was flowered and as she reached up to unlatch the window, her bare arm glimmered smooth in the sunlight.

'Mami. Mamusia,' his lips formed round the syllables.

Warmth coursed through his veins, a happy anticipation. He waved, prepared to race into the courtyard and up the stairs.

And then there was a kick and thud at the back of his knees. He crumbled. The building heaved and turned upside down. He started to shout, shouted louder, but the shouting didn't reach his mouth that had gone bone-dry. The screams exploded in his head instead, one explosion with each kick and thump – in his stomach, his groin, his back, his face. Each punch came with the punctuation of vile curses he wasn't allowed to use. All of them ending in the word *'Jude'* – 'Jew' until the taste of blood was the taste of that word, and the world ended.

*

He hurt everywhere. His eyelids were too heavy to move. But he heard her voice, soft with meaning. There was a smell too, which tickled his nose. Antiseptic, a pomade for his cuts and bumps. She was talking to someone. Talking about Nazi thugs and a beating endured. Talking to his father. His father was back. A lump came into his throat. He forced tears away and eyes to open.

Bruno focussed through harsh glare. Focussed with difficulty as the kaleidoscope twisted and turned through time. He was in a cubicle of a room. Various medical appliances crowded around him. Strangers stood at the foot of his bed. A man in a white coat. A doctor. Not his father. And a woman, a woman with clear blue hooded eyes. She met his.

'He's awake, Doctor. Awake.' She was speaking in English. Careful but colloquial English, with only the hint of an accent. 'What a relief.'

The doctor was taking his pulse and murmuring something about possible concussion.

'I saw it all,' the woman said. 'I was on my way to visit the Freud Museum and I saw it.'

Bruno made a croaking sound.

'Yes. Yes. A youth on a skateboard. Wearing one of those peaked caps they all turn backwards and a baggy sweatshirt with a skull and bones on it. He crashed into you. Just up the street. Didn't mean to, I don't think. You stepped backwards, and he couldn't stop. Nasty. He got scared when you toppled, and he whizzed away. Then this woman rushed out of the building. She'd seen it too. From her window. She called an ambulance. We were so worried. And I recognized you. From the hotel. Someone pointed you out. Someone who admires you. Professor Lind, isn't it?'

He signalled agreement and raised himself in the bed. His body creaked but moved. Nothing broken. That was good. Just this fog in his head to get rid of. And too many ghosts. Too many dreams in this city of dreams. He concentrated on the woman. Yes, he recognized her now. She was the one who had called out the name. But she couldn't know how it had affected him. Like a trigger aimed at an unused part of his brain.

'I'm Irena Davies, by the way.'

'And you're a neuroscientist?'

There was perhaps too much gruffness or scepticism in his unused voice, since she laughed with a lilt that turned into nervousness.

'It's that obvious, is it? No, no. I'm a…'

'Not obvious, no. It was just that you'd mentioned…'

'I see. Freud. Not your kind of neuroscience.'

He demurred, would have added something, but the doctor intervened.

'You should be still. Very quiet. Nothing is broken, but we must check…' He tapped his own head. 'You rest now.'

'Yes, you took quite a fall. Bumped your head. I'll go back and alert the organizers. They'll be devastated. We'll all be… Are there any messages you'd like me to convey?'

When he didn't answer, she hurried on, 'I'll come and see you tomorrow, if you like. Hope you feel better quickly, Professor Lind.'

She slipped away, and he closed his eyes again, happy to be alone. Happier still, perhaps, to be relieved of the burden of speech giving. He had made far too many in his time. They would find someone perfectly adequate to stand in for him.

Funny how he had altogether forgotten that attack in front of the childhood apartment until this afternoon with its painful near repetition. Forgotten because so many worse events had come in its wake, displacing it in a sequence of horrors. It must have been the physical act of falling which had awoken the young Nazi thugs who had leaped on him in 1938. No, no…that wasn't quite right. It was the whole associative sequence, this city, the street, the woman bending towards the window, one thing after another, a whole series of cues activating the neural networks to give him the memory again.

The city acted on him like Penfield's electric probe, all those years ago in Montreal, when he had watched the great doctor operating on his epileptic patients, their skulls unwrapped to his prodding. As the probe moved across different areas of the brain, they re-enacted their forgotten pasts for him, smelling it, speaking it.

Yes, his mother used to stand at the window like that. Waiting for him to come home from school. He would see her and then race up the stairs impatient for the cool gentle hand ruffling his hair, the scent of sweetened cocoa waiting for him on the hob. That day, there had been no racing. He was carried, instead, a small figure wracked by silent sobs and pretending they didn't exist, though his shoulders heaved. The doctor arrived. Voices were hushed. Except for his little sister, who cried and cried. He remembered that. And Mamusia was all tension beneath the show of calm, as she dabbed at the blood that oozed from his brow.

The attack on him must have taken place not long before his father had gone. Had been taken, in fact, by two Nazi officers while Bruno was at school. When he asked where he had been taken, no answer came. But in the adults' whispers, he kept hearing the word 'camp', which seemed harmless enough, so he expected his father's return at any moment. At first, when his mother announced that they were leaving Vienna, he protested stubbornly saying they had to wait for '*Vatti*' to come home. Did he feel responsible in some way? Had the forgotten attack on him propelled his fiery father into some mad attempt at retribution?

He would join them, his mother promised.

Bruno shifted in his bed with growing restlessness. He shouldn't have come to this city. That was palpably clear given where he was lying only a few hours after his arrival. Yet the invitation had been so flattering. It had also come just as he was emerging from the cocoon he had inhabited since his wife's death. Not that he had emerged a butterfly. Far from it. But something about the proposal had stirred his curiosity. Perhaps, without wanting to admit it to himself, it was precisely to revisit those now dim years of early childhood that he had come. His wife, who had anchored him to his Western life, was gone, and her death seemed to bring all those other earlier ones in its train. As if he had neural nets that encoded death for him, and Eve's had somehow activated the whole system. Then, he was also getting old. And as the novelists always implied when desire goes, memories come. But that wasn't altogether right either: it was the chemicals which emotion produced that helped to bind memories in the brain.

So much they still didn't know, despite the genetic information. Despite the new technologies with their astonishing speed of calculation that provided those startling images of the brain.

Maybe he had come here to act as the subject of his own memory experiment. Bruno chuckled to himself. A scientist's ultimate challenge had always been to test his hypotheses by performing his experiments on himself. If he travelled the byways of his past now, he could assess whether new memories cropped up, and by what they were triggered; see too whether old recollections were altered, and decay had set in. Though he had probably left it all too late: the decay had taken over and he could no longer monitor himself. For instance, he hadn't remembered that the parental home was on the same street as Professor Freud's, but as soon as that Davies woman had mentioned it, he recalled his parents' bringing it up, indeed had an image of his mother talking to a quaintly hatted woman on the street and saying, 'That was Frau Freud, *Schätzchen*. A kind lady. They live above the butcher's.'

But he gave little scientific credence to the Freudian unconscious. It was too elaborate a concept, even in the little he knew of it. Not efficient. As far as he was concerned, to be unconscious was a state, the brain's way of preserving the body in an emergency. The brain was a voracious consumer of oxygen and glucose. It consumed at ten times the rate of other tissues. Fall down unconscious, become horizontal, and it takes less energy to pump the blood through. Just for a few minutes, mind, otherwise the comedy is quickly over.

Bruno lay back, altogether horizontally on white sheets. Was it because of his intimate childhood links with Vienna that he had always kept away from Freud, a figure who was part of an internal landscape he would have preferred to obliterate? Or did he simply share in the usual neuroscientific consensus – that Freud was old hat, at best misguided, at worse a wrong-headed charlatan?

That very question, he suspected, was already one that rose with the city's polluted vapours, infecting him at every turn.

'Herr Professor Lind.' A nurse stirred him from darkening thoughts. With able movements and a no-nonsense smile, she helped him into a wheel chair he didn't want to use and propelled him to an X-ray room, where he underwent a CT scan.

A few hours later, without anyone being the wiser, Bruno Lind slipped out of the hospital, effectively discharging himself. Yes, he had a mild headache, and he was bruised and stiff, but his vision wasn't disturbed, nor did he feel dizzy or nauseous. As for memory, he seemed to be suffering from an influx, rather than a loss. Whatever harm his fall had caused, if any, he would tend to it himself when and as the symptoms manifested themselves. He was too old now for the luxury of time lost lying about, particularly in environments he had no wish to be in. These last years he had spent too much of the wrong kind of time in hospitals.

He took a taxi back to the hotel. After a shower, he thought of heading off into the city. No one, but no one, would know for once where he was. The anticipation of that, for a man who lived within a strict schedule of duties and commitments, was delicious.

Instead, with a kind of perversity, he found himself walking towards the mock-Gothic university building on the other side of the Ring, where – all things being equal, which they weren't – he would at this very moment have been coming to the climax of his address to the audience.

The hall was large and filled to capacity. Before focussing on the speaker, his eyes were drawn to the magnificent ceiling where the seven pillars of wisdom emerged in the high decorative style of Gustav Klimt. Looking beyond the sea of heads, he now recognized the burly bearded figure of Andrew Wood behind the large oak podium. An inspired choice to replace him, Bruno thought. In fact, Wood should have been asked in the first place to do the keynote. He was far more adept than Bruno himself at blending the political with the scientific. And with his easy style of address he could draw an accessible picture – even for the lay non-English speaker – of the complexities of research into the hundred billion nerve cells and the hundred trillion interconnections that go to make up a human brain.

A memory man, just as Bruno had been at points in his long career, Wood had evidently been talking about his chicks, the model-systems his lab preferred, but now he was evoking the ageing brain and the abnormal amyloid protein build-ups found in Alzheimer's sufferers. Like the unabsorbed waste products of a city or a nation's history, Wood was saying, these abnormal build-ups were destructive and un-recyclable.

Bruno could see where the analogy was heading. Austria, like its neuroscientists, had to contend with this waste matter of the past, the plaque in the system, and somehow disperse it, or the patient's and the nation's ability to function, which was also an ability to remember, would be utterly destroyed. Without an agreed-upon memory, there was no possibility of community. Austria's full role in Europe, Wood was suggesting, would only come when the country ceased to see itself solely as a victim state of Nazi annexation. For too long Austria had hidden behind its supposed 'victim' status. It now had openly to confront its active role, not only in the wartime atrocities committed against Jews and political dissidents but also in the forced takeover of never-returned property.

Wood paused. A message had been passed to him. As he read it, he smiled broadly and gestured towards the back of the large auditorium. Simultaneously, a young man approached Bruno and asked whether he would be good enough to follow him. Moments later, Bruno found himself on the stage shaking hands with Wood, gazing down onto a sea of expectant faces, listening to a far too fulsome introduction to his own modest achievements. He glanced at his watch. Five minutes…just enough time to thank Wood and offer his apologies.

It surprised him then, when he heard himself saying: 'Friends, our science has advanced by leaps and bounds in the last decade. But the links between mind and brain remain deeply mysterious. Today…' He moved for a moment into German and felt the familiarity of the speech on his tongue, despite the sudden strain on his lips and cheek as long dormant muscles were prodded into action.

'Today, I suddenly found myself in front of my childhood home. I had no real intention of going there. Nor, if I had set out to find my way, do I believe I would have remembered the direction quite so efficiently… As Shakespeare might have said, if he joined us now and didn't have a wondrous way with poetry

"There are more things in our synapses and hippocampus than are dreamed of in our science," dear friends. Yes, we have made great strides, but our understanding of memory, which must be the foundation of mind, is still in its infancy…'

2

Irene bent towards the mirror and wiped the excess mascara from her lashes, then deftly reapplied maroon-red lipstick. She added a hint of blusher on cheeks that had grown gaunt. She looked tired. The strain of the day was scattered round her face like used ammunition. Shadows, crevices. Pah. There was nothing for it. She shrugged for the benefit of the woman beside her and went back into the fray.

The fray consisted of the select crowd gathered in the hotel banqueting room for after-dinner coffee. It was clear that, sooner or later, one of them would discover that she was here under false pretences. Irene smoothed the skirt of her best suit, adjusted the amber pendant and put on her opaque smile. She reminded herself that not all her pretences were false . She was, after all, someone.

As she wound past little groups engaged in intent conversation, Bruno Lind greeted her from the head table, where he still sat flanked by the mayor and some other notables. She nodded in return.

Funny how she couldn't make up her mind about the man. Maybe it was simply the difference between him this afternoon – frail, supine, pale, first on the ground then in the hospital bed – and now. Now the vulpine face, with its clear intent eyes and bristling white-grey hair, was full of energy. The kind of energy that burns. Yes. It was a face that might have been painted by some old master, one who specialized in the lines and furrows of truculent character. The fall, which had seemed so serious, had evidently had little effect on this erect, barrel-chested figure, more like an aging pugilist than a man of the mind. And he had thoroughly disproved the sad tale of accident and slow recovery she had told the worried conveners.

What she had forgotten was that all these Westerners worked out, even if their names were preceded by the word 'Professor'. Or maybe this one had tried some of his own remedies ahead of any clinical trials. Like Picasso with his monkey glands. Or that strange German, Frossman, she had read about, who had stuck a tube up the artery in his wrist to prove his theory that it would reach the heart. And so, at the risk of suicide, had become the founder of angioplasty.

No, she was speculating wildly. In fact, apart from hearsay, she had no idea at what stage Professor Lind's work on cognitive enhancers was.

So why did she feel she didn't trust him? Couldn't. Wouldn't. Was it the seductive charm he had turned on her when he hailed her as his saviour as they waited to go into dinner? She was never at ease with that kind of charm, had in fact long schooled herself against it. It was the charm the older man deployed with the young woman, all teasing fondness and subtle persuasion. But she hadn't been young for a long time, forever it sometimes seemed, and Bruno Lind could hardly be blind to the fact.

'Ms Davies, Irena, may I call you that?'

She jumped back, surprised at his sudden appearance beside her, his hand on her shoulder.

'Forgive me. You look a little lost. I thought perhaps I might introduce you to some of the confraternity. I know quite a few of them.'

'That's kind,' she said, her tone too regal for her words. She bridled under the hint of patronage. That was it, she thought. This Lind was just a trifle pompous, full of himself. Urging the little Eastern European she was into the bright light of the Western day. They were all like that. When they were kind, that is. They wore that air of bestowing favours. Making lordly assumptions about what was for the best, when they had no idea. No idea about anything, really.

The chip on her shoulder, Irena noted, was in danger of metamorphosing into a millstone. She forced a gracious smile to her lips.

Lind introduced her to some colleagues – a Spaniard with an impossible accent, a handsome woman from Berlin and then to the Englishman who had stood in for him. Wood seemed to be a genial man, and the conversation bubbled and flowed. She envied the easy camaraderie amongst them, the liveliness. They had ready-made topics to hand, gossip about people she didn't know, shared interests. Like members of some wandering community that regrouped whenever it met.

Lind had obviously caught her blank stare and was now trying to explain something about peptides to her and how a particular set of sequences Andrew Wood's lab was working on could convert weak memories into stronger ones – and thus potentially be of use in preventing the full onslaught of Alzheimer's disease.

'Where are you attached to, Ms Davies?' Wood addressed her directly for the first time.

'No, no. You've misunderstood. I'm not attached to a lab. I'm a journalist.'

The temperature of the group seemed to drop a few notches. A wariness crept in.

'With a London paper?'

Before she could answer, Aleksander Tarski came over to their group. He was balancing two cups of coffee, and he handed her one with a murmur.

'I'm a freelance,' she said softly, using the moment.

Lind took a step backwards as if he were on the verge of leaving them.

Trapped in the growing silence, Irena hastily filled it with introductions, babbled something about how she was writing a piece about the conference and in particular the Polish delegation.

'Oh yes?' Wood seemed to breathe easier. He engaged Tarski, whose English was remarkably good, in conversation. It turned out they had a friend in common in Warsaw, and she watched him navigate Tarski out of earshot to query him about his work. What was it she had overheard him say earlier? That he came to these meetings because you learned things in informal ways and without having to wait for what was at least the eight-month delay of

publication, by which time an experiment could already have been disproved. Yes, that was interesting. Camaraderie married to competition. Sharing but with a level of secrecy.

She could still feel Lind's disapproval. It seemed to have extended to the whole group. No, he wasn't an easy man. He hadn't taken in that she was a journalist before. Irena excused herself. She wanted another drink. But in a moment he was at her side again.

'Shall we get a refill? They have decaf too, if you prefer. And *petits fours*. I'm afraid I'm greedy. I can never resist.'

It would have been rude to refuse. But she decided to challenge him and get it all out of the way. She had always preferred directness, though for much of her life it hadn't been an option open to her.

'You don't approve of having journalists here?'

'No, no. Not at all. It's just useful to know who they are before... Well, let's just say before anything gets mistranslated or hyped as miracle. Do you have a background in science?'

She chuckled. 'So far in the background, you might say it has disappeared. I'm afraid my one distinct memory of a laboratory dates from schooldays and has more to do with the boy's terrorizing the girls with Bunsen burners and blistering acid than with the subtlety of equations.'

'I see.' His tone was noncommittal, and she instantly regretted her frankness.

'I did prepare myself, however. For this assignment. I did a lot of reading. And memory, you know... Well, it's a subject that spans a great many disciplines, not all of them scientific – as the mayor so kindly reminded us this evening.'

'Yes, yes, he did. An elegant cull of the dictionary of quotations, I thought. Including Roosevelt – Franklin D that is – from his address to the booksellers of America in 1942... Did you know it before?' He put on a low but oracular voice. '"No man and no force can abolish memory. No man and no force can put thought in a concentration camp forever. No man and no force can take from the world the books that embody man's eternal fight against tyranny of every kind." And so on. Stirring stuff. Even now. Most particularly I imagine for officials in countries where a pretty good attempt was made at abolishing memory.'

'Alzheimer's abolishes it even more effectively.' Irene muttered beneath her breath.

They had reached the long table on which the coffee pots stood at the ready in front of white-gloved waiters.

'I'm sorry I didn't quite hear you.'

'Nothing. Nothing. I didn't say anything.'

'Yes, you did.'

He paused for a moment, assessing her from those wolf's eyes. A Siberian wolf, she thought. He had a way with listening, did it with so much expression, that you would be forgiven for thinking he had spoken reams.

'And which paper is it that you write for?'

'Oh, I doubt that you'd know it.'

'Try me.'

'The *Tygodnik Powszechny*.'

'Polish?' He flashed an odd look at her.

'Very good. Most wouldn't even know that. It's quite a famous weekly. It even played a role in bringing down the Communist regime.'

He didn't reply. He was still staring at her.

'So you're really Polish? You write in Polish?'

'I do. Is it a crime?'

'No. But a surprise.'

She laughed. 'What did you think?'

'Well, to tell the truth, I thought you were English.'

'Which means you're not.'

'Evidently.'

'I did live there for many years.'

'Oh?'

'Yes. Almost twenty to be more or less exact.'

'You can't be more or less exact.'

'About life, I imagine you can.'

He didn't answer. He was sipping his coffee as if he had forgotten she was there. He was staring in the direction of Wood and Tarski. That suited her just fine, Irena decided. She chose the moment to offer some lame excuse and slip away.

But he was right. It had been a stupid thing to say. What had made her say it? As if she were about to engage on a confession.

Was she flirting? Heaven forbid. No more men for her. A nun, that's what she was. It's what she had always wanted to be in a way. Even before she had left England. And Anthony had left her. Suddenly. With no warning. Not verbal in any event. All those years ago. Twelve to be exact. This time she could be. Could probably be even more exact than that if she concentrated for two seconds.

November 9, 1989. The day the Berlin Wall came down. It was nice to have world historic events coincide with the merely personal dramas in one's life. It gave a certain heft to things. Helped one to remember the date – which she would certainly have forgotten if it was simply a question of Anthony, his face a sullen mask above the wine-red scarf, walking out the yellow door of the Maida Vale flat and never again bothering to return. Except to collect two cases and three boxes containing the things she had packed for him as distinctly his.

Irena blinked to chase the rising tears from her eyes. Stupid woman. Still weeping. She chastised herself. He had called her that too. She had begun to lose her magic, it sometimes seemed to her, as Poland ceased to be a site of alien difficulty, of daily struggle against Communist odds. With its freedom she got hers. From Anthony in any case. She no longer needed saving.

Or maybe he just preferred younger skin.

She didn't really know which version of events she favoured. Or indeed, which was closer to the truth. Or whether any of it mattered anymore. She had held on in London for quite a while without him, though the friends who had largely been his had begun to drop off or manifest too overtly how sorry they felt for her. Some urged her to hideous divorce proceedings and made her suspect they had all along been envious of Anthony and now wanted revenge through her. She had been too miserable for any of it and Anthony, in any event, had been generous enough. Financially, if not humanly. He may have lifted her out of her little Polish gutter, but he had no intention of dropping her back into it. He had too much pride for that – or maybe he just feared she would take the advice of his friendly enemies. Whatever the case, she was in no state to do anything, except perhaps fling herself out of the window into the common gardens at the rear. But she forced herself to carry on. And everyday she felt more bereft and more foreign.

Utterly alone, a bit of flotsam on the turbulent sea of London. Yet too proud to return to Poland divorced and beaten.

The work at the BBC Polish Service kept her busy, a semblance of life to keep the empty husk moving. There were articles for the Warsaw papers, too. More and more of them with the opening out to the West. But then her mother had needed her and she had decided to come home, though home was changing so rapidly, it wasn't always easy to define it as familiar. Certainly, everything had changed in her own life.

Irena accepted a glass of brandy from a passing waiter. She downed it in a single gulp, revelling in the burn, and wove her way through small groups to hunt the man down for a second.

Yes, she had done a lot of burning in these last years. It filled her with a welcome aridity. But there always seemed to be more things to clear away. More and more to burn. This last quest of hers was a signal of nothing more than that.

Another few glasses and it too would probably disappear from the horizon, and she could fall into bed with a welcome emptiness all around her.

The breakfast room wore starched pink tablecloths, matched with napkins moulded into rigid cones. Its buffet gleamed with laden silver casseroles, interspersed with platters of fruit, cold meats, cheeses – more food than a bed-crumpled woman could bear to contemplate of a morning. Irena walked toward the far corner, nodding at any of the conference participants she had met, and found an empty table, a chair facing away from people. She ordered a pot of coffee, took out her pad and started to scribble some questions in preparation for the day. She was mad, she told herself. She should eat, be self-indulgent, enjoy her respite. For once, she was free of cares.

'May I?' Bruno Lind laid a hand on the chair opposite her.

Despite herself, she nodded politely. 'Of course, Professor. How are you feeling today?' He was balancing a bowl of muesli and a newspaper. The arrangement looked precarious.

'Fine.' He examined her. 'You should drink two cups of warm water and then eat something sustaining before putting that caffeine into your system.'

She didn't hide her surprise.

'I know about these things. I'm a lot older than you. Go on. Go and get something for yourself.'

She went off like some slip of a girl. When she came back, his eyes were narrowed in anger.

'Have you seen this?' He jabbed at the newspaper and handed it to her.

'I'm sorry. I don't read German.'

'You don't need German to recognize the photograph of me. As for the rest, I'll translate loosely. It says some garbage like the esteemed Professor Lind suffered an accident yesterday on his way to the Freud Museum, home of his precursor in the field of neurology.'

'I didn't talk to anyone. I didn't. How dare you suggest that...?'

'Didn't you? Who talked to them, then? And it gets worse, if that's possible. "The Professor, who is here for a conference on memory and blah, blah, might have wanted to set eyes on his childhood home, not so far from his predecessor's. In fact, perhaps he has returned to Vienna in order to lodge a claim for restitution against the city, take memory to court. The theft of an apartment, certainly – and there may be more, an art collection to equal the contested Rieger horde, extracted by the Nazi state when the family left the city. Professor Lind's father was a well-known social democrat..."'

'Is all this true?' She stared at him.

'If it were true, would I be sitting here fuming, finding my breakfast impossible to digest?'

'So it's not true?'

'It's a mixture of truth and lies of the kind your colleagues are so good at serving up. An ignorant and offensive mishmash. An invasion of privacy.'

His forehead had grown warm with perspiration. Irena suddenly felt frightened for him. 'Don't let it get to you,' she reassured. 'It's just insinuation. I promise you I had nothing to do with it. All I did was tell the convenors that you were in hospital. After that...well, it's not very difficult for some reporter to put two and two together and get five.'

'It makes me so angry, I could lodge a claim out of sheer rage.'

'That's why most people do it.'

'Current rage. Not past rage.'

'A claim against the press, then. Which bits fit the facts?'

'The childhood home. I don't know about any picture collection. Maybe there was one.' He grumbled. 'It's the tone. It makes everything meaningless. And my father never left the country.'

There was something in his face that didn't let her press further. He was a man, she thought, who was probably good at rage, though had learned to contain it, maybe deflect it. She sipped her coffee and stirred some honey into the yoghurt she had selected as looking least indigestible.

'Will you be going to any of the conference sessions today?' she asked to change the subject.

He didn't answer, and she let the silence grow. It grew so thick that she was relieved at Aleksander Tarski's approach. She remembered now that in a garrulous moment – or was it because she was thinking of her article? – she had suggested they breakfast together. She gestured him to the seat beside her, moved away the cone of a napkin so that he could deposit his plate.

'You have met, haven't you?' she said for lack of anything better.

'Yes, yes. And I had hoped for a quiet moment with you, Professor Lind.' Tarski's voice dipped, polite with Polish formality over the 'Professor'. 'I don't know if you had a chance to look at the offprint I sent you, the one I wrote for the *British Neurological Journal*, four maybe five months ago.'

'You sent me something? With your name on it?' Lind gave the man a stare that was almost rude with doubt. 'No, no. I don't remember receiving it. You're certain?'

Irena intervened. 'Professor Tarski works on cytokines, their role as messengers between immune and inflammatory cells and looks at how they modulate brain activity.'

Tarski gave her an encouraging smile as if he didn't quite believe her flow of science. 'Yes, we're interested in Il-1, Il-6 and TNF, the tumour necrosis factor, and how they contribute to amyloid deposition and tissue destruction in the formation of Alzheimer plaques.'

'Oh yes?' Lind's demeanour was less suspicious now. 'And how do they?'

After a few minutes, Irena noted, Lind began to wax enthusiastic, and Tarski was gradually transformed, as if the older man's enthusiasm, slow to be roused, acted as a tonic, stirring the younger one's face, his mind, even his body, which now seemed more erect, more vigorous. Irena watched, rapt. It was like watching a mental infusion of some magical elixir or the charge of an electric rod. With the new intensity in his face, Tarski had suddenly been turned into an attractive man. Was this what people meant when they talked about 'so-and-so's' particular brilliance at heading a lab, at getting the best out of their post-docs, that slew of younger researchers who seemed to move round the world like an elite corps of scientific backpackers, sussing out through some impenetrable grapevine which beach or lab was the perfect one for them.

She wished that Lind could infuse her with some of his energy. Not that it would necessarily help her penetrate the arcane matter they were now talking about. If she had come here with the veiled hope that she might learn something that would help her deal with her mother, she was fast giving up on the notion. There was a Gobi of blinding sandstorms and unquenchable thirst to cross between these brain scientists' descriptions and her mother's experience, let alone her own, of the slow sadistic killer that Alzheimer's disease was. Would understanding the nature of a cytokine or the biochemical workings of a memory cascade explain why her mother too often insisted Irena was someone quite other than Irena, someone she called out to with love in her voice, only moments later to sit frozen in terror in the armchair she was increasingly reluctant to leave? Could anything visible only through an electron microscope at a ten-thousand time magnification tell her why, when her mother occasionally blundered out of the building, she would lose herself on a street she had walked on daily for too many years, while she could describe in minute and repetitive detail the night of Irena's birth in a small town hundreds of kilometres away, the name of the midwife, the birds and flowers she had listed so as to mute the pain of the labour – names she still chanted with parallel and rising urgency? Would anything gleaned at this conference help her deal with her mother's sudden rages, so vicious that she felt reduced to pulp when they were over? She doubted it.

If only there were someone to share it all with.

Which is why, of course, she had come. To try again, after all these years. To try and find a possible kin.

Bruno Lind's voice penetrated her absence. 'I'm sorry if I was rude, Ms Davies. You'll have to forgive an old man.'

'No. No.' She had no idea what he was talking about.

'I'll leave you now. We'll see each other later, no doubt. You, too, Professor...Professor...'

'Tarski,' the man filled in for him.

'Yes. Yes, of course. Tarski.'

The next time Irena saw Bruno Lind was in the hotel lobby that evening. He was with a striking chocolate-brown woman, who was slightly taller than him and who had her arms round his neck in what could only be called a passionate clasp. Irena tried not to, but she felt a mixture of envy and disgust.

3

'I want to see. It's important that you take me.'

Bruno Lind ushered Amelia away from the crowded conference buffet. All eyes were on them. And he knew exactly what the mental processes behind those eyes were conjuring up.

'You shouldn't have come here.'

'I knew that if I didn't come, you'd find some excuse. A message left for me at reception. Important paper, blah...blah... More important meeting...' She laughed her low sonorous laugh. 'Admit it.'

Bruno threw his head back and joined in Amelia's teasing laughter. They were outside now, on the busy midday street. A tram rattled past. 'Am I that transparent?'

She didn't answer him directly. 'It's important. Important for me too. I want to see it all. Particularly after you got me here under false pretences. Which way?'

'Let's take a taxi.'

'I'd rather walk, if you're up to it. I've been sitting too much. Feel as if I've been on planes for weeks. And I spent most of last night tossing and turning.'

Bruno nodded and matched his step to her long, loose stride. 'I didn't ask them to send for you, you know. The hospital must have found your name under next of kin in my passport. They did it without asking me.'

'So you've already told me. But they had reason. You were out cold. And not exactly in your first youth. They were right. Altogether responsible. So stop complaining. Anyhow, I'm thrilled that you're up and about. I had you nicely stretched out in a long, low coffin by the time the plane finally landed. And when the hospital managed to explain that they'd lost you, I thought...' She rolled her eyes like a silent film star. 'Never mind all that now. I'm thrilled to be here. Overjoyed. You should have asked me in the first place, Pops. I would have come with you in a flash. I did come in a flash.'

She wound her arm through his, and he patted her hand, again aware of the blatantly disapproving stares of strangers. Let them stare. Let them eat their petty hearts out. Let them have fantasies of miscegenation and stoke the ardour of their barely hidden race-hatred. He adored the big, black, beautiful woman at his side. He adored his daughter. Loved her throaty voice with its whoops of laughter, her humour, sharp and cajoling by turn, her wit, her long gangling limbs, which still left her with a residue of the baseball-playing tomboy she had once so emphatically been before she transformed herself into a bewitching woman.

Now that she was beside him, he realized again how much he missed her now that distance separated them. Easy, spur-of-the-moment encounters were out of the question. London and Los Angeles were just a little too far apart for a last-minute dinner or concert or a casual walk. And a disembodied voice on the telephone was good but not the same.

'Must have been difficult leaving work and...and everyone so quickly?'

She gave him a look of mock severity. 'I'm a very efficient woman when needs be, Pops. And the Agency provides me with assistants who can talk to the clients well enough. Then there's always this,' she patted her jacket pocket where she kept her mobile, 'for emergencies and for those poor, despairing writers blocking on a sixth rewrite. As for the rest of those "everyones" you're too polite to ask about, nothing has changed since we saw each other over Christmas. There isn't one who minds. So I'm all yours.'

It had always puzzled Bruno that this wonderful woman who was his daughter wasn't besieged by suitors. Unless men had changed so radically that he could fail to identify one, it seemed to him that the choice must be hers. That she kept them at bay after the unhappy episode of her first marriage.

'I'm all yours, that is, if you don't go all secretive and moody. I don't see why you can't just march me to the old family home and ask to see it properly. I know...I know, the accident was unfortunate, so you're a little wary. And the memories can't be of the best... Still... You've come to a conference on memory, not amnesia. So you'll just have to follow suit.'

Her voice was an invitation to tell the story he had always avoided, never filling in anything but the barest details. As if he still had the need to hide. Even now. Today. The habit of disguise went deep. He hadn't shown her the newspaper article with the vile insinuations that had so troubled him. Or confessed that the accident with the skate-boarder had brought graver scenes in its train.

They were crossing a green in front of the massive Votivkirche. His father's voice suddenly rang in his ears. His father telling him in that sweet serious way he had, as if he were addressing an adult to whom one had to be especially kind, that the massive church with its two monumental steeples had been built on the very spot where Emperor Franz Josef had survived an assassination attempt by a rebellious Hungarian. Bruno heard himself repeating this piece of information to his daughter in the same tone of voice then adding: 'And this bit of park is named after a one-time neighbour of ours.'

'Sigmund Freud Park.' Amelia read the street sign with emphatic disbelief. 'You never told me he was a neighbour.'

'The blow on the head must have brought it back,' Bruno offered with a touch of mischief.

'Is that a suggestion that I take up beating you?'

'Don't think so.'

'You're strange, you know. You always used to encourage me to look into the past, to find out more.'

'That was different. You were different. You were curious. You wanted to know. I already know too much. And all of it is bad.'

Without realizing it, his voice had dropped to a murmur.

'But I like bad. Especially big bad men. Maybe that's your doing. So I should be told why. And I'm curious about you. Now that I'm old enough to see that you really did manage to be alive before I appeared on the scene.' Her self-mockery teased him.

They crossed the busy Wahringerstrasse, and Bruno let his feet lead them. This was home ground. His school wasn't very far away. Had they already taught him the rudiments of English there? No, no. There was a tutor at home, and his mother would sit in on lessons because she too wanted to learn and as she said, her little *Schatzen*, her little treasure of a boy, couldn't be allowed to be cleverer than her. Not yet, not yet. So they had repeated the names of objects together as an Englishman in a tweed jacket that sported strange brown patches on the sleeves had leaped about the room pointing with a ruler to everything that could bear a tap, including Bruno's legs and arms.

'My mother was a very pretty woman,' Bruno said.

'I wish you had photographs of her. And your father.'

'So do I.'

It was difficult to remember the faces of childhood. Perhaps one never did, not formally, as an image in the mind, though one recognized faces if they turned up. Remembering and recognizing were not identical functions, as all the experiments showed. What he remembered of his mother was a presence, a gracious turn of face or arm, cool fingers in his hair, a scent spiced with lemon and... No...no. He wouldn't go any further.

'It was different for you, Amelia, you know. You never knew your biological parents. And when the time came that you wanted to, it seemed right to encourage you.'

Eve and he had agreed on that. Had agreed way back in the sixties when they had adopted the tiny mite who was to grow into the woman beside him. They had always told her, ever since she had begun to ask, what was effectively a child's version of the truth. That she had been chosen. That her mommy, Eve, couldn't have babies – she had left it too late, what with the death of her first husband in the war, then her medical training and work. Bruno had met her when she was already forty, six years older than he was, though she looked utterly girlish, a dark, slim, darting creature with curling black hair and red lips that burst into lavish smiles, sunlight after the storms of her cares. The miracle was she had chased him. Had eventually proposed in a matter of fact way, or he would never have thought of it.

It wasn't that he didn't want to settle down. Or that he didn't like women. There had, in the welter of circumstance, been perhaps too many. His desires seemed not so much unassuageable as somewhat random, unpredictable. Yet he had benefited from the kindness of women. And he had loved them in turn, passionately at times, best as he could at others. But somehow he had never settled. It wasn't quite an inability to commit, as the modish agony aunts would have it. It wasn't as if he was even hoping for bigger or better or simply other. It was just that, what with work and the person he then was, a little retarded in some spheres, the whole possibility of anything as wonderfully ordinary as marriage and its supposition of a future didn't enter his line of vision.

Until Eve put it there squarely, all details pre-considered. She said to him, you want to lay down roots for the future. Roots in the future rather than in the past. He had liked that. It had calmed him. Over the years she had taught him kindness, gentleness, all those qualities the war had destroyed in him. And he had loved her as he hadn't loved before, perhaps because she had been so open and frank and had refused ploys and mystery, had loved her loyally, responsibly. Had suffered with her when the babies refused to be conceived, had thought at one point that it could just as easily be his problem as Eve's, since there had been no conceptions yet. In the event, he had readily agreed to adoption.

Eve had arranged everything. Her work in obstetrics meant that she knew about services and agencies. He had also suspected at the time, though he didn't say anything, since he trusted her to tell him if she wanted to or if it was important, that she already had a baby in view, that she already knew of a prospective mother, that there was a complicated story in the case. He had only really guessed at the story when they had gone to fetch the baby. And by then he didn't care whether she was black or white or blue. It was love at first sight. The round, staring, rich chocolate eyes, the little folds in arms and legs, the tuft of hair that stood straight out as he folded the mite in his embrace, woke something in him, spoke to him in some deep preverbal tongue so that he knew he would protect this babe with his life.

It was only later that he learned Eve had indeed met the mother who was all of seventeen, who was desolate at having conceived as the result of a drunken night's partying, and who was terrified that her father would kill her when he found out that the youth – who was now off doing army duty in Vietnam – was black. He might kill her in any case, simply for being pregnant. Which was why her mother had brought her from Pittsburgh to Boston, where she had a cousin, on the pretext of enrolling her in a good secretarial college.

All this Amelia had discovered at the age of eighteen, when she set out in search of her birth parents. Her biological mother was by then living in a Philadelphia suburb, and she had agreed, though a little reluctantly, to a meeting with Amelia in town, far from the home she now shared with a husband and three young children. Amelia had described the meeting as the closest thing to a non-event one could imagine between mother and long-aban-doned child.

'I think she took one look at me and that was the full extent of her interest. That and making sure that I wasn't about to start call-ing on her at home and making demands and wanting to meet my half-siblings. One hundred percent white siblings, of course. Her husband was a good Christian, she told me at least twenty times; another twenty went to exonerating herself and assuring me that she knew she had put me into good hands, safe hands. Better hands than her own. Well, she was right on that count, at least.'

Amelia's father, they had learned a little later, had died in Vietnam.

'Is this it, Pops?'

Bruno hadn't realized he had slowed his steps to a standstill, and they were standing on the very spot where he had been toppled by the skateboarder, a second toppling. First time as tragedy, second time as farce. Yes, but far better in most instances, it occurred to him, for history to take place as farce.

'This is it. The Lind family residence from…well, I'm not sure, perhaps my birth until 1938.'

'Imposing.'

'Middle-class.'

'Imposing, whatever class.'

'We only had one of the apartments on the second floor.'

'And servants, I bet.'

He tried to remember. Yes there had been a fat housekeeper who always wore black, and when his sister came along, there was also Basia, no, no…Stefcia, a plump playful girl with pale silky braids wrapped round her head, who seemed barely older than he was.

'There's a woman staring down at us.'

Bruno looked up. 'Yes, she was there the other day. That was the apartment.'

'Why don't we ask if we can have a look?'

'Don't be ridiculous.'

'Come on. What are you afraid of?'

He met Amelia's eyes and wondered what indeed he was afraid of. Would there be ghosts lurking in the walls, odours to choke him springing up between floorboards, stray messages from his mother lost behind sofas, like the notes she used to leave lying about signalling a treasure hunt, sometimes in English. Dandy Lion, he suddenly recalled. It was all so long ago. He really didn't want to go up there. In case there was a fall. Like in the dream.

But what was a dream anyway? Not a sign. Not a prophecy. Just brain activity. Random. There was always more random activity going on up there than in response to any external stimulus. In sleep some of that activity coalesced into images. Fine. There was your dream.

Now researchers believed that memory was 'consolidated' in dreams, the short-term somehow becoming long-term. You could tell by the rate of protein synthesis. Okay. Okay. So what had he stored up? What had he learned somewhere along the way that he didn't any longer recognize? No idea. Not a scrap. Some of them said it was beneficial to dream though. When they cut out the dreaming bit, the bit that also transmitted dopamine, the patients grew listless, apathetic. No more driving urges. Maybe he should have it cut out. Leucotomy. No more dreams. No more falling. Of course these days there was not much cutting either. It would all be done, a little erratically, through drugs.

Amelia was staring at him with all the brave innocence of someone who thought both dreams and history were an adventure, a
voyage of discovery. As far as she was concerned, when truth came
to light it was always for the best. Bruno, despite the scientific
optimism behind which he generally breathed, couldn't rid himself of the feeling that this time it wouldn't be for the best.

And then the woman with the bare arms and the light-brown
hair burst from the heavy door like some explosive force and flung
a barrage of words at him which at first he could make no sense of.
Though the tone of hostility aimed at both him and Amelia was
palpable.

As he accustomed himself to the idiom, he realized that the
woman was berating him. Berating him because she had acted like
a good Christian to save his life, which might have been in danger,
when in fact he was only coming here to rob her of her home. She
should have let him die on the pavement. Yes, she had read all
about it in the papers. And she wasn't just going to lie down and
let it happen. They had paid a good sum in key money for the
apartment, and they hadn't known anything about whom it had
belonged to before them, Jews or Nazis or Turks or alien invaders
or good Austrians, as she was... It made no difference. Their
money had been taken, and she lived here legitimately now. She
had two school-age children he should know so she could only
hold down a part-time job, and her husband had left her last year
for some flibbertigibbet of a vamp in his office that was part of a
multinational, so he was now off in Kenya... She threw Amelia a
dirty look as if she were somehow a representative of Kenya. So
there. And she burst into tears.

'What's up, Pops?'

'She thinks I've come to claim the apartment.'

'What?'

'I'll explain later.'

He soothed the woman, politely asked her name, thanked her
for ringing the ambulance the other day, told her he had no intention of making a claim, that the newspapers as usual had got things
wrong just to fill their pages; and in any case when these things
happened, the claim was usually against the state, which had a fund

set up for such matters. He talked and calmed until the woman started to breathe normally and, as she did, he heard himself asking whether they might have a peek upstairs, just for memory's sake, since she had already come down to greet them. He had spent happy years in the apartment with his parents. And he'd like to show his daughter the childhood home. He patted Amelia's shoulder.

'Daughter?' Frau Berndt looked from one to the other of them with lingering suspicion, now mingled with a bored woman's curiosity. She shrugged her shoulders. 'Is your daughter in the movies?'

He nodded, letting the little white lie do its work. Amelia had an artless glamour about her that drew the eye. It was there in the long-legged swing of a hip, the casual toss of the head, the wide curling lips and cheekbones. He watched it do its work on Frau Berndt, who might have preferred prejudice but for Hollywood's power.

With a little flurry of excitement and another glance at Amelia, the woman acquiesced... If he was really certain he had no other intention but to have a look.

'What did she say?' Amelia queried.

'She's inviting us up. She likes your pretty face.'

'Good work, Pops. I knew you had it in you. Did you tell her I was Jewish?' Her broad grin elicited what was almost a smile from an unsuspecting Frau Berndt.

The apartment had either been subdivided or had shrunk – because he had grown or because every corner was stuffed with painted chests and heavy oak wardrobes, sofas and armchairs, as if Frau Berndt ran a second-hand furniture business on the side, which wasn't doing too well. The whole bore little relation to anything he remembered and he was now disappointed, sorry they had gone to the trouble. Even the rooms seemed to be in different places.

When Amelia, out of politeness, commented on a painted chest, Frau Berndt seemed to understand and explained that it came from her mother, who had died recently. She pointed to other bits of furniture – a loden-green leather armchair, an ungainly cupboard with clawed feet, a refectory table, all with the feel of a country tavern... He just stopped himself in time from saying it aloud. In case he was wrong. In case Frau Berndt heard the displeasure in his voice. It was then that he realized she was wearing a dirndl, a peasant get-up: a piece of folklore in the city. Come to think of it, he had seen other women wearing them too. And they hadn't been waitresses in mock-country restaurants. Hitler's handmaidens.

Didn't they realize what it conjured up?

He needed to get out of here. The place was airless. Like a tomb. His father must be turning in his unmarked grave at the thought of a dirndl-wearing woman in here.

Then suddenly, he heard them. The sound of heavy boots on the stairs, coming closer and closer. The knock. Heavy. Commanding. Threatening. The men bursting in, their uniforms shiny with bars and eagles, their faces cruel. The drawers searched, the house invaded, the money found hidden behind underwear. His father frogmarched away, the sorrowful backward glance, part shame at failure, part courage, consolation, urging future hope.

Bruno shivered with cold perspiration. But he hadn't been there. Hadn't been there when they came for his father. The images weren't his. Not memory of a lived event at all, but memory of an experience imagined, his father's plight, reinforced by countless films and books, perhaps even by his mother's narrative or that of others, a memory solidified by repetition, so that it became a part of him, was felt – a collective memory which was also individual, his own. Here. Recorded in these walls.

Flashbulb memories. That's what they called them in the profession. Shocking, traumatic experiences or images, reproduced by the media time and again, and bringing with them great floods of adrenalin and steroids, picked up by the amygdala and the hippocampus, imprinted. Here, inside. In his brain. As if he had lived it himself.

History wasn't bunk. It was a long trail of flashbulb memories. Countless details coalescing into received images, tableaux, icons, simply because it was these our synapses registered over and over again, learned, until the emotion which had made them memorable in the first instance became trite, third-hand, voided. And then entire sequences disappeared into oblivion until they were discovered afresh.

He forced the racing thoughts away and concentrated on the physical reality of the present.

His childhood home had been airy, uncluttered, modern. Nothing like this.

Frau Berndt opened a door into a child's room and then another and another, a concatenation of doors, and suddenly Bruno had the impression he was running wildly, racing, ducking, pushing one door open and then another, into his sister's room and then out again and round through another door into his own. Round and round, chased by Stefcia, when Anna was just tiny, a package on a bed. Out of breath, he would nip down behind a chair. Hide and seek. Until Stefcia found him and, laughing, picked him up, called him her little man, he must have been five or six – no, more, more because Anna was there – eight or nine probably. Stefcia tickled him, tickled him until he roared and pleaded with her to stop, and the tears poured from his eyes.

Now that could only be his own memory.

'You okay, Pops?'

'Yes, yes. Fine. This was my room, I think.' He looked up, and there, above where his bed had been, tucked into the corner of the high ceiling, was a single figure from what had been a stencilled frieze: a boy drummer, dressed in blue, beating out a marching rhythm all along the walls of his room. What was the song his mother had sung? Sung in Polish? Yes. Something to do with freedom. A horse and freedom. No, no, a little soldier who went off to war with bravery and seven horses and came back with one. Only one... But the words wouldn't coalesce any more.

'Did I ever tell you my mother used to talk to me in Polish when we were alone? Sing too.'

'In Polish? No. No, you didn't. How come?' Amelia was gazing at him intently, as if he had suddenly grown a pair of wings or sprouted fins. 'Maybe we've had enough of this for one day, Pops.

Let's go and grab a cup of coffee. Or something stronger. You look as if you could use it.'

At first they mistook *Philosophie im Boudoir* for a café. But it was a furnishings shop. Salacious sheets and cushion covers were draped over a couch, just a joke's throw from the Freud house. The only neurologist in history to spawn his own kitsch, Bruno thought, unsure whether he reckoned that was a good or a bad thing.

They had to turn a corner before they found a place, a sizeable establishment with *Jugendstil* flowers etched into its windows. An old ceiling fan had been pressed into service and gave their conversation a slow, sultry, timeless feel.

'So your mother was Polish?'

'Galician. It's what the Austrian-ruled regions of Poland were called. Galicia.'

'Like Spain.'

'Like Spain and unlike Spain. Cold and wintry, really, but southern by Polish standards. The lazy south. Anyhow, my mother's family was from Krakow. And they had a country place as well... Further east, towards what's now the Ukraine. Borders shifted a lot in that part of the world.'

'You're telling me. One minute I have an Austrian father, the next he's turned into a Pole.'

'Does it make any difference?'

'Maybe it does. I don't know. I'm just beginning to find out.' She assessed him with her frank gaze. 'Good coffee. And you should eat something. You're looking too white. Can't be right. Gotta get some colour into you'

Bruno laughed. He loved the banter they had developed about colour. Eve had started them off, always sensitive to the slights Amelia might suffer, acknowledging her difference, but not wanting to make too much of it. Colour, race needn't be an ultimately defining characteristic, she would argue with a rebellious teenage Amelia, who had abandoned all her white friends for black, though she didn't feel at home with them either. Colour wasn't the whole of her identity. She was also a woman, the child of middle-class professionals, a lover of books, a champion swimmer, a layabout with the world's untidiest room. And when Pops shouted at her, she knew full well it had nothing to do with her being black and everything to do with lip; just as when she shouted at him, he didn't label her anti-Semitic – it might not be the Jewish bit of him, whatever that was, that she was railing at. As for feeling at home, home was what you turned it into. And so it went on, until adolescence and Amelia's marriage were over, and they reached the age of jokes.

Then, too quickly, Eve was gone: Eve who had been his cherished companion for all those years, first in Boston, then San Diego, then New York, then back to Cambridge, where the end had come. Too soon. The cancer had eaten her up, until she said to him at last: 'That's it. I'm about to lose my most precious sense. Please, please get them to up the morphine. I want to go smiling.' He didn't know if she had somehow managed to convince one of her colleagues, but she went soon after that, faded into her pain and out. Leaving him and Amelia clutching at each other, utterly bereft.

'A penny for those black thoughts that always make you so pale.'

'The furniture. It got to me.'

'It wasn't where you left it?'

'That too.'

'I don't believe you.'

'I know. I can't talk about it yet.'

'Okay. But I'm not leaving you. Not leaving you until I've heard a little more about this Polish mother. A lot more, in fact. I need to know, Pops. Really, I do. I never talked to Eve enough about her family, and then she upped and vanished on me. Parents are altogether unreliable, that way.' She gave him a smile, half rueful, half persuasive.

'Maybe we should go to Poland too, while we're so close. You owe me a story, Pops. A big one, I imagine. A history. To think you've kept it from me even after I became a half-orphan.' She shook her head in mock mournfulness, which did nothing to hide the real feeling beneath. 'Even after I took on the faith. Well, a bit of it.'

It was true. Some years back – for reasons he didn't really understand, except that people did these things in the mysterious country that America continued to be to him whenever he paused to consider it – Amelia had decided to join a temple. She had decided to become Jewish, she told him with a lazy smile, because the Jews knew deep down about the workings of prejudice.

There, Bruno had to acknowledge, she had a distinct point. And if he, himself, knew little of belief or faith, he had an intimate acquaintance with the harsher end of prejudice. Beatings, killings, terror, the inner tremblings of disguise, these were not subjects he had ever before taken up with her. Now it looked as if he was going to have to, though he still didn't feel they were matters that he knew how to broach – even with himself.

He had spent so long dealing with memory as chemistry that having to confront his own past as narrative, whatever the ruptures and blanks, presented itself as a daunting task.

4

Irena Davies tiptoed quietly to the back of the conference room and slipped out. She'd had enough for one day. Probably enough altogether. Certainly more than enough notes to write an article from. She now knew that the cerebellum and the basal ganglia – which was affected in Parkinson's disease and Huntington's Chorea – were responsible for controlling tacit or automatic memory, habits and skills, but not memory of facts and events, which was a function of the cortex and that little seahorse called 'the hippocampus' and probably lots of other bits as well, including electric currents generated by them. She knew that biochemical cascades resulted in structural modifications of synapses and dendrites, and that this was the microscopic trace of learning or laying down memories.

She had also learned that over the ages various metaphors had been used for explaining memory, all of them attempts to understand how the mind worked. There were seals leaving traces on soft wax; vast storehouses with many chambers and ranks of pigeonholes, some secret; elaborate palaces with thousands of rooms each named. There were metaphors from photography in which memory acted like a chemical, leaving ghostly images behind; and from archaeology with its shards and relics, all needing sifting and reassembly. Meanwhile, from the digital world came hard and soft discs and neural nets. There were also homunculi and mystic writing pads in which scratchy traces or scars were left on a hard plate that was continually being overwritten. A little like the more recent long- and short-term memory model really – which was a model and not a metaphor, because there had been experiments to test and prove it in a lab.

In all this nobody had told her whether automatic memory was linked to unconscious memory, in the sense that her mother was on automatic pilot when she was remembering something but utterly unaware of what was going on around her. But maybe that wasn't interesting to the scientists.

On the other hand, she had learned a little about pre- and post-synaptic potentials in cells and the strengthening of links between them – the links being the chemical equivalents of memory. She had also learned about the conditioning of giant slugs, called 'aplysia', who had giant neurons easily visible if you knew how to get at them through the goo. And about target receptors, Morris mazes, fearful rats, not to mention various proteins and peptides that played a part in making memories.

And maybe that was quite enough to try and digest. Which only left attending the session Tarski was chairing. And, of course, seeing him on his own for a while – the train home would be perfect for that. He seemed to be rather a good sort, and not all her hopes were quashed, but nor had she let them rage. She would just have to bide her time and put discreet questions to him when the moments came right. Maybe, just maybe…

But for now, what she wanted was a drink, a chance to be on her own for a while and to do some sightseeing. She might never have the opportunity of visiting Vienna again.

She thought of hopping onto a tram that seemed to be going in the right direction but remembered what she had been told about the city's radial structure and crossed over instead, past the overly impressive Burgtheater into the inner city, where she chose a small unobtrusive café to pop into and down a glass of the cold white wine they called *Heurige*. She wondered why she had refused wine at lunch only to relish it now. She was becoming a secret drinker. Like some aging Edwardian spinster who hoarded her sherry. Maybe it was that she preferred the secrecy to the drink. She rolled the thought round her tongue for a while and decided it was bollocks. The bigger secret, the one she couldn't bear to divulge until she knew more about it herself, was what drove her to the little one, the drink, which at least had an element of pleasure attached to it. And pleasures were few and far enough between these days.

When she had rung home and spoken to Hela this morning, the friend who had kindly agreed to look after her mother for a few days, Hela's voice had been full of awe. 'It's so mysterious, Irena, and so scary. When I greeted her today, she asked me who I was and my age and where I lived and how my mother was, all in tones of the greatest formal politeness, and as if I were a young girl; then a minute later when I brought breakfast, she asked me again, and again after we'd had a stroll round the room. Then all of a sudden she was telling me about the farm she grew up on and about the wheat harvest, and she started naming all the servants on the estate as if she spoke to them daily.'

Irena had thanked her over and over again.

Yes, this interest in memory must in part be due to a generalized fear that they were all about to lose it, as more and more of the population grew older. Or was it because they had given up so much of it already to devices that did the remembering for them – computers and palm pilots, tapes and CDs?

Irena caught a glimpse of herself in the mirror behind the bar. She could do with a personal organizer. It would beep to remind her to find a present for Hela. She must do that straight away. She wasn't all that flush this month, because of the painting and maintenance work that had had to be done on the London flat, but still, she would find something lovely for her.

Sometimes she thought that the fact Anthony had left her the Maida Vale flat had been her downfall. Since she had had to come back to Poland for her mother, she had supported them both on the rent it brought in. Though things would soon change, given the rise and rise of prices, it had meant that up until now she hadn't had to work much, not that work in any case brought in all that much. Though she worried constantly that Anthony would suddenly decide to take the flat away from her. He had always been so much cleverer than she was about such things. And even though she knew from friends that his media company was doing well, and that he hardly needed more income, she worried. Maybe she worried because she no longer knew how to do much else.

Irena downed her wine and strolled out into the sunny streets. It was a fine city, Vienna, the lofty spires rising unexpectedly out of intimate lanes, the flowers spewing out of window boxes, vibrant against the pale stone. And she liked the higgledy-piggledy quality of it all, the lack of straight lines: the lack too, if she dare admit it, of any real sense of the twentieth century, let alone the twenty-first. It felt as if nothing had changed much since Mozart's day, certainly Schubert's. Maybe it was because she had taken the train in, bypassed the airport, and had hardly strayed from hotel and university. The city felt small, intimate, pre-modern. Krakow was like that too.

A moment later, Irena felt she had generalized too soon. To the side of the square upon which she had stumbled stood a strange concrete mound that could only be a piece of contemporary sculpture. There was something frightening about it in the midst of this old square. She walked towards the mound and realized she had happened upon the much-contested memorial to the Austrian victims of the Shoah. The piece was a concrete cast of a library, its volumes eerily visible from the back, inside out, a fitting monument for the people of the book.

No sooner had the thought coalesced than Irena felt the rise of a niggling counter-thought. Why was there no equivalent memorial here, or indeed anywhere, for the Shoah the Nazis had perpetrated on the Poles? In the tide of deaths, three million was hardly a negligible figure, and they too had been part of Hitler's master killing plan. But no one cared about Poles. She had come to that realization in London. Oh, it was fine and well when for a moment they could be classed as romantic rebels, solidarity workers united against the iron fist of Communism, but as soon as that was over, bye-bye heroism. What stuck far more solidly, like some champion brand of superglue, was that her lot were somehow complicit in the Holocaust, anti-Semites from Hell, akin to the Nazis, their eternal abetters of evil in some absolute scale of good and bad. Oh yes, she had experienced those glassy looks even at London parties, let alone the few trips to New York she had taken with Anthony, where she sometimes thought she might have perpetrated the death of millions single-handedly. But history wasn't like that. Not unless you bought into some American comic-book version where good and evil tackled each other like Batman and the Joker.

Not that she bought into the cleaner than clean version of Polish patriotic history either, she hastened to tell herself. That was almost as bad. Inside Poland you suffered from the latter, outside from the former. Maybe she was still oversensitive to the former. At least Poles couldn't be part of the terrorist evil. That was clear. They were the wrong colour of religious. And what would the Pope say?

In fact, after London, it seemed to her that Polish cities had no colour at all.

Right on cue, as if perhaps the subliminal sight of them had prompted the thought, Irena saw Professor Lind and that girl-friend of his. She had to be a girlfriend. She was certainly too young to be his wife…or could one permit oneself such flights if one was a famous scientist? Why not? Why ever not? Certainly, he hadn't bothered with Irena since the woman had appeared on the scene. And she was beautiful, she had to grant him that. Quite deli-cious, Anthony would have said. So there was no question that the great Professor Lind was going to pay attention to her little note telling him that Aleksander Tarski would be deeply honoured (though he would never dare ask) if the Professor could make a little time to drop in on his session at the conference. It seemed he was a great admirer of the Professor's work, etc. etc. It also seemed that Irena had been a fool even to suggest she could work such miracles.

She suddenly felt overwhelmingly tired. There was no point really. No point jollying herself along with her little ploys and silly asides. Even she couldn't be bothered to muster an interest in her-self. No point. Childless women like her might as well be shot when they reached the age of fifty, so as to be put out of their misery. Her only use was in looking after an even more useless mother.

'Ms Davies. I thought it was you.' Professor Lind was suddenly upon her. 'Thank you for your note. Yes, of course.' He gave her one of his penetrating looks so that she began to wonder if he could secretly gauge the level of alcohol in her, or the state of her hormones. 'Of course, I'd be happy to attend Aleksander Tarski's session, if he'd like me there. But wait a minute: you haven't met Amelia yet. Ms Davies, my daughter, Amelia.'

'Daughter?' Irena stumbled over an uneven cobble and struggled to right herself. How cynical she must have grown over human relations never to have had that thought even cross her consciousness. She had locked herself in with her mother too much. She must make an effort to get out more, air her prejudices. Lind helped her steady herself. 'Yes. I'm a uniquely fortunate man, don't you think? She flew over to rescue me from the clutches of the hospital I'd already fled.'

'He'll do anything to get filial attention.'

Irena didn't know whether she had heard the sardonic note in this altogether surprising daughter's words. She stretched out a hand.

'The Professor is wonderfully resilient. If I'd been the object of that rash skater's board, I think I'd still be stretched on the hospital bed.'

'You were there, of course. I should thank you for coming to his rescue. You weren't to know that Pops has developed a late allergy to hospitals.'

'I can't say I blame him. Though the place looked rather more hotel-like than the death pits you get at home.

'Home?'

'Ms Davies, despite her accent is from Poland, Amelia. Look, there's Andrew Wood with Bob Wells. You remember Bob. From San Diego.' He waved across the square and started to walk in the direction of the two men, who were visibly arguing.

Amelia grinned but she didn't follow Bruno.

'Did my father mention, Ms...'

'Call me Irena, please.'

'Did he mention that his mother was from Poland?'

'No, no he didn't. I had no idea.' Irena stared at her. 'But his mother must have been...must have been Jewish.'

'Does that make a difference?'

'No, no. Only...yes. During the war...you know...'

'Well, I'm not altogether sure I do. Not really.' Amelia looked down at her shoe, which was flat and delicate and striped. 'I only learned about it today. He hasn't exactly been advertising the fact.'

'And your mother?' For once Irena felt more curious about the present than the past.

'Dead, I'm afraid. Almost three years ago now. We all miss her. Particularly him. She was a force.'

'And she was?'

'Oh, I see. American. A doctor.' She paused, cast a sidelong glance at Irena. 'I'm trying to get my father to make a little trip to Poland. To take me there. Now that we've come this far already.'

'Why?'

'I don't know. It's just this hunch I have. It would be good for him. Perhaps you could invite him to your Institute.'

Irena giggled. 'My institute consists of one patient, who happens to be my mother, though it's true that – as you might say – she's challenged in the memory department.'

'I'm sorry.'

'It's not your fault. But I know someone who would be delighted to extend an invitation to your father. Though I fear the Polish Institutes can't always afford to pay.'

'That's not the kind of incentive he needs.'

'What, then?'

Amelia shrugged. 'I'm not certain. But anything is worth a try. I just feel that. You know he wouldn't come with me to the Holocaust Museum in Washington when it opened. A friend of mine worked on it and...but he wouldn't come.'

'Maybe he's had enough of all that.'

Irena felt her uncomprehending stare.

'But never mind. I'm certain an invitation would be no problem.'

'Oh, excuse me.' Amelia dug into her pocket and brought out her ringing telephone. 'California's just waking up. I'll have to take this.'

Irena caught up with the men. Andrew Wood was trying to explain to two Japanese tourists that he didn't really want to snap a photo of them in front of the memorial to the Jewish dead. It wasn't appropriate.

Meanwhile, Bob Wells, lean and casual and altogether un-professorial in blue jeans, was reading from his guidebook and pointing at a statue. 'Gotfried Lessing. A great enlightener. He wrote a book called *Nathan the Wise* that was tolerant towards the

Jews. So when the Nazis came into Vienna, the statue was pulled down. Apparently, a new cast was made just after the War.'

'But it says right there...' Bruno pointed, laughed, waved over Amelia, 'the statue wasn't put back on its plinth until 1982. Thirty-six years later. Guess they forgot.'

'Almost a case of wilful amnesia, I imagine,' Amelia noted as she tucked her phone away.

'At that rate, my much publicized, if non-existent, case for restitution should take until approximately 2040.'

'We learn our contemporary history through the histories of our monuments,' Irena heard herself say.

They all looked at her.

'It's true. Up they go and down they come, depending on the regime. Up, down, up down. Like a game of musical monuments. Captions graffiti-ed over, changed, rewritten along the way. Just wait till the Lenins start going up again in the Soviet Union.'

'You really think so?' Wood looked at her intently.

'It's as possible as anything else.'

'We edit internally too. Don't we, Andrew?' Lind intervened. 'When you pump some 2-Dgal into your chicks or give them an electric shock, they forget what they've already learned.'

'They do, indeed. Though only if they've learned it superficially. If the memory's become long-term, it'll come back with the appropriate triggers.'

They walked on a little and Irena paused to look at a house that was far older than its neighbours. An intricate relief showed a river baptism scene.

'Strange to have this on the square and so close to the Shoah monument, don't you think?'

Amelia shrugged. 'What does it say?'

'My Latin's a bit rusty. Something about Baptism in the Jordan ridding one of sin, disease, evil. Ritual cleansing.'

'Oh, I read about that.' Bob Wells joined them. 'The relief describes a pogrom, another great instance of the state using the Jews as scapegoats for various ills. In 1421. Albrecht V, I think it was. He had Vienna's poorer Jews stripped of the little they possessed and forced them down the Danube on rafts, while the richer ones were tortured until they revealed where they'd hidden their wealth. Then they were burned alive. Many chose suicide instead of torture. It's one of the great historical instances of ethnic cleansing. According to my book.'

'I think I've had enough history for one day,' Bruno said quietly.

So had Irena. Pyres had leaped up around the square while the man talked. She could almost smell the charred flesh, hear the screaming children.

She excused herself. 'I'd forgotten. I'd arranged to meet someone. And to buy a present. I've got to get back.' She looked at her watch, made hasty goodbyes.

'One always forgets things at conferences about memory.' Andrew Wood threw her a smile that wasn't altogether reassuring.

Irena had lied. No one was waiting for her. But she had wanted to get away. Away from these Brits and Americans with their certainties about right and wrong, about Jews and Gentiles, blacks and whites. Had she imagined it or were they all staring directly at her when that Bob Wells was going on about that pogrom almost six hundred years ago?

The trouble was they didn't seem to realize every bit of ground here had been the site of some battle or siege or horror. Some plague of rats or locusts. You never walked except to step over bodies. Turks against Poles, against Austrians, Russians against Poles against Turks against Prussians, Hungarians against Romanians against Bulgarians, Lats and Liths and Ruthenians and Moravians and Bohemians and Slovaks and Lemks and Czechs and Croats and Serbs.

And that wasn't even to get into the French or Italians or Germans, let alone the Brits and their ships, ships everywhere, unheard of bits of the world. In her school days, they were given names of battles to memorize, whole lists of heroic resistances against invading Turks and Russians and Germans and Austrians and French. And because the Brits had never been occupied, well not since the Normans, they somehow felt superior. As for the Americans, they promptly forgot all those Indians they'd done away with and behaved as if they had a monopoly on virtue. That Amelia must know better.

She was tired. Overreacting. She shouldn't have left them. But all this effort of concentration after being cooped up with her mother was too much. Her mind had gone to seed, had lost its resilience, its agility.

She sometimes really thought her mother's condition was contagious. That she, too, was growing demented. Several days alone in her mother's presence and the sharp outlines of the real faded, blurred, metamorphosed under the charge of the old woman's insistent emotion. For several months her mother had been certain that a neighbour was breaking into the house, that he was climbing up onto the roof and lowering himself down a chimney in order to invade her bedroom and her lounge and steal her most precious possessions. She would grip Irena's arm with the force of panic and breathlessly recount the experience as if a massed raid had taken place. She insisted that the police be called.

Indeed, one day when Irena was out, the poor woman had called them and Irena had found a bemused policeman comforting her mother when she returned. Irena had, first patiently, and then with growing impatience explained that it was hardly likely that the neighbour would break in, that there was nothing to steal, that he was too fat and drunk to get down the chimney, that reason dictated otherwise. But her mother's nocturnal fear spread through the house and gathered in dark corners.

One sleepless night it leaped out at her, creaked across floorboards, produced ominous shadows that fluttered wildly past curtains and pounced on her, so that she thought she would suffocate. She was certain that a burglary was in progress. Unable to get up or reach the phone, she just managed to burrow under bedclothes. She tried not to breathe. When first light finally came, she tiptoed out of bed to see what had been taken, what mess had been left. Nothing had been touched. She had grown as demented as her mother.

Yes, contagion.

On another occasion, her mother had talked of a Jana, who was coming to visit on the weekend. The best china had to be brought out, something special prepared, because she was a dear, dear old friend. Her mother, who rarely anticipated anything but disaster seemed so happy at the prospect that Irena put extra effort into preparations, bought special food, a good bottle of wine. She wanted to make her mother happy. On the appointed evening, no one came. Irena realized that she had been completely taken in by a fantasy, or a memory, or a hallucination, whereas her mother, when it came to the evening in question, had forgotten all about Jana's supposed visit.

Yes, Irena told herself, she now inhabited a world of shifting shapes, where the real and the imaginary blended with disquieting effect. It was likely that the story her mother had told her all those years ago when she hadn't suspected Alzheimer's or senility or anything at all was as demented as all the rest. Why else, having kept it secret for some forty years, should the woman suddenly decide to orphan her, to tell her that her father wasn't her father at all, to tell her when all the relevant parties except her mother were probably dead and buried? It was an act of maternal aggression that could be considered certifiable.

Lock her up. Lock her up, a voice in Irena now raged. Yet Irena had accepted it all, at first. She had added a romantic veil and a knight on horseback to her mother's pedestrian image; had readjusted her sense of herself too, had even made some cursory inquiries about a man called Tarski, and then gone back with a new tale to tell Anthony in England. In the light of her life then, filled with future potential, what did all those stories of long ago matter? She wasn't really interested in distant, dusty fathers buried in Polish soil.

And then since her return to Poland, it had all begun to niggle at her. Now that she could no longer trust any of her mother's words, it was as if the dementia reached backwards and arched over the years. Every bearing she had grew wobbly, uncertain. Why hadn't she grilled her mother sooner? She had left everything too late. Why hadn't she paid better attention to all those stories of her mother's early life? And whose daughter was she, anyway? Her assumed father's: Witek Kanikow, the only father she had known, a kind enough man, solid, reliable, a railway engineer who shied away from rows or even debates, left those to his fierier wife and daughter and seemed happy enough simply to get by?

Or was there really someone else?

She sometimes felt, as she heard her demented mother shuffling along the floorboards of the small house they shared some twenty minutes from the centre of Krakow, that they were two of a kind. While her mother wandered through the cobwebs – or was it plaques and tangles? – of her disintegrating brain, she, Irena, dreamed gossamer dreams, created fantasies of rescue involving rich and interesting fathers and brothers, even sisters, who would whisk her into a new life – or at the very least, help with her mother and provide an anchor against loneliness.

Now that it was clear there would be no children of her own, in her most secret core she wished herself a new family in which she could feel at home.

Yes, they had become horribly similar. Behind the folds and furrows the years had brought, she and her mother, with those eerie clear blue eyes turned inward, were just two girls – watchful, fearful, yet somehow innocent – still hoping the world would bring them no harm, perhaps even an occasional kindness.

A sombre cloud had settled over the city with no warning. Moments later a deluge fell on the streets, thick, warm drops like pellets, leaping up where they hit the cobbles. Irena took refuge inside a church, a pretty church with a small baroque dome aflutter with angels and puffball clouds. There was a lingering smell of incense in the air. She knelt and crossed herself as she had an intense memory of doing in the small country church of her childhood. She offered an unspoken prayer and then lit a candle for her mother

Two days later, without knowing quite how it had happened, Irena found herself sitting on a train bound for Krakow. It was not the sitting that was bizarre, or the train that was as shabby-genteel as the last one with soft, slightly sagging seats, though the windows had been scrubbed, and at least they could see out. The surprise was who was sitting with her in the compartment. For one there was Professor Aleksander Tarski. Next to him sat Amelia, gorgeous in jeans and a casual jacket with bits of glass beads on it that caught the light. And opposite them by the window, looking out gravely, as if he might conjure up bits of landscape and bring them in for microscopic examination, was Professor Bruno Lind.

For once, Irena thought, coming home held out just a little excitement.

5

Bruno Lind leaned into his seat. The even repetitive rhythm of the rails produced a dream-like somnolence. Greens and browns and blues of varying hues rose and fell before him A herd of spotted cows came into focus only to disappear just as quickly, followed by a regal house with a vaulted dome, small hillside vineyards, and in the mysterious distance, the purple folds of mist-covered mountains, their shapes as inconstant as their constancy. The train might be moving forward, ploughing towards some destination, but the sensation was that of being held in a capsule, one that lulled, produced a hole in time.

It had been an age since he had spent more than a necessary hour on a train. And those weren't real journeys. The one before him was.

He still had no idea why he had succumbed to Amelia's insistence, coupled with Aleksander Tarski's charming invitation and Irena Davies's more diffident persuasion. It felt to him a little as if they were all in cahoots. Certainly, the man and his daughter were keeping up some kind of patter now, which he couldn't quite bother to tune into. But he could see that Amelia was relaxed. That was good. As for this Tarski, if she had any idea of the thoughts he aroused in Bruno, she would probably have dragged her father back to LA in the flash of a credit card. But there was no need for her to know.

If he thought about it, the last time he had been on a train journey of any length in Europe must have been in the autumn of 1946. He could barely remember himself then, imagine himself from the inside. His past was inhabited by a stranger bereft of feeling. Though he must have felt something. Must have felt some hope now that the ghastly war was over. That was what the books said. Liberation. New hope. New beginnings. But if he could conjure up a glimpse of himself, all he could see was a tanned face, an arrogant slit of a mouth and cold blue eyes, eyes that expressed nothing. Except sometimes rage. He had met those eyes in a cracked mirror once or twice. They weren't his. Had nothing to do with him. There was even something a little mad about them.

He was eighteen, a lean, hardened and filthy youth who hadn't changed his clothes in months. A wild youth, who knew about guns and knives and explosives and hatred. Who acted, who sometimes even planned his actions, because, yes, he must have planned. He remembered making calculations, the kind which went: 'If I can hitch a ride on a truck as far as the river, I can then ford over by the bend where no one ever goes except the horses and then...' Yes, he could plan, but he didn't think much. That was probably too dangerous. As for hope, if it was there, it didn't reach his eyes. It was simply part of the body's instinct, a survival mechanism that moved it through the days. If there had been thought or hope, cruelly shattered at so many turns, he probably would have given up, wouldn't have gotten where he was. Which was to a quasi-clandestine room in Krakow, a small, dusty room with a window so dirty no light came through, where a Zionist organizer was going somehow to get him papers that would take him out of Poland. Away. Away from all this. To Palestine or Cuba or America or Timbuktu. Anywhere that was away.

He had come there after a two-day trek from Katowice, sixty kilometres mostly on foot. He had come from a Russian prison where he had been interrogated for what must have been two weeks, though he had lost all sense of time, questioned over and over, day and night at random intervals, about his links with the Polish partisans. Not for the first time. Questioned about names, about plots against the Communists, since the war really wasn't at an end. It was just in a new phase where the Germans, but not their legacy, were out of the picture. At last, he had given them some names, and they had let him go. They didn't seem to know that they were the names of the already dead. He had no illusion but that the next time he was caught, he would be transported to a more serious Soviet prison, a camp on their home soil in the frozen north.

And now, and now this man with a permanent frown on his thin face in this dirty little room in Krakow had taken it into his mind that he was a Pole or a *Volksdeutscher*. A Nazi collaborator masquerading as a Jew so that he could more easily become a displaced person and escape retribution.

The man told him to leave. Abramski was his name. Natan Abramski. He was wasting Natan Abramski's valuable time. He felt like punching him, but he let his hands lie flat, relaxed. He had learned that. And as he stared into the man's eyes, a figure from his past materialized in front of his eyes. A past that was several worlds away, so long ago did it seem, so innocent did the Bruno who remembered seem. A figure from his childhood. An old man with a long beard. A wise man, his mother said. Two children, three, around him. In Kazimierz. 'Play with the children, *Schätzchen*,' his mother said...

'Is Pan Wilmer still alive?' Bruno asked Abramski in a low voice 'And his children, Miriam, Adam? If so, ask him about me. Tell him. Bruno Lind came to see you. The son of Pani Hanka. Grandson of Pan Adek. He'll vouch for me. I'm sure of it.'

'Old Wilmer is dead. And the children too, as far as I know.' Abramski examined him afresh from behind thick spectacles.

'If I were pretending to be a Jew, don't you think I'd have taken the trouble to dye my hair black, done more to play the part adequately?'

The words emerged with a feral laugh and a mad reflection. He had hidden who he was for so long, had masqueraded as an Aryan for so many years, there seemed to be no going back. Lies had grown into truths.

The Nazi logic of race had taken them all over. They were trapped in its stereotypes, its subdivisions of subdivisions – all of them, Poles and Ukrainians and Germans and Jews. 'You want me to lower my trousers?' he had said at last, and Abramski had told him to come back the next day, he would make some enquiries.

A bare week later, the necessary pass in hand, he was on his way. On his way to becoming an official displaced person.

A train had taken him part of the distance, a cattle or goods train. Did he know then about those other trains, the ones that abutted at the death camps? Yes, he must have. Had known about the transports, in any case. But he didn't know the way he knew now, the way one knew in retrospect, a piece of public knowledge made indelible by repetition and photographs and external confirmation. Then, suspicion, distrust, one's own lies had become so much the norm of existence, that a shadow of disbelief hovered over every piece of information, whether because of the brutality it contained or its lack, which appeared as a false hope. The atmosphere was such that he sometimes didn't even trust his eyes. They might not want him to take in what they had seen.

The real could be a moveable feast, in this case a moveable cemetery.

Oh yes, he had known death. Savage, ugly, coming from nowhere death. But his train journey in the boxcar held no special percussive meaning. It was just another uncomfortable way to travel, though through the moving bar at the top of the car, if you were tall enough, you could watch the scenery go by. Where there were no tracks, where they had been bombed or shattered, transport was better. From the back of the trucks that bumped across rutted roads, you could breathe cool air, see storks soar across the sky, sniff fern, sometimes even blueberries and mushrooms which he had foraged for so often that his nose would lead him.

The camp itself was in Germany. Where else could these endless ironies of the supposed post-war take him but through Austria into Germany? The enemy – hated, feared, plotted against, fought, outsmarted too late. He had a feeling the German soil would belatedly swallow him up never to regurgitate him.

Reached at nightfall, the camp – not far from Munich – was an ugly affair of huts and disused barracks strung along muddy paths that seemed to stretch as far as the dark distant hills. Its only other salient feature was the queues. Polyglot queues full of poor specimens like he now was too, deathly pale with blank inward-looking eyes helplessly tuned to an internal slide show. Even the children were like that. Thin, muted, they clung to the arms of kin. When he managed, through some clown's antic, to make a little frazzle-haired girl smile, he felt heroic. But he was quickly reduced to the passive indignity of the queue again as a huge American with too many teeth doused him with DDT. Up the sleeves then down the neck. He heard the word 'deloused' in English for the first time. It was not the last.

The second queue took you to the registration officials. Members of UNRRA, the United Nations Relief and Rehabilitation Administration, who grilled and questioned largely in English with the help of translators. This machine-gun grilling about identity, which felt as if it was calculated to trip you up, turned the interrogators into the kin of the Russian or the Nazi police. Police of any kind. It transformed them into the new enemy, whatever their supposedly good intentions.

The refugees were now doubly displaced, from their homes and by their rescuers, who mostly spoke the languages they didn't. Yiddish, which Bruno didn't have, though he eventually learned to adapt his German vowels to a semblance of it, functioned as a lingua franca amongst a good percentage of the displaced and very occasionally worked with an official.

Bruno withstood the initial grilling. He got the right name at the right time with the right history. There were so many. He was handed his displaced person's official ID, and he got into a third queue. This one led to food tickets. The next, the fourth, led to room numbers and blankets and pillows. As he waited, another queue rumbled before his eyes. The queue with Stars of David on its armbands. He hadn't joined that one. Everything had colluded in making him refuse. And now here he was: utterly alone. And queuing even so. He didn't like queues. In his experience, there was rarely anything at the end of them that was worth having.

The quarters didn't prove him wrong. They lay down an endless track where the grey mud gripped at his shoes, and the rain fell with a melancholy rhythm on tin roofs. The room itself, inside a basic wooden structure, contained three pairs of bunk beds and some metal cabinets, all grimly lit by bare bulbs.

If he hadn't been so tired, if there had been anywhere to go, he would have fled on that first night. He was somehow more dispirited by the bare ugliness of the camp, its prison-like containment, than by so much else in these last years. Perhaps because he had let hope trickle through; had lowered his guard. As it was, after a cursory greeting to the others in the room, he hoisted himself up into the single remaining empty bunk and promptly fell asleep.

In the morning, he met a few of his fellow roomers. There was a bald, broken old Jew, with a splayed nose, who moved slowly, on limbs that felt unreliable. Kazik. There were two young Hungarians, who had spent so much wartime in a cramped cellar that their backs had taken on a permanent curve. They feared they weren't healthy enough to be accepted into the fighting force for the new Palestine, the Haganah, which was where they wanted to be. This he learned slowly and with difficulty, through their broken German. And there was Janek from Podhale, a bear of a mountaineer who had fought with the Partisans in the Tatras and lost his entire family.

It was Janek who had shown him the warehouse space where he could forage some bits and pieces for himself – a rickety chair, and what looked like the top of a child's sloping school desk, which he brought back to the room because something about it spoke of home, that early home, before everything else. Janek also told him where he could get a saw, some nails, perhaps some bits of wood to make the desk usable. He accompanied him to the refectory where thin soup was ladled out by German women who looked as if they might recently have served in more nefarious positions. He also eventually took Bruno into a bomb-scarred Munich where a black market thrived, and the care parcels received in the camp with their odd assortment of unheard-of American products – teabags, peanut butter, powdered soup – and cigarettes could be sold or traded for winter clothes. It came to Bruno, late one night, that Janek, who was hoping for a visa to America, thought that he was a Pole like him. Not a Jew. Perhaps more troubling, Bruno also felt more at ease with Janek than with the others.

But it was Kazik, not Janek who told him he should go and see the camp doctor. A cough still trailed him from his weeks in the Russian Prison.

In the infirmary he met the man who was to have a decisive effect on his future. First, though, there was the inevitable queue.

This time his intolerance of the enforced passivity of the process met with someone else's and got him into trouble. Behind him in the queue that reached outside into the mud under a makeshift tarpaulin, there was a commotion and suddenly two men came racing past him to the front of the line, elbowing women and children in the process. Bruno erupted, shouted at them to get back into their places. Within minutes, there were fisticuffs, and he was on top of a wiry man, beating at him as if he would never stop. Meanwhile the second man had leaped on his back and was pulling at his hair.

Dr David Gilbert might have been undersize, underweight and physically altogether unprepossessing, but when he raised his voice and fixed his unblinking eyes on you, you listened. Within moments, the brawl was at an end. Bruno fully expected another cell. Instead, the men were treated like naughty schoolboys, told to wait their turn, which would now come at the very end of the queue. For the time being, since they didn't seem to be dying, the sickbay needed its floor swabbed. Mops and pails were in the cupboard.

When Bruno's turn with the Canadian doctor finally came, he had the dawning sense he was speaking to someone for the first time in years. Really speaking, which was an act in which another heard you. Intelligence, perspicacity, good will emanated from the man like beams of sunlight after a bitter grey winter. Or so it felt to Bruno when the Canadian doctor gently prodded his chest and with equal gentleness asked him questions about his past, his war experience, his activities in the camp. He asked not in the way of the camp interrogators, but as if he really wanted to listen, as if he fully believed he was speaking to another human being who had an equal grasp on experience. Who wasn't demented or lying. When Gilbert saw that Bruno was following much of what he said without having to wait for the interpreter, he sent the latter away.

A few more minutes of prodding and tapping, a bit more history, and a reconfirmation of Bruno's agility in German and Polish, his smattering of English, and Gilbert asked Bruno whether he had any regular occupation in the camp. He then explained that one of his assistants had received a visa and recently left, so he was now looking for a replacement. He needed someone who could be trusted not to steal drugs and resell them on the black market, who could follow instructions rigorously, who could translate when necessary and who would be willing to help out daily and sometimes at night. Was Bruno willing?

In return for his stunned 'yes' he was told instantly to sign up for the camp's English classes. He was also presented with a military first aid manual, a German-English dictionary and told to read and come back the following week.

Gradually, as he began to work with Dr Gilbert in the infirmary, Bruno received the education the war years had robbed him of. Somehow, amongst the population of the camp Gilbert found people who could tutor him in maths, chemistry and biology. For English, he had a ragbag of teachers, some English, some American, so that his pronunciation always remained a mixed matter.

In the clinic, Dr Gilbert taught as he worked, even at his busiest, even during an outbreak of diphtheria when quarantine units had to be set up.

Bruno worshipped him, gobbled up whatever knowledge came his way like a starving man. He followed Gilbert's instructions with great precision, worked hard in order to earn a rare smile from his mentor. What he couldn't admit to Gilbert, barely dared admit to himself, was that he didn't really like the contact with the sick. But for some reason, he loved assisting in the operating theatre. Watching the cut into flesh, the violence of an incision that was nonetheless benignly administered, calmed him in the way nothing else did. At those times, the images of war that plagued him, still fresh with their horror, receded into a distance where they could somehow be kept at bay: be controlled. One form of physical invasiveness seemed to stem another. The incision made into the body, the tamping of blood, the sewing gave him a kind of low thrum of hope, as if death could be turned back, as if he were penetrating the mystery of life and that dark edge where it faded into something else or nothing at all.

He spent almost two years at the camp. He watched the floating population come and go, a stream of desperate haunted people, who wanted only to find a place that wasn't a place of transit. Bruno had begun to feel that he might have found just that at Dr Gilbert's side.

He did everything the doctor asked of him and more. He would gladly have spent the rest of his days with him, but with his unflinching generosity, Gilbert had managed to get him papers for Canada. On top of that, he had magically organized a place for him on a pre-med course in Montreal. Bruno knew that he couldn't not go, and before the winter of '48 closed in, he was on his way, first to Paris then to Le Havre and then across a wave-tossed Atlantic, so savage it felt as if it wanted to wash the war away.

The ship docked at the port of Halifax in Nova Scotia. Once past the immigration controls, Canada felt innocent. As he walked the quiet streets of Montreal, in search of a rooming house someone had recommended, he looked around him in a daze. He realized he was looking for those men in uniform, any kind of uniform, who had so dramatically punctuated his existence until now. They were few and far between. He had to adjust his behaviour. It didn't fit. It wouldn't do to lurch up and around whenever there was the sound of footsteps behind him. It wouldn't do to finish everything on his plate in record time, so that his neighbours at the student cafeteria stared. Nor would it do to pretend an arrogant disdain and barge through every obstacle, as he had so effectively learned to do in imitation of the SS officers who had so long been a part of his life. And finally, he had somehow to learn how to put this incommodious past behind him: no one here wanted to know, not really, not after the first moments of bland politeness.

From his lodgings in a sprawling stone house on the lower end of Crescent Street, he could walk to the university buildings sheltered beneath a slope that, for a brief few days after his arrival, was ablaze with red and russet leaves. These gave way to gusting winds. Snows followed in their wake, and the city took on a coat of white. He loved the white and the stillness that came with it. The American bomber jacket he had acquired with pride in the streets of Munich might barely be enough to keep out the biting cold, but on Sundays, when he could, he hitched rides into the countryside. The rolling hills outside the city had a quiet that seemed to soothe the tumult inside him, and the blinding whiteness obliterated the images he no longer wanted to see.

He was intent on his courses. His first experience of a laboratory came with what he would later call a thrill of recognition. The business of making up a slide – the thin delicate glass, the fine slice of whatever matter, paper-thin, the drop of chemical from the pipette, the second sandwiching glass precisely placed, the microscope adjusted, the moving, crawling, swimming enlarged world within, so remote from anything he had seen, yet intricately related – filled him with a delight he couldn't name. It was a little like the snow. It swallowed everything outside and made it invisible.

He spent far more than the requisite hours on his stool. As difficult as he initially found it to make contact with students who were mostly younger, certainly less experienced than he was, he had no difficulty in talking to his fellows about the world they shared on the other side of the microscope. He loved its infinite mysteries and the paradox of its containment, its rigorous exactitudes. The business of mixing and observing and measuring felt like a newly acquired and better nature than any he had known.

The problem was he had to earn his keep. Dr Gilbert with whom he corresponded regularly and who kept sending him addresses of new people to visit – which Bruno rarely did – had seen to it during the latter part of his stay at the DP camp that he was paid. But his savings were small and soon run through. It was then that he heard orderlies were needed at the Montreal Neurological Institute.

He knew nothing yet of its famous director, Wilder Penfield. Nor did he have any idea of the work the Institute was engaged on. The inscription above the heavy doors of the imposing eight-storey building on the slopes of Mount Royal, gave him pause: 'Dedicated to the relief of sickness and pain and the study of neurology.'

'Professor... Professor Lind.'

'Pops, are you okay?'

Bruno opened his eyes. He hadn't realized they had been closed.

'We were thinking of going to have some lunch. Will you join us?'

Bruno blinked over Irena Davies's words.

'Are you all right?'

'Yes, yes.' He found his voice and a smile he hoped wasn't a grimace. 'I think I was awake. I was remembering my early days in Montreal.'

'Montreal?' Aleksander Tarski queried. 'Of course. At Wilder Penfield's Institute. You must have known him.'

'You've heard of him? I thought he was utterly out of fashion now.'

Tarski grinned. It gave his long, rather pallid face, a raffish air. 'Under Communism we sometimes learned peculiar things. Not that Penfield is peculiar…only that a distant Canadian should have made it onto our syllabus. He had good early relations with the Soviets, you know. They saw him as someone who was furthering the work of their own great Pavlov and indeed confirming his findings on conditioning.'

'I see.' Bruno stood up slowly, testing his legs and his bearings.

'We were recommended his book on epilepsy and the functional anatomy of the brain.'

'But you never visited the Institute in Montreal.'

'No, no, our possibilities of travel were not great. Moscow: yes, when I was a student in the late seventies and eighties. Montreal: no.'

Bruno waited to speak until they had reached the dining car and been shown a table. He found a neutral topic. 'For some reason I was wondering whether, if Penfield were alive and working now and had the new brain imaging technologies to play with, would these have changed his insights, perhaps even his pursuits?'

'Inevitably, since tools are never simply that.' Aleksander's voice grew warm as he rushed on. 'Once they're there, they begin to shape our questions, don't they? Alzheimer himself would never have made it as a name into the diagnostic manuals if it hadn't been for the new distortion-free microscopes that magnified tissue by several hundred times. Not to mention Nissel's new method for tissue staining. These were what allowed him to see the tangled bundles of fibrils and clusters of plaques that bear his name. See them only after the patient was dead, of course...'

Amelia interrupted, teasing. 'This calls out for note-taking, Professor Tarski!'

Tarski stopped, as still as a startled creature. He turned his face to the window with a gesture of apology.

Bruno rushed in. 'No, no. You're right. Penfield would probably now be busy identifying mutated genes in inherited epilepsy syndromes and certainly in imaging sites of seizure origin, or maybe even moving into gene-chip technology, pioneering implants. You know, Professor Tarski,' he paused on the discomfort saying the name induced in him, 'I was half dreaming before about my first visit to the Institute. There's this frieze...no, no, I'm confusing it with the frieze in the reception hall which shows all the great neurologists, and then at the centre of the back wall there's a woman pulling back a veil and underneath her, a caption: "*La nature se devoilent devant la science.*" "Nature unveils herself before science."'

'They wouldn't dare do that to women now,' Amelia challenged.

'Or perhaps to nature,' Irena offered and quickly added when there was no response: 'Our environmentalists would be insulted, no?'

'I think you're right.' Bruno smiled. 'We were all much more cavalier in our ambitions then.'

'So your time at the Montreal Neurological proved interesting?' It was Aleksander's turn to prompt.

Bruno tried to answer him without hedging. 'Yes, in a way it made me. It pointed a direction. And Penfield himself... Well, I can only say he was charismatic. A tyrant, of course, but a benevolent and brilliant one. I watched some of his operations – you know the ones in which the patient helped to map brain areas in response to the doctor's probe. It was most peculiar, humbling too. These people conjuring up forgotten episodes, seeing relatives in the room, finding acute smells, and then everything would disappear when the probe moved. Penfield talked of a storehouse of memories: a film superimposed on a part of the brain in either or both hemispheres that comes to life when triggered. And pursuing the film language, he talked of flashbacks…'

Bruno stopped abruptly as if the word itself had attacked him. They were lashing back at him these flashbacks, lashing out. They didn't want to be kept back. People running. Crowds. Children staring. Processions. Whips. Marching. Marching. He speeded them up, sent them on their way. Go away.

'You don't see eye-to-eye with Penfield, then?' Aleksander brought him back.

'Was I suggesting that? No, no. He was brilliant. He and Milner, after all, led us to discover the strategic role of the hippocampus in laying down long-term memories. Intuitively, I think he was on the right track. No, I was thinking of something else.' He shook himself into the present. 'As you know, there's so much that still remains unexplained. Biochemically, above all. It's a question of mapping plus much more. Penfield was a great surgeon, by the way. I'm not. I ended up working on the eighth floor. Research. I don't know if my mentor, Dr Gilbert, would have been pleased. He died just before I made the decision.'

Bruno faltered again, still in the grip of his own memories. He saw Gilbert as he had seen him that last time in Toronto, shrunken to child-size, already gone really, but he had made an effort to squeeze Bruno's hand, and Bruno had cried his thanks, cried for perhaps the first time since he was a boy. Gilbert had been a good man. A giant.

'Did Penfield lecture?' Aleksander asked

'I think I first heard him at a meeting. The first meeting of the Canadian Neurological Society, which took place in 1949. I slipped in under some pretext… I think I was acting as an usher. And I heard Penfield make one of his rousing claims. Heard him say that the splitting of the atom was child's play when compared to the task of charting the mechanisms of the central nervous system on which thought and behaviour depend. Guess he was right, there. We're still at it.'

'And so you will be. For a long time to come.' Amelia intervened. 'The last thing we want is your lot pretending you understand everything. You'll just feed us more and more pills, pills for everything until the pills go wrong, and we have to take new ones to get over the damage.'

'But Amelia, if there had been something for your mother to take, you would have been happy.'

'That's different, Pops. That was cancer. Not her mind.'

'Amelia is a pharmaceutical Calvinist,' Bruno explained.

'That must make me into a hedonist for once. I would be very happy if there was a pill for my mother's mind.'

'Oh.'

They all stared at Irena.

She squirmed. 'Yes, yes. She has Alzheimer's.' She said it softly, quickly, as if she didn't want anyone really to hear. As if a kind of infectious shame came with it.

'That's hard,' Bruno offered. 'Hard on her. And everyone around her.'

'The trouble is,' Irena burst out, 'we want mental processes to have a physical base. And at the same time we don't. We want to be free, not to think of ourselves as utterly controlled by proteins, hormones, chemicals, even genes. But if something goes wrong with our minds, we don't want that wrong to be attributed to us, to the way we lead our lives. We want the simple chemical diagnosis, the instant pill. Well, I do.' She met Amelia's stare.

'Lucky for the pharmacologists amongst us.' Aleksander turned his hangdog look on Irena. Its irony was uncertain.

Impetuously, she squeezed his hand across the table and then exclaimed. 'Look, look, we've reached the Tatras.'

Past Present

6

1938

'The Tatras, Bruno, look. They're beautiful.'

Bruno refused to look up. His gaze was stubbornly fixed on his knees. They were knobbly. There was a smudge on them. It looked like ink. Why hadn't they let him put on his long trousers? Grandpa and Grandma, when they came to meet them at the station, would think he was still a baby, like Anna. There she was lying in Mamusia's arms, not even bothering to stir and look up at the mountains, no matter how beautiful. He could make her look up, though. All it would take was a little prod. Even a big prod. She didn't cry when she knew it was him. He had been her first word. 'Bru', though it sounded like 'Boo'.

He didn't want to look up. Didn't want to see anything. He hadn't wanted to leave Vienna. Mamusia was wrong. Stefcia was wrong too. It was wrong to go before Papa came back, even if the grandparents were waiting. And the border guards had been horrible, scoffing at them when they came to check their papers, and Mamusia had prompted him again just before to remember to say that he was Polish and going home. As if he could forget after all the times she had told him. Again and again. As if he didn't already know all his times tables and some Latin and the capitals of most of the countries of the world and kings and emperors and some English alongside German and Polish. As if he would trip up, because they were always on at him not to tell lies and suddenly they were telling him the opposite.

'Horses, Bruno. Do look. They're galloping.' This time it was Stefcia urging.

He looked up inadvertently. The horses were galloping very fast. Two of them. Running away from the noise of the train to the opposite end of a long field. Their muscles strained. They were moving towards a house with a steep bright-red roof. It glistened like jewels. Behind the house the pines were very tall. Almost as tall as the sky.

Stefcia ruffled his hair and then smoothed it down again. 'Good horses, aren't they? Told you so.'

'I suppose Grandpa will let you ride the stallion this year. When he sees how tall you've grown.'

'Do you think so?'

His mother smiled.

She was so lovely when she smiled that he wanted to stroke the place where her smile made a little crease in her cheek. She hadn't been smiling much recently. Not really since those boys with the swastika shirts had beat him up. It was horrible. He hadn't been able to fight back. Only a kick or two and then they had held his legs. There were too many of them, and they were too big. They were everywhere too. Gangs of them. Marching. Looking so proud of themselves. They had beaten him up because he was a Jew.

He had never thought much about being a Jew until some of the boys in school had made it an issue. He had had to ask Papa what it really meant and what was wrong with it, and all Papa had been able to tell him was that mostly everyone had been a Jew until Christ came along. He had muttered that and something else and then told him that Hitler and his Nazi Party with all their police forces were blaming the Jews for Germany's and now Austria's problems. All the problems since the last war, including the loss of the last war. It was convenient to have a group to blame things on. But that kind of lazy thinking had to be fought, and his father's party was fighting it.

Bruno thought that those scary men with their shiny uniforms had come to take his father away because he had gone to fight the boys who had beat Bruno up. Probably their parents, as well. Arthur, his best friend, had said that was silly. His father wouldn't do anything so stupid. Arthur and his family had left Vienna now. Papa had lent them money and arranged for their papers, for special letters of invitation to come for them from England. Bruno had overheard his mother talking to him about it. Father had done the same for other people too. There was a drawer in the house he wasn't allowed to open. High up in the back of the pantry. You had to get a chair. A secret drawer, but his father had told him a few months before that should anything happen to him, he was to open it. There might be money there he could use. Other things. But when he had gone to the place just two days ago, it was empty and his mother had scolded him. She must have been there first.

Mamusia was passing Anna to Stefcia to hold and wrapping her arm round him, urging him to look at the hills, blue and purple in the distance. He didn't know whether he ought to squirm away and sit up straight. What if the conductor came and saw him all curled up against Mamusia? But he couldn't resist.

She had tried to make him understand again last night. That Papa wanted them to go, just like Arthur and his other friends. She had cried a little then quickly wiped the tears away. He couldn't bear to see her crying. It made him angry too. Angry at her. But more angry at everyone else. He mustn't let her cry again. He would take care of her. And Stefcia. After all, he was in double fig-ures now. And he had Papa's binoculars. They hung black and solid against his chest. He flicked open the snap on the leather case and adjusted them to his eyes, first the little knob in the middle, then the two separate lenses, just like Papa had shown him. Now he could see the trees from up close, could almost make out the details of leaves and yes, a fat brown clump of cones, clinging to the needles of a pine behind. But it was hard to keep it all steady with the chugging of the train.

The Krakow station was noisy with the rattle of porters' trolleys and voices blaring Polish over loudspeakers. It was hard to under-stand what they said. It was two years, no three, since they had come here, because his grandparents had been to stay with them instead, up in the hills above Vienna so that Papa could come and visit on weekends. But here was his grandfather now, trying to lift him up in his arms and then with a laugh giving up and hugging him instead, his little man. His big moustache was a soft scrubbing brush tickling Bruno's face. Grandpa had round smiling eyes, and his hair was cut like a porcupine, all bristly, and he was grinning and grinning, kissing Mamusia, even kissing Stefcia and holding Anna high up in the air and bringing her down again, up, down, so that her curls tumbled round her plump cheeks and she chortled and then laughed that joyous laugh of hers, like some wild bird.

A porter put them and all their things into a beautiful black car. They hadn't really brought very much, though his mother had allowed his beetle collection, because he wanted to add to it over the summer, and some of his favourite books. The car took them round the big square with its covered central market, the Sukiennice, his grandfather said, asking him to repeat it so he did and then passed a church which looked even bigger than the Stephansdom and had a tower topped with lots of spires. He could just see them if he bent forward.

Home, as his mother loudly announced was only a few minutes away, round one corner into a narrow street, then another, and they were there in a big pale yellow house, with curly windows and grandma was inside and the hugging started again. Grandma didn't look the same. She had grown smaller, and her hair was streaked grey and white and black, but he remembered the softness of her voice, which had a kind of lilting music. He was going to have his own room she told him, but not here. Here he would share with Stefcia, which he didn't mind at all, since they chatted like old mates way into the night. First though, there was dinner at the huge linen-covered table that sparkled with silver and crystal. He watched his grandmother light candles and mutter some strange incantation as she wafted the smoke of the candles towards her. He noticed his mother and Grandpa exchanging looks and then a shrug and then they were all eating, and Grandma explained to him that she had been praying, welcoming in the Sabbath and thanking God for the good things they were about to eat. His grandfather seemed a little impatient with God and made a joke, saying that women always turned to him and to ritual when their men failed them. His grandfather was always making jokes Bruno wasn't too sure he understood. But Grandpa gave him wine to drink, which made him feel very grown up.

Later while he was laying out a game of solitaire his grandfather had shown him how to play, he overheard him talking to his mother. Talking about his uncle Pawel whom he had met once but when he was so little he didn't remember. 'She holds it against me,' his grandfather said. 'Pawel doesn't want to leave France, even though there are problems with papers, and his law studies are at an end, and there's little money. He's taken up with a French woman on top of all that. So she wants me to go and fetch him, bring him home at once, but you know your brother. If he's set his mind on something, I'm not going to convince him. Maybe Otto would have some effect.'

At which his mother burst into tears. 'Do you know where those pigs have taken my Otto?'

Bruno rushed over to comfort her. She held him so tightly he couldn't breathe.

That night, when Stefcia wanted him to say his prayers along with her, he held back. He hadn't done so before. There had seemed little harm in making Stefcia happy by saying the occasional 'Hail Mary' with her when she popped into a church on a whim. Or offering the evening prayer she recommended. But somehow, the proximity of his grandmother and those other prayers, the whole stormy matter of how he was a Jew, now made these prayers, which he knew were Catholic, seem wrong.

Two days later they were on their way to the country house. Grandpa spent more and more time in the country, now that he had been made to retire from the University in Krakow where he had taught law. He had been made to retire because they were cutting the numbers of Jews. 'Quotas', his mother called it. But it was also because Grandpa was getting old.

First they boarded a train that said it was heading for Odessa. He knew that was on the Black Sea and they wouldn't be going as far as that. Instead, they got off after some three hours at a small station surrounded by fields. The sun was high and everything glistened – the wheat and barley, which his grandfather distinguished for him, waving gently in the breeze, the tiled rooftops, the silvery leaves of the birches in the copse, the horse's rust-brown back and paler mane. The women and Anna had gone off in the car, leaving his grandfather, the man who had come to meet them, the luggage and him to the adventure of the clattery wagon.

Grandpa let him hold the reins, showed him how to tug this way and that, how to talk to the horse, coax him along so that he did his bidding. Both men laughed when the old mare suddenly stopped dead in the middle of the road and nothing Bruno could do would urge her up and away until Grandpa's whip cracked through the air without quite touching her back. By the time they reached the sprawling shaded house, a late lunch had been put out on the old wooden table under the apple tree to the side. They all tucked into cucumber and radishes and soft white cheese on large hunks of buttered bread, followed by berries and cream and sugar-sprinkled cake. As if to celebrate, Anna then took her first unaided steps on the prickly grass, racing towards Bruno on plump uncertain legs and collapsing in a giggling heap in his waiting outstretched arms.

The rest of the summer passed in a dream. He did everything with his grandfather who had decided, against the odds, to turn him into a countryman. Together they collected wood and made bonfires, prodding potatoes under the embers until they were ready to eat, hot and smoky and delicious on the tongue. They fished in the river, catching silver-spangled perch and pink-fleshed trout. He learned to remove their innards in two cuts of his grandfather's army knife, soon earning his own. The fish might find their way onto the bonfire or were brought home for cook to prepare. Soon he could handle the oars on the small boat his grandfather used on the river when the current allowed.

The knife was also used to fashion a slingshot out of oak twigs. He learned to take aim and earned praise for the keenness of his eye, the summit of which was that his grandfather brought out his rifle and let him practice on a roughly constructed target. He began to feel like a hero out of the Wild West books he adored. Next year, his grandfather promised, he would take him hunting. Boar and lynx and elk. Bruno walked tall, already a marksman in his own imagination.

Best of all, he learned to ride far better than he had ever done before, if not the stallion then a comfortable mare who was closer to his size. He rode and rode and brushed and dressed and curried the animal, sometimes sitting by her side at night and stroking her bristling flank. He named her Bessie after a horse in one of his books.

The children from a neighbouring estate came to visit and after an initial stiffness, they made friends. They plucked cherries and apples from the trees in the small orchard and stuffed them into mouths or pockets. Now, when Bruno wasn't with his grandfather or spending the obligatory hour with little Anna, he was roaming the countryside with them. They collected beetles in tobacco tins and watched their antics when released. They urged their horses across fields and through woods. They took them for swims, paddling alongside them, or holding on to their manes in the swift cold waters. They pretended to be cowboys and Indians, drawing inspiration from Bruno's collection of Karl May, which his mother had allowed him to bring along, hooting their way through copses, chasing each other madly over dirt tracks. At night, they lay in the long grass and gazed up at the stars, sometimes singing songs in the soft language Bruno increasingly felt was becoming his own.

At home too there was music in the evenings. In the lounge of the house stood a shiny grand piano, its vast extent lovingly polished by Grandma herself, who stroked the keys with the same tenderness as she washed Anna's baby-soft skin. Both Mamusia and grandma played – lilting waltzes, haunting sonatas, bittersweet melodies to which his mother sang along in her clear voice. Sometimes there was even a little of that jazz that made you jump up and down and which his father loved. But as the summer wore on, his mother banned the jazz without explaining why.

One day, they made a trip to the neighbouring town of Przemysl, close to the Ukrainian border. For some reason that no one explained to him, his mother had business to do with a solicitor. The rest of them walked around the hillside town while Grandpa explained about Ukrainians and Ruthenians, Tartars, Poles, Russians and Austrians and how all had vied throughout history for this pretty little place, whose sole misfortune was that it lay on an important trade route east and more or less marked a border. Stefcia went off to offer a prayer at one of the huge churches that flanked the slopes, while the rest of them admired the three bells at the side of the Uniate Church and even had a peek inside to gaze at the ornate pulpit shaped like a ship. At the top of the town, stood the remains of King Kazimierz ancient Castle and fort all but destroyed during the Russian siege in the Great War. From here, they could see the dark folds of the Carpathian Mountains in the distance, a dream landscape half covered in mist.

Two days later, in less time than it takes to crack a whip, the idyll was over. When Bruno returned from a morning's riding with his friends, his mother was gone. She must have been planning to go, but she hadn't told him. Hadn't bothered to say goodbye. His stomach churned, and he was sent to bed. He lay there, the curtains drawn, staring at the ceiling. He felt both bereft and betrayed. The abruptness of it all, the failure to take him into her confidence worked and worked on him. Nothing could mitigate his desolation: the excuse that she hadn't wanted to worry him, that he had been taken up with other things, that she would be back soon, no promise that he could ride the stallion or that cook would prepare his favourite apple cake.

Why had she gone without telling him? Why hadn't she taken him along? No one would say where she had gone, but he knew in his bones. Knew that she must have gone to Vienna. Because of his father. It was clear that his mother had been worrying while he wasn't paying attention, was enjoying himself. It was his own fault that she hadn't taken him with her. That made him doubly desolate.

A week later, the day after his grandfather took him on his first mushrooming expedition, Stefcia was gone too. Her father came to fetch her to bring her home. She was needed there. And there might be a marriage in view. Stefcia cried. She didn't want to leave. She cut off a piece of her silky plait and gave it to Bruno. He sobbed. He couldn't see his way to dinner. He hid his tears in the room, stored the plait in a tin.

After those two departures, nothing any longer brought any pleasure. He gave up seeing his friends. He did what his grandparents asked, but no more. He sat listlessly for long hours with Anna, turning over cards, or watching her root around in the grass for the tiny things she seemed intent on finding. At the end of August they left for Krakow, and still Mamusia didn't return. There was a letter from her for him and Anna, but it said little except that she hoped they were well.

Grandpa said he had to go to school. Bruno didn't want to go to school here. He wanted to go back to Vienna. He was tired of addressing everyone as 'Pan' and 'Pani' instead of 'Herr' and 'Frau'. He was tired of bowing politely to all and sundry, tired of Polish and Poland.

Grandpa told him he was unreasonable, that these were difficult times for all of them and they had to make do as best they could. He expected Bruno to help out with the women, not make more difficulties. At this Grandpa winked, hoping for a taste of that jolly complicity that had reigned all summer between them.

School was impossible. Bruno didn't listen. He could speak Polish, but he couldn't write it, and the teachers were always on at him. Then came the anti-Semitic barbs, which somehow got confused with anti-German ones when he tried to explain that he could spell perfectly well in German. His grandfather moved him to a school in Kazimierz, where the population was largely Jewish though most of them didn't seem like him at all. In fact, some of them were distinctly exotic. They both attracted and repelled him.

The men wore strange, round, fur-trimmed hats, long black coats and big untidy beards. The boys had long curls at the sides of their cheeks, and their lips were very red against faces that were very pale. With study, his grandfather filled in for him, as he filled in about the origin of the coats and hats, what he called the Chassidic style, though it seemed more serious than a style to him, since it never changed. They also talked a language he didn't know, which had German strewn through it and large hand gestures and loud exclamations. His grandfather took him to the synagogue with the big dome, where they all prayed in what seemed like random murmurings and wails and bobbed up and down to their own rhythm. They stayed around in the courtyard afterwards talking to all and sundry, but even then Bruno felt shy. It was difficult to make friends.

His grandfather hired a young law student to teach him written Polish. The law student was a dreamy sort of fellow who made him read fat romantic novels about Polish history. Bruno now spent days pretending illness so that he could lie in bed and gobble up books by Zeromski and Sienkiewicz. His grandmother, he discovered, was happy to discuss *Quo Vadis* for hours while she did the darning. Her eyes glowed then, almost as much as when little Anna bellowed out one of her laughs. Though she did that less and less the longer Mamusia stayed away.

At the end of September they told them in school that Hitler had signed an agreement in Munich that guaranteed peace. The Poles were protected by their great allies, the British. Grandfather didn't share the teacher's optimism. When a bare week later, the Nazis marched into the Sudetenland, he shook his spiky head in a manner that said his pessimism had been proved right, though it didn't make him happy. Not even the fact that the Poles had grabbed back a piece of Silesia at the same time could do that.

Then on November 9 the papers and the radio brought news of the terrible attacks throughout Germany and Austria on Jews and their enterprises. In Vienna alone, eighteen synagogues were razed. *Kristallnacht*, they called it, because of the sound of breaking glass, his grandfather said. The sound brought Mamusia home three days later. She was thin, white as a sheet, her eyes and nose too large, and she held on to Bruno's hand as if she might fall over at any moment or he might vanish. He suddenly knew with a grim certainty, though she said nothing, that his father was dead, that he would never see Papa again. He was afraid to ask, in case she disappeared again at his questioning.

Little Anna should have been pleased to have her mother back. Instead, she grew increasingly fretful, sometimes pretending that Mamusia wasn't in the room and running to Bruno instead. Maybe she didn't recognize her after all this time. Or because she had grown so thin and didn't look like herself. Grandma must have thought that was it, because she fed Mamusia non-stop, standing over her as she consumed borscht thick with sour cream, dumplings stuffed with meat and cabbage or apples and jam, morning cups of buttermilk to supplement the preferred coffee.

By March, Mamusia had regained some of her colour and her composure. Little Anna went to her willingly. Bruno decided that he could now venture to ask her directly about his father.

She met his eyes for a moment with a fierceness that seemed to leave his skin blistered. 'Your father is dead,' she said softly. 'He died a hero. When times are better, we'll raise a monument to him.'

When he could find breath enough, he asked how he had died. 'The Nazis killed him,' she said in the same soft monotone. 'Never forget that. They killed him in cold blood. Shot him like a dog because he opposed them. At one of their camps. At Mauthausen.' Then she turned away.

Three weeks later she brought a stranger home with her. A lawyer, a Pan Leszek, she said had helped her while she was in Austria. Bruno didn't like him. He didn't like his dark stiffly waving hair. He didn't like the lemony scent of him, like a woman. Even less did he like his bluff good humour that promised favours. One day, Bruno saw him hurrying away as he was coming home from school. He hid at the street corner. When Pan Leszek passed him, he aimed his slingshot at his back. He had the pleasure of watching the man stop and look round him in confused annoyance.

Soon Mamusia had a job. She went to work in the lawyer's office. She left home early and came back late.

His grandparents discussed it all in low voices.

'It's good for her,' Grandpa claimed. 'It keeps her busy, as well as bringing in some money. So she feels useful. And she's young. She can't mope for the rest of her life.'

'But it isn't good for the children,' Grandma said in a stubborn voice. 'It isn't good...' She stopped talking when she saw Bruno and gave him a forced version of her quiet smile. He was carrying a protesting Anna, who could speak quite a lot now, a garbled form of speech, but speech it was. Polish speech in which she often asked for her Mamusia.

Grandma deflected her by taking off her amber necklace, in which ancient insect fossils lodged, and putting it round Anna's neck. Anna loved that, but Bruno could only think about what he had heard. He doubted he could ever agree with Grandpa about this. He tried. He tried not to mind when Mamusia didn't come with them to the country house for the summer. She had to work, she told them. She would join them later on in August.

Three days after she joined them war erupted, trapping them in South-Eastern Poland. For a brief while Bruno lived with the secret thought that war wasn't so bad, if it kept that horrid lawyer away from Mamusia.

7

'He said "no". And I wondered…I wondered whether you might try to persuade him.'

Irena gave the lemon in the tea she had ordered a little prod then sipped without meeting Amelia's hazel eyes. Their pallor was disconcerting. As was the woman's beauty. Passers-by in the square gawked. And it wasn't only because seeing a black person in Krakow was a relatively rare occurrence. Maybe they thought she was an emanation of the black virgin of Katowice and would perform a minor miracle.

'Me?' Amelia had an astonished air. She gestured for the waiter, who for the first time in Irena's memory came running.

They were sitting at one of the terraces in what Irena called the tourist side of the central Krakow square, the side of the Sukiennice on which the flower vendors displayed their wares beneath bright yellow parasols. The side from which you could see the full splendour of the Mariacki Church. The other side of the old cloth hall, now a jewellery market, Irena and her friends thought of as theirs, because it housed the cellar which had served them as cabaret and meeting place during the emergency years and through the eighties. It was here she had first met Anthony. So better not to go there, really. Better not to remember. Better to sit here with Amelia in Krakow's rediscovered splendour, shown to best effect on this limpid spring day.

'He doesn't listen to me, you know. Not unless I put my best bully's attitude on and rarely even then. He's hardly talked to me in fact since we got here, was it three days ago? Certainly not about the past. Either he walks about in a more or less stony silence or he spends his time with Aleksander at the Academy of

Sciences, so I have to go there if I want to see him. Not that I think he likes Aleksander, but at least it's science and not the past. I might join them there for lunch. Want to come?'

Irena shook her head. 'I have to see to my mother. And I should finish this piece on Aleksander and the conference. Though I still need to ask him some questions.' A lot of questions, Irena thought. Her best-laid plans had been scuppered by the presence of Bruno Lind and his daughter. The journey home on the train hadn't provided the solitary moments she'd hoped for. And now, her brilliant idea of doing a feature on Lind was going nowhere as well. She had even imagined doubling it up as a radio feature for the World Service. She still had a good enough tape recorder, and she had learned so much about his field, it seemed a waste not to use it.

'It would make such an interesting piece.'

'The conference?'

'No.' Irena hadn't realized she had spoken aloud. 'I was thinking of your father. Polish scientist revisits…oh, forget it.'

'The great Bruno Lind is allergic to journalists. Didn't he tell you? Always has been. And I imagine that dumb piece in Vienna did your cause no good.'

'I wouldn't produce lies.'

'Not even the occasional half-truth?' Amelia teased. 'But it's not that. He just won't talk. Can't, maybe. During our walks he's been meticulous about describing the occasional building or giving me a disquisition on Leonardo's lady and her sexy ermine in that old house museum of yours but not a word about the war years. Not since Vienna. I thought being here would launch him into it. But it hasn't. Not yet, in any case. Even when he took me to his grandfather's house. It's not far from here, by the way. Nor will he go to Auschwitz with me. I'm trying to be patient. Meanwhile the hotel's allowed me access to their office and email late at night, so I can catch up with California days and ways.' She stifled a yawn. 'I had a late start this morning.'

'I understand, really. They're all a bit like that.'

'What?'

'The people who went through the war here. Or maybe it's the same with any war. Any period that transports you too brutally out of the norm. Equivalences can't be found with which to convey all those terrible emotions, which you probably want to forget, in any case. What those who know say is that the survivors may have talked at first, but nobody listened much 'cause it was time to concentrate on the present, which was terrible enough here in a different way, what with the Soviets. All that pain and turmoil, shameful things too. Acts of cowardice or blindness or avoidance. Better to put it behind one.' Irena paused. 'It was like that with my mother. When I was little, and she talked, I would tell her to stop going on about it. Then she stopped. And by the time I came back from Britain, when I wanted to hear, there wasn't much sense in anything she said.'

'Why do you think you suddenly wanted to hear?'

Irena laughed, unable to keep the bitterness out of her voice. 'Because my future was all behind me, and I was ready for the past.'

'Do you think that's why I want to hear?'

'No, no.' Irena was mortified. 'It's different. Different for you. It's a different time now too, what with Communism gone. Everything's more open. To foreigners. And about the past. On top of that, the survivors are growing so old, they'll be gone soon, so we want to know before it's too late.' She was already blushing so she felt she might as well plunge on. 'And you're American... It's such a distance to...well, to travel into that time. And you all seem to have this cultural thing about finding roots, 'cause your country's so new, so disparate. Here, we have the sense of having been rooted for so long that we don't always want to know how tangled and warped those roots can be. We prefer blaming things on our various invaders.'

Amelia stared at her. 'You speak very good English.'

'I spoke little else for a long time.'

'There's a love story in there, I can feel it.'

'Can you?'

She nodded, slipped her sunglasses down to the end of her nose and peered over them playfully in the guise of a wise professor. 'I have an infallible instinct.'

Irena managed to laugh.

'So what do you think of this Aleksander Tarski?'

'I'll give you the article when I'm done. Maybe tonight. Your father can translate.'

'I wasn't really referring to his scientific acumen.' Amelia put down her coffee cup. 'Why don't I come home with you and keep you company while you see to your mother? Then we can both go off to the Academy.'

Irena stared at her.

'Am I being forward? It would be fun. I haven't been inside a Polish place yet. And I doubt anyone's going to invite me.'

'Of course, of course. You're welcome. But it's not going to be a barrel of laughs.'

'Try me.'

They took a tram on Amelia's insistence from the other side of the tree-lined Planty, a ring road of gardens. On her return from London, Irena had used her store of capital to buy a small house on a leafy street, not too far from the centre. Everything had been so cheap then with sterling to hand. Here her mother could have a ground floor to herself, while Irena was still free to have something of a life. That had been the theory in any case. But with her mother's growing infirmity, Irena was often too afraid to leave her on her own for very long. So she had set up a workspace in a tiny backroom downstairs.

Children were playing on the street in front of the house. Her mother was sitting on the porch with another old lady whom Irena paid to stay with her on occasion, though she suspected that in this last year Pani Maria had grown almost as batty as her mum. Still, she managed to make a cup of tea and carry it to the table. And she picked up the telephone, which her mother had ceased to do, as if the object had grown utterly unfamiliar to her and she didn't know which bit to put to her ear. When Irena had tried to show her, she grew frightened at the voices she heard at the other end.

For the moment, the two old women looked benign enough, resting in the sunlight in their floral dresses topped with cardigans and staring out at the children. Irena, who had long wondered why old ladies wore only patterned dresses or dark colours now had a theory that it had to do with how much food flowers and dark colours could absorb before demanding a wash. Maybe if she had had children, she would have already known about these things. But then, maybe if she had had children, she wouldn't have been here now. Anthony had never wanted any. Before had been too soon. And now it was too late.

'Do you have children?' she suddenly asked Amelia, who shook her head.

'I'd like some, though. Trouble is, I'd rather have them with a man. And before you ask, I'm divorced.'

'A common enough state. I'm divorced. Aleksander Tarski is divorced too.'

'I suspected as much. He has the air of a man who's been hurt by women.'

'Only one official one as far as I know.'

'To give him his due, unlike some of my fellow Americans, he hasn't already told me all about it and complained vociferously about the settlement. Are you interested in him?'

'Interested in him? What do you...? Oh, I see.' Irena calmed her rising panic. For a moment she had thought that Amelia could mind-read. 'No, no, nothing like that.'

'Are you sure?'

'Yes, yes.'

'Good. 'Cause I find him intriguing. Which is a rare event these days. And he seems gentle.'

'Pani Irenka.' Plump smiling Maria was waving at them and getting her mother to raise her arm and do the same.

'Is that your mother?'

'The taller one. The one who isn't calling out. Yes. Marta. Marta Kanikowa. Kanikow is the family name.'

'What a handsome woman. Wonderful bones. She must have been a great beauty.'

Irena hadn't thought of her mother's beauty for a long time. She tried to see her through Amelia's perspective, which was unclouded by familial anxiety, and saw wispy grey hair neatly clasped in a bun, a jaw line that was still firm and clear blue eyes. These for the moment had a dreamy serenity about them.

'Yes. Yes, I suppose she was. When I was in my teens, my friends used to say she was pretty. But she never did anything for herself. Not that in those days there was much we could do, unless you had those extra privileges that came with being part of the party machinery.'

Irena introduced Amelia to the two old women. Both of them stared at her, which in her mother's case, Irena reflected, meant that, despite the rudeness, at least she was paying attention, and the present-tense barrier had been scaled.

Amelia stopped her apologies. 'Don't worry. It doesn't bother me.'

Irena ushered them all into the house. Suddenly from behind her back she heard her mother say: 'Pretty baby.' She veered round. Her mother had spoken in English. Distinctly in English. Though her mother didn't speak English.

'Pretty baby,' she said again with a lilt in her voice and a rolled 'R' as Pani Maria helped her into her customary chair beside the table. She was still staring at Amelia.

'She's singing,' Amelia said. 'How nice.'

'She doesn't sing. Or at least she hasn't for years and years.'

'Well, she's singing now, honey chile. She sure is trying to sing. She's singing Josephine Baker's "Pretty Baby".' Amelia laughed, altered her voice, chameleon-like, so that it came out as a croon, high-pitched.

'Beautiful…marvellous.'

Her mother started to move her head from side to side in a swaying motion to Amelia's rhythm. Her lips were definitely eking out some English syllables in the midst of an audible hum. The words were like a birdcall or a child's song, at once eerie and joyous.

'Pretty little baby, I love you.'

'Hey Irena, your mom is a Josephine Baker fan. She's a swinger. Would you like to hear Bessie Smith, Pani Marta? I do a mean Bessie.'

Marta, who was still humming, had what was almost a smile on her face, though Irena had thought her facial muscles had disappeared, and she couldn't anymore. It was so long since she'd seen a smile.

'She's happy.' Pani Maria said to Irena. 'She's really happy. Look.'

Irena translated and added: 'Carry on with Josephine Baker, while I get some food together for her.'

Amelia sang, sashayed round the room.

'You should get her some CDs. I can send them to you if they're not available here. Better still, I'll order them online for you tonight. She loves it. Just look at her go. My dad once told me about this experiment they did with old people who had Alzheimer's. In a home somewhere. The music is really good for them.'

Irena had a sudden wave of guilt. Why hadn't she thought of that for her mother? It was true that she was always calm when there was some Mozart or Chopin playing, but it had never occurred to Irena to try her on music from her personal past. She would do that now. Almost too late.

Luckily, Pani Maria didn't have to go home to look after her grandchildren and could stay for a few hours. So Irena quickly prepared a large omelette with yesterday's potatoes and put some cold meats on the table, together with a pitcher of blackcurrant juice, a glass and the slowing-down of Alzheimer's tablet her mother took supposedly to inhibit the breakdown of acetyl-choline, a chemical which allowed neurons to talk to each other. They didn't much, as the disease progressed.

Maybe the pill was working a little at last, since her mother was talking to Amelia with some enthusiasm, even though the woman had no idea what she was acquiescing to with all her nods and smiles. In fact, her mother was asking Amelia whether she was from Paris and how kind of her to come and visit and wouldn't she come again please, since she was sure her father would love to hear her sing. She held on to Amelia's hand like a talisman.

Irena didn't know what pocket of time she was caught in, but since she seemed to be happy in it, it really made no difference. For a good many months now, she had stopped trying to reason her mother into the present. Or indeed to insist that she was her daughter and not any other figure in the repertoire her mother conjured up. Most recently, she had realized, her mother often addressed her as her own. They had switched roles. Sometimes she would say she wasn't feeling very well in her throat, and could mama possibly have cook prepare some broth with noodles in it.

It was the first time that she firmly took on board that there had been numerous servants in her mother's early home. Now she could add to this knowledge the uncertain fact that her grandfather had enjoyed the songs of Josephine Baker. She remembered now, something that she had known as a child, known in that half-grasped way which children have since there's no repertoire for them to fit the knowledge into: that her grandfather had indeed been to France in the thirties. In a mournful tone, when Irena was just a little girl, her mother would repeat, 'How I would have loved to go to Paris, like your grandfather. How I would have loved to take you. What stories he told us when he returned.' Then she stopped talking about it. There was no use in having a father who had been a diplomat, not in the depths of the Soviet days. Even a dead diplomat might prove dangerous. It was better not to know about anything foreign, in fact: particularly if one worked, as most people did one way or another, for the state. Her mother worked as a junior schoolteacher, and that made her particularly susceptible to stray words or bits of unwanted information. So she 'forgot' her past. Forgot it, instrumentally. Until now.

So many ruptures. So many discontinuities. It was no wonder people didn't want to talk. Couldn't make sense of it all, all the layers of accommodation, of writings and rewritings, of lies that became truths, and truths that became lies with changing regimes. Narratives were supposed to make sense, personal memory somehow fit into collective memory. Instead there was repression, the state kind as well as the Freudian kind. What you couldn't speak, or didn't want to think, you eventually forgot. She didn't blame Bruno Lind for refusing to allow himself to be interviewed. For not wanting to talk. Words were linear and intended for sense. And there wasn't much sense to be found in that generation's past, awkwardly bundled in too many ripped and tattered layers of history.

Strangely, her mother was free to say and think anything she wished, now that she could no longer really think in any conventional sense. The doubling of that tragic irony was that Irena, who was now free to listen – would even have liked to know – could make little sense of what her mother was saying. Like today, now, with Amelia. 'Pretty Baby.' She wouldn't have known that was a Josephine Baker song unless Amelia had been here. And her mother, who no longer had recourse to a set of explanations that made everyday sense, couldn't have explained.

'We can go now, if you like,' Irena said softly.

Amelia extricated her hand from the old knobbly one that held on to her, smiled, said how nice it had been to meet.

'And she's says that it's been a great honour, and won't you come again? You've made a big impression.'

'Well, I guess it's not every day Josephine Baker drops in,' Amelia laughed as they slipped out of the house. 'Nice place. Bright. Fresh. I think I had a fantasy of crumbling plaster and lots of cobwebs. And walls of yellowing books and a hideous old hag.'

Irena nudged the omnipresent chip off her shoulder and managed to say with wryness in her voice, 'You should have come ten years ago. Pre-Ikea. Though the old hag wasn't one yet then. And you put her in a good mood, so she wasn't even that today.'

'I'm sorry. I shouldn't have said that. I liked her. She's very sweet. You're lucky in a way. At least she isn't in pain.'

'Your mother was?'

'For too long. At the end it was ghastly. And she understood everything that was happening to her.'

'Yes. I guess oblivion is a kind of blessing. I think, though, when the forgetting was beginning to take hold of my mother, she suffered it. Suffered from it. Not directly, 'cause you can't know what you don't know. But you can know there have been gaps. And there was confusion. That scared her. Panicked her in fact. She was horrible to me then. Always attacking me. As if everything in the world was somehow my fault. Especially the fact that she was no longer who she once was. I didn't realize there was anything wrong with her, so I assumed she was simply being critical of me, hateful in fact. Full of hate. And it was a bad time for me, in any case. So when the diagnosis came, even if it was a terrible diagnosis, I was somehow relieved. At least she had an illness. Something with a name. It wasn't only that we hated each other. Sorry, I'm going on. I think we should take the car. It'll be easier, despite the traffic.'

Irena didn't usually like to drive with visitors from the West. They always sat a little nervously in the clapped-out old Fiat that had made one too many trips to England in the old days. But she had held on to it. No one bothered to break into it and, apart from needing a push on very wet days, it was pretty reliable. And she had other expenses to consider first.

Amelia curled her long legs into the front seat without so much as a whisper of 'cute car' and sat back with admirable ease as Irena pulled out.

'I had all that Josephine Baker stuff in my head because one of my writers has been doing a script on her. Don't know if it'll ever get made. She had this terrific record of Resistance work in France. Altogether an admirable woman.'

'My mother had a connection with the Resistance here. The AK. *Armia Krajowa* or Home Army. Which was the nationalist faction, so it wasn't much talked about in my youth, 'cause the Russians didn't like to know it had been there, in case they didn't get the full credit for liberating Poland, and someone reminded Stalin of how he had gone back on earlier promises. I never got the full story from her. And it's too late now.'

'You should repeat that for my father's benefit. Emphasize how sorry you are that you don't know. Maybe it will nudge him. Is it far, by the way?'

'On a good day ten minutes. On a bad day, you could get to Vienna sooner.'

Rain started to fall, utterly unexpected. It grew heavier and heavier as the traffic ground to a halt in front of the high-rise student city until the Fiat's old windscreen wipers squealed with the effort of their labour, and the car grew fuggy with steam.

'So what do you know about Aleksander's divorce?' Amelia suddenly asked.

'His wife left him for a German. Not a happy fate for a Pole.'

'But a happy fate for a Polish woman, one can only imagine.'

'Well she's still there, apparently. It was some years ago. Eight or maybe ten. It happened when Aleksander was working in a lab in Munich.'

'Munich. Central European Capital of Decadence,' Amelia intoned.

'Have you been there?'

'No. Just joking. I haven't got a clue.'

'Well it must have felt pretty decadent back then, compared to Poland. I remember how shocked I was when I first came to London. The freedom. The jokes. Don't forget, we not only had a fair helping of Soviet Puritanism; we also had the Catholic Church in the background. Anyhow, she met someone and stayed on. With their son. I can't imagine that made Aleksander very happy.'

'Have you got any brothers or sisters?'

Irena shook her head. 'I'm a singleton in all ways.'

'Ditto. Though there are three little step-siblings wondering around somewhere who have missed the pleasure of little ole me.'

Irena threw her a quizzical look.

'I'm adopted. Didn't you guess?'

'I didn't think, no…'

'You thought sweet-as-sugar Bruno Lind found himself a nice little Josephine Baker and made yours truly? No, sweetheart. That just wasn't the way. And glad I am of it. 'Cause the woman he found for himself was a real honey of a mom.'

Irena laughed. Amelia had a way with sending herself up. 'So you were chosen. I used to think I might have been dropped. By some passing bad fairy in the shape of a stork, but that wasn't the case.' She veered off into a side street where the trees where so thick it was like a green tunnel. A tunnel that now dripped fat droplets of water everywhere. 'Sorry I almost missed it. It's just up this road here.'

This outpost of the Academy of Sciences was an indistinguishable fairly new block that could have been a set of accountant's offices as easily as a prestigious set of labs. The only marked difference was that the receptionist behind her wide cloakroom counter addressed them formally and treated them with consummate respect.

Bruno and Aleksander were waiting in the latter's lab on the third floor. The place wore a cosmetic sheen, as if each counter top and flask and Petrie dish had recently been washed and polished. For some reason, Irena had expected an animal smell, but it was clear that no animal experiments had ever been carried out in these precincts, unless they took place virtually on one of the two computer screens visible in a cubicle off the wide bright space.

Their knock had clearly interrupted an intense conversation, the marks of which lay in a pile of unreadable diagrams and equations on the table in front of them. She read bits of words: 'synthetic neurosteroid ganaxolone = 3ß-methylated analogue of allopregnanolone'.

'Hope you don't mind. I've brought Irena along. Or rather she brought me. And did so most efficiently.' Amelia hugged her father and threw Aleksander a melting smile.

'Not at all.' Bruno gave Irena what she thought was a decidedly weary look. 'As long as she doesn't hold up anything I say to public scrutiny.'

'Pops, how can you? After the woman more or less saved your life.'

'Indeed, my rescuer. Always grateful.' Bruno bowed.

'I'm sorry you don't want to be written about, Professor Lind. I thought the stages of your rediscovery of Poland might make an interesting feature.'

'Like the Stations of the Cross.'

Irena flushed. 'No, no. Certainly not.'

'Shall we eat?' Amelia interrupted and looked to Aleksander. 'I'm ravenous.'

'Of course, of course.' He moved his long lanky body into action. Irena could see that his confusion around Amelia was growing with each passing minute. 'I've reserved a small table for us in the canteen. I hope we won't be too bothered. Professor Lind's seminar was such a success that I fear we may be.'

'I'll act as his bodyguard. I'm used to it. All those students over the years... I'm an old hand.'

Their table in the canteen was next to a large window. The sway-ing trees seemed about to drench them with the weight of the con-tinuing rain. Amelia chatted and amused, while they swallowed some indifferent borscht and a tired salad. She told her father about her visit to Irena's mum.

'You should go and see her, Pops. She's a Josephine Baker fan. She can sing "Pretty Baby". Really. You could take her for a little turn round the room.'

Irena felt this was bordering on bad taste. She shook off the comment like an uncomfortable splash of rainwater. The Professor seemed to notice. Or did she imagine his slight twitch before he turned to her with his customary courtesy? 'Do you have brothers and sisters, Ms Davies – a family to help you? It can be difficult, I know.'

She shook her head.

'Amelia's right, as you've probably already been told. Music, old familiar music can be very soothing. I had a friend who sadly developed Alzheimer's, and the only thing which seemed to give him pleasure – or shall I say relief from that process of perhaps somehow feeling one's brain unravelling, and I don't doubt that people do experience it in various mysterious ways – was listening to Frank Sinatra. Really, he was transformed when the records, or should I now say CDs, were played.

'A neurologist recommending a music cure?'

'Not a cure, no. We have no cures, whatever the miracles the press and indeed some of my peers love to tout every now and again. I think Dr. Tarski will agree. For your mother, I imagine our science will have come too late...'

Irena tried to remember what she had told him about her mother's state.

He filled in her silence. 'It's very painful to deal with. Does she still know you?'

'In a way.' Irena wondered why she was lying. She corrected herself. 'To be more specific, she may not always know I am her daughter, but I suspect she feels she knows that I'm someone who looks after her regularly.'

Bruno nodded, his face chiselled in sympathy, waiting for her to say more. She didn't. She was thinking that what she had said had only just recently come to her and never been articulated. It had come with the sudden sense that when she walked into the room, her mother seemed happy to see her although she didn't really recognize her. Except with an animal awareness. And an animal sense in Irena responded. Everything took place on the level of sensation. She didn't want to call her mother an animal out loud.

'That's very well put, Ms Davies,' Aleksander Tarski intervened, as if he had heard what she hadn't quite said. It was strange that he still addressed her formally, but now called Amelia by her first name. 'We had a case in my family too.'

'Your father?' Irena jumped in.

Bruno spilled his tea. It formed a small torrent as it ran down the table and cascaded into Amelia's lap.

'I'm sorry. I do apologize. Hope I didn't burn you. I didn't sleep well last night. I'm a bit tired.'

'It's nothing.' Aleksander was dabbing at the table.

'Don't worry, Pops.'

'You were saying…about your father…' Irena tried to steer the conversation back to where she wanted it. 'Was he a scientist, by the way?'

'Yes, yes. He was. A chemist. Though he worked in the industrial sector. Altogether different really.'

'Are you okay, Pops? I think I'm going to take him away from you, Aleksander. He needs a rest.'

'Why don't you get me another cup of tea first, Amelia?'

'I'll do it.' Aleksander followed after her.

Irena and the Professor sat in companionable quiet for a moment. Then Bruno asked: 'And does your mother still talk to you?'

'She talks. Though I don't particularly think it's to me.'

'That's good. You know one of the ways people think about the progress of Alzheimer's is to use a reverse developmental scale. Piaget's is the favourite. You chart the way a child develops the abilities we largely take for granted in the first months and years – holds up her head, smiles, sits without help, speaks a few words, controls bowels – then on, up through the years where she can dress herself – say, around the age of four or five – and adjust bath temperature. Then up again until age twelve when she's mentally sufficient in the sense that she could hold down a job or run a house, more or less. You take these indicators and you apply them to the abilities people with Alzheimer's lose, moving backwards towards childhood and infancy. So you begin with some memory loss, then the inability to maintain a job, prepare meals, handle finances, say, and then you move back down the developmental scale to points like the inability to dress appropriately, to dress at all, to adjust bath water temperature, to control bowels. Towards the end speech is lost. First there can be a kind of babbling and slurring, then gradually there's silence. In the last stages, the patient is like the tiniest babe: can't walk or sit up or smile.'

He paused. 'I'm depressing you.'

'It's getting a little Shakespearean. The seventh age. "Mere oblivion. Sans teeth, sans eyes, sans taste, sans everything."'

'But your mother is still talking. So there's a long way to go.'

'Today even talking English,' Irena laughed. 'When I got back from Vienna, it was a long speech about butter. How there was no more butter. The Germans had taken it all. She kept repeating that. Taken the chickens and the eggs too. She was apologizing to someone. Rather desperately. Telling him or her not to despair.'

'She's back in the war, I imagine,' Bruno mused. 'All that – butter, eggs, any food really – was rather important in wartime. Very important. So sad that it's the traumatic moments that impress themselves on our brains so violently that we repeat them. A little like the lines of Penfield's epileptic fits Aleksander and I were talking about. The fits, he saw as he charted the damage in his patient's brains, would follow pre-marked paths, the paths the violent current had taken before. Over and over. Sorry, sorry. I'm babbling. Butter, you said.'

8

1939

Bruno toppled Anna to the mossy ground: half covering her with his own body, pretending it was a game. The droning was faint but coming closer and louder. He lifted his head just a little and through the tops of the trees he saw the sparkle of a silver body. It was quite low. Much bigger than a stork, but with a shorter beak and this one wasn't yellow. It wouldn't eat frogs either. On the fuselage, he could make out a swastika.

Grandpa had warned them to watch out, to take great care, even in the little woods near the house. Yesterday he had ridden to the station to see what news there was. Krakow was being evacuated. The Polish army was moving east, already in retreat after only a few days of war. There were hardly any trains along the track, only hundreds of people trekking eastwards, tired, hungry, carrying small bundles, asking for food of the occasional wary peasant. Then a plane had come: not a large plane. Perhaps the people couldn't see its markings in the sunlight as Grandpa could from his position. Some waved. The pilot didn't wave back. Instead the plane emitted a *rat-tat-tat*, and machine gun bullets ricocheted against stone, flailed the ground and pebbles and people. They fell, bleeding to the tracks. Grandpa had brought one young woman home on his horse. He said they would all have to pack up and go east. They could stay in Przemysl with his cousins, the Rosenbergs. The Germans wouldn't get that far.

Mother and Grandma argued that they would wait it out here. Pan Mietek, the neighbouring farmer who managed their fields would help. In any case, the British would come soon. Even if the brave Polish army were no match for the Germans, the British would certainly be. All that apart, Mamusia added, she had agreed to meet Leszek here and she had to wait for him.

Bruno was torn. He wanted to stay with Mamusia and Anna. And his horse. He was good at helping now. Pan Mietek had said so. He had done a lot of helping these last weeks, because Grandpa was preoccupied. Even if he was a little small for the scythe, he had helped with the tying of the hay, and he was as good as anyone at pulling up potatoes. He wasn't bad either at milking Pan Mietek's cow and churning the butter with his wife. But he wanted to go with Grandpa too. Grandpa had been a soldier in the last war and he knew about war. Grandpa said they all had to stay together.

The plane circled overhead once more and then the vibration of its drone moved further afield. He could hear the wood's own sounds emerging again. The birds and creatures had been frightened too. Bruno wished he'd had his Grandpa's rifle. Maybe he could have hit the plane with it. Brought it tumbling to the ground. He said this to Anna as he tugged her in the direction of the house, and she laughed. She had her funny hat on that made her look like a mushroom, and she threw it up in the air and made a 'boom-boom' sound. Then she held on to his hand tightly.

At the house there were soldiers. Polish soldiers. Two of them. Tall and handsome in their uniforms, but they didn't seem to be sure of anything. One kept saying they should get going, while the other one helped himself to another piece of Grandma's cake and asked for more coffee. They were requisitioning the car, Grandpa told him, that meant taking it over for the army's use. They too were heading east, trying to link up with their regiment. All of Poland was heading east.

'Why don't we all go together?' Bruno said.

'All together,' Anna repeated.

For some reason that seemed to clinch it.

A few hours later, they were squashed into the car with the few belongings Grandma had packed strapped to the roof and the giant picnic hamper stuffed with food on her lap. It was like going on some outlandish picnic except they had an armed escort. The soldiers trusted Grandpa to drive because, he explained, he knew all the small dirt roads where they were less likely to meet enemy planes, like the kind that had strafed the tracks. One of the soldiers sat next to Grandpa. The other one came in the back with him and Grandma. Mamusia had refused to come at the last minute. She said she had to take care of Alina, the wounded woman, and in any event there wasn't room for all of them. She hugged Bruno to her and told him to take care of his grandparents and that she and Anna would see him very soon.

The presence of the soldiers made the parting easier. He didn't cry, not even when Anna did, clinging onto him like a limpet. He was a man after all, like them.

Closer to the city, the traffic grew so heavy, they decided it would be best to leave the car with a peasant at a small farmhouse. They gave him some money to look after it. Bruno was sad at having to abandon it. But when they rejoined the road, he saw just how necessary it had been. The road was jammed with every kind of vehicle, with horses and carts and wheelbarrows, and with people trudging east.

Only one of the two bridges into town was still functioning in addition to the railway bridge. Even that wouldn't be there for much longer, Grandpa feared, since the retreating Polish army would want to make life harder for the pursuing Germans. The soldiers were still with them. One of them was carrying Grandma's hamper, and people stepped aside to allow them to pass whenever this was possible. They didn't leave them until they had crossed the river.

By the time they reached the cousins' house, which was up a steep hill, it was dark and very late. Grandma could barely stand on her legs anymore, and Grandpa had to bang hard on the door to get the guardian to open it and then had to pay him for his inconvenience.

The door to the cousins' apartment posed less trouble. Old Rosenberg hugged Grandpa to him and made them welcome. The place was full of people, all chattering at once, planning, speculating, worrying, contradicting each other. It seemed everyone in Poland who knew them had decided to come and make use of the Rosenbergs' spare beds, sofas and even, for the children, their floor. They were all on their way somewhere: to Russia or to join the Resistance they had heard about already forming in Hungary or Romania, or to Sweden the long way round, even to Turkey and Palestine.

Bruno camped out on blankets on the floor next to the bed that had been found for his grandparents and the younger man who had been ousted to make room for them. Not that anyone slept much.

In the morning, he went for a foray with Grandpa to gather news and to see an apartment that Pan Rosenberg thought might be available if a sum could be fixed. The old people who lived there wanted to move in with their children. The place was small, cramped and dank, but Grandpa said it would do, as long as they could move in straight away. They did so that very afternoon.

From the window there was a view out over the valley past the river, but Grandma only looked glumly at the grubby walls and dirt-stained floors and ugly furniture the previous inhabitants had left behind. He couldn't work out whether the fact that there was no light made it worse or better. The electricity had gone off. Grandpa thought the Polish army might have done it on purpose. He didn't say why, but he looked grim, his eyebrows knitting together with his frown.

The next day, German troops entered the city. Grandpa and Bruno had gone out early to get what provisions they could, when suddenly near the big yellow train station, there was a hail of bullets, quickly followed by an explosion. They ducked into a courtyard to get out of the way and listened intently to the drone of planes and the blasts of gunfire. When the noise receded a little, they bolted, hiding in doorways, shops that hadn't quite managed to close, tripping over bodies Grandpa had to pull him away from, arriving home so desperate and out of breath, that they could barely make it up the stairs.

Przemysl was now in German hands. A curfew was imposed. After five o'clock no one without a special pass was allowed out. Grandma worried over Mamusia and Anna. By contrast, she was now pleased that her son had determined to stay in France. The Germans would never dare attack Paris. She wrote to Uncle Pawel with all the news and insisted, one morning when things seemed relatively quiet, that Bruno go and post the letter. As if the Germans would let letters through, Bruno thought. But Grandpa winked at him, meaning that he had to humour her, and said he would come along.

They went to the big post office. On Mickiewicz Street, one of the town's busiest, they had to stop at the crossing because of some kind of procession. No, not a procession. People in terrible straits were running past them in a ragged line. Their shirts were torn, their chests naked, raw and bleeding. Their hands were oddly clasped behind their heads. The line was long. German soldiers moved alongside it, bearing whips and revolvers. They hit and beat the running men whenever they slowed. It was horrible.

The men were chanting something. In German. '*Juden sind Schweine*'. Bruno understood that. He knew those words too well. They were the same as those shouted by the youths who had beat him up in Vienna. Except now it was these poor men, with their torn clothes, who were chanting that Jews were pigs.

His grandfather tightened his grip on his shoulder. 'Scum. Monsters. ' All around them people were crossing themselves. Bruno did so too, automatically. He couldn't quite make out what he was seeing. The German soldiers looked so young, so ordinary. Yet they were beating these old bearded men, these skinny, hollow-chested youths.

His grandfather turned him around. 'Come on. I'm taking you home.' When he dropped him off at their building, he said quickly and with an intensity that felt as if it was burning itself into Bruno's temples: 'Those poor men were Jews, Bruno. That's the treatment the Nazis intend for us. We have to be careful. Very careful. You go to your Grandma now. If anyone comes to the door, don't open. If you hear German, reply only in German. Tell your Grandma to be silent. I'll be back as soon as I can.'

When his grandfather returned, he looked grimmer than Bruno had ever seen him. He told them that all the men they had watched earlier had been machine-gunned, their bleeding bodies left in full view on a hilltop of a neighbouring village, where he feared the buzzards would get to them before their wives did.

The humiliation in the streets followed by the massacre was a warning to them. They must take heed. He had already dropped a note for the Rosenbergs to say it was best to take cover and pretend not to know each other until this terrible moment was over. Meanwhile, they would lie low. Few people in Przemysl would recognize them as Jews or as anything else, and that in itself might prove a blessing.

A mixed blessing came from elsewhere first. Two weeks later, the Russians by prior agreement with the Nazis, took over Przemysl. The Germans stayed on the western side of the river, building a substantial camp there. Well-off Ukrainians who, according to his grandfather made up about a third of the population of the border town, alongside the Poles and the Jews, fled to the Nazi side. Strangely, the town teemed, and the population seemed to increase instead of going down. People, who had initially fled Poland, poured in from the east in the hope of making their way back. Meanwhile Jews, fleeing the Nazis, poured in from the west. To top it all off the new Russian administration arrived in the wake of its soldiers and border patrols, commandeering the best premises. After the fighting, many houses were uninhabitable. Soldiers with missing limbs, tattered travellers and the destitute slept rough in streets and squares. The Russian way of dealing with overpopulation, the poor and the housing shortage, Grandpa told them wryly, was to expel anyone who wasn't native to the city or Russian enough to deserve one of their passports and the accompanying work permit.

From his early childhood, Grandpa could speak some Russian. He felt, as he explained to Grandma and Bruno, that it would be best to stay on the Russian side of the war and the river. The Russians had no particular gripe against the Jews. That was one thing that could be said in favour of the Soviets: religion was officially anathema to them.

Bruno watched with fascination the way his grandfather went about obtaining Russian passports for them. First a stamp-maker was found who for a little bribe provided them with a stamp with a Polish eagle on it. Then on a blank page of Grandpa's existing passport, the blue-inked eagle magically appeared beside an official address in the town of Przemysl, half-typed, half written in the same copperplate as the other entries in the pass. Grandma's and Bruno's names appeared too, since neither of them had their own passes. Then Grandpa presented himself at the appropriate office, held himself very straight and looked the clerk in the eye, all the while making use of his best Russian.

A few days later they were issued with the necessary passes.

'Normal rules don't apply in wartime,' Grandpa repeated, always beneath his breath, but always loud enough for Bruno to hear. Bruno recognized that the ability to outwit authority – illegal authorities who ran rogue states through maximum force – was a lesson in survival as important as any his hunting and fishing grandfather had taught him.

Soon after the passes came through, Grandpa, who had been looking for a job since their money had run desperately short, was offered one in the very same issuing office. He had made a good impression; and his translation skills, it seemed, would come in useful. He didn't tell them he was a lawyer, since the Russians had more respect for ordinary workers.

The first item Grandpa brought home with his pay coupons was a radio. He had traded for it. Coupons came with work and could buy a little food. Some people didn't have either. They were fortunate. Every night now they huddled in front of the radio and listened for news.

Food was scarce in the city. Money couldn't buy it. There weren't many peasants bringing supplies in because, as Grandpa explained, they didn't trust money. They were shrewd, and there had been too many changes in recent months, from zlotys to marks to roubles, all of which were worthless and could buy nothing, so they preferred to eat what they had and barter the rest for necessaries.

Bruno was always hungry. His grandmother pretended to have no appetite so that she could give him most of her share. But even that wasn't much. He was growing too fast, she said. He began to get up very early, before light, to go and see if he could meet up with those farmers who still occasionally brought food in from the neighbouring villages. He went to the easternmost edges of the city and further and began to make himself useful. He carried boxes of potatoes or cheese or dill for gnarled women in coloured headscarves. He scavenged old bottles from city streets and brought them to red-cheeked farmers who filled them with vodka or some brandy-like concoction that cleared your nose with its fumes alone.

Men with strong arms were scarce. They had been recruited for Russian labour or had disappeared into the military where they might at this very moment be serving time as prisoners of war... Bruno had seen a sorry trainload of these prisoners one day, waiting to be moved from the Russian to the Polish gauge of train: which was what happened just beyond the Przemysl station, where the Germans and Poles took over from the Russians.

Not yet a man, Bruno's energy was a commodity in short supply. He was happy to supply it and in return earn some potatoes or cheese or a large round loaf or a sausage that he rushed home to his granny with in triumph. She was grateful. But she told him he should be going to school. He argued with her. What was the point of Latin and Greek in the midst of all this? She told him all this wouldn't last very long, and he would have wasted his time. That was on the good days. On the bad days, she said nothing. Sometimes when he looked at her, he had the distinct sense she was fading in front of his eyes. She started to talk about his mother. Talk as if she might never see her or Anna again. Everything always returned to the subject of her poor daughter Hanka and dear, sweet little baby Anna. He promised that he would try and get across the river as soon as it was possible.

Winter had come early. It was colder than anyone could remember. Colder than the mountains in Austria. Colder than your feet turned if you had been skating too long on a bad day. In their rooms, you could see your breath. Bruno scavenged for coal, for firewood, for anything that burned. He met a boy who told him that if they went to the coal cooperative, one of the many cooperatives the Russians had set up, and could give the men a little extra on the side – woollen mittens, say, or children's hats, or sweaters, even some warm cloth – then coal would find its way to them.

His grandfather wouldn't allow Grandma to work, even though the extra coupons she could earn would prove useful. Bruno knew she could knit, probably even sew. She had made wonderful berets for him when he was little, and Anna's wardrobe was scattered with her products. With his new friend, Tomek, he scoured the city and beyond for suitable materials. In the cellar of a derelict building they came across a treasure trove – abandoned bales of cloth, still wrapped in stiff brown paper that had since gone mouldy and was now frozen with the cold. They split the loot and helped each other to cart the fabric to their respective homes, stealthily, at night, always alert to the Russian soldiers and policemen, who turned out – when Bruno and Tomek were once stopped – not to be averse to bribes.

Now Bruno began bartering in earnest. He made friends with the workers in the various cooperatives. He acquired large scissors, needles, thread. He traded chunks of fabric for whatever he could find, rationing it to last. Grandma sewed, slowly, meticulously; but the clothes she fashioned fetched good prices. Though food was as scarce as ever, they now had enough coal. There were also a few new chairs, some brandy for Grandpa, and for Grandma a lamp for reading and sewing by, when the electricity functioned, and some new books to feed her imagination. He even managed to get her a chunk of the butter for which she had yearned for so long, instilling into that single foodstuff all the pleasures peacetime now represented.

When he gave the butter to her, she didn't eat it straight away. She just stared at it, letting the light from the small lamp play over the glistening square. Then she carefully dabbed a small amount onto a slice of bread and handed it to him. Her face was wet with tears.

Sometimes he would catch her looking at him from the corner of her eye and shaking her head. She had begun to treat him more as a man than a boy, though she often said to him: 'You're not yet thirteen, remember.' He knew she disapproved of his activities, though she refrained from asking him what he was actually up to. His grandfather had no such compunction and gave advice wherever he could.

Grandpa walked more slowly now. The indoor life didn't suit him as well as their outdoor summers. He didn't have his old fire. But none of this stopped him from insisting that Bruno now also learn at least a modicum of Russian, which would do instead of Greek, since the alphabets were so similar.

Time took on a strange quality through those days. It moved both with startling rapidity and excessive slowness. Perhaps, Bruno thought, it was because they were in a state of constant vigilance. They were always waiting, like animals with their ears alert, poised for the killing shot or the frantic escape. Expectant, watchful. Waiting for the next strike from above or running for their lives.

People still said the British would be coming at any moment. They would return the world to normal.

Meanwhile anything else could happen, and all of it would be terrible.

With the first breath of spring, he could wait no longer. He now had to make his way to Anna and Mamusia. His grandparents agreed. They trusted him. Grandpa made careful enquiries of colleagues. He hung out at the train station to try to pick up what information he could about the geography of German troops just to the west of the city. The railway bridge was now the only one that connected the city to the rest of Poland, so other means of crossing had to be found.

Together, he and Bruno studied maps and drew new ones, which added all the elements of the countryside Grandpa was familiar with. He showed Bruno the points at which the river was at its narrowest and might be swum safely if the current wasn't too strong and if no soldiers were visible. Or more likely at this time of year, a raft or boat would be necessary. It shouldn't be too hard to find one, since the farmers in that part of the world often made use of them.

In case he was stopped, Grandpa provided him with a pass that he had stolen from his office. Into this he now carefully wrote Bruno's name in both Russian and Polish script. He told Bruno not to worry, but to be careful. The official Russian seal should do its work with any Germans who would bother with a mere lad. As for the rest, chances were, no one would be able to read it. The story was the true one but with no Polish addresses given, just in case. He was going to visit his family from whom he had been separated during the invasion.

Grandpa gave him a loaf of bread and some sausage for the journey and clapped him on the shoulder. 'Enjoy the fishing. And don't forget. When you reach the other side, you're not a Jew.'

Bruno left home at dawn, feeling like a soldier or an explorer on a dangerous mission. He went north first of all, to get away from the Nazi encampment on the western flank of the city and only then headed towards the river, which divided Russian- from German-controlled Poland. What neither he nor his grandfather had altogether realized was that clandestine passages across the San were constantly being made. Boatmen ran a lucrative trade in ferrying people.

As he walked carefully along the bank, he saw one rowboat disgorge far more passengers than it seemed safe to carry and two more speed along with the current. On the second of these boats, there was a commotion, a row about payment from what he could make out. The boatman hit one of his passengers with an oar. The man fell into the water and struggled towards shore. He didn't swim well, and Bruno ran downstream to thrust a stick his way and help him up onto the bank. From his accented thanks, it was clear to Bruno that the man was a Jew. He was shivering, frightened. With a guilty nod, Bruno hurried along, reluctant to confront the rest of the party when they docked.

He realized he needed to choose a prudent strategy for making his way across the river. It seemed he could buy his passage, but that might prove treacherous. One could end up beaten and robbed of everything one had. He scaled a bank-side tree and sat amidst its branches, resting, waiting, watching. Then he had an idea. He found a longish stick on the bank and carefully tied the length of string his grandfather had insisted he pack in his small rucksack, together with a hook, onto it. A worm was easy to come by. He stretched out by the bank with his fishing rod in place, just as if he really was the young boy he was. It wasn't long before he felt a tug, and a smallish perch flew out of the water. His grandfather had always said he was a lucky fisherman. Another soon followed and after it came a boatman.

'What you got there?' the man asked greedily. He was big, his hands gnarled, and Bruno didn't think he was a match for him.

'Lunch.'

Before the man could look around him to see if anyone was about to prevent him from stealing them, Bruno said: 'They're yours, if you just take me across.'

'What else have you got?'

'Nothing. But I know a really good fishing spot on the other side. And if you come back in a few hours, I'll share the rest of my catch with you.'

The man considered this with a visible effort of mental arithmetic. 'All right. Hop on.'

Bruno watched him carefully, his makeshift fishing rod at the ready, and jumped out almost before they had docked. 'Okay, see you later. It's about a kilometre that way.' He pointed and hurried along. 'Enjoy my lunch.'

After that, things didn't go quite so smoothly. He blundered onto a road and saw two Nazi cars coming toward him. With a pounding heart, he leaped back into the shelter of trees and stood quietly until they had passed. It was difficult to get his bearings. The sky was overcast and he didn't know the exact point of the sun or quite where he had reached on his grandfather's map. In his mind, he rehearsed German. It was so long since he had used it. He walked and trudged, keeping to dirt tracks and woods, greeting the people he met as if he were just a youth on an expedition. Night fell before he had reached Mamusia. It was pointless to go on. He made a bed out of twigs to keep himself dry and forced himself to distinguish the forest sounds, the hoots and calls, as he remembered them. The effort put him to sleep, despite the chill air.

He was woken by the sound of voices. He lay motionless until they had passed, hoping his breathing didn't give him away. Then, as soundlessly as he could, he scaled a tree. There, not very far from him, a small group of people were making a bonfire, roasting something. From his distance, their hair and eyes looked wild. Their clothes were torn and tattered. He moved away from them, stepping as silently as he could, hoping that the sound of the fire would mute his footsteps.

With the first milky light, he drank a little water and ate a hunk of bread. He wasn't frightened, he told himself. He had a stout stick in his hand now, and he looked just like a peasant youth on his way home. He would soon be in familiar terrain. It was a bright day, and the sun would help him. He doffed his cap to a farmer in a field. Walked confidently into a wood and promptly got lost. Hours passed before he came across a turn in the land he definitely recognized. He almost shouted with joy. He restrained himself. If he were right, there would be some houses just round the bend. They were there. He marched past, waving to the old man and woman, who were chopping some wood.

When at last he reached the house with its pretty shaded porch, he could feel his heart racing. A woman was walking towards the little orchard to the far side. 'Mama, Mamusia,' he started to run and shout, but when she turned it wasn't his mother, and he almost fell to the ground with the terrified pounding his heart set up.

He heard his grandfather's voice counselling him. 'If, by any chance, anything has happened to them, behave as normally as you can and find out what. But don't get yourself into trouble, if trouble means being a relation. You understand?'

With what he felt was a superhuman effort Bruno doffed his cap. '*Prosze Pani,*' he said politely. 'I'm looking for a Pani…' He stumbled and for some reason used her old family name. 'Pani Torok.'

The woman gazed at him. She had dark hair and almond-shaped eyes. Suddenly from behind her, he heard a child's shout. 'Bru, Bru.' Little Anna was racing towards him, leaping into his arms. He held her so tight. He didn't know he could hold anyone so tight, so warm. But when his mother appeared before him, he suddenly felt shy, a stranger. Until she too stepped towards him and tripled their embrace. They stood like that for a long time.

'I said Bruno was coming. Didn't I? Didn't I, Mamusia?'

'You did, my brave girl. You did.'

'But you gave his horse away.'

'I didn't give her, Anna. You know that. They took her.' She turned to Bruno. 'I…I've been so afraid for you. And…and the others?' She lowered her eyes. She wasn't sure she wanted to know.

He told her his grandparents were both well. The pallor stayed in her face, but her smile was radiant. She held on to his hand. She held it a lot that summer. And it was a happy time, despite the absence of his horse, despite the visits from the Nazis or their stewards who robbed them of their food.

Mamusia was worried that they would steal him away too. Boys his age under the new regime mostly no longer went to school, but to work. They were kidnapped away from their families, sent to labour in mines or factories in Germany. She determined to get Bruno a work permit, so that his stay in the house had documented sanction.

Mamusia was good with the Germans, fearless. She spoke with them in German. She had convinced one of the chief Wehrmacht officers – a major – in the neighbouring town that she was the widow of a *Volksdeutscher*, a Pole of German origin. The war had caught her out at their summerhouse and she had determined to see it through by engaging in farming. They all knew how short food was. The major had found a cow for her, and an old bicycle. While Bruno was there the man occasionally arrived bearing little presents, which she accepted with a fluttery thank-you. He had red-gold hair and watery eyes and was hardly, in Bruno's view, a prepossessing figure, except for the weapon he carried in his leather holster.

Bruno, the story went, was Mamusia's nephew who had come from the eastern frontier to help out for the summer. It was to the major that Mamusia went to facilitate the acquisition of a work document, together with an account of how the silly boy had omitted to bring a birth certificate with him, but since it was only for a temporary stay, she was sure the major would be kind enough to help out. The major did as he had already done for Alina.

Alina, Bruno realized by this time, was the woman who had been wounded in the first days of the war and whom grandfather had picked up on the railway track. Officially, she was employed by his mother as a labourer, both servant and farm worker, but she also worked part-time at an inn the Germans liked to frequent. She was well educated: spoke German too. Bruno didn't want to ask whether she was Jewish. He didn't want to ask anything. He was just happy to be with his mother and his little sister in the fields and woods he now considered as home. A whole lifetime seemed to have passed since he had last been here. He sometimes felt he had returned as someone else, but someone who loved them both with an even greater passion than before.

Mamusia wanted him to go back to Przemysl and somehow fetch her parents. She wanted them all together, though she was worried about whether they would manage through the winter, what with the food shortages. The cooperative, which had quotas to fill for the Germans, never left them much. Still she had a secret stash of pretty things to barter in the attic. She had stored them away after the first raid by passing soldiers and now took pieces out one by one when need was greatest. Antiques. Pictures. Some Germans had a taste for such things, and they could fetch a good winter price. She convinced herself they would manage.

Bruno didn't think his grandfather would acquiesce. He had said to him quite firmly one day before he left, that he would prefer to be dead than to suffer humiliation at Nazi hands. He was constantly tormented by the memory of those Jewish men they had seen forcibly marched to their deaths in the early days of the Nazi invasion. Since then, it seemed he had heard worse stories still, which he didn't want to sully his tongue with or relay to Bruno so as to give him fresh nightmares.

Bruno explained to his mother, pointed out that if anything, her father wanted him to urge her and Anna to Przemysl.

Yes, Mamusia finally admitted. She could understand Grandpa's fears. It was harder for men. She looked at him as if he were one and added that, all things considered, he too was safer on the Russian side of the river, much as she would like to keep him with her. As for Anna and herself, it seemed a little mad to take the risk of moving and finding new premises and new papers, if they were coping here. She also had a feeling that everything would be better soon, that the British would get here at last.

As she said that, she rushed to kiss Bruno and Anna.

Bruno had never loved his mother so much. Or trusted her. She was so beautiful, so kind and wise. When he left the country house in September, his sack replete with provisions, it was with a sadness he couldn't put words to. He had to square his shoulders repeatedly to keep the tears from his eyes.

Perhaps it was this, or the fact that the women had instilled him with too much confidence, but he was utterly unprepared for the wagon that emerged from the haze on the horizon and stopped short beside him. Two men leaped off its front bench and stopped his progress. One was old and grizzled: the second lame, but with a mean face and a pitchfork that he brought up short at Bruno's chin.

'You're the Jewboy, aren't you? Get up there.'

He felt a prod of the pitchfork but he stood his ground.

'What are you talking about?'

'Work,' the old man grinned to show a single tooth. 'That's what we're talking about. We need another pair of arms. Yours look just right.'

'How much are you paying?' Bruno heard himself ask.

'Paying,' the man laughed. 'You're paying me. Paying me not to go to the Germans and tell.'

'Just what Germans are we talking about?' Bruno heard his voice coming out far cooler and more confident than he felt. 'Major Hans Meyer himself organized my work permit. And if I do some work for you now because you need help with the harvest, the Major will expect me to be paid.'

'Major, ha. I'll give you "Major",' the old man narrowed his eyes cannily and put a remarkably strong hand on his shoulder. 'We'll talk about pay when we see how you work.'

Bruno felt another prod of the pitchfork and leaped up on the wagon. But his mention of the major had tempered the man's tone a little. He decided he would bide his time and then make his escape. He didn't really want to have to go to the major or anyone else just now with the accusation of 'Jew' trailing him. Nor would Mamusia and Anna be served by it.

He toiled in the fields, bringing in the harvest for a week and slept in the tumbledown wooden barn next to the restless old farm horse. Though the threat of exposure was always there, they didn't try and steal his rucksack nor particularly mistreat him. He ate onions and bread and an occasional bowl of barley soup with the farmer's lame son, at least he assumed it was his son, though the man rarely spoke, and Bruno began to think he couldn't. One overcast night, he made his escape walking for some three hours in what he hoped was the right direction before bedding down in a little copse until a bright clear dawn set him on his way again.

Military traffic increased as he headed further east and got closer to the main road. He didn't care. He kept his head high. He whistled. He thought of what the bastards had done to his father and he whistled even louder, making sure his walking stick hit the road in vigorous rhythm. His route landed him straight into what had been the western side of Przemysl. The streets were crowded, the banks of the river equally so. He had forgotten it was Sunday and even the Nazi soldiers seemed to be having a day off in the balmy weather. Hardy swimmers braved the river. Further along fishermen dotted the grassy embankment. He had miscalculated. It was not the right day for trying to make his way to the Russian side of the city.

He walked on, wondering if he should simply lie down in the sun like everyone else and pretend it was a holiday. Then he saw some boys mucking about with a makeshift raft, diving off it, clambering back up, tugging it towards shore. People had given them a wide berth, preferring quiet to their rowdiness. He watched them for a while, then on impulse took off his cap and waved. When one of them gave him a look that wasn't altogether hostile, he walked towards them and asked if he might join them.

The squat, heavy-shouldered youth who seemed to be the ringleader shrugged and said why not.

'Is it stout enough to get across the river?' Bruno asked.

'What's it to you?'

He met the boy's eyes. 'I want to visit my grandfather. He's all alone on the other side. I'll pay you if you just take my stuff across so it's dry and throw it on the opposite bank. I'll swim along beside.'

The squat youth laughed, winked. 'So no one can see you, right?'

Bruno shrugged.

'You're a smuggler.'

'No way.'

'What you got in your rucksack?'

Bruno looked at the boys. At a struggle, if he held on to his stick, he could take them on.

'Sausage. For my grandfather. I'll give you some right now, in payment.'

The boys looked at each other.

'Come on. Worse comes to worse, I can speak German.'

They laughed.

'Show us.'

Bruno gave them a rendition of a Nazi officer. And added, in Polish. 'And if you double-cross me, just wait and see what I'll do to you.'

'Okay, jump in and hold on,' the squat one said. He seemed keen for an adventure. 'Just see how fast we'll get you there.'

Bruno tucked his clothes into his rucksack, took out a sausage and gave it, together with the sack, to the leader, who seemed to be the one who was going to sit on top of the raft and navigate with his makeshift paddle. The two other boys and Bruno jumped into the cold waters and propelled the raft across the river, only their hands and bobbing heads visible at its side. When they reached the opposite bank, Bruno ducked under the raft and swam towards the shore. As he scrambled up, the leader heaved his rucksack onto the bank and waved. It was all done so quickly, Bruno doubted that anyone had noticed. This side of the river, at some distance from the castle hill, was quiet.

He felt like flinging his hat in the air and celebrating. He had managed to get back in one piece. All in all, it had been a heady summer. And the crossing hadn't been so hard. He would return to see his mother and sister with the first breath of spring. Maybe even earlier, he promised himself.

9

The Wisła was high and mud-tossed brown from the recent rain. Bruno Lind, walking along the curve the river made with the old Kazimierz area of Krakow, felt an uncharacteristic spring in his step, like the tingle of limbs set for adventure. The lightness no longer belonged to him. He wondered that the thirteen-year-old Bruno had had it then, in the midst of war, as if his whole youthful existence were a boy's own story of challenges and feats, while the war itself was merely a bit of history in the background. Was he misremembering, exaggerating his one-time sense of risk and mastery, slipping over the dire grimness because he didn't want to remember, didn't want to kneel again by the cow-shit they had on occasion been driven to eat? And because he was already anticipating the worse that was to come when adventure gave way to tragedy. Turning everything into the inevitable dramatic narrative of the great 'oneself', which is what memory that tapped autobiography did in story-fed humans.

But no, he contradicted himself. The thirteen-year-old that was then himself, seen from the inside, would have enjoyed the risks and the opportunity to prove himself. Even the edge of cruelty. He was a boy like any other boy, after all, though already hardened by the loss of his father, his nerves tempered by the brutality he had witnessed. Only if he put the boy into three dimensions plus time, saw him from the back and all around and moving, did his, yes, pleasurable sense of adventure seem incredible to the old Bruno. Like those psychological tests in which the subject is asked to remember from the inside of an action or field and then from the outside. Emotion comes with the first form of recall, and apparent coolness, distance, if not altogether objectivity with the second. Maybe that was one of the differences between history and memory – the first from the outside, the second from the inside – that made it a slippery faculty, prone to distortion and suggestion. But experience was like that. And it carried its own truths.

Young Bruno hadn't known when he returned to Przemysl in that autumn of 1940 that in a few brief months, his boy's-own-story sense of the war would be thrust backward to a period of the war's innocence. He had no way of knowing that by next June, the Nazis' pact with the Russians would be at an end and their hideous war machine would be marching east. Nor did he have any way of knowing that their murderous battle against the Jews had only just begun.

Bruno allowed himself a chuckle. Perhaps if his younger self had kept a diary of that first year in Przemysl, it would have contained more about the girl in the newspaper kiosk and his adolescent longings than anything else. War too had its dailiness, a repetition that, no matter how terrible, blurred in the memory. Humans, it seemed, created habits or went mad. The mundane was a part of war too. But those versions of himself, the boy in love or the bored youth, would have been far more unrecognisable than even what his memory chose to present him with now.

Bruno paused to lean against the balustrade. Across the river, Podgorze looked pleasant, even pretty. There was nothing to tell him from his present vantage-point that the crammed, disease-infested, wartime Ghetto had eventually been located where those innocuous houses now clustered just south of the river. Geography was an innocent.

In fact, nothing in what he had seen of the city was familiar. Even though he had recognized the building in which the Torok apartment stood and had pointed it out to Amelia, he felt less than nothing at its sight. Certainly no sense of homecoming. It was as if a giant broom had swept over his childhood topography and rendered it as indifferent and dull as a stretch of new town.

Yet even if the buildings failed to trigger it, he was nonetheless in the grip of memory. Maybe it was the sound of Polish all around him, though it seemed to have grown harsher with the years, less pleasing than the childhood intonations he thought he remembered. Maternal tones those. Not brutalized by war and years of oppression.

His own tongue stumbled and blundered over the language now, like some blinded bull. He was unable to come to terms with its sibilant riot of consonants. But its presence everywhere provoked unruly bits of recall – the bristle of his grandfather's hair, the cool prod of the pitchfork under his chin, the scent of dill on white fish. Such sensations in turn brought scenes. The train had started it all, with its hypnotic motion.

Bruno followed the curl in the river beyond the Pilsudski Bridge then for some reason turned and retraced his steps in the opposite direction. Coming this way, everything looked different. The distant mound where the camp had been grew clearer. Pigeons swarmed over blackened roofs and settled with a menacing air. Shadows played like falling ash over sand-coloured stucco. Kazimierz itself, so recently anodyne, now filled him with a low thrumming anxiety he couldn't identify, like the frantic beating of a bird's wings.

The black-coated man who emerged to confront him from the shadows of a lane felt as if he had materialized from the floodtide of memory that threatened his mind. He had a long, ragged Chassidic beard, a fur-trimmed hat, and he held his hands crossed on his stomach as if it were a prosperous and capacious one that might at any moment bend and sway in prayer. His skin was paper-pale against the reddish beard. His mild washed-out eyes creased into weary canniness as he addressed Bruno in accented English.

'Good morning, sir. Welcome to our beautiful city. You would like some help, no? Some help in interpreting the remains of what was once the centre of Jewish Krakow?'

With a click of his heels and a swivel of his hat, he broke into a dance, his long thin lips curling around a mournful Yiddish plaint.

The bad taste of it grew thick and acrid in Bruno's mouth. He turned away, walked quickly.

The man was persistent. He matched his step to Bruno's like a stray dog that had recognized a likely homeowner. 'Of course you are interested, sir. I can feel it in you. See it. And I, Pan Marek of Szeroka Street, can show you. Tell you. Tell you everything. The way it was. Tales of kindly tailors who had more lore in their thimbles than all the doctors of the world, and their beautiful wives, their secrets modestly hidden beneath their lowered lashes. Such secrets, sir, buried within these dilapidated walls. Not all the scientists of the new world together could find them.'

'What is this nonsense?' Bruno erupted.

'No nonsense, kind American sir, but the truth. The truth. For a few dollars more I will deliver you into ancient Kazimierz the way it was. The way it still is for some of us. Its streets dancing with ghosts and wise spirits and fearful *dybbuks*. I will tell you tales of boys falling in love through the peephole of a window, of fortunes lost and found and lost once more, of the wisdom of the Tzaddik in concluding contracts.' He started up his infernal melody again, with its comic moans, its Klezmer whines.

Half hypnotized into helplessness, Bruno pulled some bills from his pocket. He had to get away, but his legs were reluctant. 'Your name. Marek. Marek who?'

'I see the American sir is knowledgeable. You wish to know if I am a Jew, like you. Believe me, sir, a name is not enough to distinguish us. Pan Marek to you. Come, come, let me take you into forgotten corners, the bathhouses where the pretty damsels bathed, the noble synagogues, the little rooms where study was done...'

The man had recognized him. That hoary wartime truism leaped into his mind. Poles and Jews recognized each other. Germans were less dangerous. They couldn't detect the subtle differences. He had once masqueraded as a Pole. This Pole was masquerading as a Jew now that the Jews of Kazimierz had been exterminated. But masquerading as a Jew out of folklore, a *stetl* Jew wearing fancy dress. It was like watching a minstrel show where the whites blackened their faces to perform a pastiche of black life. Watching it in a slave graveyard.

Bruno stuffed bills into the man's hand. 'Go on. Leave me. I'm not interested in your theatre. Leave me alone.'

The man scurried away, his coat flapping, his hand on his hat that threatened to pull away from his gathering speed.

'Scum,' Bruno muttered after him, his voice betraying a bitter anger he hadn't realized he felt.

Tiredness suddenly overcame him like a shroud. It made his movements clumsy.

He hated all this. History become kitsch. This turning of experience into folksiness. Like the Iroquois in Canada when he had first arrived there. Making beads on their reservations. For tourist consumption. Was this the inevitable after-effect of genocide? The unpalatable ghastliness of history transmuted into fairy tale. Dancing, fiddling Chassidim in funny hats. Winged spirits and some whining music to be fed to tourists for their pleasure along with *pierogi* and borscht. This was the city's memorial to its Jews. As if six years of gruelling killing history were just a parenthesis with no links to before or after. As if Jews were to be remembered as a costume musical rather than as modernizers, motors of the country's move into the twentieth century.

The heritage industry, that's what he had walked into. Tableaux, living snapshots of the supposed past culled from an intricate continuum and re-presented as attractions. An unruly sea trimmed into a garden pond with a couple of goldfish for effect. This was the memory business at work. The furthest end of it from his, perhaps, but related. And since there were no Jews here, memory with all its distortions was all you got. It was easier, after all, to love the extinct.

Bruno forced his legs forward over dusty paving stones and uneven grit. That was why he couldn't face accompanying Amelia to Auschwitz. A different order, that, from his masquerader, of course, but still a form of tourism. A spectacle. This time to be viewed with awe. Silent piety in front of the horror humans were capable of.

He couldn't subject himself to kneeling before atrocity. In the way Catholics kneeled before a dying tortured god. His grandfather's ironic cackle at this further turn of the screw rang in his ear like the tolling of a distant bell. Yes, he saw it now. It was as if the worst of the war could be confronted only if it were assimilated into religion. Murder, suffering made holy, transmuted into a moral touchstone, a mantra, a measure for all horror. Yes, that was why he wouldn't go with Amelia. He couldn't join the worshippers, pious or mute. Religion was about belief. Folklore about superstition. History, he hoped – like the science he had always championed – was about thought, analysis. He would say this to Amelia. Explain. It was different for her.

But it was all so difficult. He shouldn't have come here with her. Wide-eyed, expectant, she kept asking for what he couldn't give. Not yet. Maybe never. He still couldn't allow his mind the freedom to roam in those more threatening regions he had forced into shadow for so long. He didn't want the self he had then been to inhabit him. It was a nasty, suspicious, brutalized self, prone to find enemies everywhere – because in those days they had indeed been everywhere. But the self had lasted longer than the war and it carried its burden of guilt with it. The guilt of still being alive when so many weren't. A guilt that tried to wash itself clean by finding more enemies anywhere, everywhere, to struggle against. To make that deformed self a necessity. To give it a justification.

Eve in the end had quietened him, wooed him out of it, shown him that he also knew how to be gentle, how to laugh, occasionally even how to trust. Not that they had talked. She had shown him by example.

It was all so long ago now. So long since he had revisited any of that dark matter, he was half afraid that by now he might even have given birth to new monsters – like those grotesque confabulations amnesiacs come up with, asserting with quiet aplomb that they've been married for three years and have children from that marriage who are twenty.

As a preventative, that morning, he had forced himself to check on the holders of the name which had led him here, like a hound bred blindly to follow a single trail. There were four of them in the telephone directory, two at the same address. One of these was Aleksander. He would ask him. Yes, he would. Soon. As soon as he could come up with a plausible story about why he wanted to know. That hadn't shaped itself for him yet.

'Pops.' Amelia's voice startled him from his reverie. He had stumbled without thinking into Kazimierz's main square, and there was Amelia waiting for him. She was sitting at an outdoor table in front of a small restaurant partly hidden from view by the ranks of parked cars. The area, he noted to himself, was still somewhat shabby, no matter what people told you about how much had been restored over the last ten years, the Spielberg effect and all that.

'Pops, you just walked straight past us. This is the Ariel…well, one of the two. They compete, as this young man has been explaining to me.'

The young man who had startling yellow hair and one of those noses that spoke of Greek statuary or English public schools looked rather furtive as Bruno approached and hastily excused himself with a great scraping of chair legs on pavement.

'You frightened him, Pops. You're a scary person.'

'That's 'cause his intentions weren't honourable.'

'You could see that immediately, right?'

'What else are fathers for?'

Amelia stretched her long legs. 'Let me get you something. Juice. Coffee. Some lunch. Of course, it's lunchtime. They do borscht and all kinds of herrings. Look.'

Bruno studied the menu, which reminded him of West Broadway in the old days, ordered herring in onions and sour cream with tea and borscht with dumplings for Amelia from a waiter who looked like an extra on a Hitchcock set. He could feel Amelia watching him as his lips curled clumsily round the language.

'What else fathers are for,' she took up his banter in a more serious vein, 'is introducing their children to the history that made them.'

'It's not like that, Amelia.'

'Because the history that made them gets passed down, willy-nilly.'

'Nonsense.'

'Even if you don't talk about it, it's there. It's there in your silences, in your gestures, in the odd things that make you angry, like filling in forms. In your sudden starts. In the way that you used to hug me as if I might disappear down an Alice hole at any minute.'

He stared at her. Uncomfortable. Did he? More so than other parents?

'I want to understand. You're a mystery I want to understand. I want you to take me to Auschwitz.'

'I told you, Amelia. I have no interest in going. I'm not a great visitor of public memorials. Nor do I want to read explanatory captions beside mountains of shoes or words on stone. All of this is hard enough as it is. I understand that for you it's different. And you must go. Yes, you must.'

He had had to clear his throat over the mountains of shoes. As if the words wouldn't come out. Why? Only a few hours ago he had paused in front of a shabby shop window and seen just that – a mountain of shoes, all displayed higgledy-piggledy on top of each other and making plenty the only aesthetic. The mass, not the individual. That had made him think of the killer camps, as if somewhere there might be a link. But he didn't want to think about that. Enough emotional energy had gone into that kind of thinking all those years ago.

Amelia burst into his thoughts. 'You're not kidding it's different. I may be one of the few Polish Jewish Blacks in unrecorded history, and my father's too scared to take me to Auschwitz some fifty-five years after it closed for business.'

He studied her, decided that she was serious despite the mock-hyperbolic tone. They were quiet as the waiter deposited their plates, quiet for longer than usual as they ate.

At last he said: 'It's not quite the way you think, Amelia. I... No, no, that's not right. I suspect you think there's a trauma somewhere. A trauma that I won't talk about. That I can't confront. That will somehow get better if I do. If I put a narrative to emotion, even if the narrative isn't quite right. But can you imagine the opposite? Can you imagine that one of the reasons I don't want to go is that I'm afraid of feeling nothing? Nothing? Nothing at all? No emotion that can possibly meet the measure of those times?'

He gazed at her incomprehension. 'Yes, that's right. And the second reason may be that what I don't want to confront, certainly don't want to share with you, is something as simple, as ghastly, as banal, as self-hatred. Not guilt. Just self-hatred.'

'You have no reason to hate yourself.'

'I think I'm the only judge of that.'

She examined him. 'Is this linked to why you don't like Aleksander? Does he remind you of yourself?'

Something like panic rose up in him. He swallowed hard, scrambled for a voice. 'What makes you think I don't like him. I do. I do.'

'The man doth protest too much. What do you think of his science?'

'Why?'

'I slept with him.'

'I see.' He didn't see at all, but he blundered on. 'Does this have anything to do with his science?'

'Maybe. Maybe not. But it's a way of telling you.'

'Telling me you like him?'

'I do.'

'I don't understand... It's strange.'

He could see that the words that had dropped out of him inadvertently made her unhappy, wary. She looked as if she might bite back, be rude, the way she had done as an adolescent if he said anything even slightly critical about her boyfriends. These bumped along erratically between effete East-coast preppies and druggie ghetto youths, roadside mirrors in whom she hoped to see herself, but who never reflected her adequately.

'His science is fine.'

She looked at him for a moment without responding. 'Does that mean as fine as your being here? Less fine? Or more? Nobel-standard fine?'

'I'm not locking you out, Amelia.' He made an effort, though his mind was racing with this other news. If Tarski was who his fears suggested, then he shouldn't be with his daughter.

'It's just...this whole trip, it's not what I expected, that's all. Though I don't know quite what I did expect. You see...my own history was very particular. It doesn't quite fit into the most prevalent narratives. And there isn't much I can show you except for buildings. They're not what make a city. Not really. It's the people. And the people aren't here. When I was last in this particular square, as a child, it was teeming, noisy. Crowded and noisy with the babble of Yiddish, which I didn't really understand. There were Jews like me, ordinary, western, business-suited, and Jews like I really didn't know them. Exotic. They all argued and gestured and did business and tugged at their beards and haggled, and there were synagogues chock-a block at every corner and street hawkers, barrels of herring and pickles, bread stalls, horses and carts, women with headscarves or elegant feathered hats and almond-shaped eyes...and now, well now there's this – a car park with a few half-restored buildings. A few shards of the past, like at some archaeological dig, even though it's less than a lifetime away. And the ghosts have hardly begun to talk to me.'

'I don't think you're telling the whole truth.' She mimicked the childhood words she would throw at him and Eve when they simplified things for her. Kept the bad in the world at an adult distance.

'You're right.' He heard himself sigh, and his voice had a sudden hoarseness. 'You see, all this, the past, it was never part of the world I shared with your mother. She was a way of leaving it behind. She didn't belong here. With her, I didn't either. And you...well...I can't make myself feel you're part of this. You're too good.'

Amelia made a funny face and squeezed his hand. 'It's okay, Pops,'

'But I will take you somewhere. Yes I will. Not Auschwitz. But somewhere. I've just remembered. Deaths of a more ordinary kind.'

He was mumbling, talking almost to himself, in the grip of a force that was greater than him. It led him by the hand, so that he seemed to know the way. First south, then into a lane, where he vaguely thought the ramshackle youth centre might once have been a synagogue whose name escaped him, then north along a wide street where the trams clattered and east along Miodowa and under a tunnel across into the New Cemetery. The new Jewish Cemetery that was as old as the 1800's. His grandfather had told him that. His grandfather was holding his hand. His guide.

Amelia stopped to look at the memorial to the local Holocaust dead by the entrance gate where old tombstones lined a wall, but his grandfather didn't pause there. He took him into the depths of the graveyard: a dense green, overgrown and shadowy with patches of falling sunlight that shimmered through the tall leafy trees and raked over slabs. They grew alive with movement. In the distance a mist rose from moist vegetation, brooding over moss-covered sandstone, marble and granite. Carved and faded Hebrew inscriptions he couldn't read indented the tombs. Sometimes German or Polish peeked out at him.

'It's this way.' He heard his grandfather's voice, but it was his own burbling in the wrong tongue to Amelia, so that he caught himself and had to translate.

They turned and twisted along paths, sometimes dark, sometimes light, little purple and yellow wild flowers spreading to their sides amidst the dense greenery, until they came to a tall marble slab between two pillar scrolls. The name 'Torok' engraved in large letters sprang out at them, followed by a family line inscribed in German.

'This is my mother's family,' Bruno murmured.

'Torok?'

He nodded.

'You never told me the name before.'

Amelia read.

'But she's not here?'

'No, she's not here.'

'The last person in the family to be buried here was during the First World War.'

'That's right. My grandparents aren't here. No Adolf. No Sarah.'

Amelia said nothing. She picked up some pebbles from the path they had left and carefully placed them on the tomb.

'Who told you about that?' he asked.

'Stones. So the dead don't leave their tombs to haunt us. And wait peacefully for the Second Coming. I'm not as much of a stranger as you choose to think.'

'Your great-grandmother would have been proud of you. She was full of such lore. Her husband didn't have much patience for it.'

'Adolf?'

He nodded.

'You never talk about the other side of the family. Your father's side. The Austrian side.'

'Moravian, in fact. Another lost country. I didn't know them. My father, or so the story went, fell out with them. Over politics, I suspect. Or maybe it was religion. He was an adamant atheist. All before my time. So I have no idea what happened to them. They may even have died before the war. He was a good deal older than my mother, though I've only just thought about that now.'

They walked slowly side by side, pausing to look at the occasional tomb. She was waiting for him to say more. He didn't quite know where to begin. He had never thought he would come here again. Not this city, nor this cemetery; and as he stole a glance at his daughter, he wondered again what had driven him. Was it the presage to his own old age, as all the memory commentators said, a move into the past because the present had become less distinct? The blood wasn't getting through to his frontal lobes. They were shrinking. He needed some of his own as yet untested medicine. Had he come for the stimulus of recognition since pure recall no longer worked as well as it might?

Trite thoughts, he chastised himself. Another way of not talking properly to Amelia.

'This place was vandalized by the Nazis, I read somewhere. They used the tombs as paving stones for the road to the camp at Plaszow. In November 1942.'

He nodded, pleased that she had made an effort with the history he wouldn't speak.

'I'm glad they left the Toroks.'

'Left them something,' he heard himself muttering, as if some of that old anger was still intact.

She thrust him a curious glance then stopped abruptly.

'Look, Pops.'

She was pointing to a tall, narrow, white tombstone that looked more recent than its neighbours and as if it had been pressed out of concrete. It had something like a slate attached to its front. A list of names appeared on it. Amongst them was that of Adolf Torok.

'What does it say?' She gripped his hand, a small whispering girl.

He didn't answer immediately. He read down the list over and over. 'Disappeared in the Nazi terror' the inscription at the top noted. None of the names seemed to stand in any relation to each other, except for that. Disappeared. A euphemism for killed in a manner unknown – in the camps, in a street raid, in a random shooting. Death was inventive in wartime. Above Adolf Torok's name was the epitaph – 'he helped many'. Below, the inscription noted that he had died at the age of sixty-eight. Younger than Bruno was now.

Bruno gazed at the stone and then into the distance and back again. A shroud obscured the light. The graves had lost their outlines and seemed to be moving in and out of the gloom like square-cut figures on a vast receding chessboard. Forward, back, sideways, lifted by invisible fingers and thrust down again willynilly, vertiginously, without rule or reason. He held on to Amelia's shoulder for balance.

Her voice came from far away, blurring as it moved through gloom. 'Do you think it's him?'

He nodded. 'Could be. It says he died, or rather disappeared, towards the end of 1942, which is probably right.'

'But we don't know how.'

'They didn't know how.'

Stumbling, Bruno explained that this tombstone had been the gift of someone who had survived and was remembering friends. His grandfather had helped him or her, it seemed, others too. Bruno knew that was true.

He wanted to sit down at the edge of the tomb and put his face in his hands and weep. Weep as he might have done as a small boy, before everything had gone wrong. Before he had grown a thick carapace that didn't know about tears. Before those deaths.

'There's somewhere else I'd like to go. I'd like to take you,' he said at last. 'We'll hire a car. Tomorrow. Or the next day.'

The dead were murmuring to him, talking. He hadn't visited them for a very long time.

Past Historic

10

They had ended up in Aleksander's car, which was bigger and more comfortable than hers. That was just as well, Irena thought, since the Fiat wasn't really up to long journeys anymore. Not that the Professor had told her quite how long this one was going to be. Maybe he didn't know himself. The turn-off he had pointed to just past Tarnow and then so abruptly changed his mind about required a screech of brakes and a presence of mind neither her car nor she was up to. The Professor's hippocampus was evidently in decline. Wasn't that what he had told her about her mother's inability to find her way anymore – the disappearance of the internal map? Presaging the disappearance of the terrain it charted probably…

She was pretty good on the hippocampus now, and knew a little about the amygdala too, that almond-shaped bit deep in the brain with its lateral nucleus that controlled what they called emotional conditioning – or really whatever it was one remembered best. The bits of memory that came with strong emotion. Not necessarily utterly accurate, mind, and often narrow in focus, the Professor had warned her, but intense and image-based – the source of those images that recur and recur. The scenes that form traumatic memory. She wondered if the break-up scene with Anthony qualified. She could still see him altogether perfectly, like in a snapshot, fixed in time forever with his sorrowful face on, that pretend sorrowful face that was supposed to bring out the pity in her so that she wouldn't mind, wouldn't want him to be hurt, whereas in fact he was busy stomping all over her.

No, maybe that didn't qualify for the amygdala, since she could hear him clearly too. She'd have to ask the Professor. Not that any of it made a blind bit of difference to one's life. She might as well store the scene in her big toe so that she could tread on it, for all the difference it made. Though if it all went wrong, you'd want to know. Like with her mother. Bits of knowledge to grasp onto for comfort, if nothing else.

The Professor was sitting in the front with Aleksander Tarski, whereas she was in back with Amelia. She liked the Professor for liking to explain things to her. He was an enthusiast, a wonderful teacher. She'd always loved her teachers. Particularly her English teacher, who could recite great chunks of Shakespeare and Byron. And she was glad to have been asked along. It meant he trusted her, trusted her not to write about him. Maybe the visit to her paper, *Tygodnik Powszechny*, tucked in as it was by the university, had impressed him. That warren of dusty offices and serious looking people hardly had the markings of a tabloid. He had complimented her on her article on the conference too. Though she wasn't sure he had really read it all through, because of the Polish, which couldn't be easy for him anymore. But perhaps he would change his mind about letting her write about him now.

Meanwhile all this was quite pleasant, really, and something of an adventure; and she was building herself up to asking Aleksander the relevant questions. It should be easy enough, given that they were obviously travelling into the Professor's past. And one past would lead to another. That was always the way.

The only difficulty was that no one was certain when they would get back to Krakow. She had taken her mother to her friend Ida's where between the children and herself and her husband there would be someone around all the time to keep an eye on her. But, even though Ida, who had known her forever, had been altogether willing, Irena was nervous about the arrangement. It was always unclear how her mother would behave, particularly when she left her known quarters. Still, she mustn't spend the entire journey worrying about her. It occurred to her as the ultimate mother-daughter irony that her mother was now paying her back for all those occasions on which she had murmured: 'Oh Irena, you make me worry *sooo*.'

The countryside was flat here. The flatness of the great central European plain that stretched and stretched eastwards over fields and forests largely unchanged over centuries. Always a flat and open invitation to invading armies. A perfect stamping ground. No wonder the Germans had just blitzed across. Nothing to stop them.

At least the houses were slightly better than she remembered them when she had last come this way, oh so long ago now, before she had gone to England. They had probably been built by the returning American Diaspora, the Chicago Poles, who seemed now to have a monopoly over Krakow airport. Or maybe the houses were just the fruit of all those moonlighting Polish builders she'd met over the years in London? Whatever. They were an improvement over the rundown wooden shacks that used to be the lot of the peasants. Personally, she preferred the views a little further south, in the foothills of the Bieszczady Mountains. But she knew this journey wasn't about views, whatever occasional exclamations came from Amelia.

Amelia was growing more mysterious by the day. Irena, who prided herself on her understanding of people, couldn't make her out at all. She had this way of curling up into herself as if all the wisdom and patience of the ages were hers – not at all like what one expected of a high-powered LA agent, who was beautiful to boot, all in casual whites today, except for a little throw-away blue in her cardigan. Maybe all this was just an amusing diversion for her, Aleksander included: Poland as the exotic. Though reachable by mobile phone – one which juddered acutely with particular frequency after four in the afternoon. It made Irena want to laugh.

'Here, here,' Bruno exclaimed. 'We want to turn here.'

'I don't think that goes anywhere,' Aleksander murmured. 'It certainly won't take us into Przemysl.'

'Maybe not. But I'm curious. I'm almost certain my grandfather left a car in some person's house just off this road. Back in '39, of course.' He burst out laughing. Amelia joined him.

'You mean you had a car back then?'

'A beautiful old black Citroen. It was a dream of a vehicle. I used to hop onto the running board and hang on for dear life. My grandfather allowed it. He was something of an adventurous sort. Then when we were fleeing east, we had to abandon the car here because the road was so crowded with refugees. Polish soldiers too. We just couldn't get through.'

Bruno had a faraway look on his face and a sudden impish quality. 'I've always missed that car. It was beautiful. So elegant. And the smell the leather seats gave off was extraordinary...'

The road was shaded with tall trees. There was an occasional cherry, brashly in bloom near a dacha-like house, all far too new to have been there before the war. So he would probably have to carry on missing that car, Irena reflected.

Oh, those lost objects of childhood that one would never recover. Never. She had one too, though it was hardly as spectacular as a car. Hers was a violin, a tiny gleaming child's violin, with a blue-velvet lining in its case. Her mother had brought it home from school where some child who had left the city had abandoned it. She must have been four or five when the violin arrived, and it was love at first sight and sound. She had cherished that violin more than any doll. She had picked out notes with her fingers and learned to pass the little bow across its strings so that it cried or sang. She had carried it with her everywhere, like some beloved younger sister. It even slept next to her bed, and yes, she tucked it into its blue velvet every night, leaving the case open, of course. The violin watched over her.

Then the people to whom the violin belonged came back, and it had to be returned. She cried and cried. There was no solace. She'd missed that violin ever since – that perfect shape, the gleaming mahogany, the sound. A borrowed object. Maybe like her borrowed father.

'Yes, a Citroen Rosalie, or something like that. My grandfather told us that André Citroen had acquired a patent for a gear-cutting technique invented right here in Poland. Something to do with producing smooth quiet gears with chevron-shaped teeth. That's where the car got its double chevron emblem.' Bruno laughed, evidently pleased with himself. 'I've just remembered that, but I can't say any of these houses look familiar. Maybe young boys are better at cars than at architecture. They encode their shapes better. Or the thrum of the engine, in any case.'

'I think you've got yourself a Nobel-prize winning gender-disapproved theory there, Pops,' Amelia giggled from the back seat. 'He sounds a treat, your grandfather. A real character.'

'The road bends here, and then there's a turn-off away from the river,' Aleksander announced.

Bruno shrugged. 'Let's try it. Nothing looks the same. I think it's the trees. Some are new. Some are sixty years taller.'

'I think we may have more luck in town.'

'Probably. But humour me. Just carry on for a few more minutes.'

Aleksander drove slowly, until Bruno shook his head. 'No, it's no use.'

His tone was so despondent that Irena had a sudden acute sense that what was just a jaunt for the rest of them – interesting but still a pleasure jaunt – was indeed something altogether different for the Professor. Of course. She had been insensitive. The fragments of the past he was trying to piece together must have been terrifying to experience, and the car represented one of the happier moments. Hence, its importance.

She gave herself an inward shake. It was true. She had grown insensitive over these last years. It was partly to do with steeling herself against this sad life with her mother, not letting the cares get her down, the knowledge that the only future was death. And this steeling of oneself poured over into other domains, silting them over. Denying one set of emotions meant blotting out a whole set of them. So one became unsympathetic. Yes, upright and insensitive. The way that maiden aunts always appeared in books. Nasty and narrow and disapproving. That was the fate she had to guard against now. Life had all these unhappy little twists in store for one. She who used to bring home injured birds, gather up strays, weep over Dickens until there were no tears left...

'Wait a minute.' Bruno took a deep breath.

Aleksander braked, and Irena caught the sudden eagerness on the Professor's face.

'We have lots of time, Professor. There's no rush. Really.'

They all clambered out into high grass rampant with cow parsley.

'That particular rectangle of a field there. You see, the broken fence, the old struts? It makes the shape of a paddock.'

'And children, of whatever gender, remember anything to do with horses. Right?'

'You're right, darling. I was mad about horses.'

'But there's no house to address oneself to.'

'No, that must have gone,' Bruno said sadly. 'There was so much fighting everywhere around here. But this field. I'm almost sure... There was a kind of half-open stable over there, and we pulled the car up into it. And covered it. Camouflaged it. We had this innocent hope that we would be able to come back soon and fetch it. Funny how at all points over those six long years, everyone seemed to think the war was about to end at any moment.'

'The car was probably taken by the first German who came along,' Aleksander said. 'They had few compunctions about appropriation. We were nether beings, after all. Didn't deserve anything except hard labour and death.'

He was more passionate than Irena had ever heard him. She cleared her throat. 'Your family had a bad time, then?'

'No, no. Not as far as it went. Not compared to others.'

'Look,' Amelia was pointing towards the sky. Two large birds soared above them, their broad wings silver-tipped in the sun.

'They're buzzards.' There was a look of revulsion on Bruno's face.

'They're beautiful.'

'Let's carry on.'

Irena intercepted the questioning look Amelia gave him. She didn't understand his gruffness, his disappointment at the car's not being here. At its leaving no trace. Irena understood that. There was so little in this scarred world to bring back innocent childhood pleasures, happier golden times.

Maybe it was just that she was more intent on Aleksander. Her hand slipped along his arm. It was a proprietary gesture. A soothing gesture.

So it had already happened, Irena thought, stilling an unwanted pang of jealousy. Good for Amelia. Come to think of it, Aleksander looked the better for it too. He was standing straighter. What a tall man he was. A good haircut, a better suit, and he would be distinctly handsome.

She asked him as soon as they were on the move again. 'So were your parents both in the Krakow area during the war, Aleksander?' In the intimacy of the car, she had started to use his first name.

'My father was, in part.' Aleksander didn't elaborate. They were rejoining the main road, and the traffic was heavy.

It wasn't like an interview, so she didn't want to press him, but luckily Amelia had her ears tuned now. She too was curious.

'In part... That's a little mysterious. What about the other parts?'

Aleksander shot a hasty glance at the Professor, and Irena had a sudden feeling that maybe this line of questioning was going to go all wrong. What if this purported father of hers was some kind of nasty? A criminal? A Nazi collaborator? What if that was why her mother had never mentioned any of it to her earlier? Her biological father, a criminal.

Professor Lind's face had turned pasty, or was she imagining it? He suddenly reprimanded Amelia, as if she were a naughty child. 'You can't push people on these things, Amelia. It always begins to feel like a criminal trial.'

'I didn't mean that.'

'No, of course, you didn't.' Aleksander's voice was soft.

'None the less, Amelia assumes that all fathers, except hers, have told their children everything about their war years.'

'Oh, Pops.'

'In fact, my parents did tell us some things...if not always wittingly.' Aleksander turned away from the wheel to look at Amelia and defend her from her father.

Irena had the feeling she had better stop this conversation right now or they would end up in an outburst of nerves and slammed hard against someone's bumper. German car or not, bumpers had a way of crumpling.

'Hello… We're already on the outskirts of Przemysl,' she said brightly. 'Why don't we stop for a coffee and talk then? I'm sure we could all do with one.'

'Good idea,' Amelia concurred.

By the time Aleksander could find a convenient place to park, they were already across the river. Perched on its pretty green hill, the town jutted towards them, looking like nothing so much as an Austrian spa complete with Baroque domes and stuccoed cloisters.

Closer to, when they got out to walk the steep streets, it was clear that the post-Soviet reconstruction had only gone so far. Churches and cloisters and their attendant buildings had been restored to their original Renaissance and Baroque glory, but ordinary houses and shops were still awaiting a long-delayed makeover.

Maybe it was this that allowed the Professor to find his way around as if he had left the place yesterday. He walked quickly, almost ran ahead of them. The Furies were biting at his heels. He was reliving it all, a boy again, pursued by Nazis or Soviets or Ukrainians. There had been some trouble here with Ukrainians too, she thought vaguely, or maybe that was now. Yes, they kept stealing across the border, claiming refugee status, or just selling their wares. Whatever the case, Professor Lind had a particularly intent look as he guided them through a courtyard and stopped at its penultimate doorway.

'Up here,' he said to Amelia. 'This is where my grandfather and I moved after my grandmother had died.'

'Died?' Amelia asked. 'Died how?'

He shrugged. 'It might have just been of despondency or fear or old age…' He laughed ruefully. 'Though nowhere near as old as I am now… People aged more quickly then. Or perhaps it's the child's eye view. Anyhow, we lived up on the second floor.'

'Looks lovely, Somehow, I think I'd imagined everything in black and white. Grim. Drab. Like all those wartime films. But in fact it's in colour.'

'It didn't have quite so much colour then, as I remember.'

'It seems to belong to the church now. Church administration.' Aleksander was reading a sign.

'It might even have done so before. Or maybe not, because this was the Russian sector. On the other hand, I do think my grandfather might have got the lodgings through a priest.'

'Befriending priests, was he?'

'Oh yes,' he winked at her. 'If you try me now I might still get through the first bits of the Catechism. In Polish only, of course.'

Irena began to recite: 'I believe in God, the Father Almighty, Creator of Heaven and Earth. And in Jesus Christ, His only Son, Our Lord. Who was conceived of the Holy Ghost, born of the Virgin Mary. Suffered under Pontius Pilate; was crucified, dead, and buried. He descended into Hell; the third day he rose again from the dead. He ascended into heaven, sitteth at the right hand of God the Father Almighty. From thence He shall come to judge the living and the dead. I believe in the Holy Ghost. The Holy Catholic Church, the Communion of Saints. The forgiveness of sins. The resurrection of the body. And life everlasting. Amen.'

They were all staring at her. She laughed. 'Of course, we all learned it. My generation, I mean. In protest. Against the Russians. The Virgin has a more amenable face than Stalin, you have to agree.'

'I wasn't questioning. Just surprised,' Amelia murmured. 'Perhaps surprised at both of you.'

'This country is full of surprises.'

Irena couldn't quite tell if bitterness or wryness prevailed in the Professor's tone.

They followed the curve of the road uphill and ended up in the café in the old castle grounds at the very top of the city. They sat out on the terrace under a large white parasol that sheltered them from the noonday heat. In the distance the river curled beneath graceful trees and when the heat mist cleared, the blue bulk of the Carpathian hills appeared.

'It's so hard to yoke moments of time together.' The Professor was sipping a cold beer. 'I have this old grid over which everything fits almost perfectly and yet nothing, but nothing, is the same.'

'But I'm pleased you've brought me here, Pops.'

'You were asking about my parents,' Aleksander began hesitantly. 'My father once took my sister and me out to the countryside to point out this estate he had worked on. He was just a kid during the war. And as soon as we got there, he started crying. He couldn't stop. Maybe it was the cherry trees in bloom. But he wouldn't tell us anything. Not even about how the old mill functioned. Maybe there wasn't all that much to tell. Or that could be told.'

Irena was listening intently. Her mother had been in the countryside too. She wanted to ask him exactly where all this had taken place. His father had been too young. Maybe that was it. Why her mother had kept it hidden. A child-father. Aleksander as a child-father ... But he was already hurrying on.

'I don't really understand the inner logic of all this, because he did tell me about a later part of the war. He was taken in a *łapanka*, you know one of those raids the Nazis carried out. Mass kidnappings, really.'

Irena was sitting opposite Bruno, and she could see his fingers balling into a fist. His shoulders had gone rigid. Maybe it would be better to stop Aleksander now. Too much emotion at his age couldn't be a good thing. Yet he was the one questioning Aleksander.

'And where was that exactly?'

'Krakow, I imagine.'

'Yes, of course, and what happened to him?'

'Well, he ended up in Germany. Working in a munitions factory. Slave labour effectively.'

He stumbled and stammered as the word 'slave' tumbled from his lips. He had the air of a man who had somehow condemned himself.

Amelia laughed. 'That's okay. I'm prepared to learn about other people's histories of slavery. Nice not to be alone.'

'So many perpetrators,' Irena jumped in. 'Too many. The ancients. All those captives they enslaved. The Africans themselves. The Nazis, of course. And our very own Man of Steel,

Stalin. I don't know if he wasn't the worse. His slave labour camps, they say, rose to kill some twenty million. And he managed all that with no particular racial prejudice. He killed anyone, really. Democratic in his killing, he was. Though he wasn't any fonder of Jews than his erstwhile German partner in crime. Nor Muslims. Or Poles, for that matter.'

She stopped. 'I'm running away with myself. You were talking about your father slaving for the Germans, Aleksander. Sorry. During the war.'

'Well...' Aleksander wore a perplexed expression. 'He claimed that, despite the beatings, it wasn't so bad. They had a little to eat. There were some pretty girls. No, the worst, ironically, came when the Allied bombing started. There they were, rooting for them, cheering the Allies on, hoping the war's end would come soon, but with each Allied attack, some of their number got killed. When the factory was evacuated, a few of them escaped. There was no way to get back to Poland, except to walk. So that's what my father and his friend did. They walked. Avoiding bombs as they went. They were very lucky.'

'Yes, luck.' The Professor had his distant face on, like a lone wolf who had left the pack too long ago ever to return.

'Luck,' he repeated. 'Those of us who came through had to have plenty of it. But unfortunately there wasn't enough luck to go around. Or enough good will amongst our neighbours.'

A silence fell and lengthened. Irena had the distinct feeling that in it the dead were being counted and the whole matter of Poles and Jews was about to explode like some kind of bomb between them. But Aleksander didn't seem to be aware of it. Maybe he hadn't spent enough time abroad. Germany was probably different. The Germans couldn't point an accusing finger at the Poles.

Irena knew she should say something, but she didn't know quite what. Some of her friends at moments like this came out with stories about how their families had helped or hidden Jews. One would be forgiven for sometimes thinking that there was a Jew in every Polish wartime closet. But she couldn't say anything as trite as that.

How did people anywhere in this war-torn world ever make relations ordinary again after these mammoth upheavals? It took so long for the emotions to go. Centuries perhaps.

She shook herself in an attempt to thrust away dismal thoughts. In any case, it was Aleksander's father she needed to hear more about. Maybe she was also misinterpreting the Professor's comment about good will. After all, Aleksander could hardly be accused of racism. He was with Amelia, which had to exonerate him. So that left her to apologize for the Poles.

Before she could formulate something appropriate, Bruno asked in some disbelief, as if Aleksander hadn't told them everything he knew: 'So your father got through the war?'

'I'm the living proof of that.'

'Yes, yes, of course.'

'What was his first name? Would I have come across him?'

'Tadeusz. I wouldn't imagine so.'

'Tadeusz. It sounds so nice when you say it. Soft.' Amelia's voice caressed.

'Nicer than Aleksander.' He laughed shyly 'But my parents decided to name me after my father's older brother. He was the hero, apparently.'

'Which means he died young,' Irena heard herself saying. What she meant was he had died too long before she was born. Could her mother have gotten names confused, named one brother for the other? Would she still remember if Irena prodded her? Was it a one-night stand or…? She felt what was almost a blush coming on. And what if she brought Aleksander to visit her mother? She must ask him somehow if he looked like his father and then bring him to see her.

'I do think we should get on.'

Bruno pushed back his chair so abruptly that the glass on the rickety table fell over and tumbled onto the gravel beneath. Strangely, it didn't break. Maybe luck was still with the Professor, after all.

A half-hour later they were walking along a track at the southern-most extremity of the town near what all the road signs promised was the Tartar Monument. Tartarus: the ancient site of hell from which the devils rose. The name the Europeans gave to the marauding Tartar hordes. Had she learned that at school? But there was no monument here to explain. No Tartar King whose rampaging legions had laced generations in the region with sparkling narrow eyes.

Instead they abutted at a dilapidated gate with a broken lock. Beyond it was a cemetery devoid of angels or crosses or any adornment. A decaying Jewish cemetery, Irena noted, with ancient mossy tumbling stones on which the writing – even had she been able to read the script – had been scratched away by time, if not by vandals. The unrelieved slabs growing out of the rank vegetation gave off a mournfulness that somehow defied human mourning. Nothing could be made good by mere human care, not here, not for these austere unreachable dead.

The air was unnaturally still. She felt odd, like a voyeur from another realm. Odder still when Bruno Lind looked around him with a vulnerable and bewildered air. Somebody should really take the man's arm, but Amelia was busy with Aleksander. She moved closer to him.

'It should be somewhere over that way. But we never laid the stone. We weren't here long enough.'

She wasn't sure whether he was addressing himself, the elements or her. Lear on the blasted heath, she thought. Even the clouds were gathering. And the wind had come up, rustling the trees into erratic action. He started to walk quickly through the thick green-ery, as if he were running from someone in fear. He kept looking abruptly over his shoulder, then from right to left. The old days, she thought. The gestures of the old days. Persecution. Not now. Not now mercifully. He bobbed, veered to the left then disappeared. Like a will o' the wisp.

She hurried after him then almost fell over when a withered old woman in black appeared in front of her.

Her mind was going, Irena thought. Definitely. Gone, in fact. Now she was conjuring up toothless kerchiefed old hags, who materialized from the air in graveyards.

'*Dzień dobry Pani, Dzień dobry,*' Irena said, polite even to ghosts.

The ancient woman barely nodded, and Irena, still wondering about her reality, reached for her purse, took out some coins, mumbled something about 'for the care of the graves'. When the woman took the coins with a kind of shuffling eagerness, she was consoled. Ghosts didn't need money.

'There's a lot to be done here,' she thought she heard the woman say, before she hobbled off in the other direction and vanished behind a mouldering stone.

Irena followed the direction she assumed the Professor had taken. She found him bent over on all fours, poking at the ground, lifting away the trailing undergrowth.

'I think this is it,' he murmured.

He seemed to be trying to trace the size of a plot from the midst of rampant vegetation and neighbouring slabs. 'I memorized the names on either side. Grandfather told me to. In case anything happened to him. This one's Goldblum and there, that's Oppenheim. I wouldn't have remembered them. But recognition, that's easier. Remember, I told you that.' He gave her a sudden vivid smile, altogether belying her earlier worries, and hailed the others.

'Your great-grandmother, Sarah. We're going at last to erect a stone for her. Rather more than a year since the funeral. Sixty-two, in fact. But better than never. Irena will know how to go about it.'

Amelia kissed him.

Irena was about to protest but found herself so secretly pleased at the man's faith in her that she kept quiet, dutifully pulled a pad from her bag and sketched a little map, noting the names on the graves around her.

The old crone appeared from nowhere again, and this time everyone greeted her. So she was definitely real. The Professor, in fact, brought forth a flood of verbiage from her. It seemed she could help with the setting up of a gravestone. A Pan Kwiatowski in Przemysl handled it. Yes, yes, she assisted him. That's why she was here. From the folds of her tattered skirt, now like some grand angel of mercy, she brought out an utterly modern printed card and handed it to the Professor.

Amelia and Irena exchanged glances. Aleksander smiled. Then, as if the old woman had jogged him into speech as well, the Professor started to talk. He was talking to Amelia, telling her about his grandparents, the time they had spent in this area all those years ago. Maybe the gracious lady even remembered...

By the time they reached the car, time had folded in on itself, grown viscous, heavy, a neither then nor now time, but both, an in-between state in which this ageing man in search of his dead was also a youth fighting for his life against terrible odds.

11

1940

Each uphill step towards his grandparents' apartment increased Bruno's unease. The buildings with their bullet-scarred stucco seemed to be baring dingy wounds to the reddening sun. Faces emerged from gaping doors like mottled masks on sticks. The streets had grown more twists in them, the ruts in the cobblestone become potholes.

He had been gone some four months. How had his grandparents fared in his absence? Would they still be where he had left them? Such thoughts only assailed him now as he was on the point of reaching them.

He had turned thirteen while he was away. His grandmother had told him in a soft voice before he left that his thirteenth birthday marked manhood for a Jew. She had talked of taking him to a Rabbi, but his grandfather had grown irate and asked whether she thought she had been transformed into Abraham and was considering the offer of more than a ritual sacrifice.

His grandparents often argued over religious matters. He couldn't help hearing them in their small quarters. Grandma said it was sinful how Grandpa behaved, denying everything, denying his people, denying God. Grandpa said he was denying nothing, simply being expedient. She would thank him later. Meanwhile, she could talk to her God silently and leave the two of them alone.

Only his grandmother was in, when Bruno arrived. She was sitting in a chair and gazing out at the dip in the valley that provided their only distant view. Maybe she was talking to God. She stared at Bruno as if he might be a hallucination then whispered his name in a soft voice and held out her hand to him. When he moved towards her, a smile illuminated her face. That face, he realized, had grown painfully thin, hollowed out so it was all eyes. The hair that cupped it was now utterly white, ghostly.

'*Brunchen*, my little one. So happy. Tell me, tell me, did you find them? Are they…?'

He hugged and reassured her at the same time. She felt so fragile, he was afraid his embrace might break her.

When Grandpa returned, Bruno felt a sob rising up in him. He too had been transformed into an old man.

Over that winter, his grandmother slowly died. She just disappeared into herself and her chair and never re-emerged. The doctor they brought for her could do nothing.

'Better,' he said ominously, as if he knew something Bruno didn't. 'She's peaceful. The rest of us are still at war.'

They buried her in the Jewish cemetery. She would have wanted that. It was an auspicious site, Bruno forced himself to think over the tears he refused to shed, just south of the city and not far from the grave of a great Tartar King who would protect her. According to tradition, there would be no stone to mark her resting place for a full year. 'Memorize the spot,' his grandfather said to him. He evidently imagined the earth would shift, and they would never find her again, so Bruno made a mental note of the names on the nearest tombstones and took a good look at the trees in the vicinity.

In direct contradiction of at least his mood at the cemetery, a week later his grandfather announced they were moving. 'We're wiping the traces,' he said, as if all their movements left a rife trail for dogs in hot pursuit, and a great effort had now to be made to send them in a different direction. Every night he listened to the radio for hours, tuning into whatever stations he could get, comparing reports, scouring the papers which Bruno brought home for him from the neighbouring kiosk, interpreting propaganda. What he knew and Bruno only learned later was that Nazi troops were massing for a great push east on a variety of fronts and that the Nazi-Soviet pact was in its last moments.

Bruno didn't want to move. He wanted to stay as close as possible to their local paper kiosk. It was run by a young woman who had become a friend of his. So much of a friend in imagination, that he spent his nights dreaming about her eyes, which appeared to him in improbable places – in the sky as giant stars, in murky fish-ponds as bright lilies.

But they moved. They moved into two tiny rooms not far from one of Przemysl's many churches which had sprung up over the centuries as if in competition with each other so that each order could outdo the next in grandeur. His grandfather had somehow struck up a relationship with a priest. The clergy were not very well treated by the Russian administration, and the man evidently felt a friend who worked for them might prove beneficial. In turn and for various favours his grandfather didn't tell him about, but which Bruno was quite certain had been granted, the priest was to provide them with baptismal certificates.

His grandfather had spent hours grilling Bruno about his experience of the German *Arbeitsamt*, the labour office, and the papers that were necessary. He had also carefully examined Bruno's work permit, and as he did so mumbled something about 'Trust the Germans to have papers for everything. And keep records of everything. Perfect students of Weber, even the Nazis.'

It sometimes seemed to Bruno that his grandfather had taken on outwitting the Germans as a personal mission. This one old Jew would get them at their own game. In revenge for what he had seen those young thugs in uniform do to those old men. In revenge for what he called their sadism. Their state-sanctioned sadism.

Now that his grandmother was gone, Bruno felt his grandfather talked to him as he had once talked to her, mulling over ideas and strategies late into the evening in the tiny kitchen where they ate their thin broth and tasteless potatoes, unless he had been able to trade more profitably.

One part of the strategy had to do with Bruno going to the priest for weekly tutorials. This time it wasn't Russian. It was Catholicism that needed to be studied, together with lists of saints and the endless drill of Catechism, Mass and Communion. The priest believed that he was the son of lapsed Catholics, who had tragically died in the first German incursion. Now, however, he was under his grandfather's aegis, a grandfather who was getting old and had seen the light despite the pressure of Soviet atheism. He wanted his grandson to embrace the true faith again. Bruno loathed the drill, but he couldn't go against his grandfather's will. He sensed that this project was the only thing that gave the old man a taste for life. And he knew that baptismal certificates, when copied into a central register, might not come amiss. The name on his was not to be the one that appeared on his grandfather's Russian pass, but a new name, born from the romance of literature. He was to be Bronislaw Sienkiewicz: Bronek, for short. All traces of the Jewish Bruno were to disappear when his grandfather said the moment was right.

At the end of May, Bruno wanted once more to head off to see his mother and sister. His grandfather insisted that they had to wait for their baptismal papers and the accompanying birth certificates before attempting any river crossing. It was too dangerous now. There were too many soldiers about. And this time, they would go together, so they needed to be properly provided for.

The priest gave them the documents on June 19. Before they had got their provisions together for the journey and his grandfather had alerted his office of his impending absence, the Nazis had entered Przemysl. They had come by train from across the river, at first hoodwinking the Russian guards into thinking they were taking just an ordinary delivery of freight. Trainloads of troops followed together with flatcars bearing tanks and armoured cars and motorbikes. Many didn't bother to stop at Przemysl but carried on further east into the Ukraine and Russia. The Russians in the town were surrounded. There was nowhere for them to run.

The fighting in the city was fierce. For two days and nights it raged, making the streets impassable. On the third day, Bruno tried to go out early to rustle up some food. Corpses lay strewn in the streets. The Gestapo marched, breaking into houses, heaving people out, arresting them or shooting them on the spot. They seemed to have a clear picture of where they were going. He raced home and bolted their door, hoping the knock wouldn't come in this tiny apartment tucked in behind a church. His grandfather just stared out the window and shook his head. Bruno began to think he was taking on his wife's old role.

Hunger forced him out in the streets again the next day, despite fear. Curiosity too. The German's didn't behave like the Russians. As he moved through his familiar haunts, he noted that the City Hall already sported a swastika, as did various other official buildings. Streets were closed off. Fierce-looking officers stood in front of them, guns at the ready. Decrees were posted on buildings. Bruno read that all weapons had to be surrendered on pain of death and that a curfew was in place from five in the afternoon till five in the morning. People caught breaking it would be shot. Everyone was to return to work. Or they too would be shot, he added to himself and raced off.

The market was empty. There was nothing to buy or steal or trade anywhere. And though the proclamations called for shops to open immediately, they looked decidedly shut. There was probably nothing to put in them. There had, after all, been little enough before, even at the Russian cooperatives.

Finally, not knowing where to turn, Bruno decided to knock at the priest's door. The man took pity on him and gave him half a stale loaf. Bruno thanked him profusely, added from some perverse instinct that his grandfather had instilled in him, that Christ would thank him too. He rushed home with the bread, hiding it beneath his shirt, and told his grandfather the priest was a good man.

He became his grandfather's eyes and ears. He ran like lightning, forking between ranked German soldiers, scudding up tiny lanes, sniffing out the lie of the land, rushing home to report on what he had seen and the proclamations he had read. His grandfather's role was to interpret the signs he brought him.

The old man decided that he would need to return to his office as the edicts ordered. It would be too dangerous to try and cross the river now. The soldiers would be shooting on sight. If nothing else, it was clear that he would need to earn what he could, since Bruno's bartering activities were too risky while everything was still in upheaval.

A few days later when he was out in search of food, Bruno noted that a new set of orders had gone up on the walls. These concerned Jews. Jews were ordered to wear armbands with the Star of David on them to indicate their nationality. They had to register immediately with the *Arbeitsamt* for mandatory labour and with something called the *Judenrat* – the new committee that administered Jewish life. They were only allowed out on the streets between two and four, unless they had papers showing they were employed. They were forbidden to be near government offices, including the railway station; they couldn't buy provisions from anyone in town or countryside, nor could they possess any of the new official currency, the German Occupation Marks.

Bruno stared at these proclamations for as long as he dared. He wanted to tear them down, run around the city and rip them from the walls. He couldn't bear the look on the faces of the two women who were reading beside him. Life was impossible under such orders. Life as a Jew was impossible.

He began to understand more clearly why his grandfather had wanted officially to cut all ties with their Jewish past and why their baptismal certificates were so important. He thought it might be time to take on his new name. He was about to hurry home, using a roundabout route as his grandfather had counselled, to bring him the news, when he determined that, no, he wouldn't be daunted. He had set out for food, and he must find some.

He hurried on, past the limits of the city. German soldiers were stationed along the country road. Despite protests, they helped themselves to whatever the farmwomen had in their baskets and were bringing to market, then rudely tossed a few pfennigs at them.

In the distance, Bruno spied the red flowered headscarf of one of the women he used to help with her provisions. He ran towards her. She had a basket of radishes in one hand and eggs in another. He asked her if she needed assistance. She shrugged and handed him the radishes under which he spied slabs of butter. He quickly stuffed as much as he could of these into his pockets and under his cap, muttering at her that otherwise, as she probably already knew, the Germans would get the lot for next to nothing. He was right. An arrogant character stopped them and helped himself casually from the baskets. The woman named a price that he merely harrumphed at. A few coins were thrust at her, and he told her to hurry along if she didn't want trouble.

By the time they reached the town, there were only a few radishes left in her basket. Bruno looked round and quickly emptied his pockets and cap of the butter and asked if he could have some radishes in return. She gave them willingly, plus an egg that she had hidden and suggested that he come a little further along the road on the morrow to help her out.

At home, his grandfather was eager for news. Bruno gave him the food first and only then, once they had eaten a little, recounted the content of the edicts against the Jews. His grandfather said nothing. He simply sat and stared, his once handsome face lined and dismal. After a while, he patted Bruno's hand. 'Remember. If anything happens to me, remember everything I have said. Tomorrow I will report to work. Everyone must work.'

Early the next morning, the sounds of heavy boots clattered up the stairs. They were followed by knocking and raucous calls in German to open the door.

Both of them were dressed, his grandfather in his shabby worksuit and tie, ready to go out. He winked at Bruno and started talking loudly in German, complaining about this new generation and their lack of manners. '*Kein beziehung.* No respect for the old.' He pushed back his shoulders that these days were so often slumped and took on his former military bearing, as he pulled open the door.

'I hear you. I'm not deaf yet. That's enough.'

Two SS men examined him with surprise.

'You speak German?'

'I'm pretty sure that's what I was speaking. I take it you do as well. There's no need to make so much noise. I'm an old man.'

The Germans looked sheepish for a moment.

'Well. Do you want to come in?'

They stepped into the small first room of the apartment on the widest wall of which his grandfather had hung an old crucifix.

'My name is Adolf Torok,' his grandfather continued. 'This here is my grandson. No one else lives here. I'm on my way to work. He'll be on his way to school as soon as you manage to open some again. Is there anything else?'

The men looked at each other.

'Good.'

'Heil Hitler,' the soldiers said automatically.

Bruno closed the door behind them and waited until the footsteps receded. His grandfather slumped into his customary chair. 'You see, Bruno? They've been taught to obey. As soon as you establish authority, they become docile. You have to give them what they understand. That's, of course, if you're lucky enough to look the part and have the additional good fortune of speaking a common language and aren't shot first. We're lucky men, you and I Bruno. Lucky men. Lucky to have the Führer as my namesake.'

There was a touch of something wild in the laugh that ripped through him. It was an unfamiliar sound. 'This time we didn't need those documents, but we must keep them close, in any case. Now I want you to accompany me to my office. We must see what my fate there may be, and perhaps we'll have a stroll towards the river.'

The office in which his grandfather had worked was shut. A sign ordered all workers to report to the local *Arbeitsamt*.

'That can wait until tomorrow. We've already had enough excitement for one day. And there'll be queues.'

They walked through the city. It had an artificial feel to it, as if nothing was quite real, neither the marching Germans, their uniforms too neat and bright against the blighted streets and their impoverished citizens; nor the open, but empty, shops; nor the once handsome buildings plastered over with their hundreds of decrees. At one junction, they saw a group of men and women wearing Jewish armbands being herded into a warehouse.

'That's how my namesake conducts his economy, Bruno. Slave labour to finance his battles. That's why temporarily he thought he had something in common with our friends to the east.'

The sight of a train rattling over the bridge caught their attention. 'I see they have the trains running smoothly again. You know what they used to say in the old Berlin just after the Great War?' His grandfather cackled. 'They said Germany would never have a revolution. Because the trains had to run on time. Did your father ever talk to you about that? No, no, of course not. You were far too young. So sad. Well, Bruno, now, despite everything, the trains are still running on time. Come, I have an idea.'

They wound their way down to the yellow railway station that always reminded Bruno of Vienna. Gestapo officers stood by the front doors. To the side, where there was a way through to the old left luggage office, a man in a railway guard's uniform hovered.

'Ah, he's here,' Bruno's grandfather smiled. 'My friend, Pan Staszek. Let's go and have a little chat with him. He owes me a favour. I arranged some papers for him.'

It was the first time Bruno realized that his grandfather's cunning extended to help those beyond their immediate circle.

The two men chatted while Bruno listened. Pan Staszek confirmed that the trains were running again. With a degree of punctuality. And yes, it was just possible to go to Krakow.

Bruno wondered if this mention of Krakow was another of his grandfather's ploys. Evidently, he didn't trust anyone. The men had lowered their voices so that he could no longer hear. He watched the station door. Most of the people coming in and out wore either German uniforms or Polish Railway uniforms. But there were also one or two women about. No men. Of course. All men were meant to be at work. His grandfather was running a risk being here. He waited impatiently, and at last his grandfather was back at his side.

'All is well, Bruno, we go to Krakow in three days' time. You come with me to get your picture taken, then leave the rest to me.'

The early-morning encounter with the Gestapo had evidently breathed fire into his grandfather's veins. For the next few days, he was all activity and when that evening he presented Bruno with his German ID, it was with the old smile of triumph he had when he had landed a particularly plump trout. 'It's as genuine as can be, Herr Bronislaw Sienkiewicz.'

He bowed to Bruno. The next day they took the first morning train to Krakow. Their papers withstood two checks by guards. Bruno watched the nonchalant manner in which his grandfather handed them over all the while carrying on a conversation with Bruno about the milling of barley or the families of fish found in Poland.

They got off at Tarnow and walked south, away from the tracks, hoping that they might meet a friendly farmer who would take them part of the way. The fields were flush with summer heat, and the walking was hard. His grandfather, Bruno noticed after a few miles, was short of breath and needed to rest in the shade. He urged him into the first copse, where a dog came barking at them, followed by a toothless farmer in an old floppy hat. He gave his suited grandfather a derisory look then looked at him again more closely.

'Is that you, then, Pan Torok?' He grinned, showing bare gums. 'Neither of us getting younger, eh? Hard times these. I'm just supplementing the farm produce,' he cackled again and pointed to the pouch he was carrying.

'Well done, Pan Tadek. We're on our way home. Needed a little rest in the shade.'

'I can give you a little something to help you along.' He tapped his pouch again.

'What have you got there?'

The old man drew out a bottle and handed it over. His grandfather took a large sip then coughed and grinned. 'You old rogue. Still brewing the devil's drink, eh? Too strong for the young one here. But thanks. We'll be seeing you.'

They hurried along after that and by mid-afternoon had reached the house. It looked oddly deserted. They cast worried glances at each other. Then Bruno ran forward, shouting: 'Mamusia, Mamusia, Anna.' A dog's fierce barking met his call. He was there on the other side of the door, but no one opened to his knock. Bruno dashed to look through a grubby window. At first he saw no one, then he spied a movement beneath the kitchen table. It was Anna, he thought, Anna hiding. A stone settled in his stomach.

He called her name again. This time she heard him and came racing to the door with a stool. She unfastened the bolts, all the while shouting at the dog to get down. She leaped into her brother's arms, while the dog prodded at him with his pointed snout. He had a shaggy pelt of indeterminate colour and mournful button eyes.

'This is Bolivar, Bruno and…and…' She was suddenly aware of their grandfather. She looked up at him shyly, uncertainly.

'Come here, my little one. Come and give an old man a kiss. They've left you all alone?'

Anna's words fell all over themselves in a confused rush as she tired to explain that Pani Alina had gone out to work and Mamusia had gone to Krakow last week to see some friends and maybe get some money, so she was guarding the house with Bolivar, their new dog, Wasn't he beautiful and everyone would be so excited when they found out that Grandpa – and she rushed to kiss him again – was here with Bruno. Bruno. Her darling brother.

Bruno worried. He could see the worry reflected in his grandfather's face. Little Anna should not have been left alone. The situation must have been desperate if she had. And she was so thin, her eyes deep caverns in her heart-shaped face.

She seemed as so often to read her brother's mind. 'Oh, you mustn't blame Mamusia, Bruno. She had no choice. She had to see a doctor.'

Bruno could see that his grandfather was about to ask for what exactly, but he clamped his lips.

'And you can't blame Pani Alina. We're very poor now. Pan Mietek has stopped helping us. And Mamusia's not very good at fishing. And they stole the cherries from the little orchard. On top of that Mamusia's German friend in the village, the major who helped us so much, has been sent east. So she had to go. She'll be *sooo* happy that you're here.'

Anna had grown up too quickly, Bruno thought. As if she were already a girl his own age, or even older, despite her smallness.

'I'll go fishing first thing tomorrow. We'll have a feast and fatten you up. Won't we, Grandpa?'

Grandfather nodded, preoccupied. 'I'm going to go and have a little word with Mietek first. You look after your Anna, Bruno. Look after her very well.'

He didn't return until evening when Pani Alina was already there and greeted him shyly, her saviour she said. But Grandpa didn't respond with his usual smiles.

'The man had the audacity to threaten me, Bruno. Me. After I set him up in style. I gave him a taste of my tongue, though. I think he'll be all right for a while. I suspect he's been stealing from under the women's noses.'

'I think so too, Pan Torok. The problem is we have no hold over him now.'

Grandfather brooded. Little Anna sat on his knee and tried to cheer him. Pani Alina told them about her day at the cement factory. It was a good fifteen kilometres away, but Mamusia had given her the bicycle her German officer had found while he was still in the area. It was so sad that he had been sent away. Some of the military weren't so bad. It was the Gestapo you had to watch out for.

Grandfather stayed with them for only two weeks. He was determined to go to Krakow. He would make contact with Mamusia there and see if perhaps life mightn't be better for them in the city. He told them to take good care of the small kitchen garden their mother had started. Before he went, he made a swing for Anna and tied it to her favourite tree. Swinging would bring colour into her cheeks, he said. Miraculously too, he came home one evening with a rooster and two chickens to fill the empty coop at the back. These were to be under Anna's special care.

The summer passed in a fretful haze. Time became waiting for Mamusia's return, until the waiting replaced the expectation of her arrival. Bruno worked in the fields alongside Pan Mietek, who had grown curmudgeonly and swigged his vodka at ever-shorter intervals. Under his boozy breath, he muttered continually, complaining he didn't know how he was supposed to take care of all of them, make up his quota for the cooperative with its upstart *Volksdeutscher* head and feed his own as well. Bruno, growing irritated, told him he was lucky to have a strong pair of arms beside him that he didn't pay for and extra fields that he robbed besides.

'Christ-murderer,' Bruno thought he heard him murmur, but he kept his temper in check. He had been with Pan Mietek when a visit from the cooperative had taken place, a routine visit which included a military presence, and he had seen the soldiers help themselves to baskets of fruit and vegetables, even vodka, while Mietek was meant to turn a blind eye or smile and nod. He hated those soldiers. It was hard to control that hatred and not somehow lash out.

Anna helped. She was always at his side, and he would do nothing that might harm her. When he wasn't working, they fished together or scrambled about in the mossy wood, gathering berries. Blue and red juices stained their lips and hands. She was never so happy as in those moments: her straw basket perched on her arm and the upside-down mushroom hat on her curly blonde head.

One evening in the middle of August when it was already dark, Bolivar started to bark angrily. The bark was followed by a knock. Bruno asked who it was in his deepest voice.

'Is that Bruno?' a man answered. 'I'm bringing a letter from your mother, from Pani Hanka.'

They opened the door inch by inch to see a dark-haired man of middle height with ruddy cheeks and a dimple in his chin. He was wearing shorts and an open-necked shirt and carrying a stout stick. He didn't look as if he had come from the city. He walked in before they had asked him to and closed the door quickly behind him.

He pulled a letter from his rucksack and smiled at them all, particularly at Pani Alina, but handed the letter to Bruno and then asked whether in turn he might have a bed, straw would do, for the night. Any extra supplies would be welcome too. He would be off before dawn.

Bruno tore open the letter before replying. 'My darlings,' their mother wrote, 'I hope to be with you before too long. Grandpa is well. You can trust the person who brings this.'

Bruno swallowed his disappointment.

'Letters are always brief these days,' the man said to him, as if he knew what his mother had written. 'Of necessity.'

Bruno only understood him after some moments, when Pani Alina had already asked him to sit down and offered him a shot from the vodka bottle.

'Do you know our mother?' Bruno asked.

'Not personally. But I'm told she's a fine woman.'

'I see.'

Bruno had to put himself into his grandfather's place really to see. Covert matters again. Everything was always hidden. Nothing straight. Everything in code. Once he had thought it was just the way of the adult world. Mirrors within mirrors. But his grandfather had shown him differently. Living in fear meant living in secrets. Hiding in one way or another. The man must be a Jew.

'Where are you going?' Bruno asked.

'Oh, just walking. A holiday,' he winked. 'I like the woods. Don't you?'

'Oh yes,' little Anna answered for him, while Bruno suddenly had a memory of the raggedy people he had seen in the woods round a bonfire deep in the night when he was travelling from Przemysl the previous year.

They gave the man a bed, but before bunking down they talked. He talked mostly to Pani Alina though Bruno listened intently. Things were hard in the cities. All of them. Even Warsaw. Food was scarce. Everything was scarce – for Poles too. The Germans had instituted a blistering regime run by their own people. Those they didn't like, the visitor looked at them intently, they forced behind guarded walls, concentrating a great many in very little space, so that conditions were foul, and disease spread like wild-fire. They were well off here, he said. There was air. At least the illusion of freedom. That's why he was going off into the woods. He turned to Bruno again as he said this. If he ever went walking, they might bump into each other again. It was always good to bring extra food along on such trips. It was also better not to men-tion to anyone that a stranger had been through.

In the morning, without so much as a single bark from Bolivar, the man was gone, together with the bread and sausage and onion Alina had put out for him. If Bruno hadn't had his mother's letter next to his bed, he might have thought he had dreamed his passage.

His mother returned with the first chill nights of autumn. They were so pleased to see her that Anna determined to bake a cake to celebrate her arrival. She stood on a stool and carefully broke two eggs into flour, added some spoons of blueberry jam Alina had made and three crinkly apples from the garden tree which they had carefully stored in the cold room alongside the potatoes and pears and dried mushrooms. The result was so sumptuous that they all declared Anna was now to be their chief baker.

Despite their joy at the reunion, it was clear that Mamusia was unwell. Her cheeks were sallow. The hollows in them had grown very deep, and her eyes had lost their sparkle. But she was still, Bruno thought, exceedingly beautiful: a grand lady in her pretty dress. He had forgotten what elegant women looked like.

He wanted to ask her what the doctor had said, what was wrong with her, but the moment didn't present itself. He hoped too, that being home would soon revive her.

Mamusia had brought with her a small hoard of German Occupation Marks that Grandpa had earned, she wouldn't tell them how. She hoped that might see them through the next months. They needed to move for the winter, though not to Krakow. Too many people knew her there.

'But what about Grandpa?' Bruno asked.

He was cleverer than she was. And it was better to separate so none would give the other away. The Nazis had become more stringent in their searches. That was another reason they needed to move. Now that her major had left, the new local authority was not to her liking. She had papers for herself and for Anna in the name of Lind, which could pass as an Austrian or Galician name. And the young Pan Sienkiewicz, her nephew, she knew was already taken care of. But the local farmers had known them for too long. And Alina was a worry. The major hadn't been able to see to her *Kennkarte* before he had been transferred. She would start making enquiries in the next weeks.

With the first snows, Mamusia came home triumphant. Because of her German, she had landed a job in the Labour Office in the substantial neighbouring town of Tarnow, far enough away and big enough for no one to know them. It was potentially a good job too, since she could do some good in it. She had also found them lodgings. They would be cramped, but no matter. Alina would have to stay behind until Mamusia could find new papers for her. Or she might even be able to devise something herself, once she saw how the office functioned. Then a transfer from the cement factory to a new job in the District of Tarnow should prove no problem. None the less, after that, for the same reasons she had already given, it was best that they not see each other.

Mamusia had tried to warn him in subtle terms he hadn't altogether understood that there were two real problems with Tarnow. The first was that he would now be going to technical school, the only kind of secondary education available under the Nazi Occupation. She wasn't worried about his ability. An accounting course would hardly stretch him. But she wanted him to be careful with the other children. He mustn't give anything away. She looked at him a little oddly as she said this, and he reacted quickly, saying that of course he wouldn't, but he would far prefer to work and bring in money, he was old enough. No, she was firm on that point. They would try school first. A job would be far more arduous. But at school, he wasn't to get too friendly with the other boys.

The second problem with Tarnow was that it contained a large ghetto. It was the first time Bruno had heard the word but when he had seen even a little of the reality, it seared itself into his mind, more indelibly than the rubber stamp with which his grandfather had simulated the authority of the Soviet State.

The Tarnow Ghetto stretched to the east of the old part of the city which was dotted with craters from the first days of the war when the Nazis had destroyed a large synagogue and other buildings belonging to the town's sizeable Jewish community. The Ghetto gate lay just past Ulica Kupiecka. Bruno had little reason to go there. But he would sometimes make a detour on his way to school and stand and watch the guards, whether Polish or German, as they brutally pushed and prodded long queues of huddled people off to their work-sites in the morning. They all wore the telltale armband with its Star of David that somehow seemed to obliterate their status as humans, suck attention into itself and away from the all-too-human face. The Star meant they could be beaten without mercy. The guards, even if they were rigorous in checking traffic as it went in and out of the Ghetto, behaved quite differently when they didn't have the Star to focus on.

Sometimes a smell would rise from the Ghetto gates like the odour of dead flesh in the woods, a sweet nauseating stink. One day, a little way past the main gate, Bruno saw a child crawl out of a hole under the wall, which had been covered over with rubble.

She caught his eye then ran away on stick legs. She wasn't much bigger than Anna.

Another day, it was after school and getting late so that he should have been rushing, he saw a youth hurl a bundle over the wall. It just skimmed the barbed wire and toppled over onto the other side. The youth strolled nonchalantly away pretending not to see Bruno. He wondered what the bundle contained and imagined it must be food.

The following Sunday, after church, which Mamusia insisted they all had to go to, instead of accompanying his mother and sister for a walk and smiling stupidly at all the churchgoers, he rushed home, packed up some bread and cheese and a cabbage, wrapped them in a cloth and rushed out again. He had been told to place a coin in the priest's collection tray. Now he would place another coin. He walked until he found a quiet bit of wall and with a heave sent his package hurtling across. He did this several Sundays in a row until Mamusia began to complain that he was eating them out of hearth and home and she couldn't come by enough food to keep him.

'Send me to work,' he challenged her, and then Anna piped up. 'He gives it away. He gives it to the poor.' His mother stared at him. After a moment she said: 'You are not, I repeat not, to go there. You're just like your grandfather. Do you want us all to be shot?'

'And what about you?' he retorted. 'What about all those little work permits you give out to...?' She hugged him, so as to seal his lips. Maybe she didn't want Anna to know. Maybe she thought it was bad luck to say anything out loud. The walls had ears.

Yes. There were eyes and ears all around them. At home, in the streets, at school. What they saw and what they heard had only one possible outcome. Death. Mamusia had admitted it at last.

12

On the other side of the level crossing, the road stretched like a taut shimmering ribbon between the variegated greens of infinite fields. An ancient horse with a long sagging back faced them across the tracks. He was tugging at a rickety wooden farm cart, atop it a driver with a battered hat and a face so toothless and weathered, he could have posed for Death in an old engraving. Time had stopped. Even the train whose passage had been announced had given up on it and refused to arrive.

Aleksander turned the car's engine off, and the stillness around them felt as palpable as the growing noonday heat. Bruno knew they must all be losing patience with him.

Last night, they had almost been pushed off the road by a police car in hot pursuit. They were its inconceivable object. The men of the supposed law, enforced by visible weapons, had pulled them out of the car and lined them up by the side of the darkened road. No threats of reports to the American Embassy had served any purpose. Amelia, in particular, had been roughly handled by the thugs. Aleksander's raised voice didn't help, and Bruno began to think that only a few dollar bills folded into his passport would. Like in the old days. Bribery oiled the wheels of both civil and uncivil society. He was about to pull out his wallet when Irena brought a cold penetrating voice out of herself, like a headmistress carrying a hefty ruler.

'If you stop for a minute and use your torches, you'll see very quickly that no one here is from Bielorus or the Ukraine, let alone Georgia or Chechnya. Just think. Think, or I'll have you reported through my newspaper straight to HQ for assaulting important visitors.'

The uniforms backed away, apologizing. Police had to patrol the borders, they grumbled. Mafia, drugs, illegal immigrants – Poland was beset by problems.

They had driven to Tarnow with an unpleasant taste in their mouths and then spent a fruitless hour scrambling through shabby Soviet-era streets in search of nothing but faceless ruins. The only open restaurant he had been able to locate afterwards had been a veritable disaster.

Yes, the whole expedition was proving a waste of everyone's precious time. And on top of it all, he found it almost impossible to talk to Amelia about the family, about the past, in front of that man. Yes, that man. Tarski. It was his own fault for chasing him to Poland. And now he was even beginning to see a resemblance.

For a split second Bruno felt something like a sob forming in his throat. He sent it back to where it belonged. He was growing mawkish. And all because... No. It wasn't the journey into a lost time. It was because of what this Irena beside him had said. She of the gracefully swaying neck and slightly hooded eyes. Clever woman. Pretty too. Could she be interested in him? Plucking at strings he hadn't known he had. Saying that life really was unspokenly hard for men. First they couldn't have their mothers, 'cause father or brother was in the way, and then they couldn't have their daughters either, because all these suitors arrived to steal them away. He had laughed, but it had thrust him into a self-pitying mood, as if he really were becoming an old fool, an old Lear.

He should clear the air by asking this Tarski outright. But he wasn't ready for his answer. And it would probably mean going to see the rest of his family.

That he would have to speak at some point, he had no doubt, given the way things seemed to be going with Amelia. But he wasn't ready. And he was half-hoping circumstances would somehow save him, and he never had to be.

He looked at her fine-boned profile. Her eyes were tightly shut. Almost as if she were concentrating on sleep. She had done that as a child, screwing up her eyes to block out the world at will until sleep took her over. She probably hadn't had any last night – and not only because of the hotel's damp sheets and heavy curtains which smelled of mould and pressed dust.

Yes, they were all losing patience with him. Even his second-in-command at the London laboratory had asked him when he had rung to check in yesterday morning, on what exact date he was planning to return. Something had come up. No, not in the experiments they were running. All was going according to plan so far. No major disasters. No delays in acquiring materials or refrigeration breakdowns or any of the other thousands of minor cock-ups that plagued laboratories everywhere. But there was a query he couldn't answer from their backers – about the timing of results. The moneymen, it sometimes seemed these days, were even more intractable than the material world. They wanted everything before it was anything at all.

Yes, patience was running out. Most of all his own. A whole morning spent blundering through the countryside, and he hadn't been able to locate his grandparents' house. No one they had asked had been able to help either. It was as if the landscape itself had shifted, taking with it distance and a sense of measure. So he didn't know where to begin. Hamlets had vanished or grown into unrecognisable villages or changed their names with new times and a succession of heroes. Or maybe it was the roads that had moved, new ones replacing the old in a generational sequence that couldn't be reversed. On top of it all in those days, he travelled largely by foot so that time and space were bound in a different, more intimate relation.

He was taking them all on a wild goose chase of the most ridiculous kind, the geese having all flown or been served up for a Christmas dinner. He no longer even knew why it had come into his head that he needed to find the house. More years than he liked to count had passed by without the need so much as hinting at its existence. And now...now it had grown into a huge carbuncle of stubbornness blinding him to everything else.

With an abrupt rush of movement, Bruno pushed open the door of the car and strode out.

'Pops.'

'Professor.'

He could hear the cacophony of voices behind him, telling him to stop, setting up a stir in the country quiet as he moved quickly across the tracks. Maybe they thought he was playing at Anna Karenina.

The wizened peasant with his battered hat was watching him from narrowed eyes. The last of a disappearing breed, Bruno thought. They might have withstood the roll of the centuries and the Communist years, but they wouldn't withstand the demands of European union and modernization.

As he walked towards him, Bruno had the uncanny feeling that the old farmer wouldn't mind seeing him mowed down by the Krakow-Odessa Express, if only to relieve the monotony of the day. But he managed to reach the other side safely and now suspicion played over the man's features. He didn't raise his hat, and by way of greeting Bruno gave the horse's hot flank a pat. That clean childhood odour of mingled straw and manure scratched pleasantly at his nostrils.

'*Dzien dobry Pan, przepraszam. Czy Pan...*' the words flowed from his lips with no seeming intervention from his will. He was asking the man if he could remember way back, his parents might have told him, there was a Krakow family living somewhere around here, the Toroks. Pan Adolf Torok. A fine figure of a man. Loved hunting. Fishing too. Planted a small orchard. Cherries. Apples.

The peasant stared at him, stared until a distant rumble at last announced the arrival of a train. '*Toroki, tak, tak.* Jews. Yes. That mad old woman used to grumble that they'd taken her for everything. Burned her out. Even her home-made vodka.' He winked.

'Mad old woman,' Bruno echoed, disbelief rising in him along with a thick gob of hatred mingled with fear.

'Yes, yes. What was her name? We were scared of her. Always muttering. Full of malice. Threw things at us. A hag. Ancient.' He laughed suddenly, soundlessly, baring his gums. 'Probably not as ancient as I am now.' He took out a small hip flask and raised it in Bruno's direction in a toast, before taking a swig.

Bruno's lips trembled. 'Are we near...are we near that farm, then?'

'Yes and no.'

'It's far, then?'

'No, quite near as the stork flies. But not all that near by road.' The peasant pointed in a diagonal across a sea of swaying grains and grasses. 'About eight or ten fields over that way. But you'll have to go round. Right round. Past the cooperative.' He formed a broad lazy arc with his arm.

Bruno took in the instructions. He was perspiring, his thoughts muddled.

'Not much to see,' the old man added, as the train whooshed past them. 'Your lot are they? Planning to build a house?'

As Bruno shrugged noncommittally, he grumbled, 'Too many new houses around here. Not for us, though. Rotten government. Going to sell us out. They're...'

The rest of his mounting diatribe was lost in noise.

As soon as the dust-cloaked train raced past them, the peasant whisked his horse into action and clattered away.

They pulled up on a muddy dirt track to the side of the road just past a little wood. He knew those woods. He was certain of it. He could feel it in the dryness of his mouth, in the erratic rhythm of his heart. And in his mind, the thickets where the rabbits hid took on a visual precision, so that each twig and bramble had an unnatural clarity. Yes he was certain of it. A brisk walk past the neighbouring fields would yield his grandparents' house.

Everyone piled out and insisted on walking with him, despite his protests. After what they considered the madness at the level crossing, they were unwilling to let him stray on his own. Perhaps they were right, but Bruno wasn't sure he really needed to be held onto the way Amelia was doing now, her arm tightly draped through his. He stopped an impulse to shake it off and had a flickering sensation of his mother at his side, silent but gravely present, observing his every motion, and his need both to thrust her aside and simultaneously keep her there.

The generations were swirling through him like a blizzard, one indistinguishable from the next, so that he tripped over his own feet, no longer sure of their size.

Behind him, he could hear Aleksander and Irena talking. He focussed on the snippets of their conversation that floated towards him. She seemed to be asking the man what his mother had been like, whether she had been much younger than his father. He wondered why she was pressing him, when she suddenly giggled girlishly and offered that her own father in rowdy moments had persecuted her mother with stories of early conquests, all – it seemed – far more appetizing than she was.

He couldn't hear Aleksander's response, though he strained his ears because now Amelia was addressing him, taking him away from the flow of that other language.

'What you thinking about, Pops?'

'Not sure. Not sure I'd call it thinking.'

'Is the terrain looking familiar, Pops?'

Bruno nodded.

'Despite these?'

She didn't need to point. Coming up on their left were three brashly new houses with sloping roofs of bright-red simulated tile.

'It's further,' he said with assurance, setting aside a trail of irritation and disappointment. 'And, I imagine, to our right.' He closed his eyes for a moment to capture an inner topography and was suddenly confronted with an unsettling image from another part of his life. He couldn't shake it off, nor did he know why it had suddenly invaded these flat fields so far from its source.

The image was of a woman in an operating theatre, so long ago that the equipment looked almost Victorian, even heavier and more antiquated than those old room-size computers. She was lying on her side on a table surrounded by doctors and nurses, and her eyes were wide open. They were staring directly at him. The peculiarity was that one half of the woman's head was shaven and her brain lay exposed to the doctor's electric probe and soft-spoken command.

Bruno knew where the image came from. He was in the operating theatre of the Montreal Neurological back in the late forties or early fifties. It must have come back to him because Aleksander and he had, a few days ago, been talking about Penfield and his pioneering work on mapping the brain. But why this particular woman, with her solemn intense gaze focussed accusingly on him?

He tried to blink the image away and was rewarded with float-ing red spots at the corner of his eyes, the kind the epileptics used to talk about as signals of forthcoming seizures. Just what he needed, he scoffed at himself.

'It's a scorcher of a day. You okay in this heat?' Amelia was gentle.

'I'm fine,' he lied. 'You're sweet to pamper me like this.'

'Your very own Cordelia. You're a lucky man.'

'Never doubted it.'

'Pops, what's special about this place?'

'I spent a lot of time here. More than anywhere. Good times as well as bad. With my little sister too. And my mother.' He squeezed her hand.

She picked a tall blade of grass from the roadside and whistled softly through it. 'What was she like? Your mother, I mean.'

'A thoroughly modern woman. Independent. Full of inner resources. Brave. Very brave. Now that I think of it as an adult, though, I didn't have enough perspective as a child to see that. Or much else. You would have liked her. And she was quite unlike her own mother. More like her Dad. Though both she and her mother played the piano. Played wonderfully. My mother even gave us the occasional racy number.' He laughed as he put adult words to it. There was that other matter he hadn't had words for then either. Lovers and abortions and racy music.

That was it. Music. Of course. The woman on the operating table. A right osteoplastic craniotomy. The incision was made just to the side of her ear. A Rahm stimulator was used with a strength of one and half volts. On the temporal lobe the strength was increased to three and then four volts. As the probe moved along the contours of the brain the patient felt tingling in her thumb, then lip, then tongue. On the cut surface of the first temporal con-volution the patient heard music.

Bruno shivered. An aural hallucination of a remembered song. She was certain an orchestra was playing in the operating room. What was the song? She had sung lines of it over and over when that particular region was stimulated. Something about walking along, perhaps. Walking along as he was doing.

Was it about that patient or another that Penfield had made the comment that so struck him, struck him probably with too much force because his own nerves were still palpably in disarray whatever he did to hide the fact? Yes. They wouldn't describe it the same way now, but the truth of the matter stood. Penfield had commented that previous epileptic discharges – electrical storms in the temporal lobes Bruno imagined them as – made the cortex more susceptible to subsequent stimulation. So that recollections could temporarily alter, interfere with, present experience.

The patient, remembering her song, insisted that it was being played out there, not in here, in her memory, by her brain. And she found things in the room to confirm her inner experience.

The doctor cut out the area affected by the brainstorm. Was it after this that he made his decision to work in neurology? The hope that a bit of him could be cut out too?

The contained violence of the operating theatre seemed to suit him then. As it had in the DPP camp. A contained violence to echo the uncontained violence of the near past. Yes. He needed the edge of danger, the whiff of brutality, the cut, to make him feel alive. Since he was mostly dead. Mostly with his dead. And then the change came. He couldn't hack it anymore. Literally couldn't hack it. The impossibility of it all. So he had moved sideways. Into the lab, a more enduring love, which demanded not drama, but an intense quiet patience and a deferred hope: that the next step, or the one after that, or the one after that would shine a bright light through the gossamer shroud of the unknown.

'Over there, Pops. What do you think?'

An old truck rattled past them, raising dust and leaving a cloud of fumes in its wake. When the air cleared, he saw a house surrounded by a cluster of trees coalescing out of smoke. He stopped in his tracks. It wasn't his grandparent's house. There were no deep wings. And yet there was something in the geometry of land and house and trees that had an aching familiarity.

They walked towards it slowly, Irena coming up behind them to say that, of course, so much had changed it might be impossible to recognize anything. There had been bombing, after all, Nazi tanks invading and then fleeing, the Russians arriving, surrounding. Raping too: the women always talked of the Russians as fearful rapists. And the Partisans in the midst of it all, exploding, setting fire, doing what they could with their limited means. She didn't think the Ukrainians had come this far, but maybe. So much terrain around here had been aggressively contested. Or so she presumed. Though she was hardly an expert. Her mother had told her something about what it was like not so very far from here. Further south, towards the mountains where she had spent much of the war years.

She deferred to Aleksander, who nodded and shrugged and let his hand rest on Amelia's shoulder and mumbled something about how one could only wish it would never, never happen again and how lucky they were to have been born after.

Bruno was only half listening. Confusion mounted in him with each step. It wasn't the house. Even if you discounted the onetime wings. The windows here were regular. And the trees were too tall. There was dappled shade everywhere. Everything was too small or too big or too hazy. Yet there was something, a feeling about the place. And as they came closer a gnarled old apple tree that had been half-hidden moved into view, its leaves ruffled slightly by the wind. A little girl sat in an old swing tied by a heavy coiled rope to one of its thick branches. She had golden hair, dishevelled by her swinging, and she sang in a small clear voice.

Vertigo took him over. A mad motorized kaleidoscope, moving too quickly for focus. He clutched at Amelia's arm, a life raft in the storm of his mind. Childhood images swirled, invaded by dreams and the operating theatre, the woman with her brain exposed, little Anna playing, figures falling, falling into ever-deeper pits, his mother at the piano, or with a kerchief round her hair, pulling potatoes, waiting for him to come back with the catch. He should have been back earlier. He shouldn't have tarried. He should have been able to do something. He should have intervened. Stopped them. Shouted, screamed, run, hit out. He should have. He should have.

13

1942

As soon as the warm weather came, Mamusia sent him back to the country. She said it was important that the summer fields be ploughed. Pan Mietek would need a hand with that and the sowing. The house needed to be prepared for their arrival too. There was no help now. She and Anna would join him as soon as she could get some leave. She piled on the reasons. But Bruno knew why she sent him off. He knew it was because she was afraid that curiosity or something else would draw him increasingly into the orbit of the Ghetto.

A few days before he left, he had wrapped a parcel of food to take to the Ghetto wall. It was then that he had seen them, crowded together just behind the gates, a throng of Jews, whole families, clutching suitcases and possessions, as if they were bound for a journey. He had questioned his mother about it, and she had thrown her arms round him. 'They're being sent further east.' The way she said the word 'east' created a pit in his stomach. Ever after, it carried an aura of death.

Despite the separation, he was relieved to say goodbye to the city. He had found school difficult. Not the courses. Some of these he enjoyed, particularly the illicit ones in Polish history and literature in which the teachers bravely engaged, an eye on the door, when they were meant to be doing some Nazi-approved subject. No, what was difficult was the pressure of contending with other youths he was meant to be civil but neither friendly nor assertive with. He had to restrain both his chatter and his punches. This had proved as hard in its way as the daily struggle for food in those first years in Przemysl, which were already receding into a haze like the one that sometimes sat over the countryside and made the fields melt into each other as the horizon shifted and bled.

The house was hostile with cold and damp and sheer emptiness. He opened windows, brushed away cobwebs and lit a fire with twigs that were still wet. They sizzled and smoked, but slowly they banished the musty smell of the rooms. The pantry was empty. Only two jars of plums and one of cherries remained hidden behind a cloth. He set out the few provisions he had brought with him then went to the barn where the horses used to be stabled and mourned their disappearance. Mice scuttled beneath his feet. Pan Mietek had inherited the rooster and Bolivar when they left. They had eaten the chickens, so now there was only him and the mice to be counted amongst the living. He determined to see if he could buy or trade for some more. But first he had to report to Pan Mietek and get Bolivar back. Bolivar would be his friend in loneliness.

Pan Mietek was more curmudgeonly than ever. His kerchiefed wife, to whom Bruno had always been polite and who used to give him warm cups of milk straight from their cow or chunks of sausage from the pig they killed each year, didn't even bother to greet him. He wondered what had gone wrong.

'That stupid beast vanished, went off when we were short of food in the winter,' she told him. 'Just as well. We had nothing to give him.'

Bruno had the hideous feeling they had eaten Bolivar themselves. He barely restrained his anger. But his mother had warned him to be civil, so he murmured something innocuous and said he was ready to begin work on the fields the next day.

'None too soon,' the old man replied. 'I was about to ask for help from the cooperative.'

Bruno worked, turning the fields, planting the buckwheat and beetroot in return for nothing more than hunks of bread, white cheese and the occasional onion. When he wasn't working, he fished and laid traps in the woods for rabbits, trading what he caught for whatever he could get for their own kitchen garden from Pan Mietek and two, more distant, farmers. One day, when he had had a particularly good catch, he went off to the village and managed to trade the rabbits for a chicken, which he brought home in great delight. The clucking kept him company in his loneliness.

A few days later Anna and his mother arrived. Miraculously, a cow came in their wake. Mamusia had acquired it through some act of unspoken shrewdness. She was worried about Anna, who had developed a persistent cough. They had come earlier than anticipated because Mamusia hoped that country air and buttermilk would cure it more effectively than anything else.

As he tugged at the cow's warm udders and tended to his daylong array of duties, Bruno sometimes had the odd sense that the war had receded. He was happy. Both Mamusia and little Anna were blooming in the country air. In the balmy evenings, they would all sit and gaze up at heavens replete with stars, and Mamusia would tell them stories about all the constellations and the ancient heroes whose names they had taken.

Mamusia always dressed Anna warmly in the evenings and fussed over her. She wouldn't let her go off into the woods with Bruno either. It wasn't warm enough, she said, or the mossy earth would be too damp or she would end up running which exhausted her. Bruno sometimes felt she was trying to make up for all that time during which she had been forced to leave little Anna to her own devices. He liked to stay close to them too and would often rush back from his necessary expeditions at double speed.

One day towards the end of summer, Mamusia told him she was expecting visitors probably tomorrow and anything he could catch would be more than welcome. Bruno went out early to check his traps and lay some fresh ones then trudged straight on to the river.

When the sun rose high, he grew impatient with the fish that were too lazy to bite and made his way home. He saw the German military vehicle from a distance and wondered whether these were the visitors his mother had mentioned and they had come sooner than expected. This might be the major she was always talking about. Her early benefactor. But he wasn't in the mood for Germans. He hated them too much. And his mother would want him to be polite. Always polite.

He stretched out at a little distance beneath the birch and watched the sky through rustling leaves. He chewed on a bit of dry bread and bided his time.

Suddenly he heard shouts: loud, guttural, commanding. As he looked up, he saw two men in Gestapo uniform pulling Mamusia out of the door and down the stairs of the porch. Their voices were raucous, ordering, hectoring. Behind her came little Anna. Before he could get to his feet there was the sound of a revolver, and Anna fell, dropping from the porch like a bird from the sky, toppling, her arms akimbo. His mother shouted a piercing shout. It exploded inside him like a bomb. And then there was the rattle of gunfire, and she fell over too, crumpling to the ground like a dancer crushed by a giant fist. The two men hulked over her, emptying their guns and before he could run or cry out, they were back in their vehicle and racing away while he stood there, his breath knocked out of him, his whole world revolving vertiginously before his eyes, a paltry creature, open-mouthed, gutted, useless.

He was only able to move after what felt like an eternity trapped in stone. He stumbled. The blood was terrible. Terrible. Everywhere and terrible. He gasped, felt himself retching. Retching unstoppably.

At last, like some automaton he had no relation to, he went and fetched a bucket of water from the well and with a cloth carefully washed his mother and sister. Little Anna was staring at him, her eyes wide in surprise. What's wrong, she seemed to be asking. Pleading. Her head was shattered in the back, grey ooze visible beneath golden locks that were bloodied and bullet-charred.

The tears poured down his face, mercifully blinding him. Overhead he could hear the scavenging birds beginning to circle and caw. He cleaned and wiped at his mother and sister madly, as if the business of tending would bring them back to life. Would force the birds away. Finally, not knowing what else to do, he went upstairs and fetched clean sheets. He covered them up to their faces then rushed in again and came back with little Anna's mushroom hat, which he gently perched on her shattered head. He sat there, looking at his mother and his sister, staring at their interrupted beauty, burbling he didn't know what words.

When it grew dark, he closed their eyes and forced himself up. He fetched a spade and, finding a space near the old apple tree where Anna had always liked to play, he dug. Dug for hours round roots and stone. One large hole. They would be together. He would have liked to lie next to them. But then there would be no one to cover them over, protect them from the predators. He carried first Mamusia, then Anna's body to the grave. He wanted to say some prayer, sing some song. But nothing came to him, so he fetched one of his mother's favourite books, Tolstoy's *War and Peace*, from the small bookcase by her bedside and his sister's old rag doll and carefully placed them beside the bodies. Then he covered the graves and lay down beside them. He hoped he would never have to wake.

Birdsong broke the stillness, high, shrill. Bruno stirred. At first he didn't know why his bed was moist beneath him, moist and gritty and too hard. It took the breath of wind on his cheek to wake him more fully. To make him realize what he didn't want to know: that he was lying in the damp earth by the graves of his mother and sister.

In the distance he heard the clatter of a wagon. And voices coming closer. In the milky light, he made out Pan Mietek. Beside him there was a bulky form that could only be his wife. He was surprised to see them both, confused too. What were they doing here so early? He was about to cry out when something stopped him. They were making for the house without calling so much as a greeting. Nor did they knock before pushing the door open. Someone must have told them, told them about the tragedy. But who? No one had been here during the night. Maybe they had found out from the Gestapo. He got up and again almost called out. No, no. He was being a fool. He was being a child. Why on earth would the Gestapo bother with old Pan Mietek and his wife?

But somehow they knew, for there was old Mietek now dragging their kitchen table out of the house with the chairs and piling them up on his wagon. And that old witch, he couldn't believe it, she had wrapped his mother's coat around herself and was tugging an armful of her clothes through the front door. It came to him with the force of an illumination. Of course, of course. They were the ones. There had been so much bile these last months. It was they who had alerted the Nazis. Old Mietek. And he hadn't even waited for the earth to dry on the family's graves before coming to rob and steal.

Bruno should have realized. Should have suspected that they would do something, shouldn't have put up mutely with their rancour. But he had been wrapped in a cocoon of summer security. And he hadn't thought. Not that.

They had reported the Jews. As all good Poles were now meant to do. Reported them to the Nazis out of malice and envy and hatred. He would smash Pan Mietek's face in. His witch of a wife's too. Yes, now. Immediately. Beat them to a pulp. They assumed him dead. That's why they had dared to come here so openly. To steal, after the Gestapo had done the dirtier work.

He started up, spade in hand, then stopped himself.

No, no. Bruno had a better idea. They had to suffer. He would give them a taste of the terror they had inflicted. Let them die slowly, painfully.

He threw a stone at the kitchen window, then another at the bedroom and started shouting in German. Bellowing, Hollering, in the manner he had heard so often. '*Raus! Schweine. Achtung!*'

As he shouted, he ran from place to place in the garden, making himself into a squad, until the two old people came out trembling and pleading. They had dropped everything they were carrying to put their hands up before their invisible assailants. But now, not seeing anyone, they made a dash for their wagon and whipped their old horse into action while Bruno continued his savage howls and screams.

That night, after having banished the hikers who had turned up earlier and asked for his mother, he did worse. He went to Pan Mietek's house and silently, stealthily led the old mare and the cow from the barn into the fields. Then he set fire to the rickety structure and threw a bale of burning hay in front of the door of their old wooden house. He watched the fire take: grow into a blaze. He could feel the heat on his face. He was tempted to hurl himself inside the flames. But he wanted to see the old people rush out, screaming. The way his mother had screamed. The way little Anna had screamed. When they didn't, he led the horse and cow back to his grandfather's house.

It was only at daybreak, as he brushed the old horse down, that he realized his madness. If the horse and two cows were found here, it would be clear to all and sundry who had done the burning. Did he care? Wasn't that what he wanted? No, no, he didn't want to be shot in cold blood by the Gestapo. Far better to shoot them. Far, far better.

Regretfully, he took the animals into a field between the two properties. He wished he could sell them, but that would draw too much suspicion. They might be after him soon.

On his way back to the house, he stopped by Mamusia and Anna's grave again. He bent to kiss the moist earth and murmur to his dear ones. He would avenge them, he promised. They could trust him. Then he would join them.

He looked around, at a loss for something to mark the graves with. There was nothing, nothing…. Finally, he managed to heave a rough-hewn stone from the edge of the well and roll it towards the spot. With his penknife, he scratched the names 'Mamusia' and 'Anna' into the stone. It wasn't much, but it was something. He would come back. He vowed to come back.

He returned to the house and packed his rucksack with all the food that could be squashed into it. Catching a glimpse of his face in the mirror, he saw that he was filthy. Hurriedly, he washed himself, slicked down his hair, found a cleaner shirt and a jacket. The jacket was a good one. It had belonged to his grandfather. Always look your best, his grandfather had told him during the bad days in Przemysl. It was his grandfather's voice that also counselled him to roll up his winter coat and put it in his bag. He would be back, but he couldn't be certain when. At the last, remembering himself, he packed his ID and inside the coat placed Mamusia's and little Anna's, together with all the money in the house and a number of the photographs that sat innocently on the piano. He was crying again. How would he ever stop crying?

He didn't really know how he got to the train station, but it was while he was standing behind a column on the platform and pretending to be invisible, that he heard two women talking excitedly about a fire in the countryside. Was this a new Nazi strategy to bring them low, one of them asked and the other shook her head and said surely not, since they were so avid for what the farms produced. Bruno started to whistle, saw a guard turn round and stopped himself. A train hooted and moments later, the one bound for Krakow pulled into the station. He squeezed onboard.

The next thing he knew he was walking along the street that led from the station towards the central square and his grandparents' old house. He didn't know why he thought they might still be there. But he did. In his mind, he was coming home after a long day at school, and everyone would be there: his grandmother and little Anna, his mother and grandfather, all plying him with questions which he didn't want to answer.

The city was crowded with uniforms. Cars raced in the streets. Perfumed women wafted past him, their lips redder than he remembered them. There was German everywhere, and he recalled through his daze that Krakow was the centre of the General Government, the German Occupation's capital. He had heard his mother talking about it, the way the Governor had installed himself on Wawel Hill in the old palace. His mother. He squared his shoulders and aped a military bearing. If he hadn't felt so removed from everything, as if the world occupied a space on the other side of an impermeable glass wall, he would have been frightened.

When he reached the house, the old caretaker, who had grown even more crooked and gnarled, stopped him at the doors. He didn't recognize him. Some cautionary instinct prevented Bruno from identifying himself. His papers wouldn't tally. He asked for Pan Torok.

The dwarf of a man tilted his head towards him suspiciously. 'Pan Torok hasn't lived here for several years, young man. There are no Jews in this building now. We are *Judenrein*.' The man cackled. 'Now only pure-blooded Germans live here. The very best. A lady dentist. A factory owner…'

Bruno stood rigid. He dared a second question, this time dipping into his pocket the way he had always seen his grandfather do when the doorman was asked to wait for a parcel or some such.

He slipped a coin into the man's hand. 'Do you know where Pan Torok can be found?'

The man gazed at him from beneath his grizzled brow. 'Where have you come from, young man? Don't you know anything? If Pan Torok is still to be found, God bless his soul, he was a kind man, it'll be across the river.' The man suddenly looked around him warily and lowered his voice. 'Don't you know all the Jews have been concentrated?'

Bruno swallowed hard. Of course, of course, had he thought for one moment, he would have known that. But his grandfather...by this time his grandfather would have another identity. Bruno dipped into his pocket again.

'Pan Torok didn't by any chance leave anything with you? A forwarding address? A letter perhaps, for friends, old clients, who might want to find him?'

The man's eyes narrowed. 'You're not by any...?' Furtively, he pulled Bruno into his small quarters away from the gate. It was almost dark in here and he squinted to examine him, his face canny.

'You're the boy from Vienna, aren't you?'

'Yes, yes, that's me.'

From outside the door, there were German voices raised high. The old man shivered. Then with sudden determination, he slid open a drawer in a ramshackle old desk, piled high with papers and dirty cups, and pulled out a dog-eared envelope. 'Here, take it. Go, no wait. Read it, then leave it here.'

Bruno tore open the envelope while the old man poked his head through the door and mollified the voices. Inside there was a scrap of paper with an address. He memorized it quickly, heard a yapping, was about to hurry away, when the caretaker reappeared with a small dog on a lead. 'This,' the old man declared, shaking his head, 'belongs to the Frau Dentist and for the moment is in my care.'

Bruno didn't pause to look at the sausage of a dog. He thanked the caretaker and raced away, realizing too late that he hadn't asked for directions and he had no idea where the address was.

He finally reached it at nightfall, when the curfew was already in place and it was treacherous to be on the streets without the appropriate permission. He was exhausted, so exhausted that he hadn't been able to turn his head in fear every time he heard boots behind him. The fear had come to him at the same time as the overwhelming wish to cry in his grandfather's arms.

He was on the outskirts of the city on a lonely little street that he imagined would in a few hundred metres give way to countryside. When he saw the dark-painted door with the number on it, he almost began to shout. He let the knocker fall several times with noisy emphasis and as footsteps sounded, he called out: 'Grandpa, Grandpa.'

The door opened on a tiny birdlike woman who at first he thought was a girl, but on second glance seemed to be about his mother's age. She was wearing a dress with a polka-dot pattern and had no shoes on her feet. He stared at her in dismay for too long before finding his voice.

'Sorry, sorry, I've come to the wrong place.' The tears that he had been holding back leaped into his eyes. 'Sorry. I was looking for...'

Before he could finish his sentence, she had pulled him into the narrow hall and closed the door behind him.

'You're Hanka's son?'

'Yes, how did you know?'

'I must have recognized you. Come in.'

She led him into a small room cluttered with too much furniture and made sure the heavy curtains were completely drawn.

'Grandfather...'

'He's not here.'

Bruno wasn't sure he had heard her correctly. His heart swooped.

'No. I'm sorry. He just...well...we keep in touch.'

'But I need to go to him. I have to go to him.'

His voice rose, and the woman put a quietening finger to her lips and pointed upstairs.

'I'm afraid it needs arranging. And it's much too late tonight. Much too late. You look tried. Does anyone know you're here, do you think?'

He shook his head and then stopped abruptly. 'I got the address from…from the caretaker at my grandfather's old building.'

She nodded sagely. 'Would you like something to drink? I could even give you a little food. I took some home from the hotel tonight.' He followed her into a second room, smaller than the first. It served as a kitchen, though again, the assortment of furniture seemed odd, as if the place were both a warehouse and an apartment. She saw him looking round and smiled again. 'I'm keeping things. For friends. How is your mother?'

A single loud sob escaped him. The effort of holding the others back imprisoned his tongue.

'I'm sorry. So sorry.' She drew him to her, held him. She seemed to know without him saying. 'You can tell me about it later. Or another time. When you can. I loved her. Loved her very much.'

He couldn't bring himself to speak, so she went on.

'Now I want you to drink something. Eat if you can.' She pulled out a chair for him and brewed a pot of tea. 'It's real, so enjoy it. I don't often get any. But we should talk before my flatmate gets back. She has a late pass tonight. Yes, it'll be fine,' she countered his query before he had posed it. 'You can sleep on the table here. I'll try and get a message to your grandfather. But it may take a few days. No, no.' She held up a hand and suddenly looked stern, despite her size. 'You're not to try and find him yourself. You'll only get everyone into trouble. Understood?'

He nodded.

'What kind of papers have you got?'

For a moment he didn't know whether it was a good idea to show her. Then when he took in her expression, he relented and pulled out not only his own papers but inadvertently his mother's and Anna's.

Her eyes filled with tears. 'Very hard. Your grandfather too will take it very hard.' She stared into space for a moment as if

there were a window in the middle distance through which something was visible to her. Then she seemed to grow bigger in her
chair.

'All right. A couple of questions. Are you in trouble? Should
you have new papers?'

'I think I may be dead,' he said.

She stared at him but asked nothing more. 'Tomorrow you
don't set foot out of here. If anyone asks, you're the son of a friend
of mine from the north. You came to bring me news and to see if
you could get a job in the city. You speak German, don't you?'

He nodded.

'Good. I'll see if I can get you a job in the kitchen of the hotel
where I'm working. The Germans use it. The food's good. The
scraps are good. And the head chef likes to be understood, and no
one does except me. Okay? You can't hang around the streets or
you'll disappear in no time. Always look busy. Remember that.
Always. Purposeful and busy.'

'But Grandpa...'

'You won't be able to stay with him. Out of the question.'

He didn't dare for the moment ask her why.

For eight nights he slept on Pani Marysia's kitchen table. Everyday he asked her about his grandfather, and everyday she said it
wasn't time yet. On the ninth day, she brought him a new identity
card in the name of Tomasz Nowak, resident in Krakow, at an
address he hadn't yet visited, and a work permit showing that he
had a post at the Hotel Francuski near the Barbican.

On Sunday, the day before he was to begin work, she told him
to wash thoroughly and get spruced up. She herself was wearing a
smart suit and a hat with a feather in it that made her face as saucy
as her high heels suddenly gave her grandeur. She warned him that
he wasn't to speak unless she spoke first. She took him to church
and then for a tram ride.

The tram ferried them across the Vistula and stopped at the
entrance to the Ghetto. The gates where the wall began were
crowded with SS men, police in a variety of uniforms and a queue
of people having their passes checked. The behaviour of the
guards, the pushing and shoving and casual brutality made Bruno

clench his fists into tight balls. He kept them like that, even when Marysia tried to divert his attention.

A Polish Police officer stepped onto the tram and stood on the outdoor step as they moved off. Bruno, staring through dirty glass, held his breath and saw into poor overcrowded tenements and downcast streets. People raced about their business rather than walked, their legs as thin and rickety as sticks. He saw an old woman carrying a package wrapped in brown paper whose weight seemed more than she could bear, a Chassid, his arms crossed behind his back, who stared at the tram as if he were waiting for some miracle. He saw emaciated children and old people lying on the pavement, their hands outstretched.

A terrible noise erupted. The tram slowed to a crawl and in the street below there was an ear-splitting rattle that he only recognized as gunfire when the bodies fell like marionettes on a stage. Splayed. Crumpled. Except that it was real blood that spilled out of them.

And then, before he altogether took in what he was seeing, they were out again beyond the other side of the wall, and Marysia prodded him to get off. There had been no stops anywhere in the Ghetto.

They walked now to nowhere in particular, still not speaking, staring straight ahead. Eventually they hopped onto another tram to make the return journey. It was only when they were out on more familiar streets again and making their way homeward that it occurred to Bruno that the reason for their journey was that his grandfather was somewhere in those dangerous decaying streets of the Ghetto.

'Grandpa,' he began, and Marysia nodded, cutting him off.

'Now you understand.'

He understood nothing at all.

'I shall go and see him. I must.'

'No, you wait. He doesn't want you there. I know. I know him.'

'How do you know him?'

She shrugged.

'Marysia, are you a...?'

She cut him off. 'No, I'm not. And don't ask stupid questions. And don't go making yourself conspicuous. There are people here, everywhere, everywhere around us, Jews too, in the pay of the Nazis. They'll turn you in as soon as greet you on the street.'

She softened the force of her response, by giving him a slice of *apfelstrudel* when they got back to the house.

'Your mother was a very good friend of mine, Tomek.' She called him by his new name. 'So I take the liberty of giving you advice. You have blond hair and a direct blue gaze. So you don't need to worry too much. You've probably grown out of all recognition over the last while, so few in Krakow can recognize you as a Torok. That's not the case for your grandfather. And here's some more advice. Tomorrow, at the hotel, remember,' she lowered her voice and looked round her shoulder to make sure her roommate hadn't come in, 'don't talk to anyone too much. The less said the better in all circumstances. And...and...' She was suddenly shy. 'You probably know this, but I repeat it anyhow. Never use the urinals, if there's anyone else in there. Your mother explained, didn't she?'

He didn't know what she was talking about. Not until later. All he knew was that his mother and sister were dead and his grandfather didn't want him at his side and had gone to join the dying.

At night, lying flat on the hard table, every time he shut his eyes, Anna flew from the porch of his grandfather's house, and his mother screamed and screamed her pain, before an agonizing silence descended on the world.

14

There had been another shift in the car's composition. Amelia sat in the back seat with her father now and held onto his hand.

It was unclear, Irena thought, stealing a backward glance, who was the parent and who the child. He looked as if he might be asleep, certainly dreaming. He was very pale. The last part of their expedition had been too difficult for him. She almost wished they hadn't found the spot. And what an announcement. So blunt, so frightening in the peace of that countryside as if to make it almost into a delusion.

'My mother and sister were shot here. In front of my eyes. They're buried near that tree where the little girl is swinging. My sister played there too. She was barely six-years-old. I promised I'd come back.'

Her first reaction had been that he was lying. He was making it up. But she knew better from his eyes.

There had been no marked graves to show them, and he hadn't wanted to talk to the people who lived there now. Had rejected Amelia's idea of erecting a stone.

'In this wilderness? Where no one was kind to them? No point.' He stared at the tree where the child played over the murdered dead, and Irena had wanted to cross herself, just to make some kind of sign, some ritual acknowledgment. Aleksander, intending to comfort, had pointed out that after all these years, there were probably few remains and a memorial in Krakow might be better. The Professor had looked straight through him. The comfort really hadn't worked for Amelia either.

That's because there was no comfort, Irena thought. No comfort for some losses, even in time – that neutral impassive force that healed most things. Probably by destroying. Destroying the cells that contained the experience. Or at least its trace. Destroying the bit that made you care. You might as well call that force God, though she had never heard of people anywhere going to war on behalf of time.

Amelia turned out to be braver than the rest of them. Maybe because she had to confront prejudice upfront and couldn't wriggle out of it like they did. Wriggle and wriggle all the time until the earth turned but looked substantially the same.

So Amelia marched right up to the door of the house and rang a bell. A youngish woman answered. Irena could see that the explanations weren't going well and that the woman was appalled, shaking her head at whatever it was she understood from Amelia's dramatic gestures. At which point Amelia seemed to grow a metre taller, stamped her feet and showed some rage.

Aleksander, wearing a distinct air of embarrassment, went to her side and started to explain, while Amelia took a pad out of her bag and wrote what Irena later learned was an inscription for a tombstone that named the Professor's dead and added: 'remembered by Bruno Lind and his daughter, Amelia.'

She then marched the woman over to the tree. The little girl had run off in the meantime, which was just as well, because Amelia pointed emphatically and made a tombstone shape in the air, around it a circle like a small wall or fence. She pulled dollars from her bag. Irena could now hear her words, though not Aleksander's quieter translation. She was saying that she or one of her friends would be back to check on progress. If her wishes weren't carried out she would start proceedings to see how this house had in fact been acquired and on whose land it stood. The woman objected, said they had come by it legally, at which point Amelia smiled sweetly and said she was sure they had, but a little digging in the historical record, let alone in the ground, might none the less prove otherwise and what she was asking was simple enough. So she expected her request to be carried out.

And then she marched back to her father and said: 'Good. That's done. You'll feel the better for it. As will I.'

Aleksander had been slightly cowed by this episode, and Irena, when she was gestured by Amelia into the front seat beside him, thought that maybe their first lovers' misunderstanding was underway. Would they survive a history that had made them so different?

Strangely, she found herself on Amelia's side. An admiring 'well done' had slipped out of her. If only she had been capable of such decision in her life, such confrontation, everything might have been different. Instead she had the Polish gift of pessimism. The romantic mantra: everything for the worse in the worst of all possible worlds. She wore it like a badge of honour, she thought, scoffing at herself and worrying once more about the poor Professor and the sudden presence of his dead, with them now in this lumbering car, like a great curtain of sadness blotting out the sky.

No one had spoken since they had left the house. The silence had grown as oppressive as the mounting heat. It was only when they reached the outskirts of the city that it was broken – and, oddly, by the Professor himself.

'Thank you. Thank you, Amelia. Of course, you were right,' he said.

Irena wondered whether he meant right for him or for herself. Perhaps for both or for all of them. She imagined the marker going up in the midst of the flat peaceful countryside. People might stop. Might wonder. Reflect. That was no bad thing. It wasn't like a state memorial or an official ceremony that inevitably always contained an admixture of contemporary politics. It was personal, an intimate record of tragic inhumanity and the grief that attends it.

'My thanks to all of you,' the Professor went on. 'You have been exquisitely patient with an old man.'

Irena turned to smile at him. There was nothing she could think of to say. All the words that came to her felt banal, unequal to that troubled face, the history the man contained.

'It's nothing, Professor Lind,' Aleksander murmured. 'It was an honour. And for me, in some ways, also an education. We live with all these scars in our country, but more recent ones have displaced them, so we don't pause to think back that far. Until there are dramas, like over the massacre at Jedwabne, and then it becomes a national event and we're pressed to take sides. But somehow the individual stories touch one more nearly.'

'And we never know quite how or why...' The Professor was staring at the back of Aleksander's head. Staring at it in a way that made Irena uncomfortable. She had the distinct impression he didn't like what he saw.

Abruptly, he shifted his gaze towards her. 'I was lucky, you know. Unusually lucky for a Jew. And not only because I got through. But in the way I got through. I was young, spoke German, spent part of the war in the countryside. And my grand-father was remarkable in his prescience. In keeping us out of the Ghetto... Yes. And I had a chance to act too. To be active. That helped.' His gaze moved once more to the back of Aleksander's head.

Irena shifted in her seat. 'Yes, yes. Passivity is terrible. Like depression. It makes one want to die before one is dead. It's a state suitable only for saints.'

Bruno turned to her. 'You understand.' He paused. 'You know, I'd like to make up for that awful evening I gave you yesterday. Somehow. Let me take you all out tonight. The best Krakow can offer. You choose. And not one gloomy word will pass my lips.'

'How kind,' Irena laughed. 'But I don't know if I can. I'd have to check on my mother first. It may be difficult.'

'You'll arrange it,' the Professor insisted. 'You know how to arrange things. We'll help. We'll take you straight to her, won't we Aleksander?'

'And I can do my rendition of Josephine Baker for all of you,' Amelia laughed.

They had almost reached Ida's house when the Professor mur-mured: 'There used to be a big bakery around here.'

'Really?'

'Yes, yes. It serviced the Germans.' He was growing excited.

'Did you get your bread from there too, Pops?'

'No, no. Certainly not that, though I had a taste. Your grandfather worked there, I think. Well, I'm not sure if he was in fact working there.' He grew quiet abruptly, and then they were pulling up in front of Ida's and there was no time to ask him more.

'I'll try not to be long.'

'I'll come up with you,' Amelia offered.

'Yes, yes. She'll be pleased to see you.'

But Irena doubted that her mother would remember Amelia at all.

'Oh Irenka, I'm so sorry. I don't know how it happened.' Ida opened the door and instantly threw her arms around Irena.

'It's my fault,' Irena's goddaughter, Nina, was just behind her. Her heart-shaped face drooped beneath the feathers of bright home-hennaed hair. 'I only went upstairs to do some homework. I thought she'd be alright...' She stopped and stared at Amelia, whom she had just taken in.

'What's happened?' Irena's heart sank.

'That's just it. We don't know.' Ida was ushering them into the lounge where a television sat in front of a plump sofa. 'Nina left her in here watching the TV. And when she came back down from her room, she'd gone. Vanished.'

'Is something the matter?' Amelia asked.

'My mother's gone walkabout. We'll have to call the police.'

'It's done,' Ida responded in English. 'An hour...no...more... almost two hours ago. And Adam's out looking for her as well.'

Nina was still staring at Amelia, and Irena introduced them quickly before dropping onto the sofa.

'Does she have any favourite places that she likes to go to?' Amelia asked. 'Or friends? Friends she might want to visit? Maybe even a hair stylist? My mother used to go to hers to relax, to have her head fondled.'

Irena tried to control her panic. 'You don't understand. She doesn't go anywhere on her own. She can't find her way.'

'I see.'

Irena took in that she had been too brusque. 'Let me think, let me think. The Planty. She likes the Planty, the gardens. But from here...'

'It's worth a try.'

'Yes, I'll come with you,' Nina blurted out in careful English. 'It's all because of me.'

'No, no.' Irena tried to make light of it, but her voice held a sob. 'Maybe she tried to go home.'

'So she remembers her address?'

'I don't know anymore. She might have it on her, if she took her bag with her. But she doesn't have the keys.' The tears gathered in her eyes. Why had she taken her mother's keys away? Because she kept losing them, of course, losing them anywhere and everywhere, even if they weren't lost but simply gone, like her mind. But Irena hadn't thought through all the eventualities, her mother's erratic stubbornness, if that's what it was. If that's what going off for a walk meant. No, she should never have left her. If anything happened...

'She took her bag. I checked. Maybe she hailed a taxi. It's possible,' Ida said. 'Did she have some money on her?'

'Okay, okay,' Amelia was patting her shoulder. 'You give me the keys, and Aleksander and I will drive to your place. Drive slowly and keep our eyes open. If we find her, we'll phone back here. Meanwhile, you head off for the gardens. I've got my phone on me.'

'And I'll stay here and monitor the phone and any calls from the police.'

'Take Pops with you. He's got his phone on him too. Just make sure he turns it on.'

Before Irena could protest or think of a better plan, numbers had been exchanged, and the Professor, Nina, and she were walking towards the Planty, while Aleksander and Amelia headed off in the opposite direction in the car.

'I was fooled by the television, Irenka. I'm so sorry. I could hear it. So I just thought she was still there. She must have slipped out very quietly.'

'She's got soft-soled shoes,' Irena said, feeling stupid. She was examining all the faces around her, as if she might somehow miss her own mother amidst the strollers who were numerous on this warm evening. At least, her mother wouldn't get cold. Die of hypothermia.

'Did she say anything to you before you went off to your room?' The Professor addressed Nina directly for the first time.

'Not really. Not specifically.'

They walked on. They could see the Castle Hill in front of them, the low sun glistening over the red roofs.

'Well, she was a bit confused.' She shot a glance of teenage uncertainty at the adults. 'You know, just rambling a bit. She does ramble, doesn't she, Irenka?'

'That's a kind way of putting it,' Irena reassured her.

'Yes, well... In the middle of all this rambling, she thought she recognized someone on the television.'

Irena laughed nervously. 'Yes. She does that sometimes.'

'It was this man. This presenter. She got a bit excited. She told me to phone the television station and invite him over straight away. She said he was her cousin.'

'That's happened before.'

'Is he always her cousin?' Bruno asked.

'Yes.'

'And have you checked that he might not be?'

Irena shrugged. 'I didn't really think... You see, the man she points at, if it's the same one that she's pointed at before, is about half, no a third of her age.... So it doesn't make sense.'

'Maybe she's gone to the television station?' Nina offered.

Irena stared at her. 'Surely they would have alerted the police if a batty old lady insisted on seeing her cousin. She didn't by any chance mention a name, did she?'

Irena waited for her answer with baited breath. The last time her mother had thought she recognized the face on the television it had born a distinct name. It had born the name of the man who was also meant to be Irena's father. Aleksander Tarski. In her mother's deranged mind, at least. And the man was far younger than Irena. Did desire persist? she suddenly wondered. Persist through all those other fallings away of body and mind? It was too horrible to contemplate. And she didn't want to involve her goddaughter, let alone the Professor, in all this madness. It was shaming somehow.

'Maybe. I'm not sure.' Nina answered her question. She was mumbling a bit, you know how she does, as if she might be talking to herself. I might have heard a name beginning with an "M". But all this was well before I left her on her own. She could have seen something else on the screen after.'

'It might be worth phoning the television station, in any case. You never know,' Bruno said. 'The people we think least able are sometimes very determined.' He passed Irena his telephone, and they paused on the side of the street.

By the time they had reached the Planty and breathed in the freshness of the city's circular green belt, Irena had ascertained that as far as anyone knew, her mother hadn't turned up at the television station reception desk to look for her cousin. She tried to call Amelia to find out about developments there, but for some reason she couldn't get through and gave up in frustration.

Meanwhile, the Professor was deep in conversation with Nina. She wondered that her goddaughter had so much to say to him. Not that she didn't adore her in all her adolescent impulsiveness or respect her intelligence, but she had rarely seen her display any interest in men of the Professor's generation.

'Nina is trying to remember for me all the things your mother talked about over the last few days.'

'You think that might provide a clue? You have experience of these things?'

'Not as much as you, perhaps. But I've read some. Lived too. A dear friend of mine, I think I mentioned him before…'

'I'm sorry.' She cut him off. 'I don't know what's got into me. I think I'd forgotten who you are.'

He laughed, trying to cheer her. 'Because I refused the profile. In fact, it's just common sense. We try and follow your mother's train of thought. Which is where her feet or a taxi might lead her.'

'The trouble is, there isn't always a train of what you call thought.'

'No planning perhaps. And no single train. But several. And there might be some kind of associative sense in them. She still has language, you've been telling me. And some recognition, from what Amelia said. She paired her with Josephine Baker, after all. She may just not be in the present a lot of the time. But then which of us is?' This time his chuckle held a note of bitter irony.

'I've just realized. We haven't checked hospitals.'

'Won't the police do that as a matter of course?'

'I don't know.'

'I imagine so,' he calmed her. 'You're a good daughter.'

'I'm not.'

Nina suddenly intervened. 'I've just thought of something else...'

Irena didn't give her a chance to finish. She had spied an old lady with white hair sitting on a bench some thirty metres away and talking to the pigeons. Her heart thumped as she raced towards her.

She stopped brusquely. It wasn't her mother. Terrible that she couldn't recognize her own mother from a short distance. Old ladies didn't wear uniforms, after all. She was a bad daughter, not a good daughter. Over these last weeks, she had not only scooted off to Vienna but then abandoned the old dear again, probably killing her in the process. The heavens wouldn't forgive her.

Irena now felt compelled to wish the strange woman a good day and found herself enmeshed in a conversation about the secret life of birds. It took the Professor to rescue her.

'Not your mother, I take it.'

'Someone completely different. Old age makes one invisible. That's what de Beauvoir said.'

'But you recognize me?' he twinkled at her.

'Because you have power. My mother doesn't. So even I don't recognize her. So humiliating. For her and for me. No wonder the old get depressed. The indignity of that, on top of everything else. We treat them as if we were all Nazis and they were all Jews.' She clamped her hand over her mouth, realizing what she had said.

'You're very hard on yourself.'

The phone rang, interrupting him. Irena passed it over, and he talked as they carried on their walk through the gardens.

'She's not at home, according to Amelia. They're going back to your friend's place.'

Irena felt doubly desolate. It was growing dark. Her mother didn't like the dark. Had never liked it really. Had even kept a light on during the nights, despite her husband's grumblings. In Irena's childhood she had said it was for Irena, though Irena didn't mind the dark. Still the light stayed on. Irena had never stopped to ask herself whether this was an old girlhood fear of her mother's. Or perhaps, now that she stopped to consider it, one linked to the war. Hadn't she read somewhere that domestic electricity consumption had been kept to a minimum. Two nights a week or some such on a rota. And in the country…who knew? There probably wasn't any at all, and you had to scramble round in the dark over insects and spiders to reach a toilet. Probably an outdoor toilet. Why hadn't she thought properly about her mother's early life before?

She suddenly realized the Professor was talking to her.

'Nina has something to tell you. It might have some significance for you.'

'Yes.' Her goddaughter wound her arm through Irena's and looked at her from darkly kohled eyes. It occurred to Irena that the young these days were allowed to look like sluts. No problem. Sluts with attitude. Had her mother thought the same about her?

'Yes,' Nina repeated. 'Pani Marta was saying something about how she had to go to Dukla. She had a message to deliver.'

'Dukla,' Irena echoed. 'What on earth for? I don't think she knows anyone there.' She paused for a moment.

'That might not be for you to say.' The Professor was gentle with her. 'She may know someone you don't. From the past, perhaps. She lived for a while before you were on the scene, I imagine.'

'Of course. Of course.' Irena rushed on. 'Dukla. That means taking a train. That means we'll never find her.'

'We could go to the station,' Nina suggested. 'We're not far. At least we can find out what trains have left for Dukla.'

'I don't imagine there's a direct line. She'll be stranded somewhere in the countryside. She'll have forgotten where she's heading.' The disasters mounted in front of Irena's eyes with far greater speed than the people now teaming out from the underpass that separated the Planty from main roads and the station. She saw her mother huddled in a carriage unable to explain where she was heading, her ticket lost, her panic mounting even faster than Irena's own. She saw some kind conductor trying to ask her where she lived and her mother not knowing. Did she even still remember her name? Irena wondered. It wasn't the kind of thing one asked one's mother. 'Hello, what's your name? Where do you live?'

If they found her, she crossed the fingers of both hands and hid them behind her back, if they found her, she would practice with her everyday, like scales. Name, address. Name. address. The Professor had already told her in Vienna that it wasn't impossible to lay down new memories in old age. It just took repetition. More repetition than previously. Like conditioning one of those slugs the memory physiologists always talked about. The ones with huge neurones. Aplysia. Like a Polish name. But her mother wasn't a slug.

The station was busy with commuter traffic. Messages blared over the loudspeakers. People were scurrying in all directions, holding sandwiches, drinks, babies. Concentrating, Irena hurried towards the first yellow schedule board she could see. It was complicated. Dukla was a small place, probably not on a main line, so there would have to be a connection. Through Tarnow perhaps. Ridiculous. They might even have waved to each other from some level crossing.

'Why don't we ask at the information desk?' Bruno suggested.

'I'll go,' Nina offered.

'No, no, there'll be a huge queue and here, here, I've just found it. She'd have to go to Krosno first. The last train is in about an hour.' Irena ran her finger up the complicated list and took a deep breath. 'I don't think she could have made the earlier one. Come on, let's go and have a look at the platform.'

They hurried down some stairs and then up again. The platform was a double-sided one and not too crowded, but as Irena looked around, her momentary hopes sank. 'I'd forgotten. There's nowhere for her to sit and wait. She'd have collapsed.'

They walked to the far end of the platform, which was a long way, and back again. Just to the other side, the street market was still active, and noise echoed over concrete and tracks.

Suddenly Nina stopped and tugged at Irena's sleeve. She pointed at some gritty ancient carriages parked at a platform to the far side of the station. 'I might have dreamed it, but I think out of the corner of my eye while we were passing, I saw someone in there. A shadow...something. It could just have been Pani Marta.'

They retraced their steps.

Sure enough, at the dirt-spattered window of the final old carriage, there was a woman. She had her head bent. Irena squinted in an attempt to make out her features. An incoming train bumped past, blocking her view. But her pulse had already started to race.

'Come on, it's worth a look.'

They went back down the stairs to the station underpass and came out at the furthest platform. It was no longer altogether easy to determine which carriage the woman they had seen was in, since she had been sitting at the opposite window; but at a quick calculation, Irena decided it must be the second one from the back. The train door here stood partially ajar.

The Professor saw it at the same time as she did and gallantly held it open for her.

In the last compartment Irena found her mother.

She was sitting there quite calmly, as if she were in her chair at home. Her grey-white hair was neatly coiffed and pulled back to reveal a scrubbed, fine-skinned face, almost free of wrinkles. Her fingers tugged mechanically, as they so often did, at the top button of her cardigan or strayed restlessly over a bit of lint. Her blue eyes were uncannily clear, though distant. As if she were blind to the world around her and yet seeing something. She manifested no particular surprise as she looked at Irena.

A shiver of fear ran through her. It had a different quality from her earlier panic. It had to do with finding a point of connection with her mother. She wanted an answering mind, some recognition.

Disappearance could take so many forms. These last weeks, whenever she called out to Marta, she was never sure what form of acknowledgement, if any, she would get.

'Mama. Mama. What a relief to find you.'

Her mother didn't answer, and Irena filled in for her silence, embarrassed as always that others would witness her vacant state. 'We looked everywhere. We didn't know where you'd got to. How are you feeling? Do you think you can get up now, so that we can take you home? I'll find us a taxi.'

Marta didn't move or speak.

Irena felt a tap on her shoulder, and the Professor excused himself, walked past her and sat down opposite her mother. He met Marta's eyes and then, after a moment, put his hands out to her.

Marta confided her own to his. Irena was startled by the change that came over her face. Her mother's lips began to curl in a small smile. One eyebrow arched slightly, and she looked out shyly at the Professor – almost, had it not been so odd to think it, flirtatiously.

They sat like that for a moment. Then Marta said softly in a voice rich with endearment, 'Little Cousin. Oh, Little Cousin. I knew you would come, Little Cousin. I was waiting.'

'And you see, I'm here.'

'Your hands are so warm.'

'Yes.'

'Oh, Little Cousin. I'm so glad you've come. So glad.'

Return

15

1942

The cold had set in, damp and bitter, so that it cut right through his jacket like a knife. The sky was an unrelieved grey. The wind had come up too, biting at his face and ears where they weren't quite hidden by his cap. He was pleased. The cold meant everyone walked even more quickly than usual and kept their eyes to the ground. Tomasz Nowak – until not so long ago Bronislaw Sienkiewicz and before that Bruno Lind, though sometimes Torok – did likewise. He had received very specific instructions.

He was to go to the bakery south of the Castle Hill, nip into the lane on the right and round the back, where he would find a series of sheds. He was to slip into the third shed. There he would see bags of flour piled on the floor. He was to go straight to the back of the storehouse and tuck himself behind the flour sacks. At six-fifty am precisely. If anyone stopped him, he was to show his pass and say he had a message for Pan Tadeusz.

Bruno was only stopped once at the main gate. He arrived as precisely as the watch his father had given him all those years ago in a forgotten Vienna permitted. He had held onto it, even in the hungriest days. He was glad now.

He stole over the creaky wooden floor and casually dipped behind a stack of sacks. No sooner had he stopped than he heard his name called from beneath him. A trapdoor opened, and a ghost emerged covered in what looked like white ash. It took him a moment to recognize his grandfather through the veil of white that powdered the air when he moved. Soon Bruno too was covered in flour. They held each other for a long time.

When his grandfather spoke, it was in a choked whisper. 'Marysia got the news to me. You're a brave boy, Bruno.'

'No, Grandpa. No.' It all came out in a rush, though he hadn't meant to say it like that, because he was sobbing, how he had let his mother and sister die, how the Nazis had killed them. With Pan Mietek's help. He had betrayed them. Pan Mietek. Yes. But he had taken revenge for that, at least. That, at least.

His grandfather held him and rocked him as if he were still a babe, not a man now as tall as he was, hushing him, crooning slightly. And then he forced him to look into his eyes. 'Listen Bruno, I haven't got long.'

Bruno interrupted. 'I want to stay with you.'

'No, that's impossible. I can't allow that. I love you, Bruno. We brought you up to be free. As bad as it is out here, it's a hundred times worse in the Ghetto. I want you to stay alive to carry on the family honour. I depend on you for that. Understand? Promise me. You will leave Krakow. Marysia will give you instructions.'

'You'll come with me.'

'No, dear boy. No. It's no longer possible. I'm too weak now. In any case, the world after won't be for me. I made my decision some months back. For your grandmother's sake, perhaps. For other reasons too. I'm old now. I've thrown in my lot with my people. In the Ghetto. It was the only path my conscience allowed. Life is getting harder there every day. Sometimes I can help just a little from the inside because I know how the system works, know people on the outside, know the dragnet of corruption and bribery. For you it's different. You must live. But remember everything I've taught you.'

For the first time Bruno took in how dreadful his handsome grandfather looked beneath the fine covering of flour. He was paper-thin, his face reduced to a skeletal outline, his neck under the overall a web of stringy tissue. His eyes had lost their old fire.

Bruno clutched at him. 'And you?'

His grandfather didn't seem to hear him. 'I say it again, more strongly after what you've told me. You can't stay on in the city. I know your temperament. It will only end in trouble for everyone. Marysia will arrange things. Listen to her. She isn't one of us, but she's utterly reliable. I want you to tell her too, that a new stage has begun. The old, the infirm, the children, they're being singled out for special treatment. Tell her to spread the news. Goodbye, my darling boy.'

'Special treatment?'

'Yes.' His grandfather had a faraway look in his eyes. 'They're moving us ever closer to God.'

Two tears trickled down his cheeks as he stuffed rolls into Bruno's pockets and patted him on the back.

'No. No, you keep them. And I almost forgot. This is for you.' He took out all the money he had wrapped into his rucksack on leaving the country house. He had hoarded it and spent little.

'No, Bruno.'

'Please. Please. I'm working. And they feed us in the hotel. Will you get messages to me?'

His grandfather nodded. 'And this will go a long way. Thank you.' He met his gaze with something of his old spirit and with another hug, disappeared down the trap door.

Bruno stood there for a long moment, before shaking himself awake. He was mad. Why had he let his grandfather go? Listened like a docile child? They would kill him. They were killing everyone. He pulled open the trapdoor and raced down the stairs into darkness. He called out his grandfather's name. A moan of an echo was his only answer.

He was in a long corridor. Moisture oozed from the walls. His footsteps squelched through wet earth. The darkness grew thicker with each step. It was hopeless. He would need a torch to find another trapdoor. He ran his fingers along the low ceiling in an attempt as he moved. Nothing. His grandfather had vanished into thin air. At last he bumped into the corridor's end. Here was a door. He tried it, rattled it, knocked, pushed. But it was securely locked and no answer came to his call. With tears in his eyes, he blundered back, now doubly frightened. He would never get out of here. And his grandfather would die. He wouldn't find the first trapdoor. But he stumbled upon it, tripping over the rickety stairs, and managed to ease it open.

Another few minutes saw him making his way swiftly along the cold streets. A thin snow was falling, floating in the air like the flour in the bakery and settling on the ground in stark patches of white.

He was late for work. Even later than he had anticipated. The delay was a boon. A few minutes sooner, and he would have been right at the centre of the crossroads where a *łapanka* was in full progress, the roadblock already half-formed. Loudspeakers blared, their orders raucous, trapping all the people in the vicinity in a deafening ring of terror. Rifle-toting soldiers jumped from armoured cars and trucks. They screamed, pushed, shoved. Bruno scooted into a narrow doorway. From the corner of his eye he could see the Wehrmacht soldiers brutally herding people together then with equal venom forcing them into two distinct groups. A mother shrieked as she was prised from her daughter; another woman had to be dragged from the side of an old man who promptly fell on his knees and started to pray. A rifle prodded him until he doubled over onto the icy wet of the street where a boot found his gut. The snow turned scarlet.

Bruno flattened himself against the wall and inched in the opposite direction. A hairbreadth stood between him and a journey to some munitions factory in Germany as slave labour. He had no doubt in which line his youth would place him, unless his Jewishness was discovered, and then there would be no more lines at all.

The Nazi habit of separating out one thing from another came home to him with the force of a death knell. Yes. Jews from Poles from Germans, old from young, mothers from children, fit from unfit. This latest separating-out within the Ghetto, which his grandfather had announced, would lead to even more murders. As each separation seemed to.

Why had he been so feeble and not forced his grandfather with him? A habit of obedience had taken him over.

Now, a pit of despair threatened to swallow him. He should just let the Germans take him this time. Sooner rather than later. What did it matter? Get it over with. There was nothing to go on for. Nothing and no one. No one at all any more. And the war would never be over. It had become a permanent state. An endless Occupation, whatever Marysia murmured about the Nazi defeats in the east. All of them had got used to the daily horror and its accompanying indignities. They were ground down, abject, barely human.

Without thinking he picked up a loose stone from the street and was about to fling it in the direction of the Gestapo when a hand touched his shoulder. He lurched around, ready to aim his fists, to kick, to yell.

A woman's hushed voice stopped him. 'In here, quick. You'll be out of the way.'

Within seconds, he was in a small courtyard, well hidden from the long reach of the Germans and with a stout door firmly interposed between them.

'Just let yourself out when you think it's over.' The woman smiled at him gently from beneath a beret pulled low over her brow. 'Take care.' She rushed up the staircase opposite.

'Thank you,' he called after her.

The simple act of kindness saw him through the next weeks. He remembered the stranger every time his spirits sank to a level so intolerable that the knife he wielded daily in the kitchen of the hotel tempted him to extreme measures.

It wasn't that the job was so bad. Stout and spectacled, Herr Ritter, who ran the kitchens with more organization than the march on Russia and more anxiety than a mother nourishing a sick child, was a reasonable employer. For a German he seemed almost human. The kitchens were warm. Bruno was fed and given scraps to take home. His particular role – slicing up and preparing the carcasses which were delivered to the hotel every week, despite hunger everywhere else – turned out to be one he had a knack for once he had served a necessary apprenticeship with the German and learned the names of the various butcher's cuts. Herr Ritter appreciated the fact that he could speak German, particularly since Marysia was mostly occupied out of the kitchen. He often used him to translate instructions to the other kitchen workers – four women and two old men. They kept their distance from Bruno, as a result.

Sometimes Ritter even confided in him, telling him he had a son of his age at home, worrying about what would become of the boy. In Tomasz Nowak, Bruno had grown younger. He was now once again barely fourteen.

On the day of the *łapanka*, which he used as an excuse for his lateness, Ritter offered Bruno a tiny room in the attic of the hotel. Bruno wondered whether he could stand being in constant proximity with Germans, but in the end he acquiesced. Marysia's kitchen table had grown increasingly uncomfortable, and it was clear that her flatmate's initial welcome was reaching its irritated end. It was better not to irritate Poles now that the Germans had blaringly announced the death penalty for anyone who helped Jews.

And, away from Marysia's constant watchful eye, he felt he could probably sneak into the Ghetto and see his grandfather.

It was after Christmas by the time he had his scheme in place. He had stolen some stationery from the hotel, and now he wrote a letter under the name of Major Schmidt, who sometimes came into the hotel kitchens to talk to Ritter. This he brought to the Ghetto gates, as soon as Herr Ritter granted him an hour's leave. Here, pretending to be Major Schmidt's messenger, he paid a guard to make sure that the letter was delivered to his grandfather. The letter, written in German, asked Lawyer Torok to make himself available at eleven o'clock on Sunday morning at the gates to discuss a legal matter pertaining to a property transaction.

Bruno counted that another bribe would see him past the guards and within the Ghetto walls, where his grandfather would be waiting for him on Sunday. He would then plead his desire to stay or devise a plan to see him out. They had to be together. He was certain he could convince Herr Ritter to come up with another cubicle at the hotel as a temporary measure. All his grandfather had to do was shed his telltale Star.

But on that bitterly cold Sunday morning, his grandfather didn't appear at the Ghetto gates. Bruno waited and waited, making himself small amidst the commotion. Brusquely interrogated by a blue guard, he went off, only to return minutes later. In this way he waited until mid-afternoon, well past the time off he had begged. And still his grandfather didn't come. At last, his feet two blocks of ice in his worn shoes, he returned to the hotel to an angry Herr Ritter who had twice sent for him. He needed extra help in the kitchen tonight. Not less. There was to be a banquet. Two of the senior Wehrmacht officers had been posted east.

Bruno apologized, almost in tears. Why hadn't his grandfather

209 Lisa Appignanesi 209

come? What had happened? He could think of nothing else. His original letter hadn't gotten through. The guard had just pocketed the money and done nothing.

He didn't want to consider the alternative.

Herr Ritter's bad mood increased in the coming weeks. He too was to be moved east. He wanted to take Bruno with him. Bruno didn't want to go. He had to find out about his grandfather, take care of him. Not knowing how to say no, he ended up confessing part of the truth to the man: he had an old ailing relative in Krakow whom he helped out. Ritter's pudding of a face creased with displeasure, but he gave in with a shrug. A week later he was gone.

A certain Müller, a thin choleric man, replaced him.

'He's a pig,' Marysia whispered to Bruno in passing as she piled her tray high with plates. 'Take care.'

Bruno had more than noticed the difference. There was no extra food now, no conversation. The kitchen became a place of grim discipline where everything was constantly measured and counted. Everything any of them did was the subject of instant and harsh criticism. After a few days under the new regime, Bruno was moved from the meat section to tend to the huge soup tureens and ever-simmering stews. One day, in Muller's line of sight, the girl who was bringing over the chopped potatoes for the soups dropped some on the floor. Muller rushed over and berated her, accused her of dropping them deliberately so they could be stolen later. He raised his hand to hit her.

Bruno intervened.

'That's not true. We wash the vegetables again and put them into the soup,' he said in German.

'Wash them and put them into the soup?' the man roared, giving him a clout across the ear. 'Was I speaking to you? Are you trying to poison our people?' A second clout followed, drawing blood. 'Just tend to your pots. I'll see to you later.'

The girl mouthed a thank-you behind Muller's back, but the next day the violence increased. Muller having tasted the cabbage soup went into a rage and thrust a ladle-full into Bruno's face. The liquid burned and blistered.

A few nights later, Marysia stole up to his room and came in soundlessly without knocking. Her face wore a grimmer expression than he had ever seen on it. Without a word, she handed him a folded piece of paper. It looked like a sheet torn from a book, but was in fact overwritten. She waited while he read it.

'Bruno, my treasure. Forgive an old man. I didn't have the strength to come to you. I am dying and forced to dictate this on the only scraps we can find. The good news is that the Gestapo failed to find and eliminate me on their last roundup of children and the infirm. So I shall die my own death. Please, Bruno. Do exactly as Marysia says. The life of the Ghetto, I fear, is almost at an end. You will live for all of us. All my love. Your grandfather.'

He held back his tears and instead smashed the battered cup he kept on the windowsill to the floor. The sound resonated in the hush.

Marysia stared at him from her large soft eyes.

'The note took a while to get to me. It's over for him, Tomasz. I'm sorry. He was a great man, a good man. He did a lot for people. Remember that. Now listen, Tomasz.' She seemed to shed her birdlike frailty and grow taller as she spoke. 'As soon as the weather breaks – one week, two – you're out of here. It's too dangerous for you with that Müller. Outside too. The Germans are getting desperate for labour. I was only waiting for word from your grandfather. And you're needed. You're a man now.'

Bruno began to listen through the haze in his mind.

He had always suspected that tiny Marysia wasn't altogether who she seemed. She knew too much. She arranged things unflappably, brought news, fixed meetings, came up with forged documents and underground newspapers. People would drop into her remote little house at odd hours. While he was staying there, he had occasionally been sent off into the small garden behind the house while they talked. Packages were delivered. He delivered some for her himself, heavy ones which didn't rattle. It was through these deliveries that he had got the idea of how to communicate with his grandfather. The tears shadowed his eyes, as he listened to her.

She would slip him a pass sometime in the next few days. Perhaps tuck it under his lumpy mattress. He was joining Herr Ritter in Tarnopol. In fact, he would get off the train much sooner and walk to his destination. Once there, he was to ask for an André Citroen. There would be a package to deliver too. She would get it to him somehow.

She came up to him and put her arms around him as he memorized the address and softly repeated instructions. She was as slight as a child and he found it odd that there should be such comfort in her presence. 'We'll triumph, Bruno. Remember that. And we'll meet again when it's all over.'

Over the next days he began to squirrel away what food he could for his journey. He watched Marysia carefully when she came into the kitchen for any signs that she might want him. There were none. But on the fourth day, he found an old dishrag under his bed. Inside it was a brown paper package and the travel pass he would need. On the package, a scrawled message read. 'Friday. Inform Müller.'

The next day was Thursday. He looked for Marysia so that he could somehow express his thanks and say goodbye. But she didn't turn up at lunchtime. By mid-afternoon, Müller was fuming at her absence, when a messenger arrived to say that Marysia had been taken in a raid. Bruno hid his despair. It was unlikely that Marysia would ever be returned to the hotel.

Early the following morning, he stole away, leaving a note for Müller to say that permission had arrived for him to travel east. By the time Müller could check it out, he would have disappeared.

He left Krakow on a train crowded with Wehrmacht soldiers. Only two carriages were destined for Polish travellers.

Once more he was cast adrift from everything that had become familiar to him. This time he was full of angry purpose.

The name and address Marysia had made him memorize took him to a small town in the southeast, closer to the mountains than his grandfather's country home and in border country once more. The trains were slow, and the best part of the day was eaten up in starts and document checks and longer stops. When he reached the region, it was already dark. He didn't want to walk by night and get lost or stopped by some German convoy, so he begged a farmer to let him bed down in his barn in return for some hours work the next day. The barn forced thoughts of Mamusia and little Anna on him and led to nightmares that had no need of sleep. He stole away guiltily before dawn, leaving a few coins for the farmer on the windowsill of the house.

The meadows still wore a covering of morning frost. As the sky grew brighter it unveiled a breathtaking panorama of rolling hills and valleys through which the Carpathian streams and rivers coursed with bubbling energy. His spirits rose and then fell abruptly. He was moved by the beauty that whispered of peace, only to be reminded that there was no peace, let alone anyone to share it with. He hurried on. By late morning, he found himself in what turned out to be a small spa town, nestling in a pretty valley. It would have been idyllic but for the presence of so many German uniforms.

He walked purposefully as if he knew his direction, all the time on the look out for a fellow civilian. At last, on a small hilly street, he spied a young woman, who rapidly indicated a confusing number of lefts and rights that led him up a hill. The house, when he found it, had the aspect of a prosperous merchant's house from another time. It filled him with uncertainty. This was exactly the kind of house that would be taken over by Germans. He looked round him to check out an escape route, in case he needed to make one. Marysia might have made a mistake.

A girl of about his own age wearing a maid's apron opened the door. He swallowed and somehow stopped himself from blurting out the code name just in time, checking instead on the address. He had indeed made a mistake. He was looking for the lower end of the street, not the upper. Tipping his cap, he raced away.

The address he wanted was a far more common residence tucked in at the back of a small courtyard where a lone child played, desultorily flicking pebbles against a wall. The woman who answered was dressed all in black but for a coloured shawl, which she draped over her hair, as if she were on her way to church. She was old and didn't seem to understand him when he told her he'd brought something for André Citroen. The codename had made him happy since it reminded him of better times and his grandfather's abandoned car, but now it didn't produce the desired effect.

He repeated his words to the woman's growing consternation and added, with wide-eyed innocence: 'Have I come to the wrong place?'

'You're German?' she said. It was only in part a question.

Bruno protested and let out a torrent of Polish about how maybe because he'd had to work for them, he'd taken on the voice, but really he came from Krakow, where the winter had been hard; how he preferred smaller towns and he named a few obscure ones, hoping this would convince her he wasn't part of the enemy camp.

At last the woman invited him into a small neat parlour, told him to be seated, said she had nothing to offer him except a hot cup of the local waters. The person he wanted to talk to wasn't in.

Bruno waited. All the while, the woman made erratic conversation. She asked him more about his place of work in Krakow, about his parents, so that he had to tell her with a thick swallow that he was an orphan now. Evening came, and he was still there, talking about the Hotel Francuski again, saying that his closest friend, a wonderful woman, had just been taken in a German raid. A sudden noise came from a backroom. A man emerged. He was tall and fresh-faced, handsome but for the disfiguring gash of a scar on his left cheek. He stretched out his hand to Bruno and grinned. 'That's enough. Welcome. You've come to join us.' He looked Bruno up and down in swift appraisal, shook his hand and then embraced him in a manly hug.

The old woman smiled at him with a warmth that suddenly gave a vibrant intelligence to a face that had been wan and dull. 'Yes, welcome. I'm sorry, but we have to be careful.'

The next months woke Bruno to a different way of life. It was one he felt he had been born to. Gone was the claustrophobia of the hungry decaying city where every glance was a potential betrayal,

where boots and armoured cars clattered over cobbles with relent-
less threat. Now, as the member of a small Partisan band, he lived
with friends. They were brave, daring, sworn to secrecy and to a
single purpose: to free Poland from the clutches of the murderous
occupier. They lived largely in the forests, foraging and hunting
for food, breathing in the cool moist air of tall, needle-thin trees
and ferns, a smell that for Bruno spoke of freedom.

As Tomasz Nowak, he was the band's youngest member, and
that first spring and summer, his duties were largely that of a messenger. He knew they were testing his nerve. He was given a work
permit that linked him to a farm in the area, run by a man who was
attached to the Partisans and who would cover for him if the need
arose. He was also given a rickety old bicycle with a large basket
and two saddlebags. On this he moved between towns and villages
and forest, carrying roughly wrapped packages that could contain
anything from sterling supplied by British sources, underground
newspapers, food, grenades or guns. He wasn't always certain of
the exact contents of a package, which was just as well. Nor did he
know where the orders that came to his group stemmed from. All
he knew with certainty was that they were part of a struggle that
would soon defeat the Germans.

He had lost all fear. It had finally gone with his grandfather and
with Marysia's disappearance. For himself, he no longer really
cared whether he was dead or alive. He never thought about it.
What he cared about with a kind of rabid blindness was the
group's mission. So he was attentive to the details of his bicycle,
making sure that there was always enough straw or bits of old
burlap and beets or potatoes to mask more important items. On
the occasions when he was stopped by German police and
checked, he merely pretended to be a dim-witted peasant. Once,
for some reason incomprehensible even to him, he had bunched a
mass of wild anemones into a bouquet and placed them at the top
of his basket. When he was stopped, a bluff German officer scoffed
to his fellows about the stupid peasant who had a flower-loving
sweetheart. In the midst of the flood of ridicule and laughter, the
officer had grabbed away the bouquet and told him to get another
for himself. There had been no other questions, nor a search. From

then on, Bruno always perched a bouquet of whatever flowers he could find atop his basket.

Every evening under the stars the band shared news of German defeats and Allied victories. Around the campfire, they sang songs of melancholy longing or rousing cheer. A shield of warm solidarity against the cold of war and night grew up around them. They also talked of more immediate matters – ambushes, assaults on military transports, barracks and tracks, raids on depots, thefts of arms and ammunition.

Early in the summer, the leader of their group, the man whose mother's house he had first gone to and asked for Citroen, was killed in an ambush near Krosno. Two others were wounded. Soon after, they had news that their Prime Minister-in-Exile, General Sikorski had died in a plane crash. Sadness pervaded the band until a new leader arrived a week later: a tall man with a pleasant face, but with rather secretive studious gestures. He brought with him a young woman who gradually took over Bruno's activities and the bicycle. He, instead, was given a rifle, and once it was clear that he knew how to use it, could also master the pin on grenades and even simple explosives, he became a fully fledged fighter. He hid in roadside ditches and held his breath as Nazi supply trucks or cars approached. At the given signal he took aim or flung the grenade. He watched men die. He watched vehicles go up in flames that looked hotter and fiercer than the one he had started at Pan Mietek's farm all those months ago. Once, wearing a Nazi major's uniform, he even managed to march past guards at an ammunitions store and fire on them from the back as his comrades rushed in for the heist. All this, plus news of a German rout near Moscow and Italy's move into the Allied camp, buoyed them up into winter.

Through it all, he sensed that their new chief, whom they called Andrzej, was suspicious of him. Maybe it was because, unlike the others, he had failed to make up a codename to use in the group. In case they were caught and tortured, they all only ever used first names and these, he suspected weren't their real ones. Andrzej had reprimanded him as soon as he had found out that the name in his documents was the same as the one he used, but now it was too late.

Maybe Andrzej was also suspicious of him because Bruno didn't altogether know how to be a full member of a group. There were Polish songs he hadn't learned as a child. There was always a slight reserve between him and the others. He was quiet: kept himself to himself, rarely spoke unless he was spoken to. He saw that the others didn't behave like this, but he didn't know how to breach his awkward difference. If there was no activity marked out for the day, he liked to go off into the woods by himself, often coming back with some bit of game for their dinner or a stash of mushrooms. Nor did he really like the burning sensation of the various rough vodkas and berry brandies which were drunk by his comrades, especially as the winter cold set in, freezing them despite the crackling bonfires. In particular, he didn't like the blanket that covered his mind and twisted the world into terrible shapes when he had drunk too much. Within its thick folds, he felt small and alone, and, yes, frightened: frightened of what he might do to batter it away. For all this, he sensed Andrzej didn't trust him.

The women in the group, however, were sweet to him, often coming to sit with him while the men drank. Above all, Joasia, the one who had arrived with their new chief, was kind: sewing up his old, ripped gloves, providing rags for him to wrap round his feet in the icy weather. She had deep-set green-gold eyes, and when she wore her fur hat she looked like a princess out of one of those old Russian fairytale books his mother used to read to him.

Just after the New Year, in the coldest days of the winter, Andrzej came back with a pair of German boots for him. Bruno was astonished. He was less astonished when he heard he was about to be sent on a mission past Dukla to deliver a message to another band of Partisans who carried on the struggle near the Slovakian border where the Nazis controlled a strategic mountain pass. He was given an address, a codename and an utterly incomprehensible message to memorize. The message seemed to be a communiqué about plants and flowers and varieties of cow. He was also given a pill, given it secretly while he and Andrzej stood at a distance from the group in the shelter of some snow-laden pine trees. 'Only if you're captured,' Andrzej murmured, looking him directly in the eyes.

Bruno nodded without exhibiting a single tremor and quickly slipped the pill into an inside shirt pocket.

Andrzej patted him on the shoulder. 'You're a brave young Jew.' At first Bruno didn't think he had heard him correctly. He didn't respond, didn't blink. How could the man know? Had Marysia said anything? No, no. He caught Andrzej's glance whipping past his flies, and he now realized that he had failed in the very area that Marysia had warned him of, all those months ago when he hadn't been paying enough attention. In the woods he had let his guard drop. Andrzej must have seen him – seen the telltale mark of his circumcision.

There was no point protesting. He pretended not to have heard, but he wondered as he set off at dawn whether Andrzej hadn't specially selected him for the mission so as to get rid of him.

The journey was cold and treacherous, taking him deep into the Beskid Niski and, as he moved closer to the border, into heavily patrolled terrain. Maybe his burly ragged coat made him look innocuous. Maybe the sudden snow that reduced visibility to a few feet was on his side. Maybe the Nazis had other worries than a muffled and impoverished peasant who walked with the exaggerated limp Bruno had decided to adopt as camouflage, so that he looked unfit for work. In any event, travelling mostly by night and following the line of the river as far as he could, he arrived at the village unharmed and delivered his message to a rosy matron, who offered him sausage and some hot tea brewed from a concoction of thistle and herb, plus a blanketed floor next to her two young sons for the night. Bruno was grateful, and he set off the following afternoon in far better spirits than he had come.

The light was bright and crisp above the freshly fallen snow. For some kilometres he considered whether, given Andrzej's words, it might be better for him to disappear than to return. But he couldn't face abandoning the group that had become his home, his family, his country, all in one. Where would he go?

He had been concentrating so hard on his thoughts that he hadn't been paying attention to the path in front of him, where two soldiers suddenly appeared from nowhere and ordered him to

halt and show his papers. With an effort Bruno drew out his identification.

'Krakow,' one of them barked. 'What are you doing here so far
from home?'

Bruno pretended not to understand the German. He pointed to
his work permit, which showed him attached to a farm at some
distance from the group's camp in the woods. It was also, unfortunately, at an inexplicable distance from where he now found
himself.

'Take him in,' the other soldier muttered. 'He's got no reason to
be here. No travel pass.'

Bruno started telling them a complicated story of how he had
been to visit his grandmother, but it did no good. They marched
him off to their police barracks in a neighbouring village. All the
while he dragged his leg, fearful that this encounter might end up
in his being shipped off either to a German ammunitions factory
or far worse. He had the pill, he reminded himself. He had no
compunction about using it. The only thing he would regret is that
he had promised himself as soon as spring came to gather a large
bouquet of forest flowers for beautiful Joasia.

When they reached the village and were about to enter the barracks, they met a convoy on its way out, and a superior barked at
the two soldiers. This was no time for the checking of insignificant
peasant passes. A fire had started at the local oil installation.

Bruno found himself abandoned in mid-street. He considered
his position. He no longer had any papers. The Wehrmacht soldiers had kept them. In the commotion, there was no question of
asking for them back. And now, he had to get away. Night was
falling. He wasn't altogether sure of his bearings. He decided that
if he proceeded downhill he would eventually come to the river
that would lead him north. The stars would help. But the stars
were blotted out by the thick smoke that must be rising from the
fire the Nazi officer had referred to. He wondered if it had been
started by Partisans.

It took him another day and night to reach more familiar terrain.

By then, the snow had started again, light dry flurries now which occasionally blurred one's view but didn't blot it out into sameness the way thicker flakes did. Even so, when he reached the location where he was certain the campsite had been within the uneven circle marked out by nine pines, there was no trace of it. The space was desolate, empty, as if he and his friends had never existed. The ground was covered, pristine, not even marred by the ashes of a bonfire. In the distance an owl hooted.

His spirits plummeted. He followed them, sinking down into the snow. He gazed up into the night. The high wolf pines wore silvery cloaks and swayed gently. The birches danced in their icy finery. Only they hadn't abandoned him: left him for softer climes. He was alone, utterly alone with the tall trees and the snow.

The sudden crack in the darkness startled him. Several more followed. This wasn't the crack of a branch breaking in the cold or with the heaviness of snow. This was gunfire. It was ricocheting through the woods, echoing around him now, even if muted by snow. And it seemed to be coming closer, whizzing with the wind through the trees.

Silently Bruno padded towards the shelter of thicker woods. It was then that he tripped over the body. It was sprawled in the snow, face down, legs and arms askew. He called softly, but there was no response. With a shudder of realization he lifted the head and in the light the snow cast, saw the features of one of the band. Janusz. Glimmering against white ground next to him was a streak of red, almost black. A grim certainty took hold of him. The Nazis must have found their camp. The falling snow had covered the traces of struggle, but in another part of the woods the battle was still in progress.

Veering between trees, Bruno moved stealthily towards the rattle of gunfire. Further on, a glimmer of dawning light showed three bodies splayed on the snow like large fallen birds. He gazed at them. They must have been hit as they ran. A massacre. There were no guns on the ground around them. Stolen. He moved closer and recognized Joasia from the raven gleam of her hair. He stared at her poor inert form, turned her over and saw the pool of blood spreading on whiteness like some strange bloom. He kneeled down beside her and put his ear to her lips. No sound. No whisper of a breath. She was dead, cut down in mid-flight. Like the others. A moan escaped him, as low and throbbing as a wounded animal's, and suddenly he saw his mother lying there and Anna too. His grandfather. His father. All of them murdered, slaughtered. All of them lying dead in the snow: helpless, inert.

He started to scream, to shout at the very top of his lungs so that the woods echoed with his savage wail. He ripped a branch from a tree, wielded it like a weapon, ran, thwacking the stick against trunks, creating a havoc of pain and sound. Through the trees he thought he saw the glint of a uniform. Another. Nazis. Other figures too. All coming towards him. He screamed with banshee wildness and flung himself in their direction, hitting out.

The flash, the sudden low whine and crack of bullets didn't deter him. He rushed forward through a small clearing, his stick flailing, thrashing above his head like a whip.

The impact knocked him over, flung him backwards into the snow. He seemed to fall for an eternity. Above him the trees whirled round and round, lashing him with their fronds. In their midst, a face appeared. Andrzej's face. Huge above him. Mouthing 'you fool'. Scowling with hatred. And then everything was black.

He woke with a terrible pain in his shoulder and arm and chest. His flesh burned and his mind with it. Everything was confusion. Confusion trapped in searing pain He tried to move and had a dim sense that the burning was the cold: a freezing tundra had overtaken his body. He forced himself to move again, to sit up.

A streak of pure icy light illuminated the clearing. Daylight. It hurt his eyes. He could only move one hand to shade them. When he did, he saw the body stretched out beside him. Joasia, he thought through a haze. But it wasn't Joasia. This body was too big. A man's body. He crawled towards it on tottering knees and leaned forward. Andrzej. Why was Andrzej lying here? Had someone fired at him in turn? Yes. After he had shot Bruno. Of course. Bruno, the Jew. Bruno, the fool. And now Andrzej lay here. Motionless. Dead. Dead while Bruno, whom he had shot at, moved.

Had the pain and the blinding storm in his head allowed it, he would have laughed at the ironies fate had in store for them. He managed to give the body a kick. A kick of pure vicious hatred. And another, and another – one for his mother, one for his sister, one for his grandfather and one for himself – until the pain took over and he could kick no more.

He crawled towards the edge of the small clearing, gripped a tree trunk to pull himself up. He stood quietly for a moment and took deep painful, breaths. He waited for the world to stop moving, waited for the dizziness to settle. Summoning a superhuman effort, he moved back towards Andrzej, rifled through the man's pockets and found the pouch beneath his shirt where he stored his papers. These he took with him and stumbled away through the woods, lurching, clutching onto trees, going as far as his legs could carry him. He had reached open ground when they gave way.

And then he fell. Fell farther than he had ever thought possible.

When consciousness floated back after an eternity of emptiness his first sensation was of hands rubbing his, rubbing and rubbing. He opened his eyes to a blue dark-ringed gaze above him. It came from beneath a peaked cap.

'You have such cold hands,' the youth said. 'Such very cold hands.'

16

The flicker of candlelight gave Irena's small dining room, with its assortment of good prints and drawings, better gold-rimmed china and sparkling white cloth, a romantic glow. In the circumstances, it hardly seemed appropriate. There was no romance in the air. Not the teeniest little bit of it, Amelia thought, even if you got down on your hands and knees and searched under the table to where it might have sunk in fear of rearing its charm. What they had was one silent and sweetly demented woman who had not removed her weird blue eyes from Bruno's face throughout the entire evening.

He, on the other hand, was in one of his moods, by turn abstracted and curmudgeonly. He had barely uttered a word all evening, and when he did look up from his plate – which couldn't swallow the untouched Chinese takeaway – he seemed as absent as the woman at his side. Maybe Polish-Chinese wasn't his thing, though she didn't think that was it.

Had she been wrong to induce him to come here, to go through all this chasing of lost souls? Today had been too much for him: that was clear. Too much for her too, if she thought about the coldly brutal murders he had conjured up, the dead woman who might have been a grandmother to her. The poor dead child.

Now that he had started to talk, she recognized her own ambivalence. She had wanted to hear, wanted to know, but she also wanted to block her ears to the horror. It wrapped itself round you like a dirt- and lice-infested coat, at once too heavy to wear and too heavy to throw off. It made the world so sorry a place. That whole deadly history of race-hatred and race-murder. With its own quota of slavery, as Irena had underscored for her, though no one bothered to pay for the train-transported folk at the point of arrival.

It was probably because all that was in his bones that she always felt Bruno understood her so well. He knew intimately what it was like to enter a room preceded by your skin colour or the length of your nose. He knew about the murderous logic of appearances that meant that you walked into a wall of stereotyping prejudices well before you began to exist as an individual. He had learned to hide bits of himself, to use disguise, which wasn't something she could do as effectively, though both of them knew how to disguise pain. The difference was he had lived within a terrifying regime that officially made race a killing attribute. She hadn't had to confront that, not personally.

For that she thanked her lucky stars.

In her first day here, she had done some quick online research on Polish history and had been interested to find that of the pre-war Polish population, Jews had made up some ten per cent, just slightly less than the percentage of Blacks in the US. At various points through the centuries, Poles had also effectively instituted various principles of multicultural equality. But the war years had obliterated all that. Obliterated millions of people too.

So she probably shouldn't have entreated Bruno to re-enter his own killing fields. It had been selfish of her to want to know. But the fear that he would disappear before she had a grasp on his prior life, had taken hold of her ever since he had left America for Britain. Though selfishness wasn't the whole of it.

Over Christmas, which she had spent with him in London, Bruno had seemed in a bad way. She could hear him tossing and turning through the night in the room next door and occasionally calling out in panic in some incomprehensible language that had turned out to be this one. She was no Freud, but she knew when a guy was unsettled, even if that guy was her dear old dad. And she had really hoped that revisiting the damaging past would help. From the look on his face now, it had certainly not achieved that. If she thought it would do any good, she would throw her arms around him and drag him home this very minute.

Amelia's gaze moved round the table. Irena. The woman had felt remote at first, maybe even a little contemptuous. But she liked her now. There she was doing her hard-working best to keep people's spirits up, which meant chattering nervously or dramatically to cover up the gaps and failings in everything and everyone else. A little like some party organizer who had taken on the responsibility for everyone's life and was adamantly going to make it cheerful. Not cheerful in an American way, of course. But at least amusing, which could entail some scathing ironies or mock theatrics.

She wondered why she always had the feeling Irena was hiding something. Maybe it was just the extent of her mother's madness, but Amelia had also begun to think that hiding might be one way of simply being yourself around here. You never knew who might be watching and tell on you. Her father had a bit of that.

Worst of all there was Aleksander, who had somehow contrived not to meet her eyes once since they had sat down. At least she knew what that was about. It was about her announcement that she would have to go home either tomorrow or the next day. She had told him while they were driving to and fro in search of Irena's mother. He hadn't taken it the way she had hoped. Hadn't protested or asked her to prolong or said he would zoom right over and visit her in LA. He had only hunched his shoulders and gone quiet, his face more hangdog than ever. As if she were already gone and he was mourning her departure. The man had a genius for melancholy.

But then he was probably right. This was no place for a long-legged black gal who looked less at home in these streets than a prowling tiger inside a Carmelite convent. The nuns were all lined up, looking too. No, that wasn't accurate. Nuns were the only blacks she had seen around here. And that condition certainly wasn't what drew her to this country. No, the whole situation was utterly impossible. If she hadn't managed to make things work with a black man close to home, she could hardly make things work with a white, and a foreigner to boot.

She looked at Bruno, as if he could read her thoughts. She knew the lecture he would give her, if only he liked Aleksander. She knew it from beginning to resolute end. He would point out that skin and race and all those things one was born with didn't matter, not ultimately, not conclusively... After all, the brain changed throughout life, was constantly evolving in response to experience and environment. Even clones would have individual configurations of neuronal connections that mirrored their personal experience.

But it was clear that Bruno hadn't taken to Aleksander. So there would be no lecture.

Amelia took a sip of the indifferent wine and imagined herself trying to live in a tidy little house like this one, cooking dinners for Aleksander, waiting for him to come home from the lab...

The retrograde fantasies made her laugh in self-mockery. She hid the laugh in a cough. She had never, never imagined herself doing that for any man anywhere in the world. Impossible. And she'd never learn the language with all its soft slurring, all those rather flirtatious hesitations that Irena used. So she wouldn't be able to work, even if there was a job for her to do. Which was probably a bigger daily problem than race.

No, Aleksander was right. There was no point even discussing it. A little holiday fling. Soon to be forgotten.

He raised his eyes and met hers. The longing in them. No, not soon to be forgotten. She had fallen hard. It wasn't only the planes of his face and those soft deep-set eyes with the expression of a serious teddy bear. It wasn't only the quality of his appreciation: the slow step-by-step nature of his approach to her, as if each moment on the path to love gave off its own sweetness that had to be savoured. It wasn't even that everything wasn't shadowed by a sense of performance, a kind of baseline competitiveness that engendered more and more from both of them so that life became a question of winning or losing, though you were never sure quite what and simply got exhausted in the process. Aleksander knew how to be still.

She sighed. She hadn't realized it was so vocal until everyone lifted their eyes to her, even old Pani Marta, who murmured 'Pretty Lady' so that Amelia felt called upon to smile broadly. In that smile her spirits lifted just a little.

If only Bruno could be prevailed upon to do his bit and call in some favours. Then Aleksander would eventually be brought a little closer to home. She needed to see him on her own turf so that she could ground her perceptions. And those feelings that were flying up all over the place and out of control. But Bruno had decided not to like him. And it didn't even feel like his ordinary hesitation towards any man she came up with. Maybe he thought this was all a little over-determined. A scientist. A Pole. No, Bruno didn't think like that, just acted it.

She wished her mother were around. Eve could always cajole him and make him see what he was blind to. She missed her.

Probably Bruno thought Aleksander was only interested in her because of what Bruno could do for him. A scientific fortune-hunter. That would be like him, though there was nothing really wrong with fortunes in this case. Yet she sensed there was more. It had to do with that impenetrable tangled matter Bruno was carrying around with him and probably came down to a prejudice against Poles. She couldn't blame him, really, but she wished it could be otherwise. She would work on him. Work on him when he was a little more present than he was now.

'You know, Professor Tarski,' Irena was saying, 'quite a few letters arrived at the *Tygodnik Powszechny* in response to the article.'

'Tarski,' Pani Marta said in eerie echo. 'Aleksander…' But she was looking towards Bruno and getting all agitated. Her fingers worked away at her buttons.

Irena handed her a glass of water. She pushed it aside, inadvertently spilling it over her cardigan.

'So sorry,' Irena said. Her voice quivered a little. 'It's been a long day for her. I had better get her to bed.'

With low soothing murmurs of the kind mothers used to their children, she led Pani Marta away.

Bruno got up too, paced the length of the small room, pausing to examine the array of prints and drawings that hung on the walls. That left her and Aleksander looking at each other uncomfortably with nothing to say that they could say in front of her father, so she got up as well and started to pile the dishes and make desultory conversation.

'That's a good charcoal.' She looked over Bruno's shoulder at a drawing he was studying. It showed an old, rather handsome house, half-hidden by trees. It was the trees that were good. An invisible storm had made the foliage swirl and shake.

'Yes,' he said absently.

With a shrug she took the plates towards the kitchen.

'I think I'll go and give Irena a hand with her mother.'

'You do that. She'll appreciate it.' Amelia called after him, wondering again whether he was developing a soft spot for the woman. Irena treated him with great consideration, a careful mixture of respect and admiration. But then she treated Aleksander like that too. Who knew? Who knew anything in this strange country?

Amelia, piling dishes into the sink, suddenly felt a hand on her shoulder. She shivered. What was it that made skin so susceptible to one touch and not another? Was it because she had known that about Aleksander from the moment they first shook hands, that she had really persuaded Bruno to make this journey. No, no. She mustn't be that cruel to herself.

'I wish...' Aleksander's voice was soft and wondered off on a note of such pure longing that she turned into his embrace despite the water dripping from her fingers. The kiss felt as illicit as his erection. The kitchen was so neat and tiny, her father a matter of a brittle wall away. As if she were an ardent teenager again. Though now she had a clearer picture of what she might want. Not that it seemed any more attainable.

'I wish you could stay. Or that I could come to you,' Aleksander was whispering. 'Maybe after this run of experiments...'

'Oh, I'm so sorry. So sorry.' Irena's eyes were vast with embarrassment as they met her own over Aleksander's shoulder. 'I didn't mean... I'll... I was just getting a glass of... I'll come back.'

'No, please.' Amelia barely held back a giggle. 'Please, Irena. I'll get you a glass. Shall I make some coffee too? We need it, I think.'

'Yes, yes. Good idea.'

Irena stood there, head lowered, then looked up abruptly. 'Your father is quite extraordinary with my mother. Better than any of the doctors. Better than I am. He's so gentle. It's as if...as if he knows that to get her attention you have to touch her. I'd never quite realized it. But it's true. Yes. And she focuses on what he says. She doesn't wander so much.'

She seemed to be trying to communicate something special. Amelia smiled at her. 'Leave him with her and come back to us. Maybe he'll work a miracle. I suspect he's always had a way with the ladies.' She winked at Irena, all the while holding on to Aleksander's hand.

'Yes. Yes.' Irena was now looking up at Aleksander. 'I need to say something to you. I need to clear the air.'

Amelia watched her walk away. A sudden suspicion filled her. Had she quite innocently walked into an already burgeoning love affair and somehow broken it up? That's what Irena was hiding. No, no. She would have realized, wouldn't she? Or were the cues so different here that she understood nothing at all?

She hurried to make coffee, could only find some instant then heard her phone ring while she put the kettle on the hob.

'Let me.'

Aleksander took over. She switched off her phone and watched his gestures. They were precise, instinctively accurate. Did he already know this kitchen? Or was she watching the movements of a large man accustomed to small spaces?

'May I invite you back to my place later?'

She met the plea on his face. They had only been together in hotels: some good, some ghastly, but always impersonal. Places for unconsidered passion. Despite the sense of slowness, it had all happened so quickly. And she hadn't been to his apartment yet. Only his lab. Would there be unpleasant secrets hidden away in the bedclothes? No, no, she hoped not. And the invitation was a sign. She nodded.

'Oh no. Please don't. Here, here.' Irena was back. She found a tray and quickly placed everything on it, then ushered them to the table. Guests really shouldn't behave as informally as they had been. 'Please,' she said again.

They took their places. Irena's strained face threw a hush over them. She turned to Amelia first. 'I don't mind you hearing this, Amelia. But please don't think me mad. It's just that I need to know. Need to clear the air, as I said.'

She stared at the flickering candelabrum then got up again, too restless to sit.

'Aleksander…' She paced, refused to meet his eyes.

'Oh do sit, Irena. He's not that frightening.' Amelia tried to lighten the atmosphere. She wasn't sure she had succeeded.

'Of course. Of course. The thing is…' Irena stopped and began again in a great rush, as if she were overcoming a barely surmountable hurdle. 'The thing is that some years ago, before my mother was visibly ill, she told me that my father wasn't my father. I mean the man I had always thought was my father, Witek Konikow, wasn't really that at all. My real father was somebody quite different. Somebody called Aleksander Tarski.'

'What?' Amelia couldn't hold back her surprise.

Aleksander said nothing. He was standing there, somewhat rigid.

Amelia looked from one to the other of them. Bewilderment coursed through her. Wasn't Aleksander much too young to be Irena's father, since she was older than Amelia? She shook herself, realized that Irena was talking about another generation.

'So you mean…?'

'I don't know quite what I mean.' Irena's voice held a sob in suspension. 'I left it all too late, you see. Back then, when my mother first told me, I wasn't all that interested. I thought it was a kind of joke, really. Something to make my English friends giggle about. I was living in England, which made everything seem different in any case. But now I'd like to know. If my mother still remembered names back then, if she wasn't yet demented, it could just be that Aleksander's uncle was my father. Though if he died in the Warsaw Uprising, as I think you said while we were travelling, then his sperm would have had to have been frozen, and the whole thing is completely lunatic. As I suspect it is. Either that or I'm even older than I am.

'But I have to ask because, well, because I've been thinking about it so much. It's…well, it's really why I sought you out in the first place, to be brutally frank. I'm no science journalist. Though I've learned a lot. I enjoyed it. Meeting you. And Professor Lind, as well.'

She had started to cry in the midst of this, and Amelia put her arm round her shoulder. 'Don't be so upset, Irena. I understand. I understand how one has to know. How uncomfortable it all is.'

'I thought... Well, I thought if she saw you, Aleksander – you said you looked like your uncle – that she might just recognize you. But I don't think she did. So I don't know why I'm saying all this. Except that maybe you still have some relatives you could ask. Because I'd like to find out. No one's altogether clear about who was killed during the Uprising, so maybe in fact your uncle lived on. Went back to the countryside until the war was over, as so many did. I don't know. Maybe I'd just like some family.'

The tears were streaming now and the plea in her voice brought them to Amelia's eyes too. She found a hankie and passed it to Irena. It reminded her. Reminded her how upset she'd been all those years back when she went to see her birth mother. The awkwardness of it. The sense of abjection. As if one wanted something one wasn't even sure existed. The reparation of some lost unconditional love. But maybe it wasn't love from that particular person. More like love from some idealized being one had dreamed up.

It was all so strange. The way memory was so crucial to who one was, the very foundation on which identity was built, yet that crucial bit of one's identity – who one's birth parents were, even if one had lived with them for some years – was something memory couldn't deal with. You simply forgot. In those early years of a child's life, when everything was being learned, memories of that kind weren't laid down. Not so that you could recognize the person later. So bizarre. Maybe birth parents didn't really count for much unless they hung on in there until speech kicked in. Genes: yes. But since as her father kept telling her we all shared some ninety-eight percent of our DNA with chimps, not to mention some forty percent with a banana, what was a little matter of a gene or two between humans?

Yet here was Irena, desperate to know. As she had been.

'What can I say?' Aleksander was staring at Irena, as if he were trying to place a grid over her features. 'There are some photographs. Of my uncle, I mean. We could show them to your mother.'

'Do I look at all like him?'

He shrugged. 'I'm told he looked a lot like me. But that was by my grandmother, who had a vested interest.'

'And were there ever any stories which cast doubt on the timing of his death?'

It was Aleksander's turn to pace. 'No, I don't think so. The stories came in dribs and drabs, of course. He wasn't a member of the Communist Resistance but a nationalist, which might account for that. He lived in Warsaw and rarely visited during the war years unless he was on some kind of mission. But as my grandmother would have it, he came to see her in July of 1944, just before the Uprising, and he was burning with the excitement of it. Apparently, she tried to hold him back, get him to stay with her, because she had a feeling that she would never see him again. Her intuitions were proved right. She never did. A message came from one of the members of his group in October of '44 to say that he had died in Warsaw, died heroically. He remained her hero. She would recount his exploits over and over again, while my father's war experiences were never spoken of. Not until we children prised them out of him. He took his mother's view. He didn't count for much. Anyhow, there was never any other account given of my uncle's death during my childhood.'

Amelia took one look at Irena's disappointed face and burst out: 'I'm sure he'd gladly have you as a cousin, in any case, Irena. I know I would.'

Was it really truth that mattered so much in these cases? she wondered. Even if one was adamant about discovering it. She was no longer sure. She wanted to give Irena a hug, but the woman was all prickly tension now.

'By the way, my uncle was always referred to as Pawel. That was his first name. My father and mother preferred his middle name, Aleksander, so gave me that.'

'So that's that.' The tears welled up in Irena's eyes. 'Died too soon and wrong name.'

'Tarski isn't an uncommon name.' Aleksander tried to be helpful. 'And people took on false names during the war. Particularly the partisans. Maybe my uncle chose to be known as Aleksander.'

This last attempt at reassurance seemed to make Irena even more despondent.

Amelia intervened. 'Is there any one else in your family one could ask?'

Aleksander thought for a moment then shook his head. 'No, my mother died last year. Though...' He gave Amelia a quick furtive glance. 'Before he died, my father talked at length to my former wife. She loved all those family stories, family trees. Probably because of our son... I never really listened. You could, of course, contact her.'

'No, no.' Irena's eyes were veiled in sadness. 'It's too silly, really. I've made enough of a mountain of it.'

'No you haven't,' Amelia heard herself say. 'If you're not satisfied, girl, you go on and pursue it. Ask more questions. Get the bedding off. Air those ancient mattresses.' She laughed. 'You know how many children are born on the wrong side of the marital sheets? Some six out of ten of us, depending on whose statistics you decide to believe.'

'No, no,' Irena protested. 'It's not a matter of illegitimacy. At least, I don't think it is. I don't mind about that at all. It's just that I'd like to know. And I don't know why I think I'll find a satisfactory answer. It's not as if anything else in life is clear. Well, not the way things are clear under Aleksander's microscopes.'

She was right, Amelia thought. At least about this place. In the Californian light, in the scripts she handled there weren't as many shadows, as many textures, as many uncertainties. And the histories had been wiped out, left behind in places like this for others to worry over, so that America could concentrate on the future. Or just not concentrate.

She watched Aleksander, wondered about that former wife of his. He didn't really want Irena to contact her. The woman still counted in some way. Did her ex count too? Probably, to sensitive external eyes, though she thought he didn't count at all. She never thought about him. But he must have helped to shape her, produce those diminished expectations, that façade of not giving a damn. Which is why she should make more of an effort with Aleksander, not less. He was reading the remains of a second skin she had grown, a hard, laughing one.

'You could always,' Amelia said, knowing as she said it that it was altogether the wrong thing to bring up, 'you could always both have a DNA test done. It would probably come up with a relationship.'

'No. Certainly not.' Irena came as close to snapping as Amelia had ever heard her.

'Why DNA tests?' Bruno had just come back into the room. He looked exhausted, Amelia thought. They should get him back to the hotel. It had been a long day. A very long one for him. Too many ghosts. They had eaten the pounds off him.

'Oh, it's nothing.'

'Irena thinks she may be related to Aleksander through a father her mother only revealed to her a few year's back. But Aleksander says he doesn't think so.' Amelia explained quickly about the Warsaw uncle, his death, the name.

'I see.' Bruno gave Aleksander a bizarre look then eased himself into his chair and played with the small glass of vodka in front of him before downing it in a single gulp. 'I owe you all an apology. You too, Aleksander. And Pani Marta.'

'Was she all right? Shall I go in to her?' Irena asked.

'No, no. I don't think it's necessary.' He smiled at her with a touch of sadness. 'You must try not to worry so, Irena. I know it's not fashionable to say this, but death is inevitable. And it has its own logic. Pani Marta is comfortable.'

A shiver crept up Amelia's spine. She wasn't sure what had caused it. Was it the way Bruno and Irena were looking at each other? She wanted to clutch at Aleksander's hand, but he too seemed far away. Maybe, as she had half suspected all along, Bruno planned to inflict a stepmother on her, though she was well past the age of mothers of any degree. Eve would have wanted him to be happy. But she wouldn't have persuaded him here as Amelia had done, back to the terrain his restless ghosts inhabited. Eve didn't believe that if you put a narrative to things, they ceased to torment you. Or if she did, she had never told Amelia or ever felt it necessary to persuade Bruno here.

Or was it that the moment had never been right before?

Amelia wondered if Bruno's nightmares would stop after this visit. Perhaps not. He looked more haunted than ever. And he was saying something she couldn't quite grasp.

'So your mother told you that you were related to Aleksander Tarski?' His voice was so soft she had to strain. 'It's not altogether impossible.' He paused. 'Yes, yes. I owe you all some explanations.'

He got up to pace, his hand rifling his hair then clenching into a tight fist behind his back.

Amelia rushed to his side. 'You don't have to give us any explanations, Pops. You don't owe us anything.'

He met her gaze with his steady blue one. 'Come here, Amelia. Come and sit beside me on the sofa. This may take a while. I do have some debts, you know. I think I may owe Irena's mother my life. Yes.'

He looked up at the charcoal drawing with its heavy shadows and stormy foliage. 'Plato asked: can the same man know and also not know that which he knows? The answer is certainly yes. And you don't need a brain lesion to make it so.'

He paused. He was still looking at the picture. 'I'm not sure what I recognized first. That drawing. Or maybe it was her voice. Husky, yet somehow precise. Or the gestures. Those large hands with their small neat motion. You know,' he looked at them all with an air of wonder, 'I really think I'd all but forgotten that period. Or not remembered it. I needed the trigger. The stimulus of those hands and the murmur. The murmur of, "Little Cousin".'

17

1944

The shots in the woods had reverberated all night, coming first from one place, then another. She had lain there, listening to the hideous *rat-tat-tat* of gunfire. The thunder that spelled death and more death. Iniquitous death. Till there would be none of them left. No Jews, no Poles, no Slavs, no gypsies. No one except the Nazis, and then they'd probably have to start killing each other, because the killing habit would have taken hold. Like an opium addiction. *Rat-tat-tat.*

Yes, she had lain sleepless in that cold bed in the draughty house where the wind moaned its displeasure with all their lives. Even more loudly than her father did when the pain took hold of him. Even more loudly than he had when she had taken that Wehrmacht lover who had protected them. Long gone now. How she had loathed him. Loathed his lordly manner with her. His favours. Lord of creation who, with a little help from her, spilled his seed in a flat five seconds. Yes, you could tell a people by how they treated their women. Not that she supposed it was the poor man's fault. Trapped by stupidity. All of them. They were all responsible, though some were far more responsible than others. Yes. *Rat-tat-tat.*

She waited until the shooting had stopped. Had learned over the years to give the silence a chance for an extra hour, so that the armoured cars and the planes were all gone. Then she slipped into the old warm trousers and the worn tweed jacket and cap. She packed the bandages and the remains of the alcohol which served as an antiseptic and the rotgut vodka their neighbour made which could revive a dead pig, if it thought life was still worth living after swilling it. Finally she saddled her horse. Winter had turned him into skin and bone, and she didn't like attaching the two linked up child-sleighs that could serve as a makeshift stretcher behind him. But they might prove useful.

The moon had set now, and the light all came from the ground where the snow wore a thin crust of glittering ice. Her horse's hooves crunched through it. She kept him to a trot and skirted round to the far side of the forest where a track would take her to the old forester's cabin. He might have news of the partisan band, would know more accurately where the fighting had taken place. But the forester wasn't in, had probably gone off to help as soon as he heard the Germans receding.

She rode slowly, peering through the trees to see where the snow was disturbed. Yes, Pan Stanislaw had gone ahead of her. She could see his boot prints where the trail branched. Should she follow him or head off to the left? Best to follow, since he wasn't riding, and there might be some left alive for her to bring out.

She found the forester in a small clearing in the grey light of the earliest dawn. He was cutting fronds from the lowest pines and covering over the bodies. A superficial burial. But the ground was frozen and too hard to dig. There were three of them here. The wild boars would get them soon enough if the buzzards didn't. She averted her eyes, not wanting to see. She had to protect herself from the nightmares. Had to. Still.

They followed the tracks after that, too many of them. And the telltale markings of blood on snow. Maroon, almost black in the first glimmer of the rising sun. The day would be beautiful. She could feel it. She kept her eyes on the sky and watched the morning cloud scuttling above the high trees. She listened to the birdsong. She didn't want to be the first to see the bodies. Even though she was here. Even though she had come to help.

A line of poetry her father had taught her in English when she was still little came back to her. He had loved Shelley and Coleridge, the English Romantics. He had been wonderful then, her father. Before the illness.

> Ah woe is me! Winter is come and gone,
> But grief returns with the revolving year

So much grief. There was another body now, a fighter stretched in the snow as if sleep had caught him unawares.

The forester kneeled by his side. 'He's alive,' he whispered. 'Quick.'

She poured the vodka down his throat. He coughed. A strong man. The cold helped. It slowed the blood flow, slowed the heart too. She had read that in the book the doctor had lent her just before the start of the war. Read about the syphilis as well. Her father. She had thought she might study medicine.

They strapped him onto the makeshift stretcher, and slowly she led her horse back to the forester's cottage. The man opened his eyes as she prodded the wound. They would have to try and get old Dr Zygmunt over. The bullet had gone too deep for simple extraction.

The man was watching them. His lips moved.

'We should be able to get you fixed up,' she said softly, unwinding the bandages she had made from boiled rags. 'Take it easy.'

He was speaking again, too softly for her to hear. The forester put his ear to his lips.

'You want me to get a message through,' he repeated. 'From Aleksander Tarski to Bronek Kowalski.'

The man murmured a yes and closed his eyes. There wasn't much more she could do. She rode off to fetch Dr Zygmunt, while the forester dragged her sleigh back into the woods. There might be other survivors and they would have to move quickly. The Germans could well be sending men to scour for their own.

It was then that she saw them. Just as she emerged from the south side of the forest. Tracks glistening with their icy crust that was just beginning to melt. German boot prints. They zigzagged and swerved madly. The body lay at a little distance on the slope of the hill. She kept her horse trotting in a straight line. She wasn't going to make a detour to help a German bastard: that was for sure.

Then with a shrug she looped back. Some mother's bastard. And he couldn't harm anyone in his present state.

There was a shaft of sun right on him, and she found herself marvelling at the beauty of that young golden head, the fine skin. He lay so peacefully asleep, like Icarus fallen from the skies. Or Adonis, yes, more like Adonis, gored by the jealous boar. The blood was caked on his jacket at the shoulder. But the jacket wasn't a uniform, she noted in confusion. She slipped off her horse and put her pocket mirror to his lips. Seeing a trace of breath she reached for the vodka flask and simultaneously unbuttoned the jacket to see the wound as much as to check what he was wearing and what identification he might have. But she already knew that whatever his nation, she couldn't leave him here to die in the cold.

She was surprised to find him carrying papers in one of the names the fighter in the forester's cabin had mentioned. She put her perplexity to one side. The real problem was how to move him. She had to get him home. Out of the cold. A little cold slowed the blood. Too much killed. Could she heave him onto her horse?

He flinched and opened his eyes as she tried to lift him.

'Can you walk a little?' she asked in Polish, and he seemed to understand, clung to her as he got to his feet. 'I'm going to try and mount you on the horse.'

'Bessie,' he murmured, as if he had arrived in heaven. 'Bessie.' He half fell and half clambered onto the animal with her help, then leaned heavily against her while she held him upright all the way home.

She walked him into the big front room where her father dozed beneath his chequered blankets on the old wooden wheelchair. The canapé he had once used, before the business of moving him to and fro had proved too difficult without help, still stood there not far from the hearth. She helped her patient stretch out, then put more wood on the fire and stoked it into a blaze. She put the kettle on to boil. She thought she could tend to this wound herself. Would have to. If he were a German, old Dr Zygmunt would quite happily let him die.

'Drink,' she cut through his mutterings and handed him the flask. He was delirious, she thought. At least the mumblings were in Polish. 'Drink,' she ordered again. 'I'm going to try and get the bullet out.'

She undressed him to the waist, washed the skin that emerged firm and golden around the ugly welt. So unlike her father's, she marvelled as she cleaned, then prodded and pulled and swabbed with the instruments these last years had taught her to use, however inadequately. The bullet extracted, she dabbed at the wound with more alcohol, then bandaged the whole area tightly.

His cries had roused her father, who was calling for her in the hoarse groans he used now, interspersed with that hacking cough. These last months, he was mostly off somewhere in his own world. The illness had eaten up so many chunks of him. Almost better he were dead. While she tended to him, she conjured up the handsome witty man he had once been. Just, too, and generous. Had he known what she was doing, he would have approved.

Within a week, her young patient had come back to himself enough so that she was sure he understood her. None too soon, because she had had to hide him in her room while she went about her endless duties. She never knew when Pani Zablonska, the wife of the old family retainer, might trek over from her house and make a pretence of helping out while she spied and scoffed the old man's gruel. There were few one could trust in these hard times.

She repeated that to her patient. She also said to him: 'As far as I know, you're Aleksander Tarski. That's what your papers say. That's fine with me, although you look young for your age. I shall tell everyone you're my little cousin come from the north. Your parents thought you'd be better off in the country and you've come to help out. And you will help out. As soon as you're well. There's a lot to be done. We have a few cows, here. Fields too. With luck the wheat will grow as golden as your hair. I'm the only one left to work, fulltime. Apart from you. Is that a deal, Little Cousin?' She thought she might have smiled at him, because he smiled back, a warm endearing smile that illuminated his whole face. She felt it illuminating her too, as if a flame had been lit beneath her heart and sent the blood racing.

'Little Cousin,' he repeated, and he gave her his hands to clinch the deal.

Over the next months, though, she worried for him. He did everything he was asked. And more. He even took over the bathing of her father that she had performed ritualistically once a week with old Pani Zablonska's help in lifting him into the tub. Aleksander had watched her rubbing and rubbing and taken the cloth from her and copied her movements so that she wasn't sure whether her father noticed the difference.

Watching, she stilled a leaping desire.

He was good at finding food too, her Adonis. She called him Aleksander out loud, but she was sure it wasn't his name, since he hadn't answered to it in his delirium. That other man they had found that day in the clearing who had mentioned the same name was long gone, fetched by a woman with a wagon, Dr Zygmunt had told her.

So she thought of Little Cousin as her Adonis. He was a hunter even though he hadn't come to her with a gun or a bow and the Germans had long ago taken theirs. But he knew how to lay traps, and he came home with rabbits and game. When the ice broke, there were fish. They hadn't eaten so well since the Wehrmacht had been with them. He loved riding the old mare too. She wished she had a second horse, so that they could ride together, but of what was left of their stables two had died, and she had given one, together with a cart, to the Jewish family they had hidden in the early years of the war in the decaying wing of the house.

It was because of that old spy, Pani Zablonska, that they had had to go. The woman he had told her in her falsely subservient way that she knew they were there and a danger to all of them. So Marta had packed them off on the cart and hoped that, with the extra cash she had found for them, they would make their way across the border, if not to Hungary, then at least across the river to the Russian zone.

After that, she had told the old crone she had nothing left to pay her with, so she had better find some other means of support. And still she came to sniff around, claiming a loyalty to her father, supposedly helping with his personal care but really foraging and stealing beneath her very nose. Now, with her Little Cousin here, she had an excuse to get rid of her for good.

Yes, she worried for him. And not only because of the old witch. She sometimes thought there was something wrong with him. Something wrong in his mind. At first she thought it might be some defect from birth, since he spoke hardly at all. He was simple. But it turned out that he knew how to speak perfectly well, and in Polish, though only did so in response to direct questions. Then she thought he must be in a state of residual shock, because of the wound and the accompanying fever, or because of something else, something that had happened before. She was gentle with him.

Once the skin had healed, leaving only a puckered scar on the golden flesh, she asked him. How had he come by the bullet wound? For the first time, he looked furtive. But oddly so. She wasn't sure whether he was trying to hide something or find something.

'Where are you from?' she asked him.

He was quick to say Krakow and then in something like panic, excused himself, told her he had a task to perform.

Mostly they worked side-by-side, not speaking much, but somehow in tune: she in her old workman's clothes, so that from a distance they probably looked like brothers. He knew about ploughing and sowing. He knew about milking the cows too, though she wouldn't let him take the milk to the village. It was best if he wasn't seen too much, she had determined from the start.

One late afternoon she found him in her father's library, which was directly underneath the room she had given him. He jumped, startled by her approach, and she said, no, no, it was fine for him to be there if he liked to read. She noticed he had taken down a volume of Dickens, and she laughed and said it was an old favourite. They could read together, if he liked, by the fire. Her father might enjoy that too.

As the days grew longer, they read into the evenings. Poetry too. She watched his face, the rapt attention, the play of emotion. No, he wasn't simple.

In May, for her birthday, she decided to celebrate. She was twenty-five and, even though she felt a hundred, it was an age worth celebrating. The sound of gunfire had been close again. In the village the news was that the Russians were advancing, the Germans on the retreat. Either death or liberation was on the march. She was no longer altogether sure she remembered what the second meant. In either case, she felt like a celebration.

She boiled some water and washed her hair with the bar of soap she had hoarded for so long it had developed thick black grainy ridges. She unfolded the silk stockings from their wrapping of tissue paper, found the delicate silver-blue crepe dress she had last worn in the first year of the war and put on the pearl choker which had been her mother's and which the Nazis had failed to plunder because she had hidden it amidst the down in her pillow. She dressed, brushed her hair to a sheen, applied some old lipstick, put on shoes that weren't boots and had a heel. She no longer recognized herself in the mirror.

There was leftover rabbit stew for supper. It would have to do. But the table would benefit from a cloth. She had stored them away in a chest years ago and listed them in her mind as unmanageable household items, like so much else the house had once contained. But now, she went upstairs, up to the attic where she had hidden the linen, and brought a cloth down with her.

Little Cousin was standing at the foot of the attic stairs when she came down. He was all attention, and she realized he thought she might be an interloper. It took him a moment to recognize her and then he seemed to grow even stiller.

'It's my birthday,' she offered in explanation.

'Birthday,' he echoed and without looking at her again rushed out of the house.

Sadness filled her. She had frightened him. She shrugged away a sense of desertion and went to set the table. She dawdled, took her time, but still her Adonis didn't return. She wheeled her father to his place. Sang a desultory song, because she knew it soothed the old man somewhere in those unreachable depths, and she had wanted to celebrate. How she had wanted it. She found the last bottle of wine that dated from what she thought of as her Wehrmacht days, back in '40 and '41, when it had become clear that the war wouldn't be over in six months. Her father had suddenly taken a terrible turn then, and she was willing to do anything to keep him alive, to get him the treatments old Zygmunt said he needed. She dusted the bottle off, uncorked it and poured a little for him and herself. They drank. When she had finished her glass, and the dark had set in, she served the stew on the few uncracked plates. She felt more like weeping than like eating.

Then he was there, wiping his feet on the grate, rushing towards her. 'Happy Birthday, sweet cousin,' he murmured. He thrust into her hands a bouquet of tiny spring anemones, all purple and white amidst their moist leaves and still perfumed by the forest.

She smiled. She couldn't stop smiling. She put the flowers into a low bowl and gazed at them as they drank and ate. She could feel him stealing glances at her, as if he still wasn't sure she was who she was.

Afterwards she lit the tallow candle, and they read poetry. Shelley, because he was her father's favourite, and also Adam Mickiewicz. He told her he thought he still remembered how to sing 'Happy Birthday' in English, his tutor had taught him. Then he stopped himself and went silent, and she was afraid to interrupt the look on his face.

Later, at the top of the stairs, when he said goodnight, she called after him. 'Thank you, thank you, Little Cousin,' and he turned, and she stretched out her hand to him. He came towards her, and she held on to his fingers. She led him to her room that was at the opposite end of the hall. Leaning against the door, she kissed him. He didn't really know how to, not at first, not until later and by then they were lying on her bed and solemnly undressing each other by the moonlight which trailed through her window and left a silver path on her sheets. She taught him everything she knew, but he seemed to know things of his own. He knew how to run his fingers along her skin, how to explore softly, firmly, how to bury his head between her breasts and arch her against him so that she had to stop herself from crying out in case the night woke.

In the morning, he lay asleep tightly curled against her. She watched his beauty and marvelled, moving slightly so that she could take in all of him. Her Adonis. It was then that she saw it. She wanted to laugh out loud. There, there lay the explanation for everything. All the secretiveness, the probable disguises. It made her very happy. Her Adonis found wounded at the cusp of the forest was a Jew. Not a German, but a Jew. And she wouldn't let anyone, not anyone, take him away from her.

That summer, time, which had grown so thick and sluggish that she could barely wade her way through it, took on a new consistency. It was as frothy and light as whipped cream or the seeds on a dandelion, and it flew by without her being able to catch hold of it. There were poppies, and then the meadow grasses grew and grew until they were waist high and wonderful for rolling in when they could. During the days they worked enveloped in a heat that might have been sun or their own making. At night their passion electrified the air and made everything glow with the burnished gold of the wheat fields.

The serpent in her Eden turned out to be the *rat-tat-tat* that had led her to him. That summer the Partisans of all groupings and colours had intensified their activity. In August they made an attempt to free Warsaw from the Nazis' clutches, perhaps anticipating help from the Russian Army. It did nothing, and the Uprising failed. Meanwhile, in their southern corner of Poland, the fear was growing that the Russians, who were beating the Germans back inch by inch with the help of the Partisans, intended to stay. They were occupiers in a different guise. Not liberators.

Their remote corner of the countryside reverberated with gunfire and explosions. On top of the Germans and Russians and Poles, there were also the Ukrainians and the Lemks and the Boyks. Several times a week now, she and Little Cousin would go to the forester's cottage and see if there was any help they could offer the wounded.

One night, it must already have been September because the harvest was in and she had decided to force herself to make jams and preserves against the bitter winter months, they were surprised by a knock at the door. They stared at each other. She told him to go and sit with her father while she answered.

A man stood at the door and assessed her. His clothes were worn and mud-spattered. His face wore the marks of exhaustion. 'Please, madam. Two friends and I. May we sleep in your barn?'

She nodded. 'Does anyone know you've come this way?'

He shrugged. 'I don't think so.'

His tone was polite, educated.

'Are you hungry?'

He grinned, showing large teeth. 'Well, perhaps, just a little.'

She invited them in, served them onions and white cheese and thick slabs of bread and the vodka she had just that morning traded for. Little Cousin watched the three men with the nervous attention of a feral creature. And listened. Listened astutely. As the men relaxed they explained that they had come from the Kielce area to join a band of fighters somewhere in the border country. They were bringing something. But they had gotten sidetracked in their journey by the fighting and were now lost. There was supposed to have been a contact in Tarnow who never turned up.

'I'll take you,' she suddenly heard Little Cousin say. 'I'm a good tracker.'

That night he murmured: 'I have to go. I have to join them again. I owe it. I've let too many die.'

And she thought to herself, now you'll let me die. I'll die, if you go. Perhaps she said it aloud, because he answered. 'I won't leave you. I'll be back. As often as I can be. Please.'

She knew she couldn't hold him.

Time grew heavy again. The time of endless waiting. And he did come back. Came back once, sometimes twice a week, sometimes every two weeks, always with that gleam in his eye, that nervous glance over his shoulder and that visceral exhaustion that made her realize he was more than half elsewhere. She minded, but she forgave him. Because he kept his word. He came back when he could.

Then winter arrived, bringing snows and bitter cold. Her father was worse than ever. One night he gave up and died. He had already been a ghost of himself for so long, she didn't think the pain would be as great as it was. She wept and wept. She rode weeping to the village and arranged for his burial. She wished, she wished beyond anything, that Little Cousin could be by her side during the funeral.

He came, as if he had heard her call. She thought it was a miracle. She also thought news of her father's passing must have travelled with the gunfire through the forest. One thought didn't disqualify the other.

When she looked at his golden face that night, she felt that perhaps the years had made him better acquainted with death than with life.

It was not long after that she found out about the baby. She wanted to tell him the next time he came, but the moment wasn't right. She thought she might wait for spring. When the anemones burgeoned. When the war would be over. Yes.

But the Russians came first. She had an odd feeling that they might be looking for him. They didn't find him. But they filled the house with their soldiers. Only enemies of the people usurped so much space for their own use, they told her. On the second night of their stay, when she sensed that rape or perhaps worse was imminent, she saddled the horse she now thought of as Bessie and stole into the forest. She didn't find him. For a week, she stayed in the forester's cabin. Then she moved to a room in the village. She watched and waited. Waited and watched. Waited until the war was officially over, though the fighting didn't stop. Waited with a part of herself which was beyond hope.

Sometime. Somewhere she would see her Little Cousin again. Her Adonis. Her love. He would come. She knew he would come.

18

Alone on the train to Linz, Bruno thought about the strangeness of the last days – that girl's voice that emerged from the old woman's lips, the intensity of the gaze she settled on him that saw into a place in him he no longer altogether knew except in the passion of her presence. She awoke it for him with all its troubling uncertainties.

No. Science wouldn't, couldn't, give him explanations that dealt adequately with the complexity of the experience of these past weeks. He felt at ease with that knowledge now. Felt strangely light too, in the midst of a sadness, as if he would have liked to immerse himself even more deeply in that recollected world, rather than bear its burdens by avoiding it.

While Eve was still alive, he didn't think he would have been able really to hear Pani Marta – to listen and recognize that wild, slightly disjointed narrative from another world that emerged from a woman whose grasp on the everyday was far frailer than her body. Nor would he have believed her. Now he felt he should have given it all longer. So that his debt to Pani Marta could at least be in some small part repaid. She had saved him. And more.

But the calls from London had grown ever more pressing, and there was one more thing he felt compelled to do before he returned. Returned fully to the demands of the present.

He had stayed with his sweet cousin for three days. Three days of holding her hands while this old woman, who was and was no more the person he had begun to remember, had talked, sometimes coherently, sometimes in a jumble of cascading language, of those lost moments of what he was now convinced had been their shared past in the last year of the war.

Except for those stark murderous images that returned in ever-
more glaring and crystallized form on a loop, the period had all
grown so blurred for him. Icons of death and guilty terror were all
that remained for him of the war, and they were best avoided.
They had displaced much of the lived and daily reality, had somehow drawn all the rest into themselves until they too vanished,
only to come back in the wake of his wife's death.

But she, Pani Marta, had remembered. Had remembered a flow
of days, a continuity. He had forgotten, and she had remembered.
Had even remembered the name he had worn and which had
belonged to a man he thought dead, a man he had felt had tried to
kill him and he had somehow helped to kill in turn. Aleksander
Tarski.

That brutal logic of hatred and revenge, though all too true emo-
tionally, he was now almost certain had no grounding in events.

His personal memory had functioned in the spirit of what collective memory had made of the time – Poles and Jews mired in
hatreds, when the killing machine which made murderers and victims of them all had in the first instance been put in place by a Nazi
regime that despised them both. That was history.

Yes, he had once been Aleksander Tarski, had stolen the identity
of a Partisan leader he had thought dead. And Pani Marta, whom
the neurologists would have supposed to have lost her name
memory almost first of all, had remembered this through the tangles of her own forgetting.

How much longer would she still contain that part of her
history?

Had he been less of a sceptic, less of a believer in the observable
elements of the material world, he would almost have begun to
think that it was Pani Marta, herself, who had called him to her
side on the wings of her desire across the miles of time and space
and the snarls of her thought processes. She had winged him to her
side while some of the electrical currents and chemical compounds
in her brain still functioned well enough for her to speak. A tele-
pathic feat in the memory of Little Cousin.

Yet at the same time, he wasn't altogether convinced that she
recognized him. Not in the normal way. He was an old man now,

not the golden youth romance had preserved in her. But something about him, perhaps it really was the touching of hands, had triggered a supposed recognition and launched the waterfall of speaking memory. Odd, that if he hadn't been following Aleksander Tarski, which turned out to be the wrong lead, he would never have arrived at the place where her voice stirred his forgotten past.

How much did his own returning recollections echo hers?

Certainly, with the help of the drawing, her house had returned to his mind. A large shadowy place of whose location he was still uncertain, but that he had found himself waking in one day, he wasn't sure quite how. He was lying beside a decaying old man who never spoke. What was clearest for him was the old man. He frightened him in his glaring speechlessness. And the hearth, the leap of flame. He saw that. Pani Marta only entered his consciousness later. He had believed a young man had picked him up near the forest. Their actions had taken place under palpably different descriptions. What memories they had were different as a result. In a certain sense, he was even now making new ones.

What he must have been most aware of then was pain. It was not a sensation one could recapture, though at the time of the experience, it blotted out and distorted so much else. The body had to focus on rallying its survival systems.

Bruno stared out the window of the train and realized that if anyone had asked him what he had seen in these last fleeting hours, he would have had no answer. Yet, he had been looking. Only to see in the stream of landscape the workings of his own mind and that of the woman who so many decades ago had been his lover.

Yes. Old Pani Marta had used the name that had probably been instrumental in ferrying him eastwards across the seas of oblivion and bringing him to the conference in Vienna in the first place. He must have been aware of the offprint Aleksander Tarski had sent him without recollecting it, like in those Gallin picture completion tests in which subjects repeatedly denied that they remembered something that their non-declarative memory attested to. So, of course, Tarski was the first name he seemed to hear when he arrived in Vienna.

Why had the name stolen so long ago taken on so much more emotional significance than all the others he had hidden behind during the war? The technical explanation must be that in his super-stressed state of terror in the forest, the very chemical – noradrenaline – that served as the basis for some of their recent experiments must have been pulsing through his brain: through his amygdala, to be exact. It had bound the name in him forever.

Yet, from the outside, his assessment of what had happened in the clearing was utterly confused. In the scene that returned to him, he was convinced he had left Aleksander to die, had somehow helped to kill him. Because at the time he hated him, hated him for recognizing Bruno as a Jew, for sending him on a dangerous expedition that had resulted in his papers being stolen, for palpably wishing him dead. All of which somehow also entangled Aleksander in the responsibility for those earlier deaths of his mother and sister. He wanted this man, who had authority over him and over his people, dead. He wanted to take the place of that authority. And in his confused state, he had lived out his wishes. He hadn't helped Aleksander to safety. He had kicked him. Left him to die.

In turn, he was left with a terrible redoubled guilt. So many deaths at his door.

Yet Aleksander, if one were to trust the recollections of an old lady with Alzheimer's, had lived on, had been ferried to a doctor and been saved. Bruno hadn't helped to kill him. Did he trust these sources more than his own memory, which in this case was a series of hazy images, black and white and grainy like in an ancient newsreel?

He smiled to himself as he remembered Mark Twain's wonderful quip. 'It is not so astonishing the number of things I can remember, as the number of things I can remember which are not so.'

Yes.

He would have been producing opiods too in those terrible moments in the forest. He had probably been producing far too many of the morphine-like molecules ever since the barbaric attack on his mother and sister. The opiods dulled fear and pain.

They had seen him through. But they also had the effect of making certain things indistinct, producing distortions. He now wanted to believe that the real Aleksander Tarski had lived on. Not only the youth who had stolen his papers and in some senses become his double, probably ending up in Russian clutches in part because of the activities of the first. Then too, Bruno acknowledged, he now needed to clear his conscience, particularly since he would inevitably be seeing more of a contemporary Tarski, if his daughter had anything to do with it. In fact, he should thank this younger Aleksander for unwittingly leading him here. By some perverse instinct, he had followed a name he didn't want to think about, and it had led him to a seam of his past he had lost, but not, it now seemed, forever. It had been kept passionately alive for him by an old woman who contained a young one, almost intact.

Bruno took in peaceful meadows and tumbling hills. No, the mountains in the vicinity of Pani Marta's old house were far less steep than these. How well did he now remember those months with his first love? He had to confess to himself that little was altogether distinct. The effect was not unlike what he saw from the train as it picked up speed. Then time, rather than distance, had sped by, first in the daze of his wound and after that in the warm security of the woman's presence.

He thought that perhaps for the first time in a long, long period, he had felt safe. But he had had no words then, no conceptual framework, no structure with which to recognize the nature of the love she had now revealed to him. After he had mastered his uneasiness about the man in the wheelchair, the elements of that time had all blended into each other, her kind strong face with its loving smile, the fields, the soft downy bed in which they caressed each other, the dusty shadowy house which had far more rooms than his grandfather's, the purple and green hills. Yes, all merged into a haven from the horrors that preceded and followed it.

It had been different for her.

But he was more than prepared now to adopt the mood of Pani Marta's fervent recollections and give the name of love to feelings he had been too young and stupid and callous to recognize. Yes, love: somewhere within that thick carapace he had worn like a suit of clumsy armour over the hair shirt of his shame.

It came to him as he pondered the puzzles of the past that he had gone back to the house to see her only to find there a Russian barracks from which he had fled. It must have been shortly afterwards that his first bout in prison, as Partisan Aleksander Tarski, had come.

Perhaps he was prepared to believe the full extent of Pani Marta's monologue because, in this land of cemeteries, he really did want to recover something that was still alive. Alive, particularly for him. A link between past and present. And Pani Marta, who had found him at the edge of the woods and had returned him to life, was exactly that.

She had also, it seemed, given him a daughter. Somewhat belatedly. Far beyond the age when fathers mean much. But perhaps he was readier now than he would have been then – when he was nothing more than a troubled child himself.

He liked Irena, liked – now that he had accepted it – to think that they had been subliminally drawn to one another because of a sense of the other's familiarity. She was not unlike her mother. Perhaps she even wore traces of him, he told himself fancifully.

What was difficult was knowing how to behave with her. There was no pre-existing rulebook marked how to handle a newly discovered daughter who was already in her fifties. Both of them had felt rather tentative. As if it wasn't quite real. As if the coincidence of their meeting at all, as she had said, was a little more than ordinary hard realism could swallow. Both of them chasing the will o' the wisp of a proper name – which turned out to be an utterly improper name, a mere disguise. It was more like one of Shakespeare's comedies than a recovered wartime story. Though one heard plenty of far stranger ones.

She told him about babies flung from trains and raised in convents, met again in Baku oilfields. About researchers from Turkey and the US in the Warsaw Jewish archives discovering, as they dug through the past, that they were probably brother and sister. Yes, the stories and coincidences were stranger than fiction would allow. So she was happy simply to know that in her case her mother hadn't come up with this story as another hallucinatory figment thrown up by her decaying mind. Biological daughter or not, she was also happy because she had made new friends, had new extensions beyond her narrowing world.

Irena didn't really want to go in for the hard test, the DNA test, she told him. She preferred, a romantic like her mother, to keep hopes and emotions free. Perhaps he would come to visit her from time to time, and she him. Perhaps he would even grow to like her.

He liked her already, he told her. Secretly, he was also chuffed to imagine that once in his long life he had in fact fathered a biological child.

But what about Amelia in all this? Amelia who was faced with a rather tardy sister? Amelia who had prevailed upon him to make this journey, for which he now felt deeply grateful to her? He had been so reluctant at first, not wanting to rake up all that terrible matter, not wanting to dig through mud and ash and old terrors. But it had been salutary in a way. He understood a little better now, from his distance of age and time, the unspeakable course of that war. Understood particularly his grandfather's move into the Ghetto, where he knew certain death awaited him. The young Bruno, angry and guilty in equal parts, couldn't have stopped what was almost a generational resignation in the old man, let alone a wish to embrace his own people.

Strangely, Bruno now felt more benevolent towards himself as well, as if he too might be forgiven his sins, which included survival…even if not for much longer.

For all this he was in debt to Amelia. She had said, with that wonderful infectious laugh he hadn't heard enough of these last years, that she really rather liked the possibility of a half-sister from sources quite other than she had imagined. Wonderful Amelia with her courageous sense of life. To be honest, she hadn't been paying quite so much attention to him or to Irena these last days. She had been more engaged in worrying about the real Aleksander…the only one who was real because he was still alive, papers or no papers.

Amelia was relieved to find that what Bruno had against the man was a mere matter of name. Not even the taint of kinship he had suspected. So she didn't expect him to go round behaving like some raving Montague or Capulet. As for Aleksander's being Polish, surely Bruno couldn't hold that against him in any way. It had to be enough that Aleksander was prepared to make up for history and take on board a black Jew who, on top of everything else, was an American. So he had strict orders to provide Aleksander with a reference whenever he was asked – something, Bruno chuckled to himself, he had already promised to do on his first visit to Aleksander's laboratory, whatever his other suspicions.

Last night while he had lain in bed considering everything, the nightmare had suddenly confronted him again. The falling figures had risen out of the first moments of sleep. They bathed him in cold sweat as they tumbled down the precipitous incline one after another.

He had begun to think over this last while in which they kept reappearing that perhaps they weren't his figures at all, but figures that had come with the chilling events of the Twin Towers tragedy. That they had triggered some deep fear in him. His own fear of falling. Of dying. It was the future he was frightened of, even though it wore the aura of the past.

Then last night some of the faces had turned towards him. Without really recognizing them, his dream had put names to them the way dreams do, allowing recognition without resemblance. They were Anna and Mamusia and his grandfather. He knew them now. His war-dead. But his wife, Eva, was there too, and he had thought in his night-state of random associations that perhaps her death had brought all the others back, like a train which moved backwards to pick up its passengers.

And then, with a jolt that shook him awake, he had recognized that rock face with its sheer granite drop. Not a skyscraper, no. But a place he had been to: had visited briefly on his journey from Krakow to the Munich refugee camp after the war. Yes, yes. And the site could find no place in his narrative of war, which was a youth's, and for all its horrors wore a human dimension, even if these humans were at their barbarous worst. So he had thrust the place away. That visit and the impossibility of containing it in any autobiographical story. He couldn't have gone on if it had lodged there, accessible to everyday recollection. Its enormity was such that he had to put it out of mind or leave his mind. It was too much, coming on top of everything else. Too much, when the toughened youth he had been was weakened by the sudden outbreak of hope. The enormity.

The taxi brought him from the station. It was only twenty kilometres from Linz, in the kind of countryside the tourist brochures drooled over. Linz, the town that had given birth to Hitler and which in his last days he had dreamed of as his great 'city of art'. The main camp building was a solid stone structure hewn from the quarry beside it. The quarry, a sheer granite drop, nicknamed by the SS 'the Parachute Jump', was called the Wiener Graben – like the street he had stayed on those short weeks ago. It had made him edgy. Now he knew why.

His father must have been amongst the first inmates, those forced to build the HQ, the high stone wall and the watchtower in the summer of 1938. There were political prisoners, enemies of the Reich, and there were Jews. His father had qualified as both. There were also eventually Russians and Poles. Polish priests shared the lowest category with the Jews. There were thirty-eight barracks for prisoners and all around the perimeter, electrified barbed wire charged with 380 volts.

Mauthausen and its neighbour, the Gusen complex, plus forty-nine linked sub-camps in the region, were amongst the camps in the Nazi's third category: '*Ruckkehr unerwunscht.*' Return not wanted. His father hadn't returned.

According to eyewitness accounts the prisoners were divided into two groups. One hacked granite, the other carried the twenty-five kilogram slabs that rose to forty-five kilograms after the first journey – a weight designated by Himmler himself – up the 186 steps to the top of the quarry. In one day when eighty-seven men were at work, forty-seven died by eleven-thirty in the morning. Those who were responsible for hacking the granite were at the mercy of SS guards who had pickaxe handles with which to flail them. Combats in gladiatorial style were organized at the top of the quarry. Whichever opponents could push the others down were promised freedom. Instead, they were summarily propelled down the Parachute Jump, themselves.

There were other killing methods. In ten degrees Celsius weather, inmates were ordered to undress, hosed down with water and left to freeze. Benzine injections were used in baths. As were operations to remove a part of the brain. All patients died. There was a gas chamber beneath the sickbay. It was smaller than a neighbouring one in Hartheim, where Camp Commandant Franz Ziereis, shot in May 1945 by the camp's liberators, confessed to the gassing of 1,500,000. He apparently found it worthwhile to boast. Other sources estimate 30,000 deaths in that particular and small gas chamber.

At the camp's liberation 15,000 bodies were found in mass graves. Three thousand more died after liberation. Their state was beyond repair.

Bruno read and walked. Mostly he stared into the pit. Little waterfalls trickled down the granite. Here and there moss turned the black stone bright green. Flowers peeked from its sheer expanse.

The terrain around him was beautiful. It increased the enormity of what had been put in train here.

He stood in front of the sheer rock face and repeated the words: *'Ruckkehr unerwunscht'*. Return unwanted. The meaning slipped to encompass him. He had made his own unwanted return. He had returned after too many years to his father's grave. And it had cleared something in him. Even if it was also the passage to his own death.

He allowed the childhood tears, never shed, to roll down his cheeks. It was some kind of small memorial.

Acknowledgements

In its gestation, this book incurred many debts of gratitude. Professor Steven Rose, one of our foremost neuroscientists, valiantly allowed me into the Brain and Behaviour Research Group laboratories at the Open University, where memory research is carried out, and where I could observe and talk with a superb international team of scientists, including Konstantin Anokhin from Moscow. Steven Rose also permitted me to trail him at conferences and to ask far more questions than any man, even a scientist, should have to answer. On top of it all, he was an early and expert reader of the book. For all this I am deeply grateful to him – though he can in no way be held responsible for any of the uses to which I have put neuroscience.

Our work together was made possible by the Gulbenkian Foundation and in particular Sian Ede, who brilliantly weds artists, writers and scientists under the auspices of the 'The Arts and Science' programme, which has done so much to bring people from radically different disciplines together, develop ideas and sometimes find common and fruitful ground.

Ever since I wrote a thesis on Proust, I have been interested in memory and forgetting, the tricks and incompleteness of each. It was a boon to be able to place the neuroscientific alongside earlier forms of understanding.

In the writing of this book and well before, I immersed myself in a great many war-time memoirs, both published and unpublished, as well as, once more, in my parents' memories and stories. The extraordinary resilience and courage, the cruelty and generosity people manifested in these extreme conditions (each in their own very particular way) is an endless source of wonder. I owe a debt to all of them.

Thanks too are due to my first readers, Eva Hoffman, whose critical eye was a veritable boon, Monica Holmes, Suzette Macedo and of course, John Forrester. Their responses helped, as did those of Stephanie Cabot, my agent. I am also very grateful to Gary Pulsifer and Daniela de Groote of Arcadia Books, my adventurous publishers, and their editor Ken Hollings.

Oranges for the Son of Alexander Levy
by Nella Bielski

Translated from the French by Lisa Appignanesi and John Berger

Chekhovian in its deceptive lightness, Nella Bielski's fiction is a uniquely feminine meditation on death and absence: the absence of the heroine's husband Paul, of the intense life of her childhood in wartime Russia and her youth in Moscow, of friends and family who have vanished behind the tundra of the Gulag, of her parents who loved her.

'Nella Bielski writes out of the experience of obstruction, exile and betrayal, but the tone is hopeful and humane'
– Hermione Lee, *Observer*

'The book is flawless, and John Berger and Lisa Appignanesi - both eminent authors in their own right - have produced a wonderful translation'
– Jonathan Self, *Jewish Chronicle*